Jack Gelfand, M.D., assistant medical examiner of New York County, looked up from his desk. "Hello, Sergeant Ross."

"Morning, Doc." They were old friends. Many a stiff they'd shared between them. "You take a look at the headless body?"

"I wondered what brought you to my door. Just a quick once-over."

"You gonna cut him up?"

"You bet. I want to know the cause of death."

"Loss of head?" Arnie offered.

"Maybe. Maybe that's a cover-up. Maybe he OD'd. Maybe he was poisoned. Maybe anything. Until I look, I'm not going to know."

"That's what I thought." Arnie hesitated. "He was into martial arts."

Gelfand sat back. It paid to listen to Arnie Ross. "He was?"

"Calluses on the edges of the palms and knuckles. He's in terrific physical condition. Young."

"And maybe take a look to see if he was killed by a blow, or other karate-type violence?"

"That's the idea, Doc," Ross said. "Funny about the head. Can you cut better than that?"

"Not with a scalpel. Not a shred of skin above the edge of the incision. A regular surgical job. Minimal splintering of the bone."

"Maybe he was guillotined."

Other books by Nick Christian

HOMICIDE ZONE 4
INTENSIVE FEAR

NICK CHRISTIAN

RONIN

TOR

A TOM DOHERTY ASSOCIATES BOOK

RONIN

Copyright © 1986 by Edward A. Pollitz, Jr.

First printing: May 1986

A TOR Book

Published by Tom Doherty Associates
49 West 24 Street
New York, N.Y. 10010

ISBN: 0-812-52429-2
CAN. ED.: 0-812-52430-6

Printed in the United States

0 9 8 7 6 5 4 3 2 1

CHAPTER

ONE

Libby Beckman glanced at her watch as she rang the doorbell of the small brick building. She had plenty of time for her exercise class and lunch. It was a quarter past twelve and she wasn't due back at her office at Citicorp Center until 2:00 P.M., when the Foreign Loan Committee was due to convene.

She looked at the lunchtime crowd that bustled by on nearby Madison Avenue, from Sixty-second Street, embarrassed by her juxtaposition to the "Slimtronics" sign, and imagining that passersby nodded with satisfaction to see her there. Her round face crinkled in a characteristic smile. Silly Libby, she thought.

She rang again, and the lock buzzed, allowing her to push through the door into the hall. The girl at the desk didn't bother to look up from her magazine. She let up on the buzzer when she heard the door close.

As Libby walked past her through the small entrance to the staircase, she said, "Hi, Gena." When there was no response, she shrugged and propelled herself up the steps.

She wrinkled her nose as she encountered the first trace

1

of stale perspiration, penetrating even though masked by a *parfumier* burning Arpege, as it wafted down from the gym floor of Muffy Grant's Slimtronics Salon.

"Come on, old girl," she said to herself under her breath. She paused at the second-floor landing, where Muffy's office was, and looked up the remaining flight. She wrestled with the temptation to turn around and go out to a good lunch. Self-consciously, she patted her midriff with the palm of her right hand. She could feel a modest roll of excess flesh protruding above the waistline of her skirt.

"Halo, Libby. How you doink?"

Libby looked up the stairs through brown eyes under dark brows at Laszlo Dushan, Muffy's assistant and resident masseur. His fair complexion was as Croatian as his name and his accent; his body showed the results of constant exercise.

"I'm doing great, Laszlo," Libby said. "I'm ready for my workout." She moved up the stairs with an enthusiasm she did not feel. "How about you?"

"Like alvayz. I doink terrific. If I vas millionaire, I do even better." He laughed at his own joke. "Till I am tventy-six, I get up at five in mornink vit a glass of Slivovitz to be at lousy job at six. Here"—he flexed for her—"I make muscles and rub down ladies. Is more fun vatching ladies svetink in New York than vorkink like dog in Tomos factory in Koper." He trotted down the steps past her to the office. "Vork good, Libby. Make good figure."

Libby stopped again at the top step. She had found out that there was more to making a good figure than good wishes. I've managed to work at everything else, she said to herself. Why not this?

"Elbows and arms, ladies, elbows and arms. And one and two and one and two." Muffy Grant's voice was as sleek as her body. The explosion of the physical fitness business had coincided perfectly with the decline of her modeling career. Though still in her early thirties, lines of

maturity had begun to etch their implacable way into the
soft planes of her face. Long limbs, uplifted breasts, and
optimum physical condition would have kept her in swim-
suits and lingerie for a few more years, but the magazine
covers and the big money were behind her. Muffy hadn't
waited to be pushed. She'd jumped.

Two years ago a one-time lover had cosigned a fifty-
thousand-dollar note and the lease, permitting her to rent
three floors in the small building, refurbish them, and buy
some equipment. The loan was already paid off.

Libby peeked around the doorframe at the chorus of
kneeling forms, arching and twisting in unison to Muffy's
voice and the rhythm of the tape deck in the corner. They
were starting to show the strain. Ten minutes left. Then
there would be a ten-minute break, and her class would
begin.

Libby squared her shoulders and pushed into the locker
room. Athletics had never been her thing. She could play a
little tennis and swim, but she could as easily do without.
Both her inclinations and her physique had guided her
away from the playing fields and her long-limbed, agile
classmates and into the library, and, she thought sadly, the
cafeteria, the vicious circle of sloth and gluttony.

She had been born into a comfortable New York family,
and had enjoyed a good education: Riverdale, Yale, and a
master's degree at the Georgetown Institute for Foreign
Studies. She'd taken off two weeks after graduating, then
interviewed at a half-dozen places, settling on the international banking department of Citibank. She had worked
there since late September, about six months.

The dressing room was confining. About twelve feet
square, benches ran down one wall in front of a bar hung
with clothing-laden hangers. Two dozen metal lockers in
which valuables could be secured stood stacked across the
room, keys dangling from the empty ones, with rubber
bands to be worn on the wrist while exercising. Next to the
lockers there were three sinks in a fake marble vanity, and

two stall showers. A steam room and hot tub were located above on the top floor.

Libby smiled her brightest smile as she walked into the room and shrugged off her coat. Three of the ten women in her class had already arrived. They were models in their early twenties. One of them had changed into her tights and leotard. The second stood in her black panty hose, her gamin's body naked to the waist, chatting with the third girl who sat nude, casually straddling the bench, smoking a cigarette. She modeled bras and panties and had shaved her pubic hair.

"Hi, Lib. How's the working girl?" the half-naked one asked.

"I'm fine Cheri. Hi Babs, Donna."

Libby turned her back and started to take off her own clothes. Though she was the same age as the other girls, and had lived in college dormitories that offered little privacy, she was uncomfortable with the steambath atmosphere of the locker room.

She hung her gray woolen suit and blouse neatly, then stepped out of the sensible low-heeled shoes that she wore, though she was only five foot three, and wrestled her way out of her panty hose. Her one hundred thirty-five pounds were twenty-five too many for her stature, and little ripples of cellulite showed here and there on her inner thighs and buttocks. A tummy protruded just a bit above the dark brown curls between her legs. At least the legs were pretty good, Libby thought defensively. She turned her head and looked enviously as Donna rose from the bench, stretched her arms toward the ceiling, and stood on her tiptoes. Her rib cage stretched upward under dainty pink-tipped breasts. Her lower body from her tiny waist to her feet formed a single sinuous curve.

"Time to suit up, ladies," Donna said, balancing easily, first on one foot then on the other, to pull on her white leotard. She snapped the Lycra straps and said, "Showtime."

When the three girls left, Libby quickly pulled on her

exercise bra and tights. One of the subsidiary interests of Slimtronics was psyching out everybody's motivation for showing up. For the models, it was a professional necessity—like reading the *Wall Street Journal*. For Libby, it was aspiring to look like Donna. She was laughing to herself when three of the other women arrived. She nodded politely, stuffed her bag into a locker, and walked out onto the floor.

The three models were loosening up on the ballet bar in front of the wall-length mirror. They leaned forward, their heels hooked over the bar, touching their foreheads to their outstretched legs in a position Libby could imagine only as a form of torture.

She lay on the matted floor and did some double leg lifts. She was amazed to find that she could manage twenty, slowly and deliberately, keeping her feet together just a few inches above the floor. She smiled.

"See," Muffy Grant said, looking down at her, "I told you so. Don't you ever tell me again that you're a hopeless case, Libby Beckman. Just keep pushing away from the table and doing your exercises and you'll look like . . ."

"Donna?" Libby asked hopefully.

Muffy grinned. "One step at a time."

Libby's legs began to shake and she was glad to lower them to the floor as Muffy walked away. Muffy turned on the tape, a driving acid-rock beat, and five more women joined the class.

Though there were no set hours to use the ten-session packages, most clients at Muffy Grant's Slimtronics Salon preferred to attend the same classes regularly. Fifteen dollars for a single session, one hundred and twenty for ten.

In each of the past three months, of the twelve-hundred dollars she took home monthly from the bank, Libby had spent an average of one hundred and sixty on Slimtronics, going every Monday, Wednesday, and Friday. She had decided to come to grips with her body, and to stop letting it be an excuse for the absence of a social life. Men, like athletics, were not something that came easily to her.

The class was a mixed bag. In addition to the models, who worked out in lieu of lunch every day of the week, there were a couple of young matron types in their late thirties protecting their interest in the twilight of youth, a remarkable lady named Claire, who was seventy-two, tiny as an elf, and agile as a serpent, who said that her reason for coming was to stay alive, and there was Louise. She was delivered and picked up by a block-long Lincoln limousine whose license plate was simply "8." She was in her late twenties, and Libby had the impression that she had married someone much older and very rich. She arrived invariably late, dressed in designer jeans and a pullover. She took them off and threw them in a corner with her bag, presenting herself in a skintight metallic gray body suit that clung to every curve and crevice of her otherwise naked form. When the class was over, she put on her clothes again, picked up her bag, and left, with rarely a word to anyone.

"All right, ladies. Playtime's over," Muffy said silkily. "Is everybody ready to suffer?" Without waiting for an answer, she knelt on the floor facing them. "On your backs, ladies. Left leg first, lift and down. Then right. One, two. One, two. Let's have a little enthusiasm. One and two and one and two."

At first Libby felt only the rumblings of discomfort as her muscles were roused by the gentler loosening and bending movements. As the class progressed, and with it the difficulty of the exercises and the number of repetitions, her body temperature rose, and she began to perspire and to huff and puff as she slid inexorably into oxygen debt.

As she twisted her body into a parody of the position that Muffy held, and rotated her shoulders, Libby thought with satisfaction that lately it had been taking more to wear her down.

"Come on, ladies," Muffy said, jumping to her feet. "Show me what you've got. Tuck, tuck, tuck. Throw out those pelvises, ladies. Come on, Libby. Those abdominal muscles need the work. Tuck and thrust.''

Libby pushed her hair away from her face and thrust her hips in earnest. She looked out of the corner of her eye at Donna, whose body flowed in a single continuous motion. She tried unsuccessfully to restrain a smile as she wondered if the lithe model could actually do that lying on her back with a man on top of her.

"One and two. One and two. Hump, hump, hump.''

Christ, Libby wondered as her back began to ache and her muscles cramped, doesn't she ever lose her breath?

The front door buzzer rang loudly. Muffy glanced at the digital clock on the table next to the blaring stereo. One of her one-thirties must have run out of shopping money or finished lunch early. It was only twelve forty-five. She lost count of the repetitions and decided on ten more humps. It wouldn't kill them. Gena would get the door downstairs.

Two floors below, Gena fumbled for the button under the desk, then turned the page of *Town and Country* to find out where the best jewelers in Switzerland were located. She felt something cold against her forehead. Her breath caught in her throat and she looked up.

All she could see was the gun. It was blue-black, and close enough so that the conical tips of the bullets were visible in the cylinder. She licked her lips.

The voice was soft and relaxed, with the slight sibilance of a Spanish accent. "Don't be afraid. No one is going to hurt you. Stand up and turn around.''

She pushed her chair back from the desk and followed instructions, getting a brief glance at the man with the gun. He wore a stocking mask. There was a blur of other masked faces by the door.

"Put your hands behind your back," he said. When she complied, he taped her wrists together. "Now open your mouth.''

She resisted the dryness of the handkerchief only long enough to provoke increased pressure from the gun at the nape of her neck. Another strip of tape held it fast. She was pushed into the open coat closet, then the door closed and she was left standing in the dark. She leaned against the door when she heard the lock turn and allowed herself to slip to the floor. When she was seated, the fear set in and she began to shake.

Willie Lopez put his gun into his jacket pocket, motioned to his two companions, and began to walk up the carpeted stairs. Despite their effort to be quiet, Laszlo Dushan heard their oncoming steps through the half-open door of the second-floor office, where he sat eating a sandwich. He leaned forward from the desk to see who was there.

There was a moment of indecision as Slavic Heroism battled with two years of the New York Experience. Tradition won. Instead of reaching for the phone, he catapulted out of the door onto the landing.

"Vat you doink, you guys, here?" he asked in a loud voice. In sweat pants and sneakers and a sleeveless T-shirt he was brawny and formidable.

"Go in the office and lie on the floor," Willie said.

Laszlo sized him up. He was slender, perhaps a hundred fifty pounds spread over a five-foot-ten-inch frame. Laszlo outweighed him by sixty pounds and was four inches taller. If he whipped their leader, they would turn and run. He threw a short right to his midsection.

The reaction was a reflex born of practice and discipline. The first hint of motion of Laszlo's shoulders triggered a balletic pirouette. Willie rose on his toes and spun away from Laszlo's blow. He raised the heel of his right foot and completed the arc, slamming Laszlo an inch above his belt, over his right kidney. As Laszlo grunted in pain and surprise, Willie used the leverage created by the contact to reverse his direction. Lifting his right foot to shoulder height, he exhaled forcefully as momentum carried him through the blow. His foot struck the side of Laszlo's head, smashing his jaw and cheekbone, rendering him unconscious.

His two companions stood stock-still on the stairs, fro-

zen against the driving music from the gymnasium as
Laszlo toppled to the ground.

"Shit, Willie," said Adolfo Reyes. "What do we do
now?"

"Take him in the office and tape his hands and feet,"
he replied softly, "and his mouth."

When they came out of the office, Willie let his companions stand for a moment till he was sure they had their
composure, then motioned to them and climbed the stairs.

Muffy was down to the hard strokes with her class.
They lay on their backs, their knees raised, their feet flat
on the floor. They held their hands together behind the
napes of their necks and strained their stomach muscles,
touching their elbows to their knees.

"This is the real test, ladies. This weeds out the
diletantes. But it makes those ugly midriff bulges disappear. Go for it. Good. Hold it. Down. Up. Down slowly.
Pay the price. Fifteen more today. Okay, Libby?"

Libby Beckman was red in the face, her elbows pressed
against her thighs. Unable to talk, she nodded in agreement.

"One and two, and one and two . . ." Muffy's voice
stopped. Like Gena, trussed in the closet downstairs, at
first all she could see was the gun.

"Please, listen to me," Willie said in a calm, even
voice. "No one is going to be hurt. We are going to take
your money and jewelry, and we are going to leave. Lie
flat on the ground where you are. Just relax. That goes for
you, too, teacher."

He snapped his fingers and Paco Nunez, the smaller of
his companions, looked around the gym quickly, then
trotted up the stairs. He returned momentarily, shaking his
head. "Only a bathtub and stuff."

"In there," Willie said, pointing at the dressing room.

"It's lockers," Paco said, looking in the door.

Willie looked across the prostrate women toward Muffy.
His eyes caught the keys strapped to their wrists. "Get
those keys," he said to Paco. "Now, clean out the lockers. Ladies, please take any watches or other jewelry off

and put it on the floor next to you." He nodded at the tall muscular Reyes and said, "Pick it up."

Libby tried to train her eyes on the ceiling, but they kept straying toward the young man standing over them with the gun, anonymous in his mask. Dressed in jeans and a denim jacket, he was as slender as the models who lay on the floor by her side. He seemed completely at ease, she thought, like a leopard in a tree. She jerked away from a sharp poke in the thigh.

"What you lookin' at, fatty?" Reyes's voice was harsh and tense, with a guttural Hispanic accent. Even through the stocking mask she could see that his eyes were narrowed with fear. "You keep your eyes on the fuckin' ceiling." His hands shook and he smelled of perspiration.

Paco, the short man, appeared at the door of the dressing room with a shopping bag. "Okay," he said, "all done."

The gymnasium was thirty-five feet long and eighteen feet wide. The ceiling, edged with ornamental plaster molding, was supported by four cylindrical columns.

Willie approached the women and said, "Please get on your hands and knees. Please," he repeated firmly, motioning them along with the barrel of his gun. "I want you to walk on your hands and knees to the pillar nearest the stairs." Following them, he continued. "Now, sit cross-legged in a circle around the pole. Closer, so you can touch each other."

Suddenly, Adolfo Reyes stepped into the circle and grabbed a blond woman in her thirties by the hair. "Hold out your hand. Show me your hand," he said, shaking her head.

"Ow."

Reyes shook her again. "Show me."

She extended a slender manicured hand. On the fourth finger was a slim white gold band. He let go of her hair and twisted her wrist sharply enough to make her gasp. Cupped in her palm was a four-carat emerald-cut diamond attached to the band.

"Gimme that, you cunt," he snarled, pulling savagely at the ring.

She began to cry.

Willie interposed himself. "Give him the ring, lady." Then to Reyes, "Take it and leave her be."

The woman twisted the ring free from her finger and offered it up with trembling hands.

"Who else is holding out?" Reyes barked.

"Forget it," Willie said.

Donna, the model, edged her hand under her thigh trying to protect a ring worth a few hundred dollars that had been given to her by her father.

Reyes drew back his hand to strike her. "How you like I break you fuckin' nose?"

Libby Beckman had never done a thing that she considered brave in her whole life. From somewhere in her throat a stranger's voice said, "If you want to hit someone smaller than you, why don't you hit me? At least I don't make a living with my face."

Reyes obliged her, slapping her backhand across the cheek. He turned back to Donna and said, "Now, gimme the ring." White with fear, she passed it to him. "How about another smack, fatty?"

Libby touched her reddened cheek and looked up at him with angry defiance. Willie watched for a moment. When Reyes raised his hand to hit Libby again, he stepped in between them and did something with his hand that Libby couldn't see.

The tall man stepped back, white around the mouth, holding his wrist.

"I said that was enough," Willie said softly. He raised his voice and addressed the women. "We're going to leave you now. I want all of you to sit straight, face the pole, and hold out both hands at your sides, palms up."

Paco Nunez, who had rifled the lockers, took a plastic tube out of his pocket, flicked the tip of it with his fingernail, and carefully opened it.

"Keep your hands still," Paco said as he moved around

the circle, squeezing a couple of drops into each hand. "Now, hold hands with the people next to you. That's it, nice and tight."

After ten seconds had passed, Willie said, "That's Krazy Glue, ladies. It says right on the label, 'Cyanoacrylic glue. Bonds skin instantly.' If you try to get loose before somebody comes up here to get you, it's going to tear the skin right off the palms of your hands. If you just sit there and wait patiently, when the ladies from the next class come in, a little nail polish remover will fix you up as good as new." He started to leave after the others, then turned back to Libby and said with humor, "You know, chubby, you have a lot of nerve for a helpless female."

"Stuff it," Libby snapped. "It can't take a lot of nerve to do what you do. And I'll bet you're ugly without the mask too." She regretted the words before they were past her lips. *Christ, what's come over me?*

He looked at her, strangely silent for a moment, then left.

Checking the street through the peephole in the door, the three men left Muffy Grant's Slimtronics Salon at thirty-second intervals, each going his separate way.

Wilfredo Lopez pushed the lank black hair away from his forehead as he walked toward Fifth Avenue. When he got to Fifty-third Street, he dropped his stocking mask casually into a garbage can. Alone among the three thieves, he was more comfortable with it on. He winced as he recalled the remark of the chubby girl, and reached up to touch the smooth wedge-shaped scar on his right cheek where one of his string of foster parents had struck him with a hot iron for being fresh. He pulled his hand away self-consciously. It had been ten years ago, when he was twelve.

When he got to Fiftieth Street, he turned west again and went into the Guild Theater. They were playing Walt Disney's *Cinderella*. He watched for a while, then went to the men's room. He sat down in a stall and locked the door, then went through the contents of the shopping bag that he had taken from Muffy Grant's.

In accord with his usual procedure, he pulled on a pair of white cotton gloves before going through the wallets and purses, carefully removing and counting the money and discarding the rest. There were half a dozen watches. One was initialed. He threw it back into the bag.

He smiled. The woman in metallic gray would sure be pissed, he thought to himself. In her wallet there was a picture of her sitting on a white sand beach somewhere in the bottom of a bikini with her tits out in the breeze. Next to her was a heavyset man in his mid-fifties with a shock of curly white hair and thick moustaches, wearing a Japanese happi coat tied around his broad belly. A huge gold medallion gleamed on his hairy chest. Willie threw the wallet and the picture back into the shopping bag and pocketed the six thousand dollars in crisp hundreds with satisfaction.

The last of the loot was the chubby girl's wallet. She'd had fourteen bucks, a Visa card, and an employer ID with her serial number, picture, home address, and telephone number. He looked at the card carefully. It was a breach of procedure to keep anything that might serve to connect him with a crime. Prince Matsushima, for whom Willie worked, was as stern about work rules as he was about observance of the philosophy of personal conduct that bound the group together. As his chief disciple, more was expected of Willie. Nonetheless, with a last glance at the fair, round face, he slipped the card into his shirt pocket.

Willie peeled off his gloves and dropped them into the bag, then peered out of the crack in the stall door. He was alone. He opened the trash barrel where paper towels were thrown, and dug a hole in the crumpled mass. He stuffed in the shopping bag and made sure it was completely covered before he replaced the lid. Then he went out and watched the movie. He had the whole afternoon to kill.

CHAPTER

TWO

Arnie Ross bowed ceremoniously toward the empty corner of the bedroom in his apartment on Manhattan's East Eighty-sixth Street. He straightened, focusing on the confluence of the walls, measuring his breathing and gathering his concentration.

"Haiiii—ya!" In a blur Arnie's compact body snapped into a backward somersault, the black belt that held his judo coat closed flapped in the air. He bounded once, then twice. At the apex of the second leap he shot his feet out, catching the sand-stuffed canvas dummy at the point where a man's chin would be. The head was nearly torn from the base as the dummy slammed against the wall and ricocheted to the floor. Arnie tucked his legs under him and landed upright.

Sweat ran from his short black hair and runneled into the white scar that ran faintly from the right corner of his mouth almost to his ear. He wiped at it with the floppy sleeve, then set the dummy upright. He'd been working out for almost an hour. He spun once more on the ball of his foot, striking the dummy in its midsection with an

elbow and finishing with a forearm to the throat. He turned
again and bowed formally to the corner, then stripped and
showered.

He dressed in a pair of slacks, a plaid cotton shirt, and a
V-neck short-sleeved sweater. He stopped himself at the
bedroom door, and grumbling, pulled the sweater off again,
strapped on his bulletproof vest, and replaced the sweater.

In the kitchen he ate two pieces of tofu—Japanese soy-
bean curd—that he had left for his lunch, and drank a glass
of orange juice. He reached up into the fruit bowl on top
of the refrigerator and pulled down the Smith and Wesson
.357 Magnum revolver and stuffed it into the holster in the
waistband at the back of his trousers. He patted his hip
pocket and found his shield and ID—Detective Sergeant
Arnold Ross, Homicide Squad Zone Four, New York City
Police Department.

On the street Arnie let himself into his red Porsche 924
and stretched his legs out as he closed the door. His friend
and co-worker Luis Hernandez called it *el lasso de la
arania*—the spider's trap. Arnie smiled with satisfaction,
the odd hook-shaped scar pulling his left eyebrow toward
his hairline. He patted his short dark hair. For a guy with
two scars on his face and a nose in the shape of a seven,
he did his share of trapping. Oh, to be a bachelor in New
York with all those anxious single ladies yearning to be—
well, trapped. He drew a deep breath. Even with forty just
around the corner, an hour a day on the mats and an extra
hour every week at the judo-ka to stay competitively sharp
kept Arnie's body taut and agile. Of course, he thought as
he started the motor, it was self-preservation as much as
the hunting instinct that made him stay in top shape.
Somebody once told him that in combat all you've got
going for you is physical condition and good luck. In
Homicide Zone Four you took your advantages where you
found them.

Arnie drove west on Eighty-sixth to Third, then uptown
to 102nd and east again to the dingy tenement-filled block

where the hundred-year-old brick pile that hosts the twenty-third precinct is located, and parked his car.

As he walked through the door, Morry Finnegan, the desk sergeant, greeted him. "Afternoon, Arnie."

"Top of the day to you, Morry. Any action?"

"I have it on the best authority that the meter maids in this precinct are having a record day. The captain is displeased. He thinks our uniformed personnel should be getting a bigger slice of the action."

"That's interesting, Morry. Of course, it's not police work."

"Since when would that bother the captain?"

Arnie's office was on the third floor. As he climbed the worn marble steps, smoothed by thousands of flat feet over a century, he wrinkled his nose at the acrid smell of Lysol that was exuded by the very walls. The door to the captain's office was on the first landing, marked by a sign painted in large gold letters: COMMANDER. The door was closed as always, as though Benjamin P. Finkle were afraid that somebody would catch him playing with himself and take away his precious pension before the next eight months were up, and he could retire with the maximum allowable credits.

Arnie snorted. Couldn't they put the asshole in the bushes in Staten Island? The twenty-third precinct stretches east from Central Park to the East River, and north from white and wealthy Eighty-sixth Street to the invisible wall at Ninety-sixth, behind which Manhattan's poor are barricaded, and beyond to 110th Street in Spanish Harlem. The precinct commander in a tough and complex area like that ought to have the brains to work with the opposite ends of the social spectrum under his jurisdiction, and to mellow law enforcement with a sense of compromise. But Ben Finkle was a wimp.

Arnie pushed open the door to the HZ4 squad room and kicked it shut. In the year Finkle had been on the post, no matter how happy Arnie had been when he came in, by the time he had passed Finkle's closed door, and had the time

to stew about it up a flight and a half of stairs, he was
pissed off.

"Good afternoon, Sergeant Ross."

"I don't want a shoeshine," Arnie said grumpily, walking past his partner, Marvin Baxter, and into his office.

"I do walls and floors," Baxter yelled after him. He
was twenty-seven. He had been on the force only three
years before becoming a plainclothesman, and after a year
of that, up to Homicide. He was a graduate of the John Jay
College of Criminal Justice, the Big Apple's leading edu-
cator of criminologists, and studying for a law degree at
night.

"We're catching," Baxter shouted. They were next in
line for a homicide call.

"Goddamnit, boy," Arnie yelled back through the glass.
"I dealing with my paperwork. Didn't you learn nothin'
on the plantation?" Arnie looked down at the pile of case
reports and shook his head. I wonder, he thought, what
they would do if I put a match to all of this shit? DD-5.
The universal form to report on detective case work. Ross
growled and pulled a pile toward him. If he didn't get
some of this off his desk, he'd be hearing from the man
next door.

As Arnie began to deal with his burden, Francis Xavier
Flaherty looked at his shadow through the frosted glass
that separated their offices and smiled. In his twenty-nine
years on the police force, seven of them as commanding
officer of Homicide Zone Four, Lieutenant Flaherty had
never known anyone who loved police work more, and
paperwork less. He looked at his watch. Time in grade had
its privileges. At five o'clock he would go home. He
curled a lip in disgust. Ross had come in early to deal with
the morass on his desk. He still had three hours to go.

The phone rang and he pulled it off the cradle. "Lieutenant Flaherty."

"Frank." The voice was breathy, almost desperate.
Flaherty looked toward heaven. What had he done to
deserve this?

"Yes, Captain Finkle."

"I gotta real problem. You gotta come down right away. Frank?"

"I'm here, Captain."

"Right away."

Flaherty straightened his tie, took his uniform jacket off the hook on the door, and put it on. He was tempted to knock on the door of the sergeants' office, where Ross was in the toils, then thought better of it. "Baxter," he said. "If Ross ever gets out from under that pile on his desk and wonders where I went, let him know that I'm down in the captain's office."

"Yes, sir," Baxter said. Marvin Baxter ran his hand over the top of his shaven head. I hope, he thought to himself, that Arnie doesn't come out for hours. He was already all charm when he came in. Nothing like a little drudgery to add to his good humor. Marvin turned back to his own paperwork. He had survived a year as Arnie Ross's partner. The twenty-third precinct was Homicide Zone Four's address, but its responsibilities included four others as well; the nineteenth, twentieth, twenty-fourth and Central Park—Manhattan Island from river to river, Fifty-ninth Street to 110th. His year with Arnie had been an education in more ways than he cared to think.

Baxter passed a minute of peace with his own paperwork before the phone rang. He pulled it off the hook and said, "Homicide, Officer Baxter."

It was the communications center downstairs. "Got one for you, Marvin. There was a holdup at a ladies' gymnasium."

"I think you want lingerie. That's on the fourth floor, Officer."

"Even if there's a corpse in it?"

Baxter picked up a pencil and began to transcribe the report from the patrol car that had been called to the scene. A ladies' gym on Sixty-second and Madison had been robbed by three masked men. When the cops went in, they found a guy tied up in the gym office, dead.

"What are the times on all of this?" Baxter asked.

"The nine eleven was at one forty-nine P.M. The car responded and called in at one fifty-two. They phoned in the details at two-oh-one."

"And the perps?"

"No perps. They describe the crime as taking place before one P.M."

"What were they doing in the meantime?" Baxter asked.

"You'll have to ask Homicide, sir. This is Communications. We're in the basement."

Baxter hung up and looked through the window at Ross. His mouth was twisted up in the corner where the scar was. Arnie hated paperwork. Baxter thought, nothing to cheer him up like a good murder.

CHAPTER

THREE

While Marvin Baxter was taking notes from Communications, Frank Flaherty was sitting uncomfortably in Ben Finkle's office downstairs. He was the fourth captain he lived through at the twenty-third, and he shared Arnie Ross's opinion of him. Somehow, Flaherty thought, he managed to pass the exam, and then just hung there until enough people retired and his name came to the top of the list. Then he kissed ass and politicked till he got this assignment.

Finkle's gut hung over his belt. He was balding and the few strands of graying dark hair seemed windblown above his scalp. His thick steel-rimmed glasses had slipped to the end of his bulbous red-veined nose. He looked, as always, confused.

"You wouldn't believe the call I just got from downtown, Frank. Some heat."

Flaherty moved uncomfortably in his chair. He knew from experience that there was no way to learn anything from Finkle except at his own rambling pace.

"It must be somebody really important. I got a call from Carl Peterson. You know——the deputy commissioner."

Yes, for shit's sake, Flaherty thought, his face immobile. I know who all of the deputy commissioners are.

"It seems that this guy's wife was ripped off for six grand cash and a lot more jewelry." Finkle lit the short stub of a cigar that had been lying cold in the dirty ashtray. "It was at an exercise salon on Madison."

Flaherty's impatience got the better of him. "So?" he asked with asperity.

Finkle looked hurt. "Yeah, well, when they ripped these dames off, they killed some guy."

"How come I don't have it upstairs, Captain?"

"Don't ask me. I just got a call from downtown. Since this is going to end up in HZ four, I thought we'd better have a talk."

"Talk? Let's get a report in to the squad and get somebody out there."

"I got the call. I want my ass covered."

Flaherty felt himself go red in the face, but bit his tongue before it could betray him. He'd passed the captain's examination, too, and his name was wending its way toward the top of the list. If God was good, when Finkle was gone, he would still be on the force, and eventually get his promotion. "What do you want me to do, Captain?"

"Just make sure it gets handled right. Here." He pushed a slip of paper across the desk. "That's the name of the important person. I want him babied."

By the time Flaherty returned to the HZ4 squad room, Ross and Baxter were already pulling on their coats. He walked past them into his office, shouted "Ross," and flopped angrily into his chair. Baxter looked after him, startled. Charley Passarelli, dozing in his chair, opened one eye.

Arnie grabbed the DD-5's he managed to complete, signed them, and followed Flaherty. "Here. It's all I could get done. I got six more to do. Marvin and I are catching. We just got one."

"What is it?"

"Some gym got robbed. A guy got killed. It just came in."

"Well, Finkle got it first." He handed Ross the paper. "That's the name of a big *macher*. He got a deputy commissioner to call Finkle from downtown."

"The bastard must have got the news before we did. Maybe he's involved."

"Never mind the humor, Ross. Just be polite to this guy if he shows up. And treat his wife with kid gloves. As a matter of fact," Flaherty said as a thought came to him, "Baxter, come in here."

The tall black cop entered and stood next to Ross. "Yes, sir."

"Sergeant Ross has a piece of paper with some VIP's name on it. His wife was robbed at the gym you're going to. Please see that he's treated with respect."

Ross turned on his heel and said over his shoulder, "Come on, Marvin. You want to work, or just stand there and kiss ass."

When they arrived at Muffy Grant's, there were two patrol cars and an ambulance already lined up by the curb in front of the small brick building.

Inside, a pretty, dark-haired girl sat in the entrance hall talking to a plainclothesman from the precinct investigation unit.

"Hello, Arnie. Your client is in the office on the second-floor landing."

"Thanks, Nicky."

Two white-coated ambulance drivers and a man Arnie knew from the coroner's office were seated in the office. In the middle of the floor a powerfully built man with a light complexion and hair lay facedown with his hands taped behind him.

"Hello, Jimmy," Ross said to the coroner.

"Hi, Arn. This is a weird one."

Ross knelt next to the corpse. "Why weird?"

"He seems to have suffocated. I can't tell you much till

we get him to the morgue. It seems like somebody hit him with something, then when he was out cold, taped his mouth and nostrils and let him choke.''

"Nice. Any further damage?"

Jimmy shrugged. "The guys from Roosevelt Hospital are up on the gym floor now. Nobody got really hurt."

Ross clapped his shoulder. "That's good. Has Forensics been here?"

"They've fingerprinted the toilet paper in here."

"Good," Ross said, turning the body over. He studied the dead man's face for a moment, and felt about gingerly with his fingertips. Curious, he pulled up the shirt and examined the torso, first front, then back. He pointed at a darkening spot above the belt line. "Six gets you five that the something somebody hit him with was part of a human body."

"A hand makes a mess like that?" Jimmy asked.

"A karate blow. A foot. Sure," Ross said, grinning wickedly and balling up his fist. "Want to check it out?"

"I'll take your word. We'll let you know what we think after we take him apart."

"Thanks. Come on, sunshine," Ross said to Baxter. "Let's see the rest of the setup." They climbed to the gym floor, where women were sitting around in varying states of undress. Another man they recognized from the twenty-third P.I.U. was taking notes, a paramedic was swabbing one of the women's hands with cotton dipped in acetone.

Phil Shaw looked up from his pad and waved to Arnie and Baxter. They walked to where he stood talking to a tall and elegant blonde. "Miss Grant, this is Sergeant Ross and Detective Baxter."

She reached out a slender hand. "I'm Muffy Grant." She licked her lips and drew a deep breath. The rims of her eyes were red and she was clearly having difficulty controlling herself. She released the breath slowly. "I own Slimtronics."

"Please, sit down, Miss Grant," Arnie said. "I'm sure you've already been through this with Officer Shaw. Do you think you could tell me what happened again?''

She squeezed her eyelids together and nodded. ''I'll try.'' She recounted the beginning of the class, the appearance of the three masked men, and the robbery. ''Then they went down the stairs. We sat here for about fifteen or twenty minutes. I guess it was twenty after one or so when I heard the buzzer begin to ring. It was another twenty minutes or so before one of the people who comes at one-thirty called on the phone. She must have let it ring fifty times. Then she got worried and called the building superintendent. The number's on the building agent's panel on the outside wall. He opened the door with a key. When Gena—she's the receptionist—heard him call, she kicked the door of the closet where they had left her. Then they called the police.'' She swallowed hard. ''They got us loose, and found . . . Laszlo.'' A solitary tear slipped down her cheek.

Ross listened sympathetically with his arms folded, his chin on his chest, while Baxter took down her words in shorthand in his notebook. ''Did anybody else get hurt?''

''Not really. Everybody was scared to death. Everybody. One of them hit Libby Beckman and twisted a couple of wrists. But the leader made him stop. After that we were okay, except for Louise. Once they put the nail polish remover on our hands. It just comes right off.''

''What's that?'' Arnie asked.

''The Krazy Glue they put on our hands. But Louise panicked and she pulled. She tore some of the skin off her hand, and Donna Fuller's too. She was the girl she was sitting next to.'' Muffy Grant sniffled. ''I need a tissue.''

''Go ahead,'' Ross said, and watched her walk across the room toward a table near the window.

''A polite thief who kills,'' Baxter observed.

''Not on purpose, maybe,'' Ross speculated. ''Not that that will bring the poor bastard back to life. Who was he, anyway, Phil?''

Shaw flipped through his notebook. ''Name of Laszlo Dushan. Yugoslavian immigrant. He was a combination assistant, handyman, masseur. Been here about two years. Almost since she started the joint.''

"It smells of an inside job, anyway. Maybe he was bumped to keep his mouth shut," Baxter said.

Ross rolled his eyes. "About the fucking Brink's robbery? Give us a break, will you, Marvin? Use your fucking college degree. This borders on petty larceny. What was the total take?''

"Joke's on you, white man. All told, including estimated value of jewelry, on the first pass from twelve very scared ladies—call it about nine grand in hard cash and two hundred more in jewelry.'' Shaw smiled. "Maybe we should get into another business, huh, Arnie?''

Ross nodded in appreciation. "These broads had two hundred nine large on their person? We're not in the wrong business, Philly my boy, we're banging the wrong chicks.''

"Bullshit," a voice roared from down the stairs. "Get out of my way or you'll be shoveling horseshit for the mounted patrol when I'm through with you. Who the hell is in charge here?''

A woman who had been sitting against a post in the middle of the floor, staring dully, raised her head and howled as mournfully as a bloodhound, "Freddie!'' The name seemed to have six syllables. When she put her hand on the floor to push herself up, she howled again. "Owwwww!'' She was bandaged where she had ripped the skin in her hand when she had panicked. She trembled in her silver lamé body suit, made still more transparent and clinging by the perspiration derived of fear more than exercise.

"I'm Fred Federbush," the man said, bulling his way forward. He held his arms open. "C'mere, baby doll. Who the hell is in charge here?'' Louise ran into his arms, and was enveloped. He was over six feet tall, and weighed three hundred pounds, much of which protruded at waist level through his camel-colored cashmere overcoat.

This must be the heat from downtown, Arnie thought. If

he doesn't lose some weight, and stop getting apoplectic, his wife and her boyfriend are going to inherit his money even sooner than they hoped. "I'm Sergeant Ross, Homicide Zone Four."

"Terrific. I'm taking my wife home."

Arnie smiled at him. Marvin Baxter saw the smile and shuddered. Please, Lord, let Arnie not lose his temper just this one time—for me, Lord.

"There's been a murder here, Mr. Federbush. We have to question everyone. I'm sure you understand." Arnie spoke the words of calm reason. Listen, fatso, he said in his head, we need to talk to your wimp of a wife and find out if inside of the vacuum between her ears there may be some clue about who ripped her off and killed the guy downstairs.

"She's in no condition to be questioned. You ought to be able to see that, Ross."

I am not your chauffeur, Arnie said to himself. "I appreciate that she's scared, Mr. Federbush. I'm sure that she feels much more secure now that you're here. Let me ask just a few questions. You don't mind, do you, Mrs. Federbush?"

Federbush started to answer for her, and Baxter, watching Arnie's face, groaned inwardly.

"I don't mind," Louise said. "Just let's get it over with."

"What did you see?"

"There were three men. Like the three bears—small, medium, and large. All spics. They talked like spics, anyway. All with stocking masks. I couldn't recognize one if I tripped over him. I was scared to death. They made us sit over there and they glued us together. Then they took everybody's jewels and money and took off." She shuddered. "Can I go now?"

Ross nodded. "I may want to call on you later, Mrs. Federbush."

"You guys ought to worry about protecting people more than sweeping up afterward," Federbush said. "I mean, what the hell do I pay taxes for? Where's your coat, baby doll? Or did they steal that too?''

The coat was on the floor in the corner where she had thrown it. Sable, Arnie said to himself. As they passed out of sight down the stairs, he turned to Baxter and said, ''She was wearing five years of your salary, sunshine. How do you like that?''

''Very classy. You notice that she said it was spics who ripped her off. I'm sure glad it wasn't niggers.''

''Don't worry, Marvin. Your people must have been driving the getaway car.''

''And your people will be paying them ten cents on the dollar for the stolen merchandise.''

''Everybody has to do his own thing, my man. Let's talk to the girl that got beat up on.''

Libby Beckman felt much better once she had called her office. It was strange, she thought. She had been more worried about being absent from the Foreign Loan Committee meeting than she was by the robbery. Scared as she had been, she'd found it exhilarating, especially her own newfound courage. Of course, that had been before they had told her about poor Laszlo. His death made no sense to her. It was probably the one who hit her. She knew it couldn't have been the slender one with the gun.

Arnie found Libby a better witness than Louise Federbush or Muffy Grant had been. ''Even though it's hard to see through a stocking mask, I have a general impression of their faces. I know I'd remember their voices if I heard them again.'' She gave Ross heights and shapes and weights. ''The leader, he has eyes . . . like a girl, long eyelashes. He was almost nice.''

''He couldn't be too nice, miss,'' Ross said. ''He's at least an accomplice to murder.''

It was past four-thirty by the time everyone had been questioned and released. Muffy Grant's Slimtronics Salon had been dusted top to bottom by Forensics.

The press had hung around, lights and cameras winking, microphones extended, pencils cocked. After clearing it with Flaherty, Ross had made a short statement. A reporter who covered cityside for the *Post* and knew Arnie well asked, "What was the victim killed by, Sergeant?"

"We have no coroner's report yet, but I'd say he was killed by a karate blow."

"They love it," Baxter said, getting into the car.

"Murder in a good neighborhood. What could be better for circulation?" Arnie said. "Maybe Jane Fonda will add this to her exercise tape."

The day had been dull. The next edition of the *Post* headlined, ROBBERY MURDER AT GYM. Inside, working with what little they had, the story began, "At 1:00 P.M. today a gang of three masked men robbed the clients of the Muffy Grant Slimtronics Salon at Madison and Sixty-second Street. In the course of the robbery, Laszlo Dushan, thirty-one years old, an instructor at the gym, was killed. Though the immediate cause of death is believed to be strangulation, as the victim's nose and mouth were taped shut when he was bound, it is probable that Dushan died as a result of deadly karate blows. Sergeant Arnold Ross of the homicide squad indicated that the perpetrators may have been schooled in the martial arts." The rest of the paragraph came from the paper's files. "Ross, who has been on the force for eighteen years, is considered one of the department's foremost experts on self-defense. He has participated in national tournaments and has taught at the police academy."

CHAPTER

FOUR

While Ross and Baxter headed back to the precinct, Alvin Peskin stood behind a young woman in a purple down coat tapping his foot impatiently. Like the four people who had preceded her, she couldn't seem to get the hang of the cash machine. Christ, Alvin thought, it's easy enough to stick a card in a slot and push a six-digit code. The damn directions are printed for you on a display screen.

Alvin had left his office early to avoid the rush. He had expected to go to the cash machine at the Chemical Bank on Madison Avenue and Seventy-fourth Street, take the two hundred dollars he needed for his dinner date, and still have time for a haircut and a workout at the club. Cash was important. His wife went through his American Express receipts, and he didn't want to have to explain this one. He pushed his card into the slot.

Across the street Oscar Garcia gunned the throttle of his red and white Honda Passport to reassure himself that the silent 70cc motor was still running. There was no one left behind the man at the cash machine except his brother Hector.

The man turned around blindly, counting the bills he had just withdrawn from the machine. Oscar looked up and down the avenue. There was no one on the block across the street. He honked his horn twice, then cut across diagonally, just avoiding an oncoming bus.

At the sound of the horn Hector Garcia made the four fingers of his right hand rigid and tucked his thumb into his palm, thrusting them forward in a blur into Alvin Peskin's Adam's apple, while with his left hand he extracted the two hundred dollars from his grasp.

Without further attention to Peskin, Hector jumped onto the seat of the Honda behind his brother and took off down the street, and disappeared in the maze of late-day traffic.

At the same time, Flora Greenwood tucked the hundred dollars she had taken from the cash machine on Eighty-sixth Street into her commodious handbag and stepped toward the bus stop at the curb. A young man on a motorcycle like the Garcias' delivered a karate chop to the bridge of her nose. She drew a frightened, painracked breath and brought her hands to her face. The young man grabbed the purse, and slipping it over his arm, raced away.

On Seventy-fourth Street Alvin Peskin had turned to find his assailant, then realized that no air was passing into his lungs. He reached up to his throat, where Hector Garcia's fingers had crushed his larynx, pinching his trachea. He was unable even to voice his pain and indignation. He walked forward a few steps, the oxygen draining from his bloodstream, his face turning a cyanotic blue, then fell headlong on the pavement.

Several people stepped over or around his body, thinking him a drunk or an addict. Finally, a young black man in a jogging suit stopped to turn him over. Seeing that Peskin was unconscious, and that his chest was heaving for want of air, he tried mouth-to-mouth resuscitation, but was unable to force the passage. A policeman arrived a minute later, stuffed Alvin Peskin into his squad car, and roared away to Lenox Hill Hospital.

The emergency entrance of the hospital, only four blocks from the scene of the crime, opened at the sound of the wailing siren. Two orderlies took the limp form and placed it on a table. The attending resident did not bother with gloves or antiseptic. "Trach set, stat!" he yelled at a nurse, pulling away Peskin's tie and tearing the buttons from his collar and shirtfront. The cop turned his head as the doctor made an incision at the base of the throat, plucked at the windpipe, severed it, and inserted a breathing tube. There was a hesitation. He leaned his weight on Peskin's chest. There was a bubbling sound, and the chest began to rise and fall as the pipe brought air to the oxygen-starved lungs. Alvin Peskin worked out four or five times a week. He was in good shape, and only thirty-three years old. He continued to breathe rhythmically. The doctor stepped away from the table and breathed a sigh of relief. Life had been sustained. He ordered a nurse to call for a senior surgeon to meet him as soon as possible in Intensive Care. Another rolled up a Bird respirator and introduced the plastic hose into the opening in the tracheotomy tube. The doctor walked along beside the rolling table as the orderlies trundled Peskin across the main floor and into the elevator.

It had been less than ten minutes since Alvin Peskin had been assaulted. The rigorously trained nurses of Intensive Care had him undressed, antiseptic, cleansed, and plugged into an intravenous set filling him with replacements for lost fluids and life-sustaining drugs in only sixty seconds more.

They tapped his vital signs with probes that led to monitoring screens. The attending surgeon moved rapidly across the floor to join with the resident in an evaluation of the injury and a speedy decision on a course of treatment to rebuild the crushed larynx and to restore normal breathing.

Checking the green cathode tubes, they noted that all of

Alvin Peskin's vital signs were at reasonable levels save one. The time between the blow from Hector Garcia's hand and the opening of the airway in the emergency room had been too long. Alvin Peskin's brain had died on the sidewalk on Madison Avenue.

CHAPTER

FIVE

It often occurred to Sergeant Luis Hernandez that the forms of leisure activity that men and women choose are more reflective of their personalities than their professions. Life may visit a salesman's role on someone whose inclinations are better revealed by solitudinous attention to a stamp collection.

Hernandez tugged at the cuffs of his gloves to set them more securely on his fingers. The wind that blew across the Rockaway Inlet from the Atlantic Ocean gave an extra bite to the chill of the failing day. He checked his watch and increased the length of his stride. His pulse rate picked up a bit, but there was no change in his breathing pattern. He had run six miles in less than an hour, and had another two miles left to his car at the parking lot on the other side of Brooklyn's Marine Park.

Hernandez was a contemplative man. He had chosen a police career together with his lifelong friend Arnie Ross. Unlike Ross, he was married, with five children. He read a lot, and enjoyed running every day, both for the pleasure of athletic activity and the chance to contend with his

33

thoughts. He smiled to himself as he picked up his pace a bit more.

Arnie hated running. He couldn't talk and run at the same time. Much too passive, he always said. Instead, he spent an hour or two a day kicking the stuffing out of a dummy.

Of course, Hernandez thought, I don't have to live with his rage. My father, God rest his soul, was a wonderful man. My mother is cheerful, attentive, and generous. They gave us the moon from their little neighborhood grocery store as if they were Rockefellers. No, Luis thought, crossing himself, my father wasn't a third-rate gangster who beat me and my mother and sister, and who ended his lousy life bleeding from the stumps of his legs where his bosses had blown them off with a shotgun.

Luis could see the car across the broad dirt field where in a few months grass would form a softer carpet for his pounding feet. He leaned his greyhound frame into the wind and began to pump his arms. He was six foot one, taller than Ross by a couple of inches, but at one sixty-five, weighed thirty pounds less. The wind burned high cheekbones set in a narrow, handsome face, with large luminous brown eyes, a straight nose, and a placid expression. He sprinted the last quarter mile and came to the old Chevy station wagon breathing hard. He walked around the car for a moment till his pulse leveled out, then drove to his house on Farragut Avenue in Canarsie, ten minutes away.

He was greeted by bedlam. He smiled, patting heads and kissing cheeks as he made his way with imperturbable determination to the relative quiet of his second-floor bedroom and a shower.

"Luis, *amor*."

"I'm here, honey."

"You have to call in right away." Her voice came from the bedroom. "They've called three times."

Margarita sat in a straight-backed chair at the side of the bed, folding shirts, underwear, and other oddments of clothing from a large basket at her side. She was of medium height, slender, with a large bosom. Her face was beautiful, Luis thought, with traces of Carib Indian ancestry and the Spanish dons who had settled their island. Her hair was a cascade of shimmering black.

He leaned over to kiss her, a wandering hand resting for a moment on her breast. "I wonder what it is this time."

She slapped his hand, then reached up to touch his cheek. "They didn't give me a clue."

He stripped off his sweatshirt and kicked off his running shoes. Then picked up the phone. "Who wants me?"

"Flaherty."

Luis dialed the number, a frown on his face. It was unlike the lieutenant to call.

"Flaherty."

"It's Hernandez."

"Lou, you want to hurry in, please?"

"Yes, sir. What's up?"

"A mugging. The guy's at death's door. Brain-dead already, they tell me."

"Is Arnie in?"

"He's working on a stiff that was delivered at a fancy ladies' gymnasium. I'm sure you'll hear about it on the radio on the way in. Charley's waiting for you."

"Can I have him please?" Luis waited a moment while his boss transferred the call to Charley Passarelli, his partner. Twenty-five years on the force, and never drawn a bead of sweat. Very knowledgeable. Very sedentary. He heard a grunt on the line. "That must be you, Charley."

"It's me all right."

"I didn't wake you, did I?" Luis smiled. If Charley wasn't standing on his feet, it was better than even money that he was asleep. "Charley, go collect the data on this mugging victim. Where is he?"

"Lenox Hill."

"By the time I get in, I want all of the dope. Go there and see if you can contact a witness or a member of the family. Find out what happened if you can. I want it when I get in.''

Around a stifled yawn Passarelli replied, "Right, gotcha."

Luis looked at the clock. "Arnie's got a fresh case. Poor old Flaherty saw another one come, looked for me, and was afraid he might miss his pinochle game tonight."

"That gets us three phone calls?"

Dropping the rest of his running gear into the hamper on his way to the shower, he said, "I guess I'm getting cynical."

He was showered and dressed in ten minutes in a pair of gray slacks, a white shirt, and a sweater. He carried a snub-nosed .38 Police Special in a web holster under his arm. He slipped on a sport jacket and said, "Just like any other commuter."

Margarita nodded assent, keeping her eyes on the laundry. She had maintained the pretense for eighteen years so that he did not know that each time he strapped the gun to his body and walked through the door, she died a little bit.

He touched her hair as he walked by her to leave the room. He was a happy man. He had a good life. But he was not afraid to die. He had made his peace with God. Only, he could not imagine a place, hereafter or otherwise, where there was no Margarita.

He looked in on each of his children, asking about school, about homework, about sports. It was brief, but the intention was plain, and appreciated. Arnaldo lay on the floor of the room he shared with his fourteen-year-old brother. He was twelve and looked like his father. Lou stood at the door for a moment and watched as the boy snapped off twenty sit-ups. "You'll grow, chico," he said. "You don't have to rush it."

As he drove out into the street, he wondered if there was some way that his son could have inherited Arnie Ross's intensity along with his name.

When Luis Hernandez arrived at the twenty-third precinct an hour later, Charley Passarelli had laid the information that he had on Peskin on his desk. There was precious

little. There was always the temptation to enlist the aid of
the media in this kind of case. Occasionally, if you asked
them to print a special phone number for witnesses to a
crime, or information on a missing person, something
would click. In this case the only involved person had
been some good Joe who had stopped to try to give the
victim artificial respiration without success. It wouldn't be
worth the trouble to ask the press. Lou made a note in the
margin of Passarelli's compilation. They'd do it the me-
thodical, time-tested way. They'd go from door to door,
from store to store, asking if anyone had seen anything at
all on Madison Avenue in front of the Chemical Bank at
four-thirty that blustery March afternoon.

Arnie Ross was seated behind his desk fighting paperwork
when Lou arrived. "Hi, Roach," he said. *"Qué pasa?"*

"Not much, Jew. And with yourself?"

Arnie shrugged and slumped in the chair behind his
desk, which abutted Hernandez's in the Sergeants' Office.
There were two file cabinets, four chairs, and barely room
enough to navigate between them.

"How's home?"

"Fine. Mamma's coming for dinner tomorrow. You
coming?"

"If I'm alive. What's to eat?"

"I don't know." Hernandez put down the file. "Have
you been talking to Arnaldo?"

Arnie shook his head. "No more than usual. Why?"

"He's starting to show signs of Ross-like concern about
his physical fitness and the size of his *pepita*."

"You can't blame every fucking thing on me. It's the
age. You're the one with five kids. I'm a bachelor. How's
the old lady?"

"She'd punch your fat head if she heard that. She's
fine. What you got?"

"I was going to ask you. I could use some legs. Three
of your fellow Latinos ripped off a ladies' spa. In the
process they killed a gym instructor. Stocking masks.
Everybody's scared. You know the routine. I want to

reinterview everybody that was there to see if we can't get some kind of composite idea.''

"Then we can advertise for three masked Latins. I might as well help you, if Flaherty doesn't mind. I'm at a dead end. A mugger gives a guy a punch at a cash machine, steals a couple of hundred bucks. The guy dies. Case opened. Case closed. No witnesses. No nothing.''

CHAPTER

SIX

Willie entered a loft building on Sixth Avenue and Eighth Street. The old structure had been reinforced on the inside and the brick repointed and sandblasted. A savings bank occupied the lower floor. One flight up there was the Tokyo and Seoul Sauna and Health Club, an oriental massage parlor. On the third and top floor was the Ten-do Karate-Dojo.

Willie took a key from his pocket and let himself in. The room was dimly lit. Such light as there was was reflected from the thick white mats that covered the floor and padded the walls.

In the locker room in the rear he stripped and showered, washing himself thoroughly, seated on a small wooden stool. When he was dry, he put on a loincloth tied about his middle with a cotton rope, then a judo suit with flapping pants legs and sleeves. He took the money and jewelry from Muffy Grant's from the pockets of his street clothes and put them into a soft leather pouch, then knocked diffidently at an adjacent door.

"*Hai?*"

"Wilfredo Lopez, Matsushima-sama." Always *sama*, the address of deference.

"Come."

The light in the office had a red cast from two paper lanterns. An inlaid writing table of Oriental design stood in a corner beside a straight-backed armless chair. The floor was covered by tatami mats of woven grass. On a cushion in the midst, Prince Hiroo Matsushima sat cross-legged. He was of indeterminate age by appearance, though Willie knew that he had been eighteen at the end of the war, and had therefore been born in 1927. He seemed slight in a simple cotton judo suit. His hair was graying at the temples. He had a high forehead and a squarish jaw, hinting at great determination. His face was smooth and unlined.

Willie waited until he was invited, then sank to his haunches and bowed low. After he had placed the leather pouch in front of Matsushima, he looked up.

Matsushima remained impassive. When he had come to the United States for his second tour of duty, he had realized that his life as a business executive and a marriage without sons had trapped him permanently, so that the promise of his noble heritage would die with him. In the absence of a suitable destiny in this life, he had contemplated suicide.

In a year and a half fate had turned his rage into cold calculation, his despair into hope, and his impotence into effective action.

Like all philosophers, Matsushima thought as he reached out to heft the leather bag that Willie had placed before him, I would wither without disciples. The young man on his knees before me tried to rob me. He was not my match. I had it in my power to kill him, and saw that he cared as little as I. I had a vision. I was born a samurai in a world that no longer treasures their ways. He would learn them.

"Why was there violence?" Matsushima asked without emotion. His voice was a nasal tenor, his English flawless though accented.

Willie weighed his words. "A man who worked at the gymnasium interrupted us, Matsushima-sama. I was forced to knock him out."

"Were you forced to kill him?".

"I did not kill him," Willie answered. He repeated a lesson learned by rote. "It is forbidden to take life unless there is no other solution, or capture or betrayal of a clan member is imminent."

"Nonetheless, it is in the papers and on the radio that he died."

Willie wanted to say that it was impossible. He searched for other words more deferential. "I struck him above the kidney with the heel, and then with the toe to the jaw. Unless my aim was poor, they were not killing blows."

"I saw a policeman on television. His name is Ross. He is a martial arts expert. He says the blows were delivered by a man schooled in the arts."

"If he says they could have killed, then he is not an expert, Matsushima-sama."

"Just so." The calm voice took on an edge. "You may read all of what he said in the paper. Was it you who tied the man?"

"No, Matsushima-sama. It was Adolfo Reyes."

"The man was strangled by his bonds. Reyes?" There was a flicker of the eyelids. "Tell me what happened. Leave out no detail." Matsushima listened with patience. There were no Japanese in New York yearning to return to the ways of their ancestors. They had come to sell video games and learn to dance in discotheques. But there was the material of samurai there. Not the hardened criminal, but the youth without hope. To live as a samurai you cannot fear death. Willie was only the first. His clan, like his philosophy, was ecumenical. Blacks, whites, and Puerto Ricans had been accepted—a dozen of them. They had all been lost and past caring. He had given them strength through learning—Zen and the martial arts—the way of the samurai. From his discipline they had recovered a will to live. Matsushima's eyebrows rose a fraction as he experienced a moment of cold lucidity. For the propagation of their faith and his philosophy, there had to be risk and reward, and the funds to go on. For the samurai warrior in New York City in the 1980s, the only open road was crime. Disparaging of society, Matsushima never hesitated. He had attained his end. He had become a master of samurai, as his family heritage had foretold. That he had become a common criminal was of no moment. He focused his attention on Willie.

Willie finished his story, bowed his head, and waited. Matsushima asked, "Wilfredo, what are the guiding principles of the samurai?"

"Filial piety, obedience, loyalty, and the sense of one's indebtedness to one's superiors."

"How is the failure to observe these principles regarded?"

"As a disgrace."

"Is a superior not responsible for the failure of his subordinates?"

Willie's voice was very low. "Yes, Matsushima-sama."

"If you are responsible for the acts of subordinates, and they kill needlessly, are you not in disgrace?"

Willie swallowed. He could see clearly where Matsushima was leading him. A part of his mind called out to him that this was a scene from a book or a movie. The thought was immediately submerged in his total commitment. From Matsushima he had learned, like the other clan members, that there was a place for him. All that was necessary was to believe and act accordingly. If he was unable to believe, he would be where he was when Matsushima found him. He would rather be dead. "If you want, Matsushima-sama, I will commit seppuku."

Matsushima felt a rush of satisfaction. There had been a breath of hesitation, then Wilfredo Lopez had offered him his life. Such was the strength that he had instilled in Willie. That belief in the way of the samurai was what bound the members of the clan to him. He did not doubt that if he ordered it, Willie would find a quiet corner, sit down, and disembowel himself.

Matsushima let Willie ponder his fate for a moment, then said, "It is not a fitting punishment. Your fault has been in choosing your subordinates unwisely. It was you who brought Adolfo Reyes to us. He acts not like a samurai, but like a *yakuza*."

Matsushima used the word with contempt: Japanese men of low birth and poor manners. The real world beyond these walls was filled with *yakuza*. Matsushima frowned. Which was the real world? His Wall Street office, where he presided as general manager of North American operations for Inyo Lines, the largest Japanese ocean freight carrier, or this bare gymnasium, which was the headquarters of a samurai clan that existed as an extension of his imagination?

Willie heard the characteristic flapping sound of Matsushima's sleeves as he straightened his arms from his sides in a gesture of anger. "Will Reyes be here tonight?"

"Yes, Matsushima-sama."

Matsushima looked through the contents of the bag, counting the money and estimating the value of the jewelry. "What is his share?"

"You receive eighty percent. Twenty percent are kept by the samurai. Of our share, I receive forty percent and Adolfo and Paco Nunez, thirty percent each."

"So Reyes is due six percent of the total." Matsushima calculated quickly. "About five hundred dollars in cash and perhaps ten times that when the jewelry is sold." He rose and opened a drawer in his desk and withdrew one of the stacks of hundred-dollar bills with which it was packed. "When he comes to class tonight, pay him, also pay Paco, the full share. Give them each six thousand dollars."

"Yes, Matsushima-sama."

"You are dismissed. Go to prepare the gymnasium for the class and turn on the boiler for the steambath and the showers. When you are done, sit in front of the picture of Ryoan-ji, and meditate."

Willie took the money and backed out of the room, a

tremor passing through his body. Was he really prepared to take his own life?

When he had finished his chores, he sat cross-legged on the floor in front of a large scroll painting of a Japanese garden. Rocks of odd mountainous shapes thrust up at random in a sea of carefully raked sand. His eyes moved from one prominence to another, then tried to take in the whole. There was order, yet there was mystery. Was that what Matsushima wanted him to see? Like Bushido—the samurai warrior code—like *giri*—the principle of duty and obedience—the garden of Ryoan-ji demanded contemplation without the promise of understanding. Willie could see that there was beauty in the principles as well as in the garden, and that study of both would bring him closer to the truth.

He had chosen badly in bringing Adolfo Reyes to the clan.

He rose and went into the mat-filled room to begin his loosening exercises, first for suppleness, then for speed and guile, and then for devastating strength.

When Matsushima walked into the gymnasium, Willie stood in the middle of the room, feet spread to shoulder width. Keeping his hands at his sides, he bent forward from the waist until the top of his head touched the floor. He maintained the position for a moment. When he saw that Matsushima had entered, he straightened, bowed to him, and backed to the wall.

Matsushima squatted slowly, then rose again, twenty times, carefully controlling his breathing, exhaling sharply when he came upright. With the exercise his mind calmed. Having properly stretched his thigh muscles, he did a split on the floor and touched his head to each knee fifty times.

After a half hour of loosening and bending, he whirled into a frenzy of activity, spinning around the room, striking out with his four limbs, in series and in tandem, in unison and alone.

Wilfredo Lopez stood against the wall, awed by the

knowledge that at the termination of each blow was the power of death over life. It was with that impact that Matsushima had changed his life—destroying utterly, then rebuilding on new foundations.

It was hard to believe that little more than a year had passed. It had been Christmas week. Willie and five friends had been marauding Manhattan in a 1962 Chevy, each fender a different color, that they had pieced together from stolen parts and an old chassis. The trunk was already full of packages and gifts that had been left in parked cars by the unwary or uninitiated. A paper bag contained cash and bits of jewelry, rosaries, compacts, cigarette cases that had come from twenty purse-snatchings during the day. As night had fallen, they were emboldened to mug a few men, hoping to find large sums of cash meant for Christmas shopping. Trying to avoid the police, they had spread their efforts from the East Side to the West Side, and from uptown to downtown.

At five forty-five Willie and three of his companions left the others in the car on Sixth Avenue and stationed themselves at the corner of Forty-seventh Street.

The block that runs east to Fifth Avenue is the diamond center of New York, and it was closing time. Willie watched disinterestedly as Hasidic Jews in their beaver hats and frock coats streamed from the stores that lined the street. He wanted no truck with them. When they were gone, the army of guards from the private detective agencies that were hired to watch over the block would be gone with them.

Willie was interested in a straggling customer, or perhaps someone headed toward the department stores on Fifth Avenue, which, in the spirit of Christmas, would be open for business until ten P.M.

As the lights in the windows winked out, Willie noticed a lone figure walking west on the uptown side of the street. There was a delivery bay half a dozen doors in from Sixth Avenue. The man would pass right by it. Willie and his friends slipped into the doorway. He was a little guy. It would be quick. They'd pull him in, take his watch and his cash, whomp him upside the head, and take off for the waiting car.

Hiroo Matsushima was preoccupied with thoughts of the office and his errands. He had had an unpleasant day with the *geigin* whose agency represented Inyo Lines. In addition, at the insistence of his wife and daughters, the *geigin* Christmas was to be kept; presents, cards, a tree.

It was a shadow on the pavement that first alerted him, then a flicker of movement. Matsushima shifted the weight to the balls of his feet and cleared his mind, all instinct and reaction.

Two of Willie's companions were to grab Matsushima by the shoulders and pull him forward into the doorway. Then Willie would hit him in the face with a gloved hand, and he would be frisked and shaken down. It would be over in thirty seconds. Then a swift kick in the groin to keep him quiet, and they'd disappear.

When the two sets of hands appeared from the darkness, Hiroo Matsushima was expecting them. He dropped his umbrella and his briefcase, and dancing away from one pair of arms, grasped the other, and using the owner's weight and leverage snapped them like matchsticks at the elbow. The hulking teenager fell to the ground, choking on his own vomit, unable to scream. Matsushima pulled the second assailant toward him and delivered two kicks, smashing his kneecaps. A third who was in the doorway ran, his coat flapping behind him, slipping and sliding on the wet pavement in his anxiety to escape.

Wilfredo Lopez stood his ground above his crippled companions.

"Run," Matsushima barked with contempt. "Run with the other dog."

"Fuck you. I ain't no dog."

Matsushima kicked a prostrate boy, who gagged and groaned. "You will finish like him."

"Fuck you. Whyn't you call the cops?"

"I need no police." Matsushima's hand flicked out so quickly that Willie would not have known that he had been struck, save for the pain. "You are common *yakuza*. Do you have a gun or a knife? Why don't you use it on me?" He struck his face again, splitting his lower lip.

Willie spit on the ground—a tooth, some blood. "Why don't you break my neck?"

"Are you afraid?"

"No."

"You know I can kill you, but you are not afraid."

"What do I have to lose?"

As Willie recalled the moment, he wondered, as often he did, what went on in Matsushima-sama's mind during the half minute of silence that elapsed in the dark doorway.

"If you have the courage to die, then you have the courage to live. Leave this place and this trash." He kicked the boy with the broken legs under the chin with his pointed shoe to still his whimpering. "If you wish to begin to climb out of the gutter, you can meet me at the bus stop in front of Madison Square Garden on the Seventh Avenue side at five tomorrow afternoon. I will wait five minutes."

"In the middle of the block?"

Matsushima struck his nose with the flat of his palm. "In the middle of the block, sir."

"Sir," Willie gasped.

Matsushima picked up his attaché case and his umbrella and walked away at the same deliberate pace with which he had arrived.

Willie wasn't sure why he showed up the following day. Perhaps it was because he had told the truth. His life had no meaning and no point, and therefore no value to him. He would never understand why Matsushima had appeared.

"Hello, boy," Matsushima had said.

"Hello," Willie had paused, then finished, ". . . sir."

"Ah, so. You learn. What happened with the others?"

"I did what you told me. I left them there. I walked away."

"No. I did as you told me."

"Huh?"

"You will learn to speak properly." There was no room for equivocation. "You will learn many things. Where do you live?"

"In an abandoned building in the Bronx."

Matsushima said, "Find a cheap hotel somewhere in downtown New York. Move your things there. Meet me here again on Monday."

"How can I get a room?"

Matsushima gave him two hundred dollars.

Willie leaned back. "You ain't a chicken hawk?" When he saw the frown on Matsushima's face, he said, "A fag, a *maricón*. I don't sell my ass to nobody."

"Ah. No." No offense was taken.

Willie accepted the money. "Monday, here, same time, sir."

"Yes."

"How do you know I won't just take off with the money?"

"Two hundred dollars in exchange for a new life?" Matsushima shrugged. "As you wish." He walked away into the crowd, leaving Willie behind him, staring with incomprehension.

Willie was brought back from his reverie by the ringing of the door buzzer. Some of the students had begun to arrive. The Garcia brothers were carrying cheap gym bags. One held their judo suits, the other the spoils of their afternoon's work. They said hello to Willie, then bowed deeply to Matsushima, who acknowledged them with a nod of his head and went back to his office.

Within ten minutes all of the members of the evening class of the Ten-do Karate-Dojo were present and dressed in their loose-fitting white suits. As they arrived, they knocked at the door of Matsushima's office and showed their respect by sitting before him with their legs beneath them and bowing to the floor. They presented their day's receipts, and then backed out to the gym floor to begin their preliminary exercises.

By seven-thirty they were all assembled, an even dozen of them, eight of Latin origin, two blacks and two whites. All were in their late teens or early twenties, and while varying in height, were uniformly supple and slender. When Matsushima opened the door of his office, they fell silent and bowed to him.

"*Hai!!!*" Matsushima cried, snapping his right fist out before him and spreading his legs in the classic posture of readiness.

"*Hai!!!*" the twelve voices replied as the movement was repeated.

For an hour Matsushima's every movement, sound, and gesture was copied exactly by the members of the class. With each succeeding moment the complexity and rhythms of the movements were augmented, till they took on the intricacy of choreography.

Matsushima stood still before them. He bowed his head. They bent from the waist, their eyes fixed on the ground before them. "Discipline," he said in his clipped tones, "is everything. I am pleased."

They raised their heads.

He squatted and sat cross-legged on the mats. They followed. He pointed at Hector Garcia and a black boy named Fred Logan. The perfect mismatch. Garcia was short and muscular, the black over six feet and painfully thin. They rose and bowed, first to Matsushima, then to the rest of the class, finally to each other.

Matsushima smiled as Garcia snapped his right hand forward with his fingers rigidly extended toward Logan's throat. We all lead with our strengths.

Logan was familiar with Garcia's pattern of attack. He spun to his left to avoid the blow, at the same time making use of his much longer reach to deliver a chop to the back of Garcia's neck. The shorter man dropped instantly to his knees, the hand brushing the top of his head. He shot out a leg, but Logan was already above the ground. A bead of perspiration trickled down Garcia's face.

"Enough," Matsushima said, clapping his hands twice. The sweat was the result of tension, not of exercise. The blows could kill. A short exchange was sufficient to maintain a keen edge.

Four more times Matsushima paired his pupils, and after brief encounters stopped them short of possible injury. Then only Willie Lopez and Adolfo Reyes were left. They rose and made their ritual bows.

Before Willie had fully raised his head, Adolfo spun and shot a leg out at Willie's groin. Willie blocked the blow with his forearm, but grunted in pain and fell back a step off balance. Reyes spun again, but Willie had used the momentum of his own near-fall to do a back roll and come up standing beyond Reyes's reach.

Matsushima frowned. With some men only the surface can be changed. Reyes had learned technique without the underlying values. He did not have a sense of honor. It was the first such problem he had encountered in his year as master of the Ten-do.

Willie had been the first disciple. He had shown up that Monday in late December with a torn canvas bag that held his every possession. He had taken a room at a single room occupancy dive in the Village in the wholesale meat district.

"It was nine dollars a night, tax included. I paid through tonight. That's thirty-six bucks. I spent three dollars a day for food. That's twelve dollars. I didn't have no money. The guys in the car had all the shit we stole. Here's the change, a hundred fifty-two bucks." He held out the money. "Sir."

"First, it is 'I didn't have *any* money.' The double negative is incorrect." It seemed strange to Matsushima to hear himself correcting the boy in his own stilted English. "Then there is the matter of shit. No one defecated. Things were stolen, not shit. You will not be vulgar.

Third, you are still growing. You are directed to eat properly. Keep the money.''

"I don't take no . . . any . . . charity, sir.''

"You will be equipped to earn your way in my service.''

"Service?'' Willie frowned.

"Where I come from . . . more correctly, where my ancestors came from . . . the concept of service was a matter of honor and pride, not shame. If you are interested in pride, I will instruct you in how to develop it through service.''

"I have never had anything to be proud of.''

"You have no family?''

Involuntarily, Willie had put his hand to the pie-shaped shadow of a scar on his cheek. "No. No family.''

"Let us go to this hotel you have found; we have much to discuss.''

Matsushima's reminiscence was broken by an explosive grunt of effort as Reyes took one, two, three, four steps forward, changing lead legs and fists in an effort to rob Willie of the advantage of quickness through an attack of unadorned power. Again Willie pirouetted away, lifting his leg. Matsushima restrained the instinct to say halt. The blow fell home in the midst of Reyes's back. His breath was a ragged gasp.

Anger and pain were a stimulant. He butted Willie with his head, catching him painfully on the point of the hip, then slapped him with an open palm, catching him across the ear. Willie's head rang like a church bell, and he was deafened. He felt a warm trickle down the side of his cheek. His eardrum must have been punctured. Reyes smiled.

Only a slight twitch of the mouth expressed Matsushima's distaste at the exhibition of bad manners.

Reyes folded his ten fingers together for a killing blow at the point of the chin and brought his joined fists upward sharply. Willie moved his head the fraction of an inch required to avoid the blow.

Reyes tried to stop, but the laws of gravity and momentum had already committed him to his course of action.

Matsushima congratulated himself on his part in the development of Willie's character. The throat was open; the chin, the nose, the chest. A thrust of a knee, or a hand or foot, and Reyes would pass his life as a eunuch. A blow to the upstretched abdominal muscles with the heel of the hands would rupture his intestines and tear his liver, leaving him a half day to die of internal bleeding or the complications of peritonitis.

Willie made a fist and rapped sharply at the middle of Reyes's thigh, not hard enough to shatter the bone, but enough to traumatize the muscle tissue. The leg collapsed under him and he fell on his back. Willie dropped with one knee on the middle of his chest and pushed his chin back with his left hand. He raised the right hand to strike at the exposed throat. Hearing no command, he brought the hand down in a lightning arc.

"Enough," Matsushima said. Not more than an inch remained between the descending hand and Adolfo Reyes's Adam's apple. Matsushima looked around at the faces of his students, and then directly at Paco Nunez, who had been on the raid of the Slimtronics salon. Though he struggled to maintain his impassivity, his lips were dry. He licked them. Matsushima-sama's lesson had sunk home.

"Take your showers. See that the blackboard is brought out," Matsushima said.

In ten minutes the class sat at his feet. All were cross-legged except for Reyes, who was unable to bend his leg under him.

Matsushima looked at the sheet of paper in his hand. "Tomorrow Logan will take the blue bike and cruise the Upper West Side cash dispensers. We have had the red bike too long. Hector Garcia will dispose of it in the water at the Harlem River pier. We will need a new motorcycle. Paco Nunez, you will get it in Queens, one hundred ccs or less, please."

He took a piece of chalk and drew a diagram on the blackboard. "This is the corner of Forty-sixth Street and Third Avenue. Because of the large number of homosexual prostitutes who frequent Lexington Avenue in the Fifties, this new cash machine of Citicorp is often visited by their customers. Note that it is enclosed, and a card is required for entry. You must slip in behind a user, or, alternatively, steal a card and make the owner tell you the code number. Tomorrow after midnight, Donald Wolfe"—he pointed to a small-boned blond boy with darting eyes—"will take a car and park around the corner. You will take Jorge Rodriguez with you. If there is an opportunity, take it."

Matsushima folded the paper carefully and slipped it into the jacket of his judo suit. "I have something to add before you are dismissed. We come from very different backgrounds. We are of different colors. But before we came here our lives had less meaning. This is as true for me as it is for you, perhaps even more. I have chosen to live by a philosophy that has been handed down to me by my ancestors. The choice has come to me very late in my life. You are young. In teaching you its value, I make up for lost years. The direction and security of spirit that you find here are a result of discipline. We walk a hard road. We can maintain our direction only through our belief in ourselves, and in each other. There was a successful operation at Muffy Grant's, but it was tarnished by lack of discipline." He raised his voice slightly. "Do you want to go back to being Puerto Ricans lost in the despair of your barrio, or blacks at the bottom of scale, or whites running from the miseries of your lives? Here there is no color, no caste. You learn to use your bodies and your minds. Here you belong." He looked out at their faces. "That is why you are here, each one of his own choice. Only the absence of discipline can put you back where you were. Here you have the strength of your belief, and of the whole of the clan. There must be discipline. There will be discipline." His eyes played over them, one at a time.

There was no question about understanding. Only Adolfo Reyes turned away.

The class stood and bowed as he left the gym. "Paco Nunez, Adolfo Reyes, you stay with me to help to clean up."

When they finished their tasks, they had an audience with Matsushima. "The error that was made at Muffy Grant's will never be repeated. If we must kill, let it be for a reason, and with the dignity of samurai, not by suffocating injured men." He nodded to Willie, who turned the packets of money over to Paco and Adolfo.

When they had left, Matsushima and Willie bathed and sat for a while in the steamy sauna. "Willie, do you think that Reyes would commit seppuku if I ordered it?"

"No, Matsushima-sama."

"Then, he must be helped. Where does Reyes live, Willie?"

"Sometimes in the street, sometimes with a girl in a housing development on the East River, around a Hundred and sixth street."

"Will he go there now?"

"He said that he was going out to eat."

Matsushima nodded. He reached for the phone and dialed. He explained to his wife in Japanese that he would not be home for dinner, and that she was not to wait up for him. There was whispered assent.

When he finished dressing, Hiroo Matsushima removed a black case four feet long from the closet. It was covered in pebble-grained black leather, with a handle and brass fittings, locks, and corners.

Matsushima drove a company car, as befitted his rank, the longest black Toyota. Willie sat quietly as they rode up the FDR Drive.

"Direct me to Reyes's house."

When they pulled up in front of the building, Matsushima looked about curiously, noting the location of the doorways, the lights and the shrubbery and walks. He parked a half mile away. "You wait for me here. If I do not return before five in the morning, you will drive the car to my parking lot near the office. Leave the keys. Don't be seen." Then he vanished, gone in the darkness between the buildings.

Only the glow of a small lamp above the portal of Reyes's house dispelled a bit of the gloom. Matsushima smashed the bulb with a stone. Standing in a corner against the wall, he opened his box, then slipped a black silk mask over his head. The other item in the case was his *tachi*. He drew the ceremonial sword, curved and mirror-bright, with the pledge that he would not return it to its sheath until it had drawn blood.

Adolfo Reyes returned an hour later, alone, reeling and smelling of beer. Matsushima stepped from the shadows. He aimed his sword at a point a foot beyond Reyes's neck and swung easily through the arc. The head tumbled to the ground like a blossom clipped from a stem. The body remained upright for a moment, blood gushing from the severed arteries in rhythm with the pulse of the still-beating heart, then collapsed in a heap.

Matsushima wiped the blade clean on Reyes's jacket and returned it to its sheath and case. Quickly, he removed everything from Reyes's pockets, including the cash he had been given earlier in the evening. He removed his silk mask and lifted the severed head from the pavement, where it lay staring sightlessly. He dropped the head into the mask and walked briskly between buildings, carrying both the mask and the case, till he reached the car.

"Willie, drive to the end of the road and then stop."

Wordlessly, Willie pulled out onto the FDR Drive, and in a moment had exited on 132nd Street.

"Wait here for me," Matsushima said, climbing out. He walked across the rubble-strewn patch of ground that separated the road from the river, stopping to pick up a piece of stone. At the edge of the water he added the stone to the bundle in his hand and tied a secure double knot, then threw the bundle into the swirling current.

He looked at his hands. There were only a few spots. He wiped them with his handkerchief. I have gone mad, of course, he admitted to himself.

He drove Willie to the nearest subway, and went home. He slept well, save for the occasional image of himself in colorful samurai armor in the midst of a crowd of *geigin* in Brooks Brothers suits.

CHAPTER

SEVEN

Willie stood against a rusty column in the 125th Street subway station waiting for a train. It was after ten. He sighed. His ear pained him, and his hip was sore. He had a busy day planned for tomorrow, and would have preferred to be in bed.

He had nothing to read. When he had sat on the bench to wait, he had been accosted twice, once by an old man offering a disgusting proposition, and the second time by a young man who expected to take his wallet. A single glance dissuaded him.

In his boredom he patted at his shirt pocket where he had kept cigarettes until Matsushima-sama had required that he stop smoking. He felt the stiff outline of a plastic card, and took it out.

Elizabeth Ann Beckman, 557 East 84th Street, New York, N.Y., ID Number 045-82-0854, 541-2773, International Division. He turned the card over. It was not a very good picture. Her hair had been askew, and her brow shiny with perspiration. She was wearing no makeup. Nonetheless, she had the large dark eyes, and the smiling mouth. And inside, the courage. She was very brave, he thought, not just foolhardy. It was as Matsushima-sama often said, character overcomes bravado. She had faced Reyes down and was prepared to suffer the consequences. Willie wondered whether Reyes had been prepared to suffer whatever consequences Matsushima-sama had seen fit to mete out to him.

A train finally rattled into the deserted station. The car smelled of urine. A bag lady, the sole occupant, looked up, fear emanating like a beacon from her rheumy eyes. She gathered her possessions around her. When Willie sat at the other end, she breathed a sigh of relief, and relaxed her grip on her assorted bundles.

At Eighty-sixth Street, the train sat for several minutes with its doors open. Willie moved restlessly, toying with Libby Beckman's ID card, then sprang from his seat and jumped onto the platform just as the doors were closing. He trotted up the steps to the street and began to walk east. At First Avenue he turned south to Libby Beckman's street, checking the house numbers.

The block was long and filled with a melange of narrow fronted buildings, none more than six or seven stories tall. Some were brownstones, some tenements with their exposed wrought-iron fire escapes, and some were small apartment houses which had supplanted them after the war. Libby Beckman lived in such a building in a garden apartment on the ground floor.

A living room in front, giving on the street, and bedroom in back, which in turn looked out on a tiny patch of green, cost only $600 per month—one half of her take-home pay. And she was lucky at that. A pullman kitchen obtruded from one wall of the living room. The bathroom recalled the old-fashioned term *water closet*. But to Libby, it was the visible evidence of being on one's own. It made her parents nervous. Among their generous gifts—mostly furniture from the attic of their country house—had been the installation of formidable-looking steel gates for all exposed windows. Libby had asked her mother in front of the installer if they made chastity belts, too.

Wilfredo Lopez was a past master at the art of melting into shadows. In his short life, he had learned that to be unnoticed was to avoid pain—whether it took the form of children's cruelty—laughing at an orphan who spoke poor English—or the kind that adults dish out; beatings, sexual abuse—he put his hand to his face—or primordial savagery. Once he had spotted the number on Libby's house, he crossed the street and hung back against the angle of a brownstone stoop, waiting.

He had no idea where in the building she lived, so when he saw her figure in the ground-floor window, he took it as a sign that his coming had not been without purpose.

Libby Beckman was mortally tired. She'd worked a hard morning, then sweated through her exercise class, only to be beaten (though she couldn't really think of one slap as a beating) and robbed. Then, there was the wait till she and the other women were freed, the shock of finding out that poor Laszlo had died, and the police questioning. Even so, she'd gone back to the bank at five-thirty to try to salvage something of the lost afternoon. After a few minutes at her desk, she'd called her parents and found her mother in hysterics. She'd heard about the Slimtronics robbery on the news, and had left frantic messages everywhere for Libby. To calm them she'd agreed to have dinner at the house. She was sorry that she had. She had found it necessary to throw an uncommon fit of temper to get them to let her go home in a cab.

It's funny, she thought, it's the kind of ego-bruising New York incident that makes most people want to run home to their parents. I can't say that I enjoyed it, but it's nice to know that there's a brave person inside of me who can peep out from time to time when needed. She smiled wryly. I wonder how brave I would feel if the big oaf that slapped me had given me another shot? I'll have to thank the leader of the pack for that.

Is that a wistful thought, Libby? she asked herself. She

shook her head. Stray dogs. Her father always said that if
he'd let her get away with it, she'd be bigger than the
A.S.P.C.A. Her concerns lapped over from dogs to people. When she graduated from Georgetown with her M.A.,
it had finally come down to either the bank or volunteer
work in South America. No one had tried to influence her.
She'd made the decision herself. She believed that by
reaching for the top of her profession inside the business
world, she'd do more good than as a lonely soul in some
godforsaken outpost. It takes a big bat to make a dent.

Libby worked one night a week during grad school in
the children's ward of a local hospital. Most of the patients
had been little black or Hispanic kids, more than half, the
victims of child abuse. She couldn't help but wonder
whether the young man at the gym had not stepped in to
protect her because he'd been helpless and abused himself.

She took a shower and washed her hair. When she was
through drying it, she stepped on the scale. Two pounds
less than yesterday—and after dinner at that. It must have
been scared off of me. She looked at herself in the mirror,
and found herself thinking disturbing thoughts about the
young robber. It wasn't because some criminal had acted
with humanity that she had to begin having sex fantasies
about him, for Christ's sake. She laughed at herself. It's
like the job at the bank and the Peace Corps. It wasn't by
sleeping with one sympathetic thief that she was going to
reform mankind. If you want some sex, Libby, you'd
better go find yourself a nice young man in a gray flannel
suit. Blushing at her own foolishness, she put on her robe
and sat at the small writing table, looking through some
reports she'd brought home.

Willie sat on the top step of the stoop across the street,
pressed against the banister. He could see directly into
Libby's room. She was dressed in a pink terry-cloth robe,
and her hair hung in wet strings about her shoulders. She
was writing something. He wished he had binoculars. He
remembered vividly how she'd looked, anger in her voice
and eyes, even after Reyes hit her. He could see the

outline of her bra and pants through her sweat-stained suit.
He wished now that he'd hurt Reyes's wrist more than he
had.

He felt an unfamiliar stirring. Though Willie was better
nourished physically, emotionally and spiritually than he
had ever thought possible, he had little interest in sex.
Matsushima had asked him once what he did for women.
He had survived three months of rigorous training, and
Matsushima had begun to treat him with respect.

"You are making progress. I would almost think that
you had come from a womb and not a gutter. Your speech
improves every day. You have finished a dozen books—
equal to the previous total, I would bet. Good food and
good habits have made good health. You have natural
athletic ability and you are learning the skills of a warrior." After a long pause, he asked, "Are there no women
in your life?"

Willie had hesitated before answering the question. He
had told Matsushima almost all there was to know about
him. "I have been with women. It was not very good."
He put his hand to his face. "The woman who did this to
me would come in to my room after I went to bed. There
were three of us. The welfare gave her money to take care
of us. She must have made a big profit. We were always
hungry. Anyway, she would come in and lift her skirt and
make me touch her and do other things. She would get
mad if I didn't." He touched his cheek again. "Once,
when I was thirteen, I lived where there was a man next
door. He was always touching me and things. I went to a
whore once, a couple of years ago. It was over in five
minutes, and I got the clap."

He remembered that he had gone on for some time
while Matsushima sat back on his heels and listened.
Willie was bathed in perspiration when he finished talking.

"One day you will find someone who will help you to
see another side of this," Matsushima said. "I think that
tomorrow I will bring you a book about love. You don't
know very much about love, Wilfredo. It is another lan-

guage. Without even an acquaintance, we are all illiterate. Perhaps, you shall read your first poetry.'' Matsushima slapped him sharply on the knee. ''In the meantime, to work. On your feet.''

Across Eighty-fourth Street, Libby Beckman looked down at the last page of the report on her desk. ''Phooey on Venezuela,'' she said. ''And double phooey on Peru.'' She stood and stretched and walked to the window. If the blinds were not closed, the sun would awaken her at seven-thirty. She had no intention of getting up that early.

She looked out into the quiet street, backlit by the desk lamp. There was a figure on the stoop across the way. She laughed to herself. Maybe he got lucky and got to see Libby Beckman in her pink bathrobe—you know the one with the catsup stain from last Thursday. He'd do better if he bought *Playboy*.

Willie could feel her eyes as palpable as the touch of a hand. Practice and instinct told him to be still, but after a moment, he fled like a flushed quail, slipping down the block with his shoulders hunched against the wind.

Libby Beckman frowned. The slender body and grace of movement . . . ''Oh, for God's sake, Elizabeth, now the fantasies have become mirages.'' She yanked the blinds shut. ''Let's go to bed, Libby. I think you need some sleep.''

CHAPTER

EIGHT

The complement of Homicide Zone Four is one lieutenant, four detective sergeants, and twenty-six detectives. It is their function to deal with the murderous proclivities of the more than half a million New Yorkers who live in their territory three hundred and sixty-five days a year, twenty-four hours a day. Plus two and a half million weekday transients.

"Couldn't this have happened on a Hundred Eleventh Street?" Francis Xavier Flaherty said as he read through the DD-5 that had been placed on his desk by Hermie Aiello, the sergeant who'd been on the twelve-to-eight the previous night.

If the headless body had been found just four blocks farther north, it would have provided a headache for the lieutenant who ran HZ6, because the son of a bitch would have been killed in the twenty-fifth precinct, Flaherty thought. And that, thank Jesus, Mary, and Joseph, ain't mine. No such luck.

He twisted in his chair to look at the roster. Who was on vacation? Who was on sick leave? Who was up to his jock in something else? It was enough to make a grown man cry. Yesterday it had been statements to the press on the Peskin guy. They were interested in him because they couldn't decide if it was murder if only his brain was dead. Now there would be more questions about the headless horseman.

He looked through the DD-5 again. They'd fingerprinted him. Georgie Ruditz, the guy from the forensics lab loved telling how the only way you can fingerprint a stiff is to break his fingers. Flaherty wondered what had been done with the head.

"Get your ass off my desk, Hermie."

Flaherty looked at his watch. What the hell is Ross doing here at nine-thirty in the morning? He's a shift early.

"Fuck you, Arnie," Aiello replied, offering him a doughnut.

"Ross," Flaherty yelled. "Come in here."

Ross looked slept in. His eyes were red and his shirt was rumpled.

"How can you come in here looking like that?" Flaherty asked.

"It's easy. I work four hours past my shift. Then I go out and eat too much, and get drunk. I sleep it off in my car, because I'm afraid to drive, and then I come in to find out if anything is going on. So I look like this."

Flaherty pushed the DD-5 across to Ross. "I'm sorry I asked."

Ross fingered the eight-by-ten black and white that went with the DD-5. "Poo. Somebody was sure mad at the sucker. Where's the missing piece?" Flaherty shrugged. "Neat," Ross said in appreciation. "Surgically neat. Did anybody make the prints?"

"Not so far. He was clean as a whistle, as you can see. Not a shoe button, a movie ticket, or a brass farthing."

"Who's on it?"

"Hermie booked it. Cassella and Welck were catching when the call came in from the precinct squad car."

"So they'll follow it?"

Flaherty looked up curiously. "I suppose. Do you care?"

"It's just funny, Lieutenant. So clean and neat. All right with you if I run down to Twenty-ninth Street and have a look at the stiff?"

"Suit yourself. You're on your own time till four this afternoon. What has Lou got on this Peskin thing?"

"Give me a break. He and Charley walked both sides of Madison Avenue for two blocks, door to door. Nobody saw nuttin'. And the guy is sure no help. The family is petitioning Judge Markoff this morning to pull the plug. Lou's going back to Lenox Hill to try to see them. Couldn't get to them yesterday. I don't know what fuckin' good it's going to do anyway."

"Routine, Arnie."

"Yeah. See you, boss."

As Arnie walked toward his car, a dark, bearlike figure approached the precinct from the opposite direction. The man was black and enormous. His hair was in an Afro six inches high modified by dirt and grease and topped with a pink cabbie hat held on with bobby pins.

"God, Albert," Arnie said, "are you the guest speaker at the policeman's ball?"

"Don't hassle me, Arnie. I ain't had my breakfast yet, and I feel mean as a snake. And on top of that, I got the hips and the ass from that moron Finkle. Oh, he's happy enough with the numbers—he counts every bust we make like a penny in his personal piggy bank—but suddenly he's noticed that the number of muggings in the twenty-third precinct is up maybe twenty percent in the last three or four months. Seems it was brought to his attention by somebody downtown. If he takes two men away from the street crimes unit to employ giving fucking traffic summonses, what does he expect?"

"Go with God, Albert. I'm on my way to the morgue."

"Next time you go, you do me a favor and take that shithead Finkle with you. He'd be right at home."

Arnie sat down in his car and started the engine, watching Sergeant Albert Ruggles climb the steps. He still limped

from where he'd been shot in the back by a loony a couple
of years back. Just the same, if Arnie Ross knew one man
he wouldn't try on for size, it was Albert Ruggles of the
street crimes unit, all six foot four and two hundred and
sixty-five pounds of him—and that was before breakfast.

Arnie knew why he came in early in the morning, and
why he worked his shift overtime, and why he was going
to look at the headless stiff in the morgue. His work was
his hobby. Flaherty knew it too. And Lou Hernandez.
They knew that every day of Arnie Ross's life was a war
against the ghost of his father. Arnie had to be better. He
was going to be better.

When the Hernandezes had moved into the tenement
where the Rosses lived when Arnie was eleven, his father
had railed against the decline of the neighborhood with the
arrival of the spics downstairs. For Arnie it had been
salvation, for they had taken him in. And now the world
was all changed. Papa Hernandez dead of a heart attack
five years. Big brother Felipe dead an infantry lieutenant
on Pork Chop Hill in Korea. Arnie's own father murdered
when he was nineteen, his mother dead of abuse and
disappointment a year later, his sister run away forever,
the day after the mother's death.

All the people in the department who had made Arnie's
life miserable in those early years because he was the son
of Eddie Ross, the hood, were long retired, and some of
them passed on. Arnie and Lou had worked their ways up
through the N.Y.P.D., and to degrees at City College at
night. Twenty years had passed. But for Arnie Ross it was
always the same—the endless contest against himself and
the ghost.

He knew the guard on duty at the door of the morgue
and was passed on through. The detritus of the city's
streets were kept in cold vaults in a wall looking like
nothing so much as a set of filing cabinets. Miss Jones,
Arnie thought, please file this under Inactive.

"What'ya need, Sergeant Ross?"

"Doe, John. No head. From last night."

"I seen him. I never seen one wit' no head before."

"You haven't met my precinct captain, Feeny. Show me the stiff."

Feeny rolled out a drawer containing the sheet-covered corpse. Arnie pulled back the cloth and looked at the body with curiosity. "You know if they're going to do an autopsy."

"Beats me."

"Who's on?"

"Dr. Gelfand."

Ross looked over the body with care. Hispanic, if he had to guess. Dark skin, dark hair. He reached out to touch the cold leg. Nasty bruise in the middle of the right thigh. Another on the left wrist. The end joints of the fingers had been snapped down by the Forensics people. He touched the edge of the hand. Calluses, thick calluses. Fighting against rigor mortis, he turned the hands palm down. The knuckles too.

"Thanks, Feeny," Ross said, pulling the sheet up again.

Jack Gelfand, M.D., assistant medical examiner of New York County, sat at his desk dictating a report into a recorder. ". . . and as a result of the intrusion of the ice pick, rupture of the superior vena cava and puncture of the left lung occurred, causing both pneumothorax and extensive internal hemorrhaging in the chest cavity . . ." He looked up. "Hello, Sergeant Ross."

"Morning, Doc." They were old friends. Many a stiff they'd shared between them. "You take a look at the headless body?"

"I wondered what brought you to my door. Just a quick once-over."

"You gonna cut him up?"

"You bet. I want to know the cause of death."

"Loss of head?" Arnie offered.

"Maybe. Maybe that's a cover-up. Maybe he OD'd. Maybe he was poisoned. Maybe anything. Until I look, I'm not going to know."

"That's what I thought." Arnie hesitated. "He was into martial arts."

Gelfand put down the recorder and sat back. It paid to listen to Arnie Ross. "He was?"

"Calluses on the edges of the palms and knuckles. He's in terrific physical condition. Young. Do me a favor and take a look at the feet for the same kind of callus, and maybe some signs of wear and tear, ligaments, cartilage and so on."

"And maybe to see if he was killed by a blow, or other karate-type violence?"

"That's the idea, Doc," Ross said. "Funny about the head. Can you cut better than that?"

"Not with a scalpel. Not a shred of skin above the edge of the incision. A regular surgical job. Minimal splintering of the bone."

"Maybe he was guillotined."

"I think you can go home now, Sergeant Ross," Gelfand said, picking up the recorder. "Guillotines are pretty heavy to carry around in the street. I'll let you know when I complete my report. I ought to be done by late this afternoon."

"Thanks, Doc." Ross turned back as he was halfway out of the door. "By the way, do you think that this Peskin thing ought to be called a murder?"

"If you kill a man's brain, I think you killed him, even if the pumping goes on for a while."

Ross nodded and closed the door. It was past eleven. Maybe he could catch Lou at Lenox Hill.

CHAPTER

NINE

Hanae Mayaki looked at her desk calendar and then at her watch. Her employer, Hiroo Matsushima, vice-president and general manager for North America for Inyo Lines had not appeared, nor had he phoned. In ten minutes, at eleven forty-five, he was scheduled to hold a meeting of the sectional representatives who were responsible for coordinating cargo bookings with their American agency. It was unthinkable that Prince Matsushima should be late.

She went into his office for the tenth time since her arrival at eight forty-five sharp to make sure that nothing had drifted out of place since her last visit. Of course, no one called him Prince Matsushima. That had been forbidden since MacArthur. But everyone knew that after the imperial family itself, the Matsushimas were the most noble. He was descended directly from Tokugawa Ieyasu, the Tokugawa shogun, who had set the course of Japanese history from 1603 to the Meiji Restoration of 1868.

Hanae considered herself lucky, and her family believed her blessed to have been chosen to serve this extraordinary man. She used her handkerchief to dust the picture frames on the sideboard opposite the desk. Mrs. Matsushima was a beautiful woman of forty, also high-born. Hanae knew her to be very modest in character, and very respectful of her husband, though she was always fashionably dressed in modern clothes, and dealt capably with her social responsibilities with foreigners. Two other pictures, of the prince's daughters, showed the indelible stamp of the square Matsushima jaw. They had both been born in San Francisco during the six years, more than a decade previous, that Prince Matsushima had been in charge of West Coast operations for Inyo. Now they were sixteen and fourteen. Hanae had the privilege of calling them by their given names.

Nervously, she checked to see that the papers were laid out in the order that Prince Matsushima demanded. He was an exacting superior, but unfailingly considerate and just. His voice was never raised, but the slightest sign of displeasure cut to the quick. Even the deputy manager for North America treated him with great deference, though he would permit no one to call him sama. Hanae left the office, closing the door behind her. He was a great democrat. Everyone could call him Matsushima-san.

She had just sat down when he walked through the door, his face serious but calm as always, bowing politely as he passed each desk. She rose to take his coat and umbrella. He was dressed immaculately in a blue pinstripe suit, with a white button-down shirt, and a tie monogrammed with the intertwined initials IL of the company logo. His Gucci loafers shined like mirrors.

"*Ohayo gazaimas*, Matsushima-san."

"Good morning, Hanae. Have there been any messages for me?"

"No, sir," she replied in English. It was her facility with the tongue that had secured her position, as well as her secretarial skills. He required someone who could keep up with him in both languages. She followed him into his office with her eyes. He was easily the most handsome man she had ever known. At five foot six, he was of average height for a modern Japanese, slender, and athletic.

She rose and poured a cup of tea, waiting until the buzzer rang. When she entered, he was glancing over the reports on his desk.

He looked at her hovering above him with the teacup, thinking of herself as a guardian angel. He reproached himself. Such loyalty was not so common that he could afford to mock it. "I had a headache this morning. I decided to sleep a while longer. I am prepared for the meeting. It should take place as scheduled. Thank you for the tea."

She placed the cup and the saucer on the desk, bowed, and retired from the room, pleased that Prince Matsushima had understood her concern, and been kind enough to allay it. How lucky was Mrs. Matsushima. She took the phone and began to call each of the representatives who were expected at the meeting to remind them that they had ten minutes left to prepare.

Matsushima spread the *Daily News* open and read the brief story about the finding of the headless body in front of a low-income housing development near the East River. It seemed that there were no clues as to the identity of the deceased. A kind word to Hanae in appreciation of her loyalty. A blow with the *tachi* to the neck of Adolfo Reyes as a punishment for disobedience.

I was born at the wrong moment, Matsushima thought. Too much of the old is still in me. And I am surrounded by the new. I was brought up to believe that to touch another person's body was an unforgivable trespass, yet I spend much of my time shaking hands with *geigin*. His nose wrinkled at the thought of beefy white hands and beefy white faces, of the smells of the barnyard veiled by the cheap scent of aftershave.

Had I only been born a year or two earlier, I would have graduated from the Imperial Naval War College, as I did from the Peer School, as is fitting for a prince. I would not have been an untried schoolboy of eighteen on the day that

the war ended, old enough to feel the pangs of shame and
defeat, but too important to have been expended as cannon
fodder. Only a few years earlier, and I might have died in
a suitable circumstance as an ensign on a destroyer or a
submarine.

As it is, I have learned to be part of the Japanese
miracle of recovery from defeat, and of the submersion of
the old values in the world of the victors. What would
happen, he wondered, if I shaved the forepart of my scalp,
and tied and lacquered my hair in the style of the samurai,
and took the robes of my great-grandfather from the ornate
trunk where they have lain since Mutsuhito, the Meiji
emperor, banned their wearing more than a century ago?

His mouth compressed into a thin line. I would be
thought either an actor or a madman. And if I wore the
two swords, and struck out at those who gave offense, or
failed to show the proper respect? I would be hanged.

So instead, he thought, looking across the room with
contempt, I carry the modern badge of Japanese honor. In
the corner an attaché case stood next to an umbrella, both
imprinted with the brown and gold initials of Louis Vuitton
of Paris. A fine symbol of status to replace the two swords.
And in place of Bushido there was the code of the modern
businessman; implacable determination, unstinting effort,
decision by consensus, and a subtle disregard for the con-
ventions by which others find themselves bound. Brooks
Brothers and Vuitton. No vacations. Hard work. Group
think. A wink at the rules. Victory for Japan.

Matsushima folded the newspaper and threw it into the
wastebasket, then buzzed the intercom. Hanae opened the
door, and the six regional representatives, each carrying a
file folder under his arm, appeared before him. He permitted himself a smile and returned their bows with a polite
nod. "Please, gentlemen, sit down. Hanae, ask them if
they wish tea."

CHAPTER

TEN

Lou Hernandez sat in the lounge on the sixth floor of Lenox Hill Hospital looking at a grim, dry-eyed Lisa Peskin. She was thirty, five foot two, and very thin, with blond hair set in tight curls, and a sharp, pointed face. "My father-in-law said we should get permission to take him off the respirator by noon." She turned to Hernandez. "Are you a Catholic?"

"Yes, ma'am."

"Then you think that taking someone off the respirator is a sin, don't you?" Her tone was not challenging. She just took it for granted that she had been judged.

Hernandez shook his head. "If you told me you were going to take a pillow and put it over your husband's face to keep him from suffering, my upbringing would tell me that's wrong. Your husband isn't suffering, Mrs. Peskin." He pointed down the hall. "He isn't in there anymore. It doesn't say anywhere in the Bible that you have to keep a machine plugged into a . . ."

"Zombie," she said. "That's what I think too. It doesn't

seem to have a purpose. Has anybody come forward yet? Any witnesses?''

"No, ma'am. Sometimes it takes a while.''

"A reporter who was downstairs told me that when we . . . disconnect Alvin, and the story appears, maybe somebody will turn up.'' She swallowed hard, but maintained her self-control.

Hernandez looked at her with admiration, then said, "Sometimes people call in right away. Sometimes they don't show up for months.''

She turned toward him. "It's very nice of you to say that about disconnecting the respirator.''

"I meant it.''

"I know.'' She frowned. "It all seems so pointless. They didn't even take his wallet or his watch.''

"No. Just the two hundred dollars he drew from the machine. We knew how much because he had stuffed the little receipt into his pocket. Whoever it was just hit him and took the money, then disappeared. He could have run, or been in a car or on a bike—anything. With no witnesses . . .''

"There is nothing to go on,'' she finished for him. "It's a waste.'' Her mouth compressed into a thin line.

After a few minutes of silence the door of the elevator opened and Mrs. Peskin's father-in-law appeared, a dignified, white-haired man in his late sixties. He nodded in greeting to Hernandez, then said, "Our attorney is downstairs presenting the court order to the administrator's office.''

Lisa Peskin closed her eyes for a moment. They shone with tears when she reopened them, but none fell. "When will they do it?''

"Now.''

"I want to say good-bye. Alone.''

The older man said, "Of course.''

Mrs. Peskin was gone for only a few minutes. Ross and the elder Peskin maintained an awkward silence. As she came back down the hall toward them, Arnie Ross emerged

from the elevator. Hernandez caught his eye and waved
him off.

"Are you going in, Dad?" Mrs. Peskin asked. Mr.
Peskin shook his head. "Let's go then." She lifted her
chin. "Thank you, Sergeant Hernandez. If we can be of
any use, please let us know. And tell us if anything comes
up."

When the elevator returned to take them away, Arnie
walked over from the corner in which he had been loung-
ing. "A lot of self-control."

Hernandez turned on him, a bit annoyed. "I can read
your mind at a hundred paces. If she isn't rending her
clothes and screaming, you want to know about her
motives."

"That's right, Roach. It's the policeman in me. But I'm
sure you've done all that."

Hernandez took an affectionate poke at Ross's arm. "I
did. Makes no sense. He's in Wall Street. Makes good
bucks. His old man's in factoring for textiles. Substantial
bucks. She has money of her own. Father dead. No brothers or sisters. They sold a big candy business. Normal
family. Married three years. No kids."

"*Diga me*, Roach, doesn't this seem to you like overkill—
you should excuse the expression."

Hernandez lifted his shoulders and turned his hands
palms up. "*Quién sabe*, Arnie. An accident. The little shit
wanted his money and hit him too hard."

"That much too hard? You know that the biggest problem with muggers is that the fuckers are so scared themselves that when they have a knife or a gun, their hands
shake. That's how they kill half the people that get wasted
in muggings."

"Are you asking if this was a hit?" Lou asked.

"Did he play? Did he owe? A broad maybe?"

"Nothing. Money in the bank. No complaints at home.
I talked to the manager of his office downtown. Solid
citizen. No drinking. No smoking. Regular exercise."

Ross raised his head. "What kind?"

"What kind of exercise? He belonged to a club on Fifty-seventh Street. He did calisthenics every day, and swam. Sometimes he took a massage."

"No martial arts?"

"Not that I know of. Why?"

"Can I take a look at the medical report?"

"Sure."

"What are the chances of getting a peek at him?"

"Come with me," Hernandez said, walking down the hall. He had long since given up trying to guess what was on Arnie's mind.

The cop at the door passed them through, ignoring the sign that said absolutely no visitors. A nurse sat in a corner chair reading a magazine. When she heard them enter, she stood.

"This is Sergeant Ross, Nurse Calli. He wants to read the chart and look at Mr. Peskin."

"You can't touch him," she said anxiously.

"No. I won't," Arnie said, lifting the clipboard from the end of the bed. It was thick with reports and charts and paperwork, though Peskin had been in the hospital for only a day.

Arnie looked through the charts, and shook his head. "Too much for me. Nurse, has the doctor been around yet?"

"Oh, yes. This morning he came on rounds." She lowered her eyes. "I think he's going to be back in a little while." The thought was unfinished.

Arnie followed her eyes to the bed. Alvin Peskin lay absolutely motionless, his head held still by two pillows on either side of his face. A collection of tubes—urinary catheter, IVs, suction—sprouted from him like new spring shoots. The respirator made Darth Vader noises as it pumped air in and out of his lungs. The doctor would be back in a little while to turn the switch and the parody of life that the tubing and the pumping were perpetuating would come to a halt.

Ross and Hernandez waited outside the door. Dr. Royce

was not long in coming. He recognized Hernandez. "Sergeant," he said, nodding curtly.

"May we talk to you for a moment, Doctor? This is Sergeant Ross. He's with HZ four too."

"I'd appreciate it if you'd let me get on with this first," Royce said. He looked down the hall, where another doctor in whites and an older man in a banker's gray suit hurried toward them. "We require three witnesses—two doctors and the administrator. If you like, you may attend."

Ross shuddered. The man's voice was cultivated, but as cold as ice. "Okay," he said.

When Dr. Royce opened the door to admit the others, the nurse was already on her feet. She looked for a cue from the doctor, who gestured toward the hall. In grateful haste she grabbed her handbag and magazine and exited.

The administrator read the court order aloud, then signed it, followed by Royce and the other witnessing physician. Royce reached out a steady hand and tripped a switch on the respirator. There was a sigh and a sudden deafening silence as the machine came to a halt. After about thirty seconds Alvin Peskin's body became rigid, and began to tremble. A rasping sound came from the tube in the hole in his chest, where the tracheotomy had been performed. The bottles on the IV stands made faint clinking sounds as the healthy, muscular body of Alvin Peskin jerked insensately against the deprivation of oxygen from its tissues and the intrusion of death. In a brief convulsion of the back muscles Alvin Peskin seemed to thrust himself forward, as though attempting to sit up. There was a last wheeze, and he fell back against the bed, dead. Dr. Royce noted the time exactly. The green life-sign monitor screens puttered along, their faces interrupted only by flat white lines. Nonetheless, Royce felt manually for a pulse, then checked with a stethoscope for a heartbeat or respiration. Then he pronounced Alvin Peskin dead.

Back in the hall Dr. Royce took a pipe from his pocket, stuffed it, and walked toward the lounge area. "You want to talk to me, Sergeant . . ."

"Ross. Yes, sir. What killed Mr. Peskin?"

"Deprivation of oxygen, Sergeant Ross. When we shut off the respirator, his diaphragm stopped pumping, his lungs stopped getting air, and he expired of a collection of ills, including coronary insufficiency. When his brain functions stopped, even his involuntary reflexive system ceased to operate. His brain didn't signal his body to go on living. In the absence of those orders, it stopped."

Ross nodded. "That's not quite what I meant. How would you describe the basic cause of Alvin Peskin's death."

"The cessation of cerebral function."

"Still further back," Ross insisted. "How about a clinical description of the injury that caused it."

Royce lit the pipe. He watched the smoke spiral toward the ceiling, then said, "When the resident called me in for a surgical consultation on the patient, he was already totally comatose, as he had been since he was brought into the hospital. Absolutely timely and skilled emergency treatment had permitted Mr. Peskin to make it as far as the respirator and the IVs, and the rest of the apparatus that kept him alive till now. His brain had been deprived of oxygen for too long—much too long. Five minutes, six minutes. I've read or heard of eight minutes. Beyond that, any recovery of life signs is a miracle, and brain damage is a certainty."

"Why wasn't he getting any air?"

"I thought that I'd made that very clear in my first interview with Sergeant Hernandez. It's also apparent from the chart."

"I'm sure you've cooperated to the maximum, Dr. Royce. But you can imagine that we're trying to cover every base. Please bear with me."

Royce lit the pipe again, blowing another cloud toward the ceiling. "Severe trauma to the larynx. Bone and cartilage contused and splintered in such a way as to exert sufficient pressure on the trachea to close the airway, this further complicated by severe trauma to soft tissue, producing both edema and hemorrhage.''

"Caused by?''

"A blow to the base of the throat.''

"Not strangulation,'' Ross persisted.

"A sharp blow.''

"Delivered by?''

Royce stopped. "I can't be a hundred percent sure. I assume there will be an autopsy. There ought to be a pathology report.''

"For now, what do you think?''

Royce exhaled. "There were four round hematomae which stood out at the base of the throat, beyond the generalized subsurface bleeding in the area. Brass knuckles? You'd know more about that than I would, I'm sure, Sergeant Ross.''

"Any traces of metal on the skin?''

"I don't know.'' Royce leaned forward. He had begun to respond with interest to Ross's line of questioning. It was well ordered and purposeful.

"May I take a look at the body?''

Royce hesitated, then knocked his pipe clean in an ashtray. "Come on.''

When they were in Peskin's room again, the doctor pulled the sheet away from the dead man's face, where he had put it minutes earlier. Gingerly, he pulled the bandage away from base of the throat, then peeled it off and threw it into the wastebasket. Above the trach tube opening Alvin Peskin's throat was a mottled purplish-blue, where broken blood vessels had leaked under the skin. Just above the larynx four darker splotches, vaguely oval in shape, were arrayed in a straight line, touching each other. Ross peered closer. At the upper part of each, a shallow semilunar mark was indented into the flesh, deeper in the first three than in the fourth.

Ross stood up and extended his right hand, his thumb tucked into his palm, his fingers rigid. "That's it.''

"What?'' Royce asked.

"The murder weapon. A blow to the throat with the tips of the rigid fingers. You see where the fingernails have cut into the skin? The force of the blow drives the nails into the flesh evenly because the pressure is distributed evenly among the first three fingers, since they are about the same length. The nail on the pinky doesn't make as pronounced a mark since most of the force of the blow has been expended by the time it gets there." Ross reached out and put his hand on Peskin's throat. "More or less a perfect fit. But you can see that whoever did this had smaller hands and fingertips than I do. Maybe the coroner will find something embedded in those nail marks that will give us something to go on."

"I doubt it," said Dr. Royce. "It's been swabbed and washed a dozen times. But we'll find out. A damn interesting lesson in detective work, Sergeant Ross."

"Eighteen years on the job, Dr. Royce."

Arnie stood outside of Lenox Hill with Lou, leaning against the fender of the red Porsche. He scratched his chin, his eyes squinted half shut. "Hey, Roach," he asked aimlessly, "you want to go back down to the morgue with me?"

"What you got in mind?"

"I want to look at another stiff."

They grabbed some lunch at a Chinese takeout place on Third Avenue and brought it up to the precinct on their way back from the morgue. They walked up the stairs and sat down on Lou's desk. Arnie's was occupied by Tom Hennesy, the fourth sergeant on HZ4, who was on eight-to-fours. They chatted for a while in low voices as Hennesy burrowed through endless reports, clacking away on the ancient typewriter.

Flaherty sat at his own desk, watching the shadowy figures through the frosted glass. Curiosity got the better of him.

"So," he said. "Where have you two been?"

"Witnessing a murder," Ross replied. "Man name of

Peskin. Fully sanctioned by the state of New York. He went quietly. Just a little thrashing and squirming.''

"Sometimes, Ross, I wonder about what goes on in your head. Is that all you have?''

"As a matter of fact, no. We know exactly how it was done.''

"You do?'' Flaherty asked skeptically.

Hernandez stood and smiled engagingly. "If you give us off from six to ten, we'll share it with you. My mamma is cooking dinner tonight.''

Flaherty snorted. "More rice and beans? You know what? Someday I'm going to get transferred, and then you can find some other poor son of a bitch to put up with you. Are Baxter and Passarelli coming in?''

"Yes, sir, and they know where to find us,'' Lou said.

"It's a deal. So?''

"A karate chop to the throat. You could even see the nail marks. Very well done. A real pro.''

"A mugger who's into martial arts. So what? Most of them are, one way or another.''

"Then we went to check out the stiff from yesterday afternoon,'' Ross said. "The Dushan guy from the gym.''

"Arnie's first instinct was right,'' Hernandez said. "Gelfand said he was smothered—tape over his nose and mouth. But before that, somebody broke his nose and jaw with one blow, and ruptured his left kidney with another.''

"Karate blows?'' Flaherty asked.

"Just like I said,'' Ross replied. "And the stiff with no head, deep bruises in three or four places, the thigh, the wrist, the back, caused by . . .''

"More karate chops.''

"Right, Lieutenant,'' Ross said.

Flaherty sat on the edge of his desk for a moment, thinking, then shook his head and stood up. "You can still have the time off, but the connection is as thin as gauze, boys. Most of the muggers in this town kick the shit out of their victims—little old ladies, delivery boys, grocery store owners. You got three stiffs with bruises, and you're trying to make a federal case that it's Qadhafi or Castro or organized crime. You'll have to do better than that before you can convince me.''

Arnie and Lou watched him go out of the door. When it closed behind him, Lou said, ''Look on the cheerful side. At least he let us have time off to have dinner with the family.''

Ross kicked a drawer shut. ''Ah, shit. He's right too. Everybody that gets killed around here looks beat up. Well, it was an idea anyway.''

CHAPTER

ELEVEN

As Arnie and Lou got into their cars to drive out to the Hernandez house for dinner, Hiroo Matsushima undertook a task that had become increasingly unpleasant for him as time in his post in New York wore on.

He pushed the intercom button and told his secretary to get the home office. He checked his watch. It was precisely three minutes to six, New York time. That made it just before eight the following morning in Osaka. Matsushima's desk was spotlessly clean save for a single written sheet on the blotter before him that related the significant details of the day's activities. There were three Inyo bottoms in the United States, one on the East Coast, one on the West, and one in New Orleans, on the Gulf of Mexico. Two were owned entirely by Inyo, and carried only Inyo-directed cargo. The third was shared by two other major Japanese carriers. Matsushima was responsible for seeing that the ships were unloaded of their Japanese cargo and refitted, repaired, and revictualized at the end of each voyage from Japan, and, most important of all, that they left to Japan with the absolute maximum in return cargo.

In view of the imbalance in Japanese–United States trade, it was difficult in a competitive market to find shipments to fill the huge ships that arrived monthly engorged with tape recorders, automobiles, television sets, and textiles from the mother country.

Matsushima nettled increasingly under the burden. Once again, it seemed to him that the brunt of the changing tides in Japanese history had fallen in unequal measure on the shoulders of his family. It had become the policy of the Japanese government, and of the business community of Japan, to exact a victory tax from the United States and its people. Using a subtle combination of the guilt feelings engendered by the destruction of Hiroshima and Nagasaki, and the ever-present threat that the Japanese people—one hundred ten million of them—would turn Communist if their legitimate aspirations were frustrated, Japan had managed to create a staggering trade imbalance not only with the United States, their largest trading partner, but, with United States sanction and protection, with the rest of the Western world. By stealth and dissemblement, postwar Japan had euchred from the world what it had been unable to wrest by force in the duration.

As a result, in the increasingly strong view of Hiroo Matsushima, the honor of the individual Japanese had been compromised almost beyond redemption. Under the guise of renouncing force as a result of suffering the only stroke of atomic warfare in human history, a warrior people had reduced their expenditures on national defense to almost nothing. Of all the treaties, trade and diplomatic, signed by the Japanese government since the end of the war, the only one observed more in the keeping than in the breach was the limitation on the national defense force. Matsushima twisted his lips in disgust. Of course, let the *geigin* spend their resources protecting our wealth and our population as we utter pious mutterings of love of peace, we who warred with all the world around us for a thousand years, then among ourselves for another thousand, who after Meiji took on and defeated the Chinese and Russian empires in a ten-year span. Where Bushido had reigned, now there was only guile. Matsushima wondered if the same ministers who spoke so strongly against violations of the defense treaties felt equally offended by their continuous series of flagrant disregards of the General Agreement on Trade and Tariffs by which international commerce was governed. If the United States had the same test procedures for Japanese automobiles that Japan exacted upon American cars, there would be as many Japanese cars in America as there were American cars in Japan—none.

The phone on the desk rang. "Good morning, Junichi-san," he said.

"Good morning, Hiroo-san," said the voice at the other end, clear as crystal in a tone rough as broken glass. Junichi Hamato, Matsushima's superior, was director of overseas operations for Inyo Lines. He was five years Matsushima's senior and had risen in the same inexorable fashion as the talented in the maze of Japanese corporate structure. When Matsushima finished his tour in the United States in two years, he would become the deputy director for one year, then upon Hamato's elevation to the next rung on the ladder—if he made it—he would become the director of overseas operations.

He read the order of the day's business to Hamato, who listened without comment. He was taking notes as fast as Matsushima could speak. He would be receiving confirmation by telex in minutes.

There was a pause after the list was finished. Matsushima ground his teeth. It was a not too subtle way to say that Hamato had expected the list to be longer. "Well done, Matsushima-san," Hamato said heartily. He had a gruff peasant's voice, for all that he had risen to the top, and it would never change. "Of course, we would be happier if we were assured that the *Sensei Maru* would leave the Gulf ports for home with a full cargo." Hamato had said what he could. He never forgot that regardless of his position on the manning chart, he was talking to a prince of the realm. "On the other hand, it seems that your organization has done splendidly with the other ships today. We are well ahead of schedule. How are we coming with our hosts?''

Matsushima permitted himself a smile. There was a certain humor in the expression *hosts*. Indeed, Inyo Lines treated their agents, in whose building they made their offices, as a parasite treats a host, by devouring its substance.

''All matters are in hand, Junichi-san. They flutter about doing what is necessary to serve our needs. While it is difficult to assess their financial position, since they are unable to do it themselves, I imagine that they have enough resources to last another year or two paying our subsidy. But then I fear we must look to our own means for a structure in the United States.''

''You can ponder about that, Hiroo-san. It will likely be your final task in America before you come home to accept your directorship. *Sayonara.*''

''Until tomorrow, Junichi-san.''

Matsushima buzzed Hanae and told her that she was free to go home. When he heard the door of his outer office close, he removed his suit jacket and stretched, then loosened his tie. He took the unread newspapers from his desk and lay down on the couch to read.

The first area of interest was the business pages. He went through them dutifully and mechanically. Then he turned to the front page and the police blotter. The reading of the paper at the same time every night was a process of transition for Matsushima. It was necessary for him to withdraw gradually from worries about filling the bottoms of the Inyo Lines to what had become his passion, his samurai life. Even the thought made him smile. Though the gods knew that he was the daimyo with the smallest constituency in the world. His samurai, all twelve of them—eleven now, he recalled—were *ichiryo-gusoko*. He stood again and laughed aloud. One suit of armor, and one plot of land. Such men had tilled the soil of Japan to eke out a living for themselves and for their families through two millennia of Japanese history. But when the occasion for courage had arisen, they had put aside their dung baskets and the rice rakes, uncovered the armor, and gone out to die with courage for their liege lords. They were impoverished knights, but knights all the same.

The police blotter prompted Matsushima to review his current position. There had been four marks of his clan in a single day. The gym instructor who had died at the brutal and unclean hands of Adolfo Reyes. Reyes, who in headless shame had paid the price for his dishonor and disobedience. The man Peskin, whose death Matsushima considered to be an unfortunate accident. And last, the mugging of the woman on Eighty-sixth Street.

It seemed imprudent to go any further. It was time to take a rest and to teach the samurai more about fealty and self-improvement. There would be no concern about money. Since the beginning of operations four months earlier, Matsushima had accumulated as his share of the clan purse over two hundred thousand dollars. It never failed to amaze him that the rewards of petty crime, intelligently organized, could be so great. He had no need of money for himself, and had never spent a cent of the money that had been brought to him. The funds, kept in cash, were dispensed only as payment to the landlord and to the samurai.

He slipped on his coat again and straightened his tie. It would not do for his subordinates in the outer office, who often worked from eight in the morning until nine or ten at night, to see him in less than perfect order.

As he removed his car from the lot on his way to the karate-dojo, it occurred to him that a halt in the forays of his clan would also enable him to resume better relations at home. His wife had begun to complain, in the ritualized way that their relative positions permitted, that he was not paying sufficient attention to her physical needs, and that self-satisfaction, though a relief, was not the same. He raised his eyebrows. Another obligation.

CHAPTER

TWELVE

Jorge Rodriguez and Donald Wolfe had loitered around the brightly lit 24-Hour Banking Center of Citibank on Forty-sixth Street and Third Avenue for most of the night. Finally, at four in the morning, they had thrown in the towel. Luck had been against them. Everyone who had come to use the facility had ducked in and out with such speed that they had been unable to approach them, or had appeared in such numbers as to make an attempt unwise.

Jorge and Donald lived together. They had found a small apartment in the East Village in a relatively clean building where there was heat. Other than several unhappy years in an orphanage for Donald, neither of them had ever lived a winter in an adequately warm place.

Donald Wolfe was eighteen. He had been born out of wedlock in the town of Dover, Ohio, a center of strict Mennonite culture. He had been cast out, together with his fourteen-year-old mother, without a cent in the world, nor a possession. She had hitchhiked to Cincinnati, where she had kept body and soul together by selling that which she had given so freely in love. When she was seventeen and he was three, a drunken truck driver had broken her neck. Donald was found wandering in the street barefoot and brought to an orphanage. Malnutrition and illness had worked together to stunt his growth. He grew up in grim loneliness, unwanted and unloved. He was a mediocre student, more from lack of interest than lack of intelligence. He developed an abnormal placidity, as he was unable to defend himself from his peers.

When he was fourteen, still looking eleven or twelve, a maintenance worker had forced his attentions upon him. He accepted these advances passively, as he did every other blow to his body and his ego. The man would often give him small gifts or treats in exchange for his services. It was the first encouragement that Donald had ever received in his life. About a year after the first episode they were caught by a supervisor.

The maintenance worker was fired, and Donald was put on a diet of bread and water for thirty days, and made to do penance on his knees for hours at a time.

When the month was up, and the period of strict surveillance elapsed, he ran away to New York, and like his mother, began to sell that which he had previously given voluntarily.

So far as Jorge knew, he had been born in a gutter. He was also short and slender, largely from the influence of an early lack of proper nutrition. He had lived with this family or that in the Hispanic ghettos of Brooklyn and the South Bronx. He had gone to school from time to time, but since he was without a permanent address, he slipped through the sloppy mesh of the educational system. He stole his first thing when he was six. It was a loaf of bread. The owner of the bodega beat him with a belt till his ragged shirt was spotted with blood. The next time, he was hungrier still, and more careful. In Jorge, small stature had bred speed and evasiveness. He was too small to fight, so he learned to run.

When Donald showed up in New York at the age of sixteen, to make his living hanging around on the street and in subways, Jorge was the same age, and living in a packing crate in the ruins of a burned-out building on Second Avenue and 108th Street.

Their paths crossed about six months later on Lexington Avenue in front of Bloomingdale's. Donald had just emerged from the underground station of the IRT subway. He leaned against the wall of the store with his hand in his pocket clutching a ten-dollar bill. He watched indifferently as the man who had given it to him for services rendered scuttled off down the street, adjusting the buttons of his blue cashmere coat, and straightening his bowler.

There had been a commotion from the block to the south.

The fat Greek who ran the all-night fruit stand was running after a small boy who darted away from him. "Stop, thief! Stop, you little *scata*! I catch you, I break you legs. Police. Police."

Donald watched with interest as the boy pumped his arms, opening the gap between him and the Greek.

A couple appeared around the corner, walking west on Sixtieth Street. They were in their late twenties and well dressed. They walked past Donald as though he were not there. When they heard the anguished cries of the Greek, they turned down Lexington Avenue and saw Jorge Rodriguez legging it up the block.

Donald saw the smile on the man's face, a leer almost. He pushed his companion aside and balled up his fist. He was about six feet tall. As Jorge drew even with him, he threw a punch and struck the smaller boy in the face.

Jorge, intent on his running, had been unaware of the man's presence till he felt the blow, slamming against the store front and ricocheting to the ground. He got to his feet, bleeding profusely from a broken nose and stunned. The fat Greek was yelling, "Hold him, mister. He stole fruit from me." Three apples lay bruised in the filthy gutter.

The well-dressed young man grabbed Jorge by the shoulder and held him, squirming. To calm him, he slapped him across the face with the back of his hand. Blood splattered.

Donald, who had never raised a hand in self-defense in his life, was moved by some emotion of which he had never been aware before. He had no knowledge of the martial arts, but he knew the source of pleasure and pain in a man's body. As the young man drew his hand back to hit the helpless Jorge again, Donald slipped away from the store wall and hit him in the testicles as hard as he could. The man gasped, then snapped forward and vomited over his immaculate trousers and gleaming shoes.

Jorge, free of his grasp, said, "Come on," and dashed around the corner. Donald followed him, stunned by his own act and propelled by the bellowing of Greek and the anguished screams of the young man's companion. Jorge, motioning frantically to Donald, ran without missing a step down the entrance to the Lexington Avenue subway. He headed straight into the men's room.

Jorge's face was a pulp, and so smeared with his own blood and dirt that Donald was unable to tell what he looked like. He was shaking like a leaf. When Donald reached to touch his face, Jorge shied away, his eyes shining with fear.

"I don't hurt people," Donald said simply. "I never hit anybody before in my whole life." His voice was squeaky and uncertain.

"Tank you," Jorge said. "I hungry, man." He looked at his rescuer, tiny and slender, as insubstantial as his voice. "Dat's how come I steal." Donald bent forward to listen attentively; the sounds seemed strange to him. "Shit. I sorry, man," Jorge said, embarrassed. "I no speak so good English. You speak Spanish?"

"No. I don't know how. Listen, you have to clean your face. You can't go out looking like that. I can do it. You want me to?"

Jorge shivered involuntarily. No one ever did anything for him. "Yeah."

Donald's hands were slender and small in proportion to

the rest of his body. His touch was more gentle than any Jorge had ever felt.

Donald took out one of the packets of Kleenex that he always carried as an item of his trade and led Jorge to the sink. It was filthy, and the mirror was fly-specked, but the water ran. When he first touched Jorge's nose, the boy recoiled, crying out in pain. Donald took great care, till finally the splotches of dirt and streaks of blood were gone, and the bleeding had stopped. Already Jorge's eyes were circled with black.

"You got a place to go, man?" Jorge asked.

Donald shook his head. "I was hoping somebody would pick me up, so I had a warm place to sleep. I got ten bucks. That'll buy a meal and a flop."

Jorge looked him in the eye. "Are you a *maricón*, man?"

It was the only word in Spanish Donald had learned. "Yes. I do it for money. That's how I live." Donald stepped back from Jorge, thinking that he would be less offended by Donald's presence if he were farther away. "I won't bother you."

Jorge was not afraid of Donald. He was not afraid of homosexuality. He had never had much interest in sex. He was too busy trying to find a place to eat and to sleep, and to stay alive. "I don't mind, man. Hey, listen, you can stay at my place. It ain't much."

"It's better than mine. I sleep in doorways. What I own is in a paper bag."

"You got subway fare, no?"

"Yeah."

They went together to the filthy hovel in which Jorge had put his few possessions. There was a candle for light, and a couple of stolen blankets and a floor of three mattresses rescued from the Sanitation Department. His water supply a dented jerry can. His lavatory was the crumbled court of the building.

Jorge learned from Donald that they could make a modest living by selling their services in the streets. They continued to live in the shattered building, but improved their conditions by the addition of a kerosene heater, and a regular supply of food. Donald taught Jorge the tricks of the trade and the English language. Jorge taught Donald that he could relate to another human being in other than the passive form. At the same time, he convinced him little by little that he could find a special kind of joy in running. And after a while, like Jorge, he began to push his pale, undernourished body farther each day, till the pain of effort was repaid by the reward of stamina. In that simple way their lives became less appalling and their misery was modestly relieved.

One day in May they were on the stroll in Central Park near the reservoir, where homosexual prostitutes can be found plying their trade in the cover of the bushes. Suddenly they found themselves surrounded by a half-dozen teenagers wearing jackets proclaiming them to be Werewolves. They pushed Donald and Jorge into the brush and forced them to give over the twenty-five dollars that they had earned in the course of the afternoon.

The leader of the pack, a wall-eyed overgrown fifteen-year-old with rotten teeth, wanted more. He wanted to feel important.

It was not that he wanted to violate Jorge and Donald sexually. If he had, they would not have been unprepared. It was their business to provide sex. No. He wanted to hurt, to inflict pain.

They tried to run, but they were hemmed in, bound, and gagged.

The wall-eyed boy sprayed them with lighter fluid and danced on their prostrate bodies, kicking and punching them. Then, laughing, he took out a match. He watched them wriggling helplessly on the ground in front of him.

"You know what?" a voice said behind him. "You are a very sick person."

The wall-eyed boy whirled, as did the rest of his troop. The voice came from a tall, slender figure leaning against a tree at the edge of the clearing.

"Fuck off, scumbag," the wall-eyed boy snarled.

"Watch your mouth," Willie Lopez said. He had happened upon them by chance while jogging the track. "Now, untie those two people on the ground, and go away."

The wall-eyed boy looked around himself in utter amazement. "You must be out of your fuckin' mind, motherfucker. You don't get out of here, we gonna stomp you fuckin' ass and burn you up along with these two faggots."

"If you don't do what I say, you will be sorry."

The wall-eyed boy made a motion with his head, and his gang began to advance on Willie. Suddenly, he was not there anymore.

Three of the boys lay on the ground writhing, one with a broken leg, the other two gagging raggedly, their hands holding their groins.

"Let them go," Willie said.

"Fuck you," the wall-eyed boy said, drawing a hunting knife from a sheath on his belt. He put his head down and charged with his two remaining companions.

Donald watched in fascination as the slender figure became a whirlwind of legs and arms, flailing and dancing. In a matter of seconds the last three Werewolves were on the ground.

Willie took the knife from the hand of the wall-eyed boy, whom he had rendered unconscious with a kick to the chin, breaking his hand and wrist in the process. Then, as an afterthought, he bent over and broke the other wrist for good measure. He used the knife to free Donald and Jorge, then threw it over the link fence into the reservoir. They took their twenty-five dollars back from the Werewolves, plus an assortment of change and bills amounting to another twenty-odd dollars.

"Have you eaten, today?" Wilfredo Lopez asked.

"No, we was working," Jorge said. "You Spanish, man?"

"Yes." Willie smiled. We are all Spanish, we impoverished Puerto Ricans and Dominicans. "Come on, let's use their money to have something to eat."

The little store smelled of the strange melange of spices unique to New York. COMIDAS CHINAS Y CRIOLLAS said the cardboard sign in the window.

Willie ordered egg rolls and rice and beans, and gandinga, a Puerto Rican stew of pork liver in tomato sauce with olives. Jorge eyed the menu. He and Donald mostly ate Campbell's soup and stew with plastic utensils direct from the can. Sometimes they would heat the food on the kerosene stove. "*Lombo acerdo,*" he said to the fat little man behind the counter, "*con frijoles.*"

"I'd like shrimp egg foo-yung," Donald added.

The food was served up from a partitioned steam table. The dishes were chipped and cracked, but their contents were savory and piping hot.

From the corner of his eye Willie watched the two younger boys eat. They were ravenous and without manners, slurping and pushing oversized bites into their mouths and licking at their fingers. He wondered how often they had a square meal.

Willie picked up the check. Over a Coke and the large desserts they had chosen, they told him a little about their sketchy lives.

"Have you even been proud of anything?" Willie asked.

"I've never had anything," Donald answered. Then he paused and frowned. "You mean of something that I've done?"

"I mean of yourself."

Donald just shook his head.

"I'm fast, man," Jorge said. "Nobody can catch me. Right, man?" he asked Donald for confirmation. "And Donald, he's getting fast, too, man. He runs with me every day. We run, man. I mean, far. We run far."

Willie looked at them. "Can you fight?"

"No man," Jorge answered. "We don't fight. We small, man. We run."

"I am not big. There were six in that gang in the park."

"How you learn to do that, man?" Jorge asked.

"I was taught by my master. He taught me it was

important to speak right, and to act right. He taught me to have respect and pride."

"Master?" Donald asked. "What do you do? Is he into S and M?"

Willie said, "You got the wrong idea. He's like the head of my family."

"We got no family," Jorge said, " 'cept us."

"Would you like to begin to learn?" Willie asked. "Would you like to begin to have a family?"

Jorge and Donald were Willie's first converts.

Ten months later, having failed in their hunt for easy pickings at the Forty-sixth Street cash machine of Citicorp, they went home and slept till late morning.

When they rose in their tiny apartment on East Third Street, they dressed in clean sweat suits and running shoes, drank orange juice mixed with honey, and went into the cool March morning. Then ran over to the FDR, jumped the barriers, and ran along the river up to 125th Street, then turned back toward home. At Ninetieth Street they saw a man in a jogging suit sitting groggily on the ground, holding his face. They stopped to help him to his feet. A black man, he said, had jumped him while he was running, then taken off down the footpath after giving him a smack in the head.

"Did he take much?" Donald asked sympathetically.

"A gold and steel Omega watch that cost me eighteen hundred bucks," the man replied with asperity, starting to feel better. "And my sports wallet—you know, one of those things with Velcro that goes around your wrist. I must've had a hundred bucks. Shit."

"You ought to call a cop," Jorge said.

"The bastard smacked me, took my stuff, and was gone like a shot. It's just going to waste my time. Shit. Welcome to the Big Apple."

"You need help?" Jorge asked.

"Thanks. No sweat. I live a couple of blocks away."

They watched him struggle over the fence, wait for a break in the traffic, and run to the other side. When he had walked up the street, they looked at each other, and began to run down the footpath, eating up the ground with rapid strides. They passed only one other jogger on their way downtown, and he was on the other side of the drive.

In the low Eighties, where the tunnel over the roadway ends, they saw a heavyset black man in his twenties in a sweat suit and sneakers leaning on the fence. He was relaxing, and counting money from a blue cloth wallet he had just dropped on the ground. They looked around for pedestrians or other joggers. The only sign of humanity were the occupants of the cars that occasionally whirred by on the drive.

"Hi," Jorge said.

The black man lifted his head and glowered. "What you want, asshole?"

"That's not nice," Donald said.

"Get lost, honky faggot."

"I bet you got a nice watch," Jorge said.

The black man stood up against the railing and reached into his pocket. He was about six feet tall, Donald judged, and built for strength rather than for speed. He looked with contempt at Donald and Jorge, who, at five foot five and six respectively, weighed less than one hundred and thirty pounds each.

"I got me a gold watch, faggot." He pushed a hamlike fist forward, exposing the Omega under the wristband of his sweatshirt. "Now, why don't you go off and suck somebody's lollipop 'fore I get mad and kick yo' ass."

Donald turned away with a sad look, then shot out a leg and kicked the side of his knee. The black man yelped, but straightened and pulled a switchblade knife from his pocket.

He lunged at Donald. Jorge hit him across the arm with a chop. The man was strong. He grunted with pain, but did not drop the knife. Though Donald had moved quickly, the blade caught him in the upper arm.

At the sight of blood the black man grinned and turned toward Jorge. Donald ignored the pain in his arm and struck the man in the ribs with his elbow. When he turned his head, Jorge brought his hand down on the bridge of his nose, smashing bone and cartilage. The man roared in anger and grasped Donald by the hair, thrusting toward his belly with the knife. Donald struck upward with the heel of his hand, catching the broken nose with all his force just where it joined the upper lip.

The knife fell from the man's hand and his eyes clouded over as the splinters of bone from his shattered septum were driven into his brain. He was dead before he hit the ground.

Jorge took the watch from his wrist and collected the cash that he had stolen from the jogger. He motioned to Donald, and together they heaved the black man's body over the fence into the East River, and threw his knife after him.

Jorge looked at Donald's arm. "It's not bad." He took a Kleenex from the handwarmer pocket of his sweatshirt, placed it against the cut, then rolled down the sleeve. He patted Donald's cheek. "You did real good." Jorge stuffed their gains in his pocket, and with Donald finished the easy run home.

CHAPTER

THIRTEEN

Sheldon Zipkin was an observer of many things. In his sixtieth year, he was five foot ten inches and one hundred seventy pounds of muscle. His hair was a mass of ill-kempt, tightly wound white curls stuffed beneath a blue wool watch cap. Wind and cold and sun had burned his face a reddish-brown. Wire-rimmed bifocals, his only concession to the passage of time, rested near the end of a round nose.

He was the master's mate on a tugboat that pushed barges around the harbor and rivers of New York.

The captain of the tug was bagged out on his bunk, three sheets to the wind. He was like that most of the time, and he had his old friend Sheldon to thank that he still had his job.

Sheldon turned up the collar of his pea jacket, and pulled down the woolen cap to shield his ears. It had been a nice day, but now that the sun was starting to come down, it was a bit sharp heading upwind, and up the East River, to dock for the night.

He pushed the glasses up the bridge of his nose and

stepped inside the bridge. "Move over, Jerry," he said to the helmsman, taking the wheel. He signaled the telegraph to dead slow. The powerful diesels slowed the propellers, and as they lost traction, the tug slewed in the turbulence of the Hell Gate tide rip.

A bit of sun remained above the buildings to the west; and glinted off of the oil-slicked gray river. Zipkin took the binoculars from the case that dangled from the compass gimbals. He squinted, then notched the telegraph ahead a stop. The tug made some headway.

"Hey, Corky," Zipkin yelled to the man at the bow. "Look off the starboard bow, in the water. Is that my imagination?"

Corky wiped his eyes with the back of his hand. "Can you maneuver a little closer, Shelly? We're maybe fifty or sixty yards off." His brogue was as thick as oatmeal.

Zipkin watched Corky's upraised hand and steered accordingly against the racing current.

Corky yelled over his shoulder. "It's a man. Facedown, he is, bobbing like a cork."

"Can you get him with a hook?"

"If we come up alongside on the beam, I can reach."

"Jerry, give him a hand," Zipkin said, reversing the engines.

They had the hook into the body in a minute, and straining and cursing had pulled it up on deck. "Okay, Shelly," Corky shouted. "We've got the bugger. He's big, black, and dead."

Zipkin increased throttle to cruising speed and pulled the tug back into her homeward-bound course. "Jerry, go downstairs and get some coffee into the skipper. I want him awake and on his feet when we dock." He carefully noted both the time and the location of the body relative to landmarks on either shore, then called in to the harbor unit of N.Y.P.D. "This is *Susan M*, over."

"Harbor unit. Officer Lanahan, over."

"Lanahan, we're in the East River Channel about a half

mile south of North Brother Island. If you look out the window, you'll see us."

"Red and white striped funnel?" Lanahan asked. He could see Zipkin's ship clearly from the harbor unit headquarters at 135th Street and Locust Avenue in the South Bronx.

"That's us. Permission to come alongside."

"Why?"

"I found a stiff in the water. I'd just as soon not take him home with me."

"Jesus. Come alongside"—he peered over his desk—"downriver from the cruiser. You can bring her in a-beam."

By the time Zipkin had moved the *Susan M* to dockside, Lanahan had alerted the captain and had hands ashore waiting to take lines.

Tommy Sheridan, the commander of the harbor unit, asked for permission to come aboard, and hopped over the side of the *Susan M*. "Where'd you find that, Sheldon?"

Zipkin produced a piece of paper. "There's my statement."

"Names of all witnesses, addresses, and telephone numbers?"

"Already there, Tom. I remember from the last time."

"How many have you done now, Shelly, these dozen years?"

"Three. He was just bobbing in the channel off a Hundred and First Street."

"Which side of the channel?"

"West. Definitely on the Manhattan side."

"Homicide Zone Four. I'm sure Flaherty will be thrilled."

"Tom, can you take statements now, or let us go?" He tapped his watch. "Union wages. We're ten minutes from the dock, and half an hour from overtime."

"I'll make you a deal. Can you take her home and then drive back here for a quick chat with Homicide?"

"Agreed."

*　　*　　*

The dinner that Lou Hernandez and Arnie Ross shared that night was very different from the one of the previous evening. They sat cross-legged on a tatami mat in a little Japanese restaurant on Second Avenue and Ninety-first Street.

A large round plate between the two men contained a few pieces of sushi. Arnie gestured to Lou.

Hernandez patted his stomach and said, "You take 'em. I just don't have any more room, Arn. God, I ran an extra turn around the park this afternoon trying to digest what Mamma did to us yesterday."

Arnie nodded. "I think I can still put these away. I love uni, Lou."

"You love uni because it's Japanese, and because almost no one else can eat it."

"Loving uni is a state of mind, Roach." Arnie picked up the book that lay at his side. "The development of inner wisdom . . ."

"Cannot stem from eating uni," Lou finished. "I have read *An Introduction to Zen Buddhism.*"

"Only because I made you do it."

"No place does D. T. Suzuki say that the road to inner wisdom can be reached by eating something that smells like spoiled fish and looks like baby shit."

Arnie stuffed his mouth and said between bites, "You are a philistine."

"I am a Puerto Rican, and a Catholic."

"I call you Roach because the cockroach is the national bird of Puerto Rico."

"You call me Roach because we have been friends all our lives, and I permit it."

"Bah," said Arnie, popping the last two uni sushi into his mouth.

"Then how come," Lou asked slyly, "you never call me Roach in front of Mamma?"

There was a pause as he chewed and swallowed. "Because she would wash my mouth out with laundry soap."

"A big strong man like you afraid of a little seventy-year-old Puerto Rican lady?"

Arnie smiled and patted his arm. "You bet your ass, Roach." He stretched and turned the book over in his hand. "Transcendental wisdom and love. Am I ever going to get there? I don't know what I am?"

"You're not satisfied with what you are. Last night you were as happy as a clam."

"Sure, I was stuffing my face with your mother's cooking. *Lechón asado!* God, I love roast pig."

"Your ancestors are spinning in their graves."

Arnie raised an eyebrow. "The only ancestors I knew are in Potter's Field. I don't remember Eddie Ross keeping a kosher house."

"Maybe that's what you need. You're terrific with children. Mine love you as much as they love me. Except for Arnaldo and the baby. I think they love you more."

"Uh-huh. Uncle Santa Claus. It's easy when you have no responsibilities. What else do I do but spoil them?"

"You're pigheaded. Arnaldo listens to you like you were speaking from the chair of Peter."

"First you complain that I'm too involved in Zen. Then you criticize me because I'm not Jewish enough to suit you. Now you complain that I speak with the voice of the pope and I don't have a big family." He raised his arm and waved at the waiter. "Will you make up your fucking mind. Check, please."

When they got into the car, Lou turned to Arnie and said, "You don't have anything left to prove to anybody. You are everything that you could want of yourself. Why don't you give yourself a break. Every time you meet a nice girl, you take it just so far and then drop it. You are generous with everybody but yourself."

" 'The head covered with ashes, the face smeared with mud,' " Arnie quoted.

"St. Augustine recommended faith and good works."

Arnie stepped on the gas and pulled away from the curb.

"St. Augustine didn't like Jews. Suzuki and Buddha don't seem to care."

When they walked in the front door of the twenty-third precinct house, they could hear the high, quavering voice of Captain Benjamin Finkle raising hell with someone on the telephone. As they trotted up the stairs they could hear him more distinctly.

"Well, you're a shit, Tommy. You know I got homicides coming out of my ears. That counts against me. That's points off. Why the hell couldn't you have reported the fucking stiff in at the twenty-fifth? Let HZ six take a crack at something. How come you never pass me any easy busts?"

They passed out of earshot and walked into the HZ4 office. "Your coreligionist, I believe, Sergeant Ross," Lou said.

"I should have had seven helpings of *lechón* last night instead of just six."

"Wait till you see what Flaherty has for you, Arnie," Baxter said, smiling.

Arnie diverted himself from the door of his own office and knocked at Flaherty's.

"Come in."

"Marvin says you want me."

Flaherty craned his neck. "*An Introduction to Zen Buddhism*. Commendable. I want you to look at a stiff. It's lying on the dock at the harbor unit."

"So that's what's the matter with Finkle."

"What do you mean?"

"He was whining to somebody on the phone as Lou and I came up the stairs."

"Tommy Sheridan," Flaherty said.

"The harbor unit commander. That's what he was doing. What a schmuck."

"Amen. Anyway, go there before the meat wagon drags him away and see what you can make of it. It's been a busy few days."

"Four in two days. That's busy." Arnie went next door to check out his desk. There was nothing on it but stale DD-5's. "What you got, Roach?"

"Just trying to follow up on that Peskin thing. Truly a waste of time. If you like, I'll be glad to follow up on the interviews from the Dushan case."

"Dushan? Oh, yeah, the gym killing. If you could just do a couple of them, I'd appreciate it."

Arnie walked out the door motioning to Baxter. "Come on, Shadow. I'm going to take you to the old swimming hole."

They pulled up at the harbor unit wharf in a beat-up unmarked car fifteen minutes later. "Good evening, Captain," Arnie said. "This is Marvin Baxter, my partner."

"Hello, Ross, Baxter. There he is under the sheet."

"Meat wagon here, sir?

"Not yet, Ross. He's all yours."

"Who dredged him out?"

"Guy name of Sheldon Zipkin. He's first mate on a barge tug."

"He worth a look?"

"He's coming back after he berths his tug to talk to you. You mean is he a possible perp? No. I've known him for years. In fact, this is the third stiff he's dropped on my doorstep."

The white truck with the orange stripes and the seal of the city rolled onto the wharf as Arnie and Baxter pulled the tarpaulin off the corpse.

"Look, Marvin," Arnie said, "I think it's a dead colored person."

"You know what the odds are, Arnie. If he's dead, and he's found on the streets of New York, it's a forty-three percent chance he's going to be black, and a thirty-one percent chance he's going to be under twenty-five."

"And if he's not black," Arnie continued.

"He's going to be Hispanic, thirty-eight percent chance."

Arnie kneeled. "I wonder how he got into the river. What do the odds say, Marvin?"

"Drunk or high, slipped and fell."

"We aren't going to know till they take him apart," Ross said. "Is this your first water baby, Marvin?"

"Yup." Baxter moved closer. This was one of those rare chances when Ross felt like teaching, and he didn't want to miss a word.

Arnie turned the head. "He isn't even stiff—for a stiff, that is. Try an arm. Go ahead. See. It moves easy. He hasn't been in the water very long. A few hours maybe. Also, when they're in a long time, they take on water and sink. It takes until they start to decompose and blow up with internally generated gases that they surface again. By then they don't look quite so human as your bro' here. They also tend to get nibbled on." Arnie smiled. "Nice, huh?"

"You have great charm, Arnie."

"Look at this, Marvin. I think that maybe somebody didn't like our friend. Check out that nose."

"It isn't cosmetically perfect."

"In fact, Marvin, we could even say that it was kind of fucked-up."

"We could say that."

"Somebody broke that nose. You see how the end of it is pushed up? Now, Marvin, you know from looking in the mirror that you flat-nosed persons don't have noses that tilt. What can you tell me about this nose?"

Marvin knelt next to Arnie on the rough concrete surface and peered closely at the dead man's face. "It looks like somebody pushed it in."

"Would you like to risk a can of Foster's Australian Lager against a four-pack of Grolsch?" Arnie asked.

"I'll split four Grolsch with you and admit that you're smarter than I am."

Arnie snorted. "I'll settle, cheapskate. I was going to bet you that I know what killed this dude."

"I know. What did kill him?"

"Somebody shoved the bone splinters from his broken

nose right up into the frontal lobe of his brain. Then they threw him in the drink."

"Here comes the M.E. team. I guess we'll know soon enough," Marvin said.

"Let's toss him. Maybe there's some identification. It would be nice to know who we pick up for a change. The last guy didn't even have a head to check mug shots from." Arnie patted his pockets, then stuck his hands into the soggy clothing. "I keep thinking I'm going to come up with a live goldfish."

"Is this for us?" a white-coated orderly from the medical examiner's office asked.

"In a minute. I'm picking his pockets." Arnie stood up, disgusted. "Let's roll him over and see whether there's anything in the back of his pants." There was nothing. "Okay, boys, he's all yours."

Sheldon Zipkin turned up ten minutes later and was very explicit and cooperative, but gave them nothing to go on. In irritated silence Arnie drove Baxter back to the precinct. When they got out, he said thoughtfully, "Another karate chop, Marvin."

"Wait for the M.E.'s report, Arnie. Maybe somebody bagged the dude with a mallet."

CHAPTER

FOURTEEN

Matsushima went directly from his office to the Tokyo and Seoul Health Club. There was a new young thing who spoke acceptable Japanese recommended to him by the patroness. She was wisplike and thin, without the stocky legs and foreshortened waist of most Korean women. She reminded him of one of the uniformed greeters at the department stores in Tokyo, babbling about the day's sales as you walked in the door.

He allowed her to strip him naked and lead him to the shower. She wore nothing but a towel over her hips. One day, he thought, the federal government will fall upon this place, and the dozens of others that have sprung up around the city as a concomitant to the Korean takeover of the retail produce business, and they will ask for green cards—the sign of resident alien status. The girls will be arrested and deported in the wink of an eye. The lucky ones will have stayed long enough to build a reserve of dollars, which they would convert into a house or a small shop in their hometown.

He sat on the stool and relaxed in the steaming water.

The girl rubbed him vigorously with a loofa mitten till his skin glowed pink. When she had dried him, she led him shyly to her dimly lit room. He permitted himself the luxury of a half-hour's massage, time enough in which to gather his thoughts for the meeting that was to take place upstairs.

With the appearance of four stories in the paper in a single day about the activities of his clan, Matsushima felt he had no alternative but to call a halt.

Though his disciples would have no material wants, he recognized that they would need a purpose. Their raids on the public, which he had taught them were a legitimate source of income, were also an end in themselves. The planning and execution absorbed their energies. Their co-operation reinforced their new identities and gave them a sense of belonging.

He had raised a standard for them, and they had flocked to it. He had defined his own values. He had not found himself in the corporate treadmill on which he had labored for thirty years, nor in his pedestrian marriage. His mind wandered more and more to the old order, which permitted each man, of high birth or low, to know his place and his course of action in every instance, guided by eternal verities.

His family had been a linchpin of the system. Then, in a period of fifteen years, from the first intrusion of the Americans in 1853 to the return by the last shogun of his commission to rule to the hands of the emperor, the system was rocked to its foundations. The verities were cast aside. No more samurai for the Matsushimas, no more rice fields, no more castles. Confiscated. The daimyos were stripped of their land and authority as the material wealth of Japan was reclaimed by the imperial power, to be replaced by meaningless titles in a European-style peerage. Two million samurai were pensioned off. Then even their swords were taken away, and their pensions with them. Five percent of the population of Japan—those that had been its heart and driving force throughout history—were cast adrift, weaponless mendicants.

Field Marshal Saigo, commander of Japan's military forces, raised an army of samurai around him to begin the Satsuma Rebellion. It was the last defiant act of the warrior class. The imperial army of loyalists and peasant conscripts met them before the walls of Kagoshima and crushed them. Saigo, gravely wounded, was beheaded by his own men.

At the massage parlor in New York, more than a century later, Matsushima turned onto his back. The Korean girl, not fully sure of her role, smoothed his body with oil, then hesitantly began to tend to his genitals.

"No," he snapped in Japanese. He was not in the mood for this distraction. Her face was filled with fear, and tears rolled down her face. He sat up and made a small bow to her. He told her that he respected her feelings. In no way was his lack of interest to be considered a reflection on her. There was no disgrace. In fact, Matsushima would be sure to express his satisfaction to the proprietor.

"What is your name?"

"Han," she replied.

"I come here often. On my next visit I will ask for you so that I may pillow with you. You are very beautiful."

She bowed low and led him back to the changing area. He tipped her handsomely.

When he had ascended the stairs and put on his white judo suit, he sat in the shadowed darkness in the lotus position. His family had lost its castles, its samurai, and its rice fields, but through its unassailable social position, opportunities presented themselves. The Matsushimas were practical men. Again they acquired possessions—rice fields, and finally the lonely island and castle that had been their home fief for a thousand years.

Matsushima clenched his fist at the memory of his father, small and dignified in his morning coat and top hat, bowing to the Americans, so tall and brawny in their informal tan uniforms, signing the document of surrender aboard the giant gray ship as it swayed gently at anchor in

Tokyo Bay. He had been forced to watch the spectacle
with the rest of his classmates at the Imperial Naval College.

Matsushima's face had been hot with shame, for everyone could recognize his father. What the Emperor had
accomplished in 1876, MacArthur had repeated in 1945.

Once again, the Matsushimas were stripped of everything—
rice fields, castle—all but the good name. Again, in time,
some of the material possessions were regained. But Hiroo
Matsushima, raised in the spirit of the samurai, and destined to be a captain of battle fleets, became a clerk in the
service of merchantmen. His father, in his eighties, sat
silent in the anachronistic castle on the unwanted island in
the windswept sea, huddled in the barren shell of his pride
and honor.

The steady rise through the ranks of the Inyo Lines had
been increasingly meaningless to him. His promotion to
general manager for North America—in the service of the
victors—seemed almost a punishment. His arrival in that
frame of mind left him at the brink of suicide. His chance
meeting with Willie Lopez had changed all of that. In a
single moment he saw his own redemption. Bushido did
not have to die with him. He could teach it to others. His
example could be his legacy.

When Willie Lopez knocked at the door a few minutes
later, Matsushima sat with his eyes closed, his fingertips
pressed against his temples. His motivation in forming his
samurai clan was clear, but its practicality often eluded
him, and he could not see how it all would end.

Donald Wolfe and Jorge Rodriguez wanted to bring him
their earnings. Willie ushered them in. They bowed low
and gave Matsushima a gold and steel watch and one
hundred and twelve dollars.

Each meeting of the Matsushima clan began in the same
way. The pupils sat cross-legged facing the master. There
was a five-minute period of silence for self-composition.
The next element of the ceremony was a unique blend of
Zen Buddhist self-realization, and Matsushima's borrow-
ing from Alcoholics Anonymous.

"Fred Logan," Matsushima said, "what brings you here? What holds you here?"

"I am Fred Logan," he said, standing. He was twenty, black, and six feet of lithe strength. "I never knew my father. My mother died when I was little. I lived with an uncle. I stopped going to school in the eighth grade. I ran away because I was beaten. I delivered groceries. I stole. I was never caught. I slept in doorways, and bus stations, and flophouses." He had made the speech many times before. At each of the meetings one of the members spoke. Matsushima was fascinated to watch as the change in the speech reflected a metamorphosis in the speaker. In language alone Fred Logan had grown in stature, now able to make a phrase without the supporting crutch of vulgarity.

"I was walking west on Houston Street six months ago. A drunk walked up to me and asked me for some change. There was another person behind me. They tried to take my money. I was cut. They ran away. I got to a doorway about half a block from Sixth Avenue. The building was all boarded up. It was just starting to get cold. I thought about going to the hospital." His eyes focused on the wall above Matsushima's head. "Then I decided not to bother. I was bleeding pretty bad . . . badly," he corrected himself. "But I didn't hurt. So I decided to die. Willie found me. He asked me if he could help. I told him to leave me alone." Logan shifted his eyes to Lopez. "He said if I didn't care about dying, he could show me how to live."

Matsushima watched Logan's face. It was true. He had been badly cut, but less near death than he had thought. Willie had brought him to the emergency room. They had sewn him up. He had been released in ten days.

"I didn't really want to die, I think," Logan said. "I think I wanted to not be a bum anymore. I think that I was better off dead than just going from doorway to doorway. I think that there was a man hiding inside the bum's body, and he needed some help to get out. I needed to have a reason to not die. Here I have what we all have. I have something to hang on to. If I act like a man, I am treated like a man."

Matsushima made a small bow of recognition. *That is our way. You are given purpose. That gives you identity. Curious,* Matsushima thought, *how the self-pity starts to drain away with time, as they begin to shift from passivity to action. Is it not the same for me? If I were not satisfied with the life I led, all that I had to do was to reach out and change it.*

Matsushima raised his hand, palm outward. Logan bowed deeply, and resumed his seat. "Today," Matsushima said, "we begin a new phase of our learning together. There will be no more gathering of tribute. Our martial skills will be sharpened only here, in the karate-dojo. Our efforts will turn for the moment from the physical to the spiritual."

Hector Garcia raised his hand. Matsushima recognized him. "But Matsushima-sama, how shall we eat?"

Matsushima suppressed a smile. He was taking his clan off the streets because he feared that as disciplined as they were, with the four deaths with which they had been associated, and the interest of the policeman trained in martial arts, the chances of getting caught had increased unreasonably. In time there would be other crimes to occupy Sergeant Ross, and any pattern that appeared to exist would have dissipated. It never occurred to Hector Garcia that he might be caught. His faith was absolute. In that way he was impractical. But his twenty-one years had taught him that he well might starve.

"What portion do you keep of what you take?" Matsushima asked him.

"Twenty percent, Matsushima-sama."

"What portion do you give to me?"

"Eighty percent, Matsushima-sama."

"Does that not seem unfair? You do the work. I take the lion's share."

Hector rocked uncomfortably on his heels. "It is not for me to question."

"Excellent. The purpose of the daimyo's share is that in

times of difficulty he may continue to see to the welfare of the samurai. My portion is untouched. You will each receive a weekly payment to deal with your personal needs until you are ordered to take tribute again. In this way you may study with clear minds." There was a murmur of satisfaction. Samurai have not changed over the ages, Matsushima thought. The rice bowl must be filled. One euphemism is as good as another; tribute for stolen goods, clear minds for full pockets.

"Now we begin to read from Suzuki." Matsushima took a book from the floor and opened it on his lap. "You are only the sum of your beliefs. To be samurai you must believe." He looked down at the page and read, "My head is covered with ashes. My face is smeared with mud. Selflessness for the general welfare leads to enlightenment."

He read to them and commented for fifteen minutes. At the end they were moving restlessly. It is not easy, Matsushima thought, to instill abstract thoughts into illiterate minds.

He led them in a vigorous exercise, and let them come even closer than usual to the sharp edge of injury in their personal combat, in the hope of dispelling their pent-up energies.

When they were done, Fred Logan raised his hand. "Matsushima-sama, where is Adolfo Reyes?"

Matsushima had prepared his answer when he had decided to eliminate Reyes. "He disobeyed. Disobedience is dishonor. Without honor, life has no meaning, and life and death are the same."

They looked among themselves in silent understanding. "You are dismissed," Matsushima said.

CHAPTER

FOURTEEN

Even for Willie Lopez it was difficult to accept the elimination of Adolfo Reyes without question. How large is the margin for error in matters of loyalty and discipline? If you are ordered not to eat lunch before two and eat at one-thirty instead, are you without honor? Or, if you kill a child?

By Willie's oldest notions of social behavior, a member of the gang was always a member of the gang, unless he turned stoolie. Adolfo Reyes failed to control uncivilized instincts that were bred into his ancestors and worsened by life as a hoodlum in the streets of New York, uneducated, uncared-for, and unwanted.

If you are left to fend for yourself, and you become an animal, how much time are you permitted to learn the new way? Willie thought about it for a long time as he walked the streets.

He decided that the answer was simplicity itself; you have shamed yourself when Matsushima-sama decides that you have shamed yourself. If your sin is great enough, you will be ordered to commit suicide. Adolfo Reyes did not behave with the dignity of a samurai. Therefore, he was not granted the opportunity to die with courage. Willie had no trouble resolving the theory with the fact. Matsushima-sama had cut off Adolfo Reyes's head like a chicken, not because he had killed a man, but because he had not obeyed orders.

By the time Willie Lopez had finished wrestling with the concepts of loyalty and discipline that clogged his mind, he found himself sitting on the stoop on East Eighty-fourth Street opposite Libby Beckman's apartment. The blinds were drawn, and the lights were out. All the same, Willie seemed to extract some kind of warmth from the proximity. The way of the samurai had finally given some meaning to his life, but secure in his devotion, he wondered whether the discipline of the samurai could be tempered by softer emotions.

He had been there an hour when Libby got out of a cab. She was carrying an attaché case, and a document case. She fumbled with her purse and the two bags, finally dropping them to the ground with a resounding, ''Oh, shit!''

Willie smiled, and watched as she was at last able to get the key into the lock. She kicked the bags inside and slammed the door behind her. Libby Beckman had not been thrilled with the course of the day.

She had gone to the office early with a report that she had spent much of the week preparing for a scheduled meeting. Her boss, an excessively neat and constipated forty-year-old Ivy Leaguer, had arbitrarily decided that her section would not be presented to the committee for another week. In short, her travails, overtime, and nervous stomach had been all in vain.

And then her mother had called her twice during the day to whine about her living alone, and to ask her to move back home. Libby had had a tantrum on the phone. Thank God, she thought, that I was in the small conference room alone, and that the sound security is high.

''For Christ's sake, Mother, if you're worried about my

virginity, you're years too late. You're not helping me or making me feel loved. You're being a burden, and asking me to soak up your anxieties. If you can't take the pressure of living in New York, I suggest that you spend more time in Florida!'' Bang. If she could have broken the phone over the cradle, she would have.

She looked at her watch. Almost nine o'clock. And if that weren't enough, that damn policeman was going to come over to talk to her. She allowed that he was trying to do his job and to protect her. And besides, there was poor old Laszlo. She doubted that they would ever catch the people who killed him and robbed the gym. They rarely do in New York.

And on top of it, she missed her exercise class at Muffy's. She'd talked to her on the phone in the morning. Muffy was going to go to Hilton Head Island for a couple of weeks. She'd open up again on the tenth of April. For the moment she couldn't think about anything. Of course, Libby understood.

She ordered her desk and papers, and hung up her coat. The rest of the small apartment was immaculate. Libby could still recall the Saturdays she was deprived of her television set for failure to meet the norms imposed upon her. She couldn't have cared less, save for the minor indignity of punishment. She waltzed through the motions required to put things in order, and then fell to her books. Her mother was never able to understand Libby's fascination with books, while her father, the prototypical intellectual, couldn't have been more pleased.

When she turned on the light, Willie could see through the half-open blinds. He pushed himself farther against the stone railing and watched contentedly as she straightened ashtrays. It occurred to him that she was expecting company, and he felt a welter of conflicting emotions. He was jealous and foolish, curious and disappointed, all in the same breath.

He knew that Libby worked in the international department of a bank. He had no idea how much she made. He assumed that she did pretty well. It wasn't Park Avenue, but her apartment was in a nicer building and neighborhood than any he had ever been in. Maybe she had money from somewhere else. From a guy, maybe. Willie was not surprised to see a fire-engine-red Porsche 924 roll up the block and park in front of her door. The motor died, and a man emerged. Willie's skin crawled when he saw him, as a cat's fur stands at the sight of a dog. He concentrated on making himself invisible.

The man was about six feet tall, Willie could see, and brawny. He carried himself lightly and with grace, despite his size. To Willie he radiated physical danger. He rang the doorbell, rocking slightly on the balls of his feet. Even in the dim light above the portal Willie could see that his face was a mass of irregular crags and angles, and when he turned, there was the flash of a scar. Willie felt at his own cheek.

When the door opened, he strained to hear and to see. For a moment there was nothing, then he saw the man follow Libby across the room and sit.

After a moment of discussion the man reached into his jacket pocket and extracted a notebook and pencil. He must be a cop. Willie mastered his temptation to flee. There was no law against sitting on a stoop.

"Thank you for cooperating, Miss Beckman," Arnie Ross said. "You know, everybody in this city thinks that criminals are never caught. They are. What helps is when the average citizen pitches in."

"I thought that once they were gone out of Muffy Grant's door, nobody would ever catch them."

"Most people feel that way. Robberies happen in a hurry. Everybody, including the perps, is scared to death. People see little and remember less. But if we can piece together a bit here and a bit there, sometimes we can pick up a scent."

"I was scared to death, myself," Libby said.

Arnie smiled. "I heard that you were as tough as an old

billy goat. You faced them down and dared them to do something about it.''

Libby's eyes crinkled in her round cheeks. "And for my troubles one of them gave me a wallop across the face.'' She turned toward him. "See. He hit me so hard I didn't even have time to feel bad about it.''

Arnie peered at her face in the glow of the lamp. It was blue over the cheekbone, and there was a little shiner around her left eye. "It isn't unique. They call it combat trauma. I was stabbed once during an arrest of a drug dealer. That's where I got this decoration.'' He pointed to the scar. "I have another more colorful one on my stomach. I didn't realize for an hour that I'd been cut. By then I'd lost blood, and I just passed out.''

"How awful.''

"As I said, Miss Beckman, I didn't know how awful it was until too late to do anything about it. Sometimes it's easier to remember things when the smoke has cleared.''

Libby sat back in her chair. "I haven't really thought about it a lot. If it hadn't been for poor Laszlo, it wouldn't have been so bad. Why did they kill him?''

"I don't know. I think that they just knocked him cold to get him out of the way. The fellow who tied him up got overenthusiastic. His nose was pretty badly broken. Someone must have hit him very hard, or with great skill and precision.''

Libby's face settled into a frown.

"Something catch your eye?'' Arnie asked.

"Jogged my memory is more like it. When the slender fellow who was the leader told the man who hit me to get away, the man didn't listen. He pulled his hand back to hit me again. The leader just . . . well, it looked like he just . . . touched him. The man who hit me recoiled like he'd been burned with a hot poker. He just stood there holding his wrist. I couldn't see his face through the mask, of course, but he seemed to be in pain.''

Arnie made a note. "He probably was. I think that we're dealing with a martial arts expert. You know, karate, judo, jujitsu. Just a poke of the fingertip in the right place can make you feel like you've been beaten with a tree trunk.''

"Do you do martial arts, Sergeant Ross?''

"It's my hobby.''

Libby shuddered. "That's scary.''

"Not really. There's much more to martial arts than beating on other people. It has to do with philosophy and self-control, both mental and physical.''

"Yes,'' Libby said. "The Way of the Tao.''

Arnie smiled appreciatively. "Don't tell me. You're a black belt.''

Libby laughed. "I'm the least athletic person in the entire city of New York. That's what brought me to Muffy Grant's. I tried listening to tapes, going to diet doctors, you name it. I was finally driven by insistent friends and an unsympathetic mirror to do something. You have been hoodwinked by the leftovers of a year of Asian philosophy at Yale.''

"What else do you remember? Any physical characteristics?''

"There wasn't much to see. They came in small, medium, and large. They were all slender and athletic-looking. I'm sure from the way that they sounded and moved that they were young, around my age, I'd say Hispanic of one sort or another. All wore stocking masks.''

"Not a word that would give them away . . . a place, a name. Distinguishing characteristics. Jewelry? A big ring? Or a big gold cross? A limp?''

Libby shrugged. "The only thing that I can say for certain is that the leader had a soft voice. And even through the mask, with his features distorted, I could see that he had soft brown eyes with long eyelashes. He was like a cat. He moved with that kind of fluidity.''

"It sounds like he made quite an impression on you. Have you ever seen him before or since?''

Libby hesitated. The form that had been on the stoop across the street. Libby was a native New Yorker, and a survivor. She knew enough not to take the subway late at night, and to stay out of the Port Authority Bus Terminal. She knew about Fox Police locks, and never to walk across the Central Park transverses in the dark. No candy from strangers. No hitchhiking. Come on, Libby, tell the nice policeman about the figure on the stoop.

"I think he tried to keep the other fellow from hurting me."

Arnie weighed his words. She was young, but this was not some wise-ass kid. This was an educated, capable lady. She was cooperating, and there was no percentage in being offensive. "You know, Miss Beckman, as nice as you may feel this young man was—I have testimony from others as well that he was helpful in his own way—you have to keep in mind that he was the leader, and probably the strategist behind the armed robbery of fourteen people, a physical assault on three more, and at least an accessory to second-degree murder. I wouldn't misplace any sentiment if I were you."

"There's really nothing more concrete that I can contribute," she said with finality.

Ross rose and extended his hand. "You've been helpful. It's the martial arts thing that fascinates me."

Libby smiled again. "I wouldn't want to think you'd misplaced any sentiments just because of a common interest, Sergeant."

"Ouch! Serves me right. Good night, Miss Beckman."

Libby leaned on the back of the couch and watched out of the window as Arnie climbed into the red sports car, revved it, and pulled away. She stared out into the darkness across the street.

When Willie saw the policeman pull away, he breathed a sigh of relief. What had they been talking about so long? There was nothing that she could have seen that would aid in identifying any of them. Even if she recognized their voices, there would be no way to prove that they had been there. Voices through stocking masks make lousy evidence. She was looking out after the cop's car. Did she

mention me? I wonder. Did she tell him that I all but broke
Adolfo Reyes's wrist because he was going to hit her
again. Did the other women tell him how brave she was?
He pulled away from the stone bannister to take a better
look.

There was a flicker of motion on the stoop across the
street as Libby Beckman turned away from the car of that
strange policeman. She froze, her eyes boring into shadows. Goose flesh crept up her arms. Perhaps he was out
there. Perhaps she shouldn't have resisted the temptation
to tell Ross that she felt eyes on her the other night. That
the man who had slipped away down the block had the
same feline body that she had seen at the gym.

If it were he, sitting there across the street on the stoop
looking at her through the window, why? Did he fear that
she could pick him out in the midst of seven million souls
by chance and run after him, pointing an accusing finger?

A tremor of panic passed through Libby Beckman's
well-ordered mind. Could he want to hurt me? Some
imagined ill, or slight? She remembered the softness of the
voice. He had admonished her to be careful, as though she
were a child playing with matches.

It was all that Willie could do to keep from standing out
in the open. She's looking for me. I know. I can tell. What
if she calls the police? His mind sprang to Matsushima.
Since Willie had become a disciple of Zen and of the
master, since he had become samurai, things were much
clearer to him. He slipped gingerly across the steps, still
seated, but away from the shadow. He would sit where she
could see him. If she called the police, he could always
run. If it seemed that he could be caught, the answer was
simple enough. He touched the switchblade knife in his
pocket. Seppuku.

Though she had sensed his presence, then and the other
night, his appearance was nonetheless a shock to Libby.
Her instinct was to casually slip over to the kitchen, and
out of his sight dial 911 and yell for help. Instead, she slid
into a sitting position and continued to look at him across

the street. He was as she remembered him, slender and lank, sitting with his elbows on his knees with his chin cupped in his hands. His face was no more visible than it had been behind the stocking mask.

They looked with their minds' eyes at what they imagined, more than what they could truly see. At ten o'clock Libby, torn between the figure on the stoop and her ingrained propriety, as she had been between the secure job at the bank and a Peace Corps village in the jungle, disappeared into the bathroom. When she returned in her robe a few minutes later, he was still there. Looking across the street, trying to pierce the shadows, Libby pulled the robe open.

He was transfixed for a moment. Then, overcome by her gesture, he rose, his penis painfully rigid against his blue jeans, and stepped forward into the light, so that she could see his face. He knew exactly what he must do. His lips formed the words, thank you. He blew a kiss from the tips of his fingers, and walked away into the night.

After working herself to exhaustion on the papers she had brought home from the office, Libby Beckman lay in bed at three in the morning, unable to sleep for the throbbing in her loins.

CHAPTER

FIFTEEN

The following evening at seven o'clock, Arnold Ross and Lou Hernandez were in an unmarked HZ4 car headed toward a restaurant on Sixth Street between Second and First avenues. It was one of a dozen on the block owned by three Indian brothers.

"Anapurna," Arnie said.

"Oh, God, Arn, my stomach. And what about Gelfand?"

"It was his idea. Everything vindaloo. Too hot to be eaten."

"Good," Lou said sourly, "that'll give us plenty of opportunity to talk."

They found a space on First Avenue and walked around the corner, past a derelict sleeping on a grating. By the time they'd gone a quarter of the way up the block, their noses were assaulted by the melange of spices and cooking meat and grease. Fifty yards beyond, a white Cadillac Seville stood in lonely splendor under a NO PARKING ANYTIME sign.

"Gelfand is here," Arnie commented.

They drew even to the car, amused. It sported every

trapping that Dr. Gelfand could acquire. There were two shields, one from the Medical Examiner's Office, and the other from the Office of the Police Commissioner. There were stickers from the Police Conference of New York, the Police Benevolent Association, and the Benevolent Association of the District Attorney's office of New York County.

"Jesus," Lou commented. "Nothing from the Girl Scouts?"

Dr. Gelfand was sitting at a table for six that he had commandeered in the back of the restaurant. It was two steps down from the street and ill lit. There were paper cloths draped over stained linen ones on Formica tables. Dr. Gelfand was finishing the last of an order of assorted hors d'oeuvres for four.

"You should talk to your doctor about that, Doctor. You keep this up and you're going to end up on one of your own slabs."

"Maybe it will cool off my mouth. How are you, Arnie? Lou?"

They sat down and ordered Eagle, the malty Indian beer, and a couple more rounds of appetizers.

"The virtues of a cheap restaurant with good food are without number," Gelfand said. "What's on your mind?"

"I thought we could talk a little shop," Arnie said.

"Over an Indian dinner? Autopsy and dinner?"

"Meat, Dr. Gelfand, is meat." Arnie took a sip of beer. "Doc, I have a half a theory. Just a guess, mind you. It has to do with karate."

Gelfand reached under the table and patted his briefcase. "I brought what you asked me to, plus a little more. I read what you said in the *Post*, Arnold."

"Can you tell me, between bites, what I want to know?"

"Mmfff," Gelfand replied around a bite of keema nan. "I love this bread. Do you like ground lamb?"

"Love it. Tell me about the stiffs."

"Let's start with the guy at the gym. His jaw and cheekbone were broken, and his nasal septum displaced by

one blow. I looked very carefully at the skin. The normal
indented pattern and bruises that come from fists were not
there. He was not struck with a heavy blunt instrument,
because compression of the tissues was not evident. He
had a scuff mark on his forehead. I scraped the tissue
sample and sent it to Forensics.''

"So?"

"So Ruditz says it's shoe polish."

"So this was done with a shoe." Arnie concluded.
"Anything else?"

"I went over him with a fine-tooth comb. There is a
severe deep bruise over the kidney on the left side. There
was a kind of V-shaped mark. I would guess that it was
the heel of a shoe. The kidney itself was damaged. It must
have been some wallop. Then, of course, once they had
the poor slob unconscious, they wanted to make sure that
he stayed out of the way. I would guess that the guys who
did him in had no idea how badly he was hurt. They taped
his hands behind his back, then rolled him over and taped
his mouth shut.''

"I thought they taped his nose too," Lou said.

"Not really. There was just so much tape that it in-
truded above his upper lip and clogged his nostrils.''

"What killed him, then?"

"A bunch of things. Certainly, shock from the blow to
the kidney. That was no tap. The blow to the face screwed
up his nasopharyngeal structure. Then there was the blow
to the back of the head.''

"What blow to the back of the head?'' Arnie asked,
looking up. "Nobody said anything about that.''

"Why do you care?'' Gelfand asked.

"How do you think this was done, step by step?''

"I would guess that they got him down on the ground.''

"Not good enough. How did they get him on the ground?
Did they wrestle him to the ground? Are there physical
signs of a struggle?''

"Not unless you call having the shit kicked out of you
signs of a struggle.''

"Come on, Doc. Were there marks on his arms or legs that would make you think that he was in a wrestling match? Did he have fingernail scratches all over him?"

"No. Okay, so there was no wrestling match." Gelfand put the fork down on his plate. "But you knew that. How?"

"The witnesses. The women upstairs. If there had been a scuffle, there would have been enough noise to catch their attention even in the midst of exercising, and with the damn music going. Those people were less than fifty feet from the landing to the gym. Nobody heard or saw a thing till the hoods walked in and yelled stick-up."

"That still leaves us with how they managed to beat up on him," Lou said.

"The bump on the head is what stops me," Arnie said.

"I would say he got it falling. I think his head bounced off the floor when he hit," Gelfand said. "But that doesn't make any sense either. They would have had to have him on the ground to kick him in the back and the face like that anyway. Maybe they made him lie down. They had a gun, didn't they?"

"They did." Ross smiled. "But that's not how it happened. The bruise on the back of the head proves my point."

"It was a twelve-foot giant that hit him."

"Wrong again, Dr. Gelfand. Would you believe me if I said that I could give you a black eye with my foot while we were both standing facing each other?"

"I believe anything you say, Arnold. As long as you will buy me Indian food, I will believe anything."

"It's the mark of a black belt," Arnie said. "This guy was standing up and the other guy just elevated himself—sprang, jumped, call it what you will. He kicked him in the back, and then he kicked him in the head. Then, with his lights out, he fell over and banged his head."

Gelfand stuffed the fork back into his mouth. "Good for you, Arnie. You want to try for two?"

"How about Peskin, Doc?" Lou asked. "Blockage of

the air passages, brain death and its sequel. A karate blow
to the Adam's apple.''

''Absolutely.''

''And the headless horseman?'' Lou asked.

''Therein lies more of a tale. Okay. Callouses on edges
of hands and feet. Score one for Sergeant Ross. The body.
Bruised in a number of places. Also, above the kidneys,
though not nearly so profound or damaging the case of our
dead gym instructor. One bad one. Right in the middle of
the right thigh. Whoever hit him meant for it to hurt, had
good aim, and knows anatomy.''

''The prints? The head?''

''So far nothing. I can tell you this. After careful examination, if I had to make a guess at what removed his head,
I'd say the world's largest scalpel. I couldn't have made a
better incision myself. Cooley and DeBakey together would
have been proud of the work. The trauma is limited to the
severing of tissue. Even the bone work is neat.''

''How about a sword?'' Arnie asked.

''As sharp as a razor, maybe.''

By the time that they had dispensed with the first three
cases, Lou, Arnie, and Dr. Gelfand had worked their way
through mountains of hotly spiced foods, and were preparing to deal with desserts.

''When you die of overeating, Doc, who's going to do
the autopsy on you?''

''Arnie, I've donated my body to the Alpo Dog Food
Company. At least somebody should enjoy the fruits of my
efforts.'' He filled his mouth, then said, ''You know that
the guy that was dragged out of the river is in a way the
most interesting case. You were right. I checked him over
from stem to stern. Mouth tissues tell me he was a smoker,
and that he blew grass. Nasal passages were slightly in-
flamed, and there were traces of cocaine. He wasn't a
heavy user. Not a mark on a vein anywhere on his lovely
body. Excellent physical health. Properly nourished. No
gunshot wounds. No knife wounds. No major organ trauma.

No circulatory or cardiac problems. Only one thing killed this dude.''

"The envelope, if you please, Mr. Medical Examiner," Arnie said.

"And the winner is . . . two blows to the nose. One from above which flattened both the bone and the cartilage, and, parenthetically, also fractured the left cheekbone. And a second blow, which was the cause of death. An instrument, possibly made of rubber, struck the base of the shattered nose with terrific force. Bone splinters from the already shattered structure just zapped back through that soft tissue into the brain. Lights out.''

"The instrument was the heel of a hand," Arnie said definitively. He reached out and rested the heel of his against the bottom of Dr. Gelfand's nose.

Lou and Arnie shook hands with Dr. Gelfand at the door. He thanked them for their generosity and staggered off to his car, full to the gills.

"It is a pleasure, Louis, to make three grown men so happy for twenty-six dollars. Let's go.''

Lou looked out the window as Arnie drove up First Avenue. "It's no coincidence.''

"Maybe. There's really nothing to tie the damn killings together.'' Arnie shrugged. "Just another one of my theories.''

Lou was prone to stick with the evidence. Over the years it had been Arnie's intuition that they had listened to, tempered by Lou's insistence on the details. "Your gut tells you it's all the same.''

"Yeah. It does," Ross said.

"It's a big city. People get killed every day. But more than sixty percent of the time it's a handgun. It's a ruckus. And it's people who know each other. I don't think for a moment that the dude without the head was killed in the course of an ordinary street crime. Somebody meant to do him in gruesomely. It could be as a warning to somebody else. I know that a headless stiff isn't much to work with, but I'd sure as hell like to find a handle on it. Alvin Peskin was killed by accident, almost in a run-of-the-mill mugging. I say *almost*. It's not that the perp meant to do Alvin in, he just used too much force. The guy in the gym died the same way. If they were real killers—no living witnesses, et cetera—they would just have killed the poor bastard. Instead, they bound and gagged him, overdid it, and he was gone. Look at the one that was fished out of the river. Call it overkill. Somebody's been taught karate, or something like it, and is using it to commit crimes, mostly robberies. But they haven't finished the course, because they don't have enough control of the art to stop before it's too late.''

"So you figure the guy in the river ended up there by accident?''

"I'll tell you what, Arn. I think he or they or whoever ripped the guy off, smacked him. He fell down dead, and they used the handy disposal unit to their immediate east.'' Lou pondered for a moment, then said, "It's like kids playing with toys they're big enough to use but not old enough to understand.''

"So we start to keep close track of every crime that has the look of martial arts.''

CHAPTER

SIXTEEN

Ross and Hernandez were able to press their attentions on their theory for less than twenty-four hours. Though Hiroo Matsushima had withdrawn the members of his clan from active operations, the rest of the population of Homicide Zone Four continued to provide Flaherty's staff with more work than they could handle.

In the absence of clear leads in the karate-related cases, Ross and Hernandez and their working partners were assigned to new ones as they came in. The first week after their dinner with Gelfand, there was a supermarket stickup in the barrio, and a couple of clerks were killed. All of the witnesses, the victims, and the perps were Hispanics. Hernandez and Passarelli both spoke Spanish, and were logical choices for the job. They made Flaherty look smart by making the collar in three weeks. Two Dominicans in their twenties, both out on parole.

A week after that Arnie Ross's luck ran out. He and Baxter had been stuck with an ugly case where a mother of two school-aged kids was found with her throat cut in the bushes in Carl Schurz Park, within sight of Gracie

Mansion, the mayoral residence. There had been a big stink.

After a lot of routine work—interviewing bereaved family members, trying to trace her steps, checking for witnesses—nothing turned up. Arnie set Baxter to looking into her personal life. It checked clean, except for a nosy superintendent's wife. It seems the victim's husband fooled around when she was in the country with the kids. How did she know? She proudly showed Baxter how she could see from her second-floor back window across the courtyard into their bedroom. She even showed him the binoculars she used.

With the sour taste that family cases always gave him, Ross cross-checked the alibi that the husband had given for his whereabouts at the time of the crime. Check. He looked over her insurance. Fifty grand. Not enough. Then he got into the guy's bank account. What had happened to five thousand dollars in cash withdrawn systematically over a two-month period with his cash machine card?

It took a week to identify the girlfriend, and half an hour to read her her rights and let her call her lawyer and her boyfriend. Baxter was waiting outside of his office when he tried to skip. The girlfriend gave up the name and number of the guy they'd hired to do the job on a plea. She would end up with a complicity rap, and a couple of years at worst. Hubby would go for murder one.

Ross and Baxter went after Max Brockhorst as soon as they had the couple under lock and key. He had a rap sheet as long as he was tall: armed robbery, car theft, racketeering, arson. He had been arrested thirty-one times, and had spent almost half of his forty years behind bars.

Ross knocked on the door and said, "Brockhorst, this is the police. Open up and come out with your hands in the air." Baxter crouched on the floor across the hall with his gun drawn.

Brockhorst opened the door and emerged with his hands up. As he stepped forward he drove his wrist down on

Ross's shoulder and tried to push him into Baxter's line of fire. Ross caught his wrist and broke it.

From behind him Ross heard a woman's voice yell "Motherfucker!" and a couple of shots. After that he didn't remember much.

Later, he found out that he had slumped to the floor, clearing the doorway. Brockhorst's blond girlfriend had been standing in back of him with a 9mm Browning. Baxter shot her twice in the chest. She died on the way to the hospital. Brockhorst ran down the hall to the stairs. Baxter hit him once in the leg, and he fell down the flight. He'd live to stand trial for murder with his employer.

The shot from the Browning had gone into the fleshy part of Arnie Ross's side, glanced off a rib, and passed through the skin just above his belt in the back. When he woke up in Manhattan Jewish Hospital, he was swathed in bandages from his waist to his armpits, and there was an intravenous tube implanted in his left arm. He got off cheap—a cracked rib, a minor blood vessel, and some torn-up tissue. Despite his protests, he'd be on the beach for three to four weeks.

Arnie Ross left the hospital and went on convalescent leave five days after he had been shot. He was not the only one who was suffering a decline in his fortunes.

Michiko Matsushima had been raised in a manner which made it both foreign and distasteful for her to meddle in her husband's personal or business affairs. Nonetheless, she had become increasingly concerned over a recurrence of sullen and solitary behavior he had exhibited recently. After his depression when they had been posted to New York, there had been a period when he was the Hiroo that she had known in her youth. He had been reserved, as always, but she could sense his exuberance. There was a boyish spring to his step, and on the occasions that he favored her with his attentions, he had been a masterful lover.

More than once she had been tempted to ask him what had brought about the improvement in his humor. Though she shared his bed, and had borne him two children, she never forgot that he was Prince Matsushima of the line of Tokugawa Ieyasu, and gave him the privacy and respect that his rank demanded.

As in Japan, it was common for Hiroo to spend long hours away from the house, and to entertain clients, but Michiko had recognized that in the past year he had been increasingly absent.

She had looked at herself naked in the bathroom mirror. Her body was slender and well cared for, and did not show the passage of time too much, she thought. She hoped that he had not found another woman whose company pleased him more than hers. It seemed to her that physically, he grew younger. When she told him so, he had seemed pleased.

"Thank you," he said. "I have found a place where I exercise. It has been very beneficial to my mind as well as my body."

Michiko Matsushima opened the middle drawer of her husband's desk. It was unlocked because such a violation of privacy was unthinkable. Hesitantly, she looked through its contents. There were pens and pencils, and a fine Japanese brush and ink stone, laid out with military precision. She took pains not to disturb them. At the rear of the drawer there were several newspaper clippings. Looking around guiltily, she removed and read them. One was dated in March, six weeks ago. It was about a robbery at a gymnasium called Muffy Grant's. The latest, which was ten days old, was about a shooting in a tenement in Manhattan, and a murder of a woman by her husband. She felt a momentary panic. When she read through the articles again, she saw that the only common items were crime, and the name of a police officer—Sergeant Arnold Ross.

She returned the papers to their place and closed the drawer. She felt unclean. Michiko sat in the sewing room upstairs and looked out at the spring bloom of the garden. As she thought about what she had seen, she realized that the decline in her husband's humor had begun at the time of the robbery of the Muffy Grant salon.

Prince Matsushima himself was occupied with the same concerns. He sat cross-legged in the Ten-do Karate-Dojo, his iron self-control strained to its limits.

"But I don't understand what 'Have a cup of tea' means," Hector Garcia said.

"It has to do with the simplicity of life, and the commonality of experience. It is also a sign of the Zen student's willingness to be of service."

Matsushima watched Hector's face. He struggled with the idea. There were too many syllables in the words. The meaning was beyond someone with only a rudimentary knowledge of the language and the process of thought.

During the month and a half since Matsushima had taken his disciples off the streets he had tried to occupy their time by stretching the limits of their minds, and to exhaust them physically with a taxing program of improvement in the martial arts. It was clear that practice short of action was not enough. They had come to enjoy their skill for more than its own sake. They needed the danger to start the adrenaline flowing. Matsushima understood. That's why he kept a dossier on Arnold Ross. Every warrior needs combat and a worthy opponent to confirm his own skills and courage.

When he dismissed them, they changed and escaped quickly into the night. Matsushima knew that the smell of disintegration was beginning to pervade the air of the karate-dojo.

He went to the Tokyo and Seoul Health Club and let Han stroke and massage him for two hours. Even the physical pleasure could not push aside the thought that his madness in trying to live like a samurai was about to lead him to a bitter end. He thought about Ross, recovering from his wounds. Didn't he live like a samurai? We must think alike, he and I. We are both out of place.

CHAPTER

SEVENTEEN

Libby Beckman's day had been spent hashing and re-hashing a presentation justifying the lending policy of the bank to South American countries. Her first public run-through had been so successful that she had been asked by the divisional director, an executive vice-president, to re-peat the performance in front of the director's committee on foreign lending. She was elated. Her boss was put out. He didn't mind enjoying the fruits of her labor, but was determined not to be outshone. He decided to make his own mark on her work. He'd had her rewrite the presenta-tion, charts included, four times.

It had taken a week out of her life. All she had time for was TV dinners and religious daily repetition of the exer-cises that she had learned at Muffy Grant's.

Finally, this afternoon, she'd straightened the lapels of her blue suit, picked up her attaché case, and marched off to the board room.

"Don't forget what I told you," Hadley Granger said in a stage whisper as they passed each other on the way in.

"Yes, Mr. Granger," she said cheerfully. Welcome to

the corporate jungle, Libby, she thought. First he's scared I'll screw up, then he's scared he'll be shown up. Oh, well, that's why they teach about stress in grad school.

"Good afternoon, gentlemen," she said, putting the first slide into the projector. Besides Granger, there were nine men in the room. They were all in their mid-forties, and cast from the same mold. "The solid red line represents our average yield on domestic loans, the blue one on foreign loans. The dotted lines represent the internal rate of return on the foreign and domestic loan portfolios." She put up another chart. "The argument is even more telling when you separate the return on South American loans from all others, both domestic and foreign."

An hour and a half later, thirty minutes past the scheduled ending time, the members of the director's Foreign Loan Committee filed out of the room. They had all thanked Libby politely. As she repacked her case she was sure that she had done at least an adequate job.

Just outside the door Hadley Granger waited like a producer in the lobby of a theater on opening night, listening for an indication from the critics.

"That kid's on a fast track, Hadley. You keep her on this South American loan evaluation."

She couldn't see who'd said it, but she was elated.

When she'd cleaned up her desk, and was looking over her diary for the following day, Hadley Granger dropped by, carrying a tightly wrapped umbrella and a suitably scuffed cordovan attaché case.

"Under the circumstances, I think it came off all right. We'll talk sometime tomorrow about what kind of improvements in approach need to be taken. Check with my secretary to see when I can fit you in."

"Yes, Mr. Granger. Good night." Libby restrained her grin till he had made his exit.

It was past six. She'd promised her parents she'd come up for dinner. She enjoyed one of the privileges that the bank offered by calling for a cab. Otherwise, she could stand on the street with the rest of the shmoes and watch the empty hacks go by with their On Radio Call signs lit.

The cab was waiting when she got downstairs. "Eighty-seventh and Park, please," she said.

When they arrived, the driver passed her a chit on a clipboard. "You want to sign, miss? Say, you're pretty young to be an executive."

"That's what my boss has been telling me. Good night." What did he think I should be doing, the old goat? Taking in wash? "Hello, Fred," she said to the elevator man.

"Hello, Libby," he replied.

As they rode to the tenth floor Libby thought that it wouldn't do to ask him to call her Miss Beckman. He'd known her since she was six.

Libby let herself into the long black and white marble checkerboard of the entrance hall and said, "Mom, Dad, where are you?"

Everything was fine till after dinner. Libby poured herself a light scotch. Her father had excused himself to make a business call. Her mother was sitting on a couch in the library with a glass in her hand. Marjorie is getting tipsy, Libby thought: Three 'tinis before dinner, wine, and now that triple shooter of Rémy Martin.

"Elizabeth . . ."

"Yes, Mother."

"Elizabeth, why don't you have a young man?"

"I haven't found one that's interested me yet," Libby replied evenly.

"The mannish clothes, no makeup . . . I really don't understand. It's difficult to talk in front of your father. It's this whole masculine attitude. I mean, I've always tried to see that you had the *nicest* clothes, dear."

"You have indeed. I couldn't have asked for more. You set a great example, Mother."

"Then why, when left to your own devices, do you hide behind all of that tailored tweed?"

Libby finished her drink and looked across at her mother

in her stylish gown. "Are you trying to ask me if I'm a dyke?"

"A what?"

"A lesbian? A homosexual?"

"Elizabeth!"

"That's my name. I work in a man's world. I don't have the personality to make the grade on my feminine wiles. And if I starve into anorexia, and work out six hours a day, I'm not going to have the looks. And if I did, I still wouldn't want to. I am an intelligent, well-trained person—not a well-trained woman—a person. My job requires a neuter with brains, not ovaries or testicles."

"God, Libby, do you have to be so graphic?"

"If that's what it takes to make the point. I like men. If I find one I like, and who likes me, I'll be glad to have him. For the moment my search for Elizabeth Beckman is confined to her intellectual skills. If anything else comes along, it's going to have to take its own course."

"Is this a wake?" Joe Beckman asked, coming into the room. "From your faces, maybe I'd do better to come back in sackcloth and ashes."

"I'm just tired, Pop. I've had a hard day. I'm going to go home and go to bed."

"Libby."

"Yes, Mother."

"I was just thinking. The first spring dance at the club is two weeks from Saturday. I want you to promise me that you'll come with us." She brightened. "If you save me this Saturday morning, I'll take you to Bergdorf's and buy you a new dress for the occasion."

Libby looked at her father and then back at her mother. What the hell? What was so bad about that offer? And besides, Libby darling, you don't have any plans for two Saturdays from now any more than you have plans for this Saturday. "You're too good. I'd love it, Mother."

Her father helped her on with her jacket and waited with her for the elevator. She was in luck. There was a cab at the door when she walked out of the building. When she

put her hand into her pocket to find some change, she
found three hundred-dollar bills. Sneaky Joe.

When Libby entered her apartment, she felt a sudden
rush of euphoria. The tough assignment at the bank and
the nerves that went with it were behind her. The difficult
scene after dinner with her parents had turned out with
everyone satisfied. She still had her freedom. Marjorie was
going to get to play dolls with Libby, and take her to the
spring dance, and Joe was relieved by the prospect of
domestic tranquility.

Libby threw her suit jacket on the couch and opened the
restricting buttons of her blouse. She made herself a drink.
As she took a swig she saw that there was no mail scattered on the floor under the slot in the front door.

She flicked on the ceiling fixture and cast an eye around
the room. The mail was neatly stacked on the small dining
table near the kitchen, next to a simple vase containing a
dozen roses.

"How about that?" she asked herself aloud. The super
must have let the delivery boy in. I wonder where the card
is? she thought. There didn't seem to be one. Who could it
be? Pop? No. Maybe old stick-up-the-ass Hadley Granger
realized that I made him a hero. Libby giggled. It would
be more likely to have come from President Reagan.

She took one of the roses from the vase, walked across
the room, and flopped on the couch, kicking off her shoes.
She took a sip from her glass, then sniffed the rose.

A thought crossed her mind. At first she dismissed it. It
had been almost two months since the robbery at Muffy
Grant's. She blushed at the thought of showing herself
naked to that boy a week later. What the hell had come
over her? Libby twisted the rose between her fingers.
What had come over her, she thought, was a taste of
mindless passion, combined with a twinge of sorrow. The
poor son of a bitch. I bet he'd like to work in a nice safe
bank. I bet his father never stuck three hundred bucks into
his pocket—if he had a father. Libby shook her head.
Libby Beckman's Emporium, stray dogs boarded here.

She looked across the room at the vase. Who could be my secret admirer? They were probably delivered by mistake. At thirty dollars a dozen? she asked herself. Not likely. She thought about the boy at the gym again. On a whim she turned and knelt on the couch. Willie Lopez sat in the middle of the stoop across the street, looking through her window.

Fuzzy from an unaccustomed intake of alcohol, Libby's mind ran in a dozen directions at once. It was him. That's where the roses came from. God, what should she do? She could hear Arnie Ross's voice—he's a robber and an accessory to murder. She was debating running to the phone to call Ross when Willie got up from the stoop and stepped forward into the corolla of light from the streetlamp down the block.

She moved as though in a dream, standing and beckoning to him. She fought against her pounding heart, her blood pulsing with adrenaline from fear and anticipation. She opened the door and stood for a moment in the light, then turned her back and walked away, leaving it on the latch.

Wilfredo Lopez was not sure that his legs would carry him across the street, so hard were they trembling. Is it possible that someone who has been burned with a hot iron, starved, beaten into almost total insensitivity, and then reclaimed by an ideal which accepts theft and violence, trembles before a young girl?

She was waiting for him in the middle of the room, standing barefoot, and a bit disheveled, with the rose in her hand. He closed the door behind him and moved slowly toward her.

Libby felt that she had been looking at Willie forever. Why, she wondered, did he hold his head at the odd angle? She could see only the one side of his face. His body movements were so controlled, so fluid, that she was at pains to see one step dissolve into the next.

When he was just out of arm's reach he stopped, his

mouth working, but unable to make a sound. He was turned now so that she could see only his profile.

It was she who made the first move. She took a single step and touched his arm. "Show me your face."

"I am ashamed," he said. "I am afraid to have you see." The s's were soft and sibilant in a tenor voice.

"And I . . ."

"You are very lovely."

"I am . . . too fat. You saw." She blushed at the memory.

"You are as lovely as the flowers."

She made another step. They were almost touching. Gently, she reached up with both her hands and took his chin between her fingers, turning his head toward her. His eyes were moist. His breath stuck in his throat. With infinite care she traced the gothic arch of the scar up his cheek.

His eyes were almond-shaped and almost too large for the narrow face, with lashes so long they might have been false. She felt his face for its texture and its shape, the straight nose, a small frown line in his brow, as though she were a blind person seeking landmarks of recognition. After a moment she pulled his face toward hers, and kissed him very softly on the lips.

Awkwardly, Willie Lopez responded. He was unsure of where to put his hands, uncertain of the amount of pressure to exert with his fingers. He settled by clasping his hands behind her waist, more trusting of the touch of his own flesh.

Libby pressed her face against his chest and held him. They stood for some minutes, mute and afraid. Finally, it was she who took his hand and led him gently to the couch. She sat down in the corner and put her legs up on the cushions. He sat on the floor beside her.

Tentatively, he placed his hand on her blouse, cupping her breast, his eyes fixed on hers, waiting for some sign of rejection.

He's so unsure, she said to herself, not at all the decisive leader of the robber gang. I don't know how to help him. She looked down at him, and he turned away, trying to hide the scarred cheek.

"Don't do that," she said softly. He pulled his hand away. "No." She reached for the hand and placed it inside her blouse. "I meant don't turn your face away from me."

Libby said, "Wait." She stood and pulled the blinds, then slipped off her blouse, turned her back, and said, "Undo the bra." It took him a minute of ineptitude. When it was done and she lay back on the couch, she could hear the breath catch in his throat.

He kissed her lips more forcefully, and fondled her breasts with an air of discovery. She could feel his pulse pounding.

When he stopped for a moment to look at her, absorbing her half-naked body with his eyes, she said, "I don't even know your name. Perhaps you don't want to tell me."

"I'm Willie. I know you from your card." His face colored. "From when I stole your wallet. That's how I found you." He rushed on. "I wanted to find you because you are very brave . . . and very pretty."

"I'm glad you tried to find me," Libby said. "I felt brave because . . . I'm not sure. I think it's because you were there."

"Is that why you . . ."

"Why I showed you my body? I wanted to. I don't know why. I have been with a man only three times before."

He looked into her face. "Three men only."

"Is it important to you?"

"I don't know."

She placed his hand on her breast again. "One man only. Not a man, a boy. It was in my second year of college. I went with him for a weekend. We made love three times. At least after that, if someone asked, I could say I did it. I didn't go out very much. I don't."

Willie swallowed. "I have never asked a woman to go out with me. My face . . . But I went with a whore once."

He laughed bitterly. "She made me sick and I had to go to the doctor. It was when I was seventeen," he said, suddenly afraid that she would reject him.

"Do you want me to take off my skirt?"

Willie nodded wordlessly.

At four in the morning Willie pulled on his jacket and bent to kiss Libby's forehead. He pulled the covers up over her naked body and left her to enjoy deep, exhausted sleep.

Libby didn't waken till nine-thirty, though her alarm had rung. She sat up and looked around in a daze. She wasn't wearing her nightgown or pajamas. She was stiff, and there was a sore spot on her shoulder. She wandered into the bathroom and looked into the mirror. Her hair was a wild tangle. The pain in her shoulder came from a row of tooth marks.

She turned on the shower and stood numbly under the hot water. After a while she snaked her hand around the shower curtain and grabbed her toothbrush and toothpaste. She leaned against the wall, lazily brushing up and down, back and forth. She felt absolutely marvelous.

She scrubbed herself thoroughly with a washcloth, then stood for five minutes more, luxuriating. Wow. She smiled. The first time had been something less than a triumph. She had been so wet with anticipation from their kissing and petting that she'd left a spot on the couch. He had throbbed with such rigid anticipation that he barely managed a single thrust before exploding like a Fourth of July rocket. After that they'd done it twice more, and it was . . . wow. She'd half-expected to find him next to her when she woke, but neither was she surprised to find him gone.

When she dried herself, she found that she could still feel the tingle of sexual satisfaction between her legs. "I will never, not ever," she said to herself aloud in the mirror, "be the same again."

As a first sign of her new persona, Libby walked nude into the living room and called the office. She spoke to old

Hadley himself. "I got hung up. I ought to be in by about eleven. When was it you could make time for me? Three. Great. Thanks."

Hanging up the phone in his office in the bank, Hadley Granger looked malevolently at the instrument. He could hear it in her voice. She got a leg up yesterday, and she knew it. She made an impression on the big boys with her first shot. Now she was on the fast track. Christ, how quickly these kids catch on.

Libby collected the things that had been thrown about the apartment the night before. Her panties were where they had landed, atop the lamp. Her bra was by the side of the couch. Her panty hose were a total loss, and she threw them, holes, runs, and all, into the wastebasket. She whistled all the way to the bus stop on Lexington Avenue.

Willie returned to his room in the Village on foot. Though he was physically tired, there was a spring in his step. He felt the need of a good stretching exercise to regulate his pulse and his circulation, which had been so recently and pleasantly disrupted.

On his way downtown he met a couple in their twenties, cockeyed and laughing as they wended their way home in the cool dawn. By the time he had passed them, he realized that rather than ducking his face behind his shoulder and turning away, he had looked directly at them and smiled. They had waved to him.

In his year with Matsushima he had been taught to use moments of physical exertion as focal points to clarify thought, and to order his mind. As he walked the long blocks, all he could manage was an occasional grin, and a light-headed flitting from one moment to another of his memories of the previous evening.

He had been ashamed that he was unable to control himself the first time. Libby had held herself to him, and rubbed the back of his neck, loosening muscles bunched with the tension of arousal and uncertain emotions. Without words and without experience they guided each other through the interlude of his embarrassment with tenderness. After a half hour the smell and feel of her body aroused him again. The second time they made love it was without anxiety, rocking together in the cradle of their new passion till they reached a climax that left them damp and exhausted, intertwined on the bed.

The sun had risen when Willie arrived at his hotel room. He showered and lay down on his bed. Before he dozed off he got up again and took from the pocket of his jacket the ID card he had stolen from Libby Beckman's wallet the day he had robbed Muffy Grant's Slimtronics Salon and murdered Laszlo Dushan. He stuck it into the corner of the mirror above the dresser, where he could see the picture, closed his eyes, and slept until the day had passed.

CHAPTER

EIGHTEEN

Lou Hernandez sat in his trunks at the edge of the Olympic-size pool in the Young Men's and Women's Hebrew Association at Lexington Avenue and Ninety-second Street, and watched Arnie Ross swim up and down its length. From time to time he slipped into the water and did a length or two himself. He had already run in the park in Brooklyn in the morning, but had decided, after consulting with Arnie's doctor, that it would be better if he came along to watch his progress, and to protect him from his natural instinct to overdo.

He looked up at the hands on the clock on the tiled wall, swam a few strokes, stood in the middle of Arnie's lane, and when he arrived, stopped him. "That's it, Arn. A quarter."

"How long, huh, Roach? How long?"

Lou looked at the chronometer on his wrist. "Thirteen minutes."

Arnie shook his head in disgust. "I ought to do a half in less than twenty."

"Relax. You're three weeks out of the hospital. I had to

147

keep Saul Rogovin from having you certified insane when
he heard you wanted to start exercising again.''

''He's a fuckin' old lady,'' Arnie said, struggling to get
out of the pool. Surreptitiously, Lou gave him a boost.
Arnie sat slumped forward on the tiles, his legs dangling in
the water. His side was still a riot of color from the
shooting. Besides his bruises, there was an angry red
four-inch scar just above his belt line on his back, and
another smaller one on his rib cage.

''You okay?''

Arnie nodded. He was a little woozy, and out of breath.
''Am I back on duty status?''

''You must be nuts. They won't put you back on full
duty status for two months.'' Lou climbed up beside him.
''Arnie, you've got to be reasonable. There's nothing
pressing you. It's just business as usual.''

''Come on, Roach,'' he said, getting to his feet. ''Let's
take a *schvitz*. Maybe the steam'll take some of the kinks
out of me.''

They sat on towels in the large cloudy room, perspiration dripping from them like jungle rain. Arnie took a deep
breath, then coughed painfully, wincing.

''Duty,'' Lou said. ''Hah!''

''What's new on the blotter?''

''All kinds pippul in dis neighbohoot tryink to kill all
kinds other pippul.''

''How's my boy Finkle?''

As they walked through the door to a blast of cool air,
Lou replied, ''Telling the world how proud he is of the
brave men in his command. He means you and Baxter.''

''Better he shouldn't say it to my face.''

''You guys are going to get commendation medals.''

''Wonderful. We can add it to Arnaldo's collection.''

It took a while to dress. ''Arnie, you come out and stay
with us tonight.''

''Don't be a wimp. You're on duty. No way I'm going
to let you drop me off in Brooklyn and come all the way
back. Besides, I got a hot date. Take me home.''

"Hot date, my ass. You'd need a snail fork to dig out that poor little thing in your current condition."

"Up yours, chihuahua."

Arnie slept for two hours on the couch in his living room before the house phone rang. He shook loose the cobwebs and dragged himself to the kitchen to push the button. "Yeah?"

"Mr. Ross, there's a man here to see you." The doorman sounded dubious.

"What's his name?"

"He says it's Ruggles. Is it a delivery?"

"No. Just let him up in the passenger elevator."

Arnie opened the door and went back to the couch. In a couple of minutes Albert Ruggles appeared with an enormous pizza box, a large paper shopping bag, and a brown envelope with the N.Y.P.D. seal.

"Welcome, Albert. No wonder the doorman got nervous."

"I'm driving a cab this week," Albert said, setting the food parcels down on the table in the dining alcove. He was wearing a soft cap on top of his mountainous Afro, a leather jacket, and corduroy slacks. "My ass is sore."

"You're a very frightening person, Albert."

"Good, then maybe the citizens won't shoot fuckin' holes in me like they do with some other folks."

"I've seen your scars. What did you bring me?"

"It's from Ray's. They said it'll feed ten. I asked them, ten what? It's anchovy, tomato, cheese, sausage, and pepper."

"No chocolate?"

"And I brought a six-pack."

"One?"

Ruggles reached into the paper bag with his hamlike hands and brought out six twenty-five-ounce cans of Foster's Lager. "That'll keep the old kidneys working."

"And?"

"And the blotter sheets from Street Crime and HZ four since the day you went off duty." Ruggles leaned forward. "Now, Arnold, I don't know which gives me more of a fright, the idea that somebody's going to find out that I've been removing restricted information from the precinct without permission, or the idea that your blood brother Hernandez is going to find out I'm helping you to work when you're not supposed to. I figure, I'm better off with the former than the latter. They can fire my ass and take away my pension. Lou, he's just liable to cut off my balls."

"We'll just keep it our little secret."

"We better had. Have a piece of pizza."

Between bites Arnie said, "Did anybody follow up on my suggestions?"

"No. There hasn't been time. I got to tell you, Arnie. I don't see any pattern."

"You haven't looked."

"To begin with, the last eight weeks, we've had a drop in the stats."

"How's that?"

"The rap sheet is shorter since just after the big week when you found the guy with no head and there was that rip-off at the health club."

Arnie took another slice and kept chewing. He gulped and said, "Have you categorized the drop?"

"I don't have any stats, Arn, but I can tell you that it's muggings, purse snatchings, that kind of thing."

"Vandalism? Sex crimes? Car thefts?"

"All ticking along. Business at the same old stand."

"Albert, would you think I was nuts if I said that the guy with no head was part of a gang that used martial arts to commit crimes, and that because he died, they went out of business?"

"I wouldn't think you were nuts, Arnie. But I sure as hell would think you were skating on thin ice. You have nothing but a twinge in your behind to go on."

"Albert, would you do me a favor, please?"

Ruggles's eyes narrowed to slits in his round face. "I hate it when you say please, Arnie. What do you want me to do, blow Finkle away?"

"Albert, I am going to make a reasonable request. I want you to get your new boss to let me go through the records of your crime reports for the last six months."

"That's not an unreasonable request." Ruggles sat on a chair next to Arnie. It groaned under his weight. "What's the catch?"

"Since I can't go into the station because the department doctor won't clear me, I'd like you to bring them to me."

Ruggles rolled his eyes.

"And I'd like to make sure that Lou and Flaherty and Finkle don't find out."

"Arnie, I've had this guy for only a couple of months. He's an administrative type. He wears after-shave cologne. Have a heart."

"Albert, there's not a doubt in my mind that you can have him eating birdseed from the palm of your hand."

"When I get suspended without pay, are you going to take care of my wife and kids?"

"Didn't I pay for the pizza?"

"Judas got thirty pieces of silver."

"But Albert, he was Jewish."

CHAPTER

NINETEEN

Willie Lopez had come to make love to Libby Beckman on the last Monday in April, six weeks after he had first seen her at Muffy Grant's.

The next day two things occurred to her simultaneously; first, there would have to be a limit on the late nights, because she was falling asleep at her desk, and second, to make an appointment with her doctor for that very afternoon. On her way home she dropped into the drugstore and got the prescription for her birth control pills filled. She kept her fingers crossed for four days, and was rewarded by the arrival of her menstrual period.

Willie had spent the day asleep. When he woke, it was with a feeling of euphoria. He had been ravenous, and gone to the diner across the street from his hotel and eaten a steak with eggs and two orders of french fries, then two pieces of pie. The counterman, used to seeing Willie nibble at food, watched him with curiosity.

At the Ten-do Karate-Dojo he listened attentively to Matsushima's lesson, and was more agile and adept than he had ever been during the judo exercises. When he said

good night to Matsushima, he was tempted to tell him
about Libby, but an inner voice warned him to keep his
own counsel. The remainder of the evening was a torment
for Willie, because he saw in his hesitation a kind of
disloyalty. When Matsushima had come upon him, he had
been like a feral animal, roaming the streets of the city
picking at scraps. After a year he was a person. He had an
allegiance. The idea that it could be divided was stunning
to him. How could he serve two people faithfully?

At first, Libby was stunned by his failure to appear on
the stoop across the street. Then she was hurt. And then
she felt foolish. Silly Libby! You're a big girl now, she
thought. In a crazy circumstance you met an attractive
dark-eyed Latin Lothario. For whatever reason, maybe it
was just time for you to do it, you let him into your house.
No, Libby, be fair; you enticed him to come into your
house. You stood at the window and showed him your
naked body. What did you expect? He sent you flowers.
That was very nice. Then he came in, got laid, and left.
You have nothing to complain about. It was the most
exciting thing that you have ever done in your life. Now
the adventure is an exciting memory, and it's time to go
back to work, and reality, Libby. All the same, she kept
taking her birth control pills, just in case.

She had gone with her mother to Bergdorf Goodman
and bought the dress for the spring dance. It was black and
white, of flocked velvet and chiffon, and it floated and
clung all at once.

"Libby," her mother had said. "That's amazing. That
size fourteen absolutely *floats* on you. The twelve is simply perfect! What's gotten into you?"

Libby glowed with pleasure. She loved the dress. She
looked terrific in it, and her mother was a fountain of
unaccustomed compliments. Libby was sorely tempted to
tell her exactly what had gotten into her, but she thought
better of it.

The dance itself had been something of a triumph.
Libby had started the evening as a third wheel at her

parents' table, and finished it hiding in the ladies' room with sore feet.

In the aftermath she had received a half-dozen invitations to dinner and had accepted them. She went out steadily for a couple of weeks, but though the men were very nice, she was not interested. She even let one of them into her apartment one evening after the theater. After a little preliminary pawing and groping she sent him politely but firmly home. Between her disinterest and the demands of her job, Libby slipped back into her routine, and stopped kneeling on the couch and looking out of the window at night, half-expecting a shadow to appear on the stoop across the street.

During those weeks Willie wrestled with his divided loyalty. In the end, celibacy, which had been his natural state, began to weigh heavily upon him. Every time he thought of Libby, the softness of her skin, her breasts, the dark curls between her legs, his body reacted with violent hunger. As the memories came to him more frequently, they became more vivid. His predicament, rather than improving, got worse.

He threw himself into the work of the Ten-do Karate-Dojo with fervor. He spent the bulk of his waking hours reading the works of Suzuki, contemplating the meaning of Zen, and stretching the outer limits of his physical endurance.

Still unable to shake his visions of Libby, he decided to do a penance. He took an old newspaper clipping that he had saved, tracing the course of the New York Marathon, put it into the pocket of his sweatshirt, put on his sneakers, and began to run. He made it in less than four hours. Shaking and exhausted, he stumbled from the finish line in Central Park back to his room in the Village, an additional three miles. He could barely climb the rickety stairs. He showered and tended to his blistered feet. It was only noon when he lay exhausted on his bed. He awoke six hours later, sore but rested, with a terrible ache in his groin. He rose and looked at himself in the mirror, his slender form interrupted by a massive erection.

A month to the day from Willie's last visit, Libby was sitting in bed watching television. Her hair was draped in a towel turbaned about her head after a wash. Her reading glasses were at the end of her nose, but she had foresaken the pile of papers from the bank for Sunday's *Times* crossword puzzle. She chewed on the end of her pencil and had a fleeting thought of Willie Lopez. She moved restlessly. A perfectly impossible idea. A criminal lover. It would have been a fine subject of conversation at the dance, or with the dates she'd had afterward.

Are you seeing anyone else? Yes, I am, as a matter of fact, Libby could have replied. Oh? Where did you meet him? We weren't really formally introduced. He was sticking up my gym. It was love at first sight.

The doorbell rang, interrupting Libby's reverie so brusquely that the pencil flew from her hand. She got up, pulling the bathrobe tight around her and tying the belt, went to the door, and looked out through the peephole. "Who is it?"

"It's me."

She hesitated only a fraction of a second, then undid the chain latch and opened the door. Willie stepped inside and stood looking at her sheepishly.

"It's your own fault if I look like a freak," she said smiling. "If you don't give a girl a warning, you've got to take pot luck. I must look like a witch. Christ, glasses on my nose, my hair in a pile, an old bathrobe . . ."

"I'm sorry I came like this," he said, "I didn't mean to embarrass you." He turned away and took the handle of the door. "I should have called."

Reflexively, she reached to hold his arm. "I don't want you to go, Willie."

He turned back to her, his face clouded with the emotions that roiled his mind. "I didn't know what to do, Libby. I stayed away because I didn't know what to do."

Libby held his hand, looking up at him. "I thought . . . I didn't know what to think. I thought maybe I was just another . . . well . . . another one-night-stand."

"No, Libby," he said in a voice charged with emotion. "That's not true."

She smiled. "And if it is? It's 1985, Willie. People go to parties, go home with other people, have sex with them, and never see them again."

"You don't, Libby."

"No, Willie. At least I haven't so far."

His hand shook as he reached out to her tentatively. "Libby . . ."

She took the hand and led him to her bed. She pushed the button and flicked off the mindless program she had been watching on television.

"I have wanted you so bad that it hurts me," Willie said. "I'm afraid that I . . . that I'm not going to hold myself again."

"It will be better the second time, then," Libby said confidently, slipping off her robe. She reached out to him and undid his pants. "Here, let me help you."

That night, as they rested from their passion, they made some rules for their relationship. "I want you to be with me, Willie. I don't know what you do during the day"—he blushed furiously—"but it doesn't matter to me as long as we don't discuss it. We can have something together if we keep the things we don't share apart. I work very hard at my job. If you come to me late in the evening, and I spend the whole night making love to you, I'm not going to be worth a damn in the morning. And, while I'd love to do it every day, I don't think I'd last a month."

"I will come to you on Fridays. Then you can sleep in the morning."

"Fridays, then," Libby said.

After two weeks they had expanded the schedule to include Tuesdays as well. The routine was always the same. He showed up at the door and slipped inside. They made love in all the varied ways that their imaginations would permit. Their conversation was limited to neutral subjects like movies and animals at the zoo, and Willie's tentative forays into Oriental philosophy, and the qualities of tea.

On their fifth Friday night, at the end of June, they decided to go out to dinner together instead of staying in the apartment. Willie had run from the Ten-do Karate-Dojo without the courtesy of a farewell to Matsushima-sama. He had dog-trotted to his hotel and changed into the clothes that he had bought for the occasion.

"Wow," Libby said. "Look at you."

He held a bunch of roses in his hand. She stepped away from the door and took them, so that she could take a better look. Willie had invested in a navy blue blazer and a pair of tan slacks. He had bought the exact same shoes and shirt and tie that he had seen in a Macy's ad for men's wear, since he had no idea, beyond blue jeans and pull-overs, of how to dress. He had paid ten dollars for his haircut.

"Do you know that you are very handsome, señor?"

"*Muchas gracias,* señorita." He looked her up and down. "And you are beautiful."

Libby squeezed his hand and walked away to put the roses in water. She'd had the damnedest discussion with her mother that afternoon. As she'd promised, she'd stopped by to say hello after she'd left the office.

"Elizabeth," she had begun. Oh, dear, Libby had thought—Elizabeth. "Is there something that you haven't shared with us?"

Libby looked at her watch. She wanted to have time to go home and bathe and change for her dinner with Willie. If this was going to be another psychodrama, it could last forever. Damn, she thought. And we've been getting along half decently too. "Why do you ask?" Libby replied.

"You look so"—Mrs. Beckman searched for a word, then settled on "good." Libby burst into laughter. "I don't mean it that way. You were always a pretty child, but—''

Libby contained her laughter and interrupted. "Oh, Mother, you are a sketch. For years, absolutely years, you have been on my back to lose weight. When I finally get up the courage to do it, you think that I've become anorexic, or have terminal cancer."

"That's not funny, Libby. You look marvelous. Confidentially''—she leaned forward—''what do you weigh? How much have you lost?"

"I've lost sixteen pounds in six weeks, and I weigh one twenty-one. I have also been working out at Muffy Grant's four times a week instead of eating lunch. And on the days I don't go there I work out at home." She stood and pirouetted. "Makes a difference, doesn't it?"

"Libby, I couldn't be more pleased. You'll have to fight the boys off."

"Men, Mother, one hopes. Also you see through the eyes of mother love."

"You really do look marvelous, though." She frowned. "I must say that I can't understand how you can continue to go to that Muffy Grant place. My God, don't the memories just terrify you? What if it happened again? The place would have the smell of death for me."

"I never think about it," Libby replied, her tone sharper than necessary. She saw the hurt in her mother's eyes. "I'm sorry. It's just not one of my favorite subjects. I didn't mean to snap."

"Never mind, dear," she said in a wounded voice. Changing to a confidential tone, she asked, "Libby, have you got a boyfriend?"

"Boyfriend? Mother, I'm going to be twenty-four years old. Boyfriend is for high school."

"Man friend, then. Have you got one?" Her tone was conspiratorial.

"What makes you ask?"

"This is where we came in. Frankly, my dear, when a young lady loses weight and becomes interested in improving her shape so much that she—who has hated even finger exercises since she was born—spends four hours a week in a gym and more hours at home perspiring, then one can only conclude that she has found . . .''

"A boyfriend?" Libby asked with a chuckle.

"Somebody to sleep with."

"Good heavens," Libby said, laughing. "I've got to run, Mother. You've been splendid."

"I hope you're being sensible, Elizabeth."

"You always suggested that I was too sensible."

"Well, maybe I was wrong."

Libby couldn't find a cab, and started to walk home. Had the millennium arrived? Mother admitting she was wrong. Now, there's a first. And what's worse, Libby thought, it's for the right reason. I'm not being very sensible.

"Since we are going out on our first date," Libby said to Willie, "and you have been kind enough to bring flowers, the least I can do is to treat you like a date. Well, Mr. Lopez, would you like a drink?"

"Got a cup of tea?"

"For you? Don't I *always*?" she said, ducking into the kitchen. Libby turned on the flame under the kettle and dropped green tea into a pot. "Someday, Willie, I must find out what makes you such a tea freak."

"Tea is an equalizer. It tastes as good to a poor man as to a rich one, to a big man as a small man. To have a cup of tea is to be part of mankind."

Libby brought him the cup without sugar, milk, or lemon, as she knew he preferred it. "That's a curious reason to drink tea." She poured herself a light scotch and soda.

"Tea is refreshing and tastes good. It stimulates the senses and makes the mind alert. The most important part is that it is available to everyone. Tea is a social benefit."

Libby sat down on the edge of the chair and looked at him. Where in the name of God did this street urchin—motherless, fatherless, uneducated—begin to grasp these

philosophical verities? I went to Yale. My father is a
consuming intellectual. What's his excuse? And how does
it jibe with . . . Libby tried to shut the word out of her
mind, but it pushed to the fore. How indeed does it jibe
with murder? Who taught him to speak like an educated
man? Who gave him the books? Who told him that the
books even existed? She pursed her lips. That was the core
of the bargain between them. If those questions were
asked, like the opening of Pandora's box, all the troubles
of the world would fly out at them, and their relationship
would come to an end. Relationship. How can they have a
relationship? She looked across at him, over his cup of tea.
When he looked back, his eyes were full of love. Libby
finished her drink.

"Where are you taking me to dinner, Don Juan?"

Willie put the cup and saucer on the table carefully.
"That's a problem."

"What's a problem?"

"I don't know any restaurants. I haven't been to many
restaurants. I eat in the diner across from where I live."

"Take me there," she said. "I don't mind. If it's good
enough for you, it's good enough for me."

A shadow passed over his face. "Don't say that again,
Libby."

"What?" she asked with concern.

"There is nothing in me worthy of the smallest part of
you. Please don't make fun of me."

She found that her mouth was too dry to reply. She got
up and knelt next to his chair, taking his hand, and kissed
the tips of his fingers. "You're wrong, Willie."

He smiled with the smile of a man who has lived a
hundred years. "Believe me, *querida*. Where shall we
eat?"

She sighed. The crack in the door had been closed.
"Okay. I'll help, but you have to help too. What kind of
food do you like?"

"I haven't been many places to find out about foods. I

eat meat sometimes. I like fish and vegetables. I never thought that I could like raw fish.''

"Raw fish?" Libby said. "You like your food like your philosophy.''

"Yes. I eat Japanese food sometimes.''

"Then you must know a restaurant?"

"No," he said uncomfortably. "I fix it myself at home.''

"Would you like to go to a Japanese restaurant? I love them.''

"Do you know a good one?"

Libby got up and smoothed her skirt. "I know lots of good ones. Come with me.'' She held out her hand.

Libby searched her mind for the perfect place and came up with Nippon. Mitsukoshi is prettier, and Hatsuhana has better sushi, but in Nippon there is a combination of good food, nice decor, and at the rear the privacy afforded by a dozen small rooms with tatami mats.

They were lucky. Someone had canceled a reservation, and they were ushered into a tiny two-mat square room with a lacquer table in its midst. The waitress was an older woman in a traditional Japanese costume. She knelt beside them and gave them menus.

"What would you like?" Willie asked.

"I want some sushi—'' Then she thought about the rice, and said, "Make that sashimi to start with, and then sukiyaki. Okay?''

The waitress returned shortly, bringing tea and water and utensils. "May I take your order, please?" Her squeaky voice mismanaged the l's and r's.

"*Domo arigato*," Willie said. "The lady would like sashimi to start and sukiyaki. For me please, sushi uni, sushi maguro, and futomaki, then mushi awabi.''

The waitress bowed to Willie and backed out of the tiny shoji-screened space. Libby shook her head. "You know about more than tea, then? Is there a philosophical significance to what you ordered?"

"I think you are making fun of me again.''

"I think that if you ever learn anything from me, Willie,

it's going to be how to accept a compliment with grace. I'm simply impressed by your grasp of the menu. For somebody who doesn't know where any restaurants are, and doesn't eat in them, you certainly handled the waitress like a pro. You can take me out anytime."

Willie made a small bow of thanks. Each day it was harder and harder not to break vows that were sacred in his heart. Each time he saw Libby, another potential danger appeared. How could he sit with her hour after hour without telling her what he wished her most to know about him? What he had been. From whence he had come. The source of his salvation and his resurrection. Willie knew that Libby would never be able to accept the principles that had permitted him to take that giant step from the gutter in which he had wallowed for the first twenty years of his life.

Revelation would mean both estrangement from Libby and betrayal of the new foundation of his life. The intimacy of the clan—its security and anonymity—could not be sacrificed for his emotional gratification. And if indeed he did expose himself and the new samurai, how would she feel about a code that approved of violence and, when necessary, killing, in the taking of other people's possessions? He knew that answer. She would find it uncivilized. She would think that the iron will and discipline by which they were bound were perversions rather than affirmations of faith.

"Were you ever in a foster home that was Japanese?" Libby asked.

Willie, deep in thought, looked up, startled at the sound of her voice. "No. God, no. Lucky Puerto Ricans get sent to nice Hispanic families. Most of them get sent to not so nice any kind of families. They do it for the money that they get from the welfare."

Libby had looked forward to the evening. It was supposed to lift their relationship to some other plateau. She hadn't been quite sure where, but to something more than skulking around her apartment two nights a week and screwing. She admonished herself. Not screwing. Making love. She accepted her hunger for Willie's body for what it was. She knew every vein now, every hair, and had traced them with her fingertips and her tongue. She blushed at the thought. But the weight loss, the sudden pride in appearance, the *difference* in Libby Beckman, came from more than that. Was it mystery? Was it a fascination with the things which were unknown and unspoken between them? Was it the disparity in their lives and backgrounds? In any case, this new plateau suddenly seemed a forbidding place. Libby could see that it was going to be the site of their first confrontation with reality. Away from the comfortable shade of their hideaway, and their physical relationship, they were going to have to deal with each other in a harsher light.

"Then where did all the Zen come from, Willie?"

"I read a lot. I've told you that." He tried to pass it off. "Ah, look," he said, as the waitress arrived. Kneeling, she placed the assorted dishes in front of them.

Willie broke his chopsticks apart, and with expert dexterity transferred several pieces of fish to Libby's plate. "You like wasabi?" he asked. She nodded. He picked a bit of the pale green puttylike mound and placed it in a small dish and poured soy sauce on top of it. "Hot?" he asked. She nodded. He mixed till there were no solid particles left, but the sauce had taken on a much lighter color and thicker texture. "Try," he said.

She picked up a piece of tuna, dipped it in the sauce and popped it into her mouth. She managed to chew and swallow it, but began to cough, as the spice bit at her tongue, and the aroma seeped into her nasal passages. "Too hot," she said, laughing and crying all at once, tears running down her face.

Willie leaned across the table and dabbed her cheeks with his napkin. "I'm sorry." He added more soy sauce to the little dish.

Libby patted his hand. "Not your fault. I said I wanted it hot. I'll never have a stuffy nose again."

"That doesn't matter," he said contritely. "I know better. I shouldn't have made it so strong."

"It really doesn't matter."

"I'm ashamed."

Libby looked up at him. He said the word in a very special way. In some way it made her angry, an unfamiliar emotion. "Ashamed? For Christ's sake. All you did was to do what I asked you to do and put too much hot stuff in the soy sauce. Is that what shame is made of?"

"Shame is failing to maintain dignity. Shame is causing someone for whom you are responsible to lose dignity. Shame is failing to honor your obligations."

Rote, Libby thought. And yet, not. Rote, word by word, because his lack of education prevented him from expressing his thoughts in such concise, polished words. Yet, not rote, because he understood each and every word. Understood, felt, believed. Not a lesson. A credo.

Libby put the chopsticks down in her plate. "Willie . . ."

It was their karma to meet. It was their karma that he had been at that gym on that day. He wanted to blame his own weakness, but it was her bravery, her *self* that had made him keep the ID card. And it was their fate that he had sought her out—insanely. That she had accepted—no, courted him—insanely. In her world, he was a criminal. In her eyes he was—something else. For the first time in a long while, as Willie Lopez tried to look around the corner of the future, he felt the stirring of fear.

"Willie, what makes you tick? We made a deal, Willie. I have to find another word for it, because *deal* isn't good enough. We made a *vow*. Some of it was spoken, and some of it not. We have to face the fact that we cannot keep that vow, and that we have to face each other." She reached out to him and touched the back of his hand with her fingers. "I want to try to understand."

Willie took a breath and exhaled. His face wore the age of his soul and not his years. "I told you, *querida*, that you would have to accept that I am not good enough for you. I cannot aspire to you."

Libby shook her head. "You have attained me already."

"Have I, Libby? Is that the truth of this minute, or the truth that will be written in the book of our lives? I came from the garbage heap, Libby. A couple of years ago I could hardly read. I couldn't put together two intelligent English sentences. I ran away from juvenile homes. I ran away from foster homes. A little bit at a time, I've told you some of the things I have seen, things that have happened to me. I lived by stealing and mugging and robbing. But there must be some native good in my head."

"Of course there is," she burst in.

"Oh, God, Libby, not how you mean. Good in the sense that I am smart and strong and fast on my feet. I was enough of a coward to know when to run. I don't have a rap sheet, like everyone else I know, the ones that are still alive. I was never caught. Because I was never caught, I became a kind of leader. I never had a second of conscience about the people that followed me. I sold or sacrificed them all, as they would me."

"You still do the same . . ." She put her hand to her mouth, trying to push the words back in.

The light that had been in Willie's eyes dimmed, and they became as bleak as the rest of his face, his mouth turned down at the corners, overcome with weariness and resignation. "To you it is the same. To me it is the difference between life and death—not of my body, because that has no meaning." *Till I met you,* a voice in his head cried out. "It is the life and death of the soul, I mean. I found out that there is an immortality, an ongoing of things, and that to pass through it with self-respect, there has to be a dignity to your actions, and an honor."

"It's all black and white?"

"No, Libby, it's all gray. Life and death are the same. It is only how you pass through them that has any significance."

Libby fixed his face with her eyes. Someone had led him to trespass on the kind of ground where men like her father walked, on the kind of ground where they showed

their children how to walk. You can't make a disciple by
shaving his head and having him run around in saffron
robes shaking bells and collecting money, Libby said to
herself. She didn't believe in programming, or deprogram-
ming of people's minds. She had come to believe that
philosophies that permit people to live by them come from
small seeds carefully nurtured over a long period of time,
not from instant transplants.

"You got all this from reading Daisetz Suzuki?"

"I got it from beginning to understand Daisetz Suzuki."

"Willie, there is a here and there is a now. If you do the
same things that you have always done, then how are you
different from what you were? A few words of English?"

"A reason. You have a reason to live, don't you?"

She knitted her brows. "Willie, I'm all the reason I
need to live. I have a future. The universe has made an
investment in me. I have a good mind. I've been the
luckiest girl in the world. I've had the opportunity to have
it tuned. Now I'm going to have a chance to learn to use it
in bigger and better ways. I'm going to build on myself."

"Have you a sense of belonging? Do you have a
tradition?"

"Of course I do."

For the first time Willie felt the sting of anger against
Libby. "I do not. I did not. My tradition is the dungheap
of poverty. I belong to the barrio. I have created my own
tradition. I have had the chance to tune my mind. Not for
so long, Libby. But when I was given the chance, I tried
very hard. And when I saw the way, I never turned my
head." He wanted to get up, overturn the table, and run
into the safety of the night. "I should never forget what I
am." She was staring at him intently, and for the first time
in weeks his hand went involuntarily to hide the scar on
his cheek. As some emotional dam had burst inside of
Willie, sweeping away feelings of confidence and security
which it had shored up, leaving him immersed in pent-up
pain, so was Libby overcome with a sense of self-anger
and remorse.

"An old Kikuyu proverb," she said aloud. "Before you take away a man's beliefs, you had better have something of value to replace them." She leaned across the table, and with some force pulled Willie's hand away from his face. "There is no scar on your body or your soul you have to hide from me. I accept you as you are. I have done you hurt, Willie Lopez, and I will be a long time forgiving myself. Please, Willie, won't you forgive me? Let's try again?"

"Try what, Libby, *cara?* To pour milk from a floor into a bottle? What we had promised not to discuss, not to think, is here with us." He lowered his voice. "How long will it be till we must face the day at the gym? How long before your traditions and values catch up with you and tell you, force you, not only to ask questions, to demand answers, but to act? To do what you have resisted until now?"

She spoke so softly that he had to lean forward to catch her words. "I can't betray you, Willie."

"Then you must betray your ideals. Those are the two edges of the sword."

"I can try to understand. I can try not to judge you—by my standards or any others. I want to understand your ideals, your standards. Can we try?"

"Can we try?" His voice was bemused. "Of course we can try. I will try, Libby, because I love you better than my life. But my life was nothing before. Till I found something to believe, I was less than nothing. It is only what I have learned, and what I believe, that permits you to care about me now. What will be left of me for you to love if that faith and the strength that comes to me from it disappears?"

"We'll work it out," she said. "You'll see. We will."

They finished their dinner in silence, then returned to Libby's apartment. For the first time Willie stayed the night. Unable to sleep, he cradled Libby's naked body against his chest, staring at the shadows of the slats of the venetian blinds cast upon the ceiling by the streetlamp, straight and confining as the bars of a prison, till the light of dawn began to wash them away. He put a hand to her breast, stroking the nipple gently with the tips of his fingers. His mind wandered to the church in which he had from time to time been raised. Did Jesus love his disciple less because he knew that he would thrice deny him?

CHAPTER

TWENTY

When Matsushima emerged from his office, he noticed that two of the boys were missing, Dennis Hollings, and George Pfister. In order to reduce what had become an ordeal in tension over the past month, Matsushima had first shortened the sessions from two hours to one hour, and then skipped Wednesdays, so that the clan met only four days a week.

In order to take the edge off their disappointment with inactivity, he pushed them harder and harder in their classes, both in terms of physical endurance and technique. In the end he had had to reduce the sessions, as their desire to prove superiority over one another in the absence of other opponents turned to dangerous violence. On two occasions he had been forced to physically discipline Hector Garcia. And several nights ago the now-absent Dennis Hollings.

He had perfected the backward sommersault into the kick. Practicing with Fred Logan, he knocked him from his feet—fair enough! But then he used a knee drop to the chest, and struck once across the angle of the throat despite Matsushima's order to stop. When he raised the hand again Matsushima had seemed disembodied in his flow across the room. The two blows were a blur. That Hollings's wrist was not broken was a tribute to the exact measure which Matsushima had of his own strength. The second blow left him gasping in the fetal position next to Logan on the mats, clutching his testicles.

"It is not permitted to strike another member of the clan with the intent to do physical harm. It is the same as striking another organ of one's own body.

"You will apologize to everyone. Get up."

Hollings straightened his legs. He was the tallest of the members of the clan, over six feet, but thin and rawboned, with the stamp of the Oklahoma prairie from which he came writ large across his face. For the first time in the six months since he had joined Matsushima, he wanted a joint, or a line of coke. It was not the pain in his balls. He had been made to feel small. He gained his feet rockily. He would have liked to touch his tender, swollen wrist, but that would have been an admission of pain and weakness.

"Repeat; my head is covered with ashes. My face is smeared with mud."

"My head is covered with ashes. My face is smeared with mud."

"Why does this signify enlightenment?"

"The physical appearance of things is deceiving. It is not the physical appearance of things which matters."

"Just so. That you are able to inflict pain does not illustrate the superiority of your mind and soul. You struck down your fellow samurai, proving that you are weaker, not stronger."

"I am sorry, Matsushima-sama. I apologize." He extended his hand to Fred Logan, and helped him to his feet.

"It doesn't matter," Fred said.

Matsushima said, "Each shall do the work of the other for a week. A week in another man's shoes is worth a month in one's own."

It had all of the sincerity of a well-rehearsed Noh play. Matsushima saw that though the lines were being properly recited, the involvement of the actors in their parts was superficial. A schism had taken place. It happened in real samurai life in Japan. There, a lifetime's training made the apologies, whether sincere or not, a meaningful act. If there was such bad blood that there could be no peace within the clan, the daimyo would simply order the participants banished, or, in extremis, to commit seppuku. Here, the layer of sincerity was all but transparent, and the training a coating of civility over a life's storehouse of bestiality.

"It is the gleam of the soul, not of the armor, that makes the warrior." Matsushima's voice sounded hollow and repetitive even to himself. The dismissal was subdued. Something of the spirit had seeped away.

Though the absence of Hollings and Pfister was self-evident, Matsushima would have lost face had he acknowledged the breach of etiquette by asking where the two missing samurai might be. He settled in his mind that he would inquire in private of Wilfredo Lopez. He glanced across at him. In the past several weeks he had also changed. It seemed to Matsushima that if nothing else had come of his efforts, at least one person had put a foot upon the path to self-understanding. The shame of his scar had dropped away from Willie Lopez. He took greater pride in his body and its accomplishments than he had ever before. As though he had crossed the bridge to enlightenment, he had developed a calm which cemented the achievements of obedience, self-discipline, and physical prowess into a whole. Matsushima felt a teacher's pride in Willie's accomplishment.

That evening's session was shorter even than the clan had come to expect. There was a five-minute reading from Suzuki, then a mere half hour of controlled exercise. When they were released, the samurai of Hiroo Matsushima cleaned up after themselves, and then dissolved into the spring evening like a mist. Matsushima waited in his office for a few minutes, expecting to see Willie Lopez, but he had gone with the rest.

CHAPTER

TWENTY-ONE

When Morris Goldfarb decided to build The Angles, he determined that it would be, at least in its physical appearance, the finest health club in the city of New York. He bought an old law tenement on Sixty-first Street between First and Second for a relatively low price because it stood in the shadow of the approach to the Queensboro Bridge. He stripped the brick and brownstone façade away, then tore out the grimy railroad flats.

On the steel skeleton he raised the height of the structure from six to ten stories, and filled it in with a monument to narcissism. The floors were connected by a glass-enclosed elevator and a hanging spiral staircase that surrounded the circular shaft. There were massage rooms and gymnasia. A running track was suspended above a floor dedicated to Nautilus machines and weights. The entire front two-story section was fronted by one-way glass, which permitted his clients to look out on the street without being viewed. From the outside the panel glowed. The basement contained a swimming pool. The roof held two tennis courts. One floor below were squash and racquetball courts, and

172

then the steam rooms. Roman baths, and saunas. On the same floor were exquisitely appointed locker rooms. It was a point of pride with Morris Goldfarb that the carpets in both the men's and ladies' lockers were changed every three months to avoid the moldy smell that so often pervades athletic facilities.

To join The Angles all that was required was money. Though Goldfarb had constructed an elaborate ruse in which it seemed that one needed to be proposed and seconded and then accepted by a membership committee of celebrities, a thousand dollars was all that was necessary to open the golden door. In fact, of course, the celebrities on the committee never appeared at the club at all, but had agreed to have their names used for what is politely called promotional consideration.

Morris Goldfarb saw to it that a number of the models from the top agencies got substantial discounts in their monthly billing, which averaged 150 dollars per regular client, and were exempted from the entrance fee.

In short order the word had leaked out, and the lunchtime exercise classes, held in the two tiered rooms, were often observed by dozens of male joggers jostling for position at the rail, looking down from the track onto the scantily clad women below. In a word, The Angles had acquired chic.

Morris Goldfarb had perceived his audience clearly. The purpose of a club, he knew, is not to belong, but to exclude others. His natural constituency were those who were financially able but socially unacceptable. Perhaps Racquet and Tennis won't have you, or the Knickerbocker or the River Club or Harmonie, but you can jiggle and sweat with the best-looking and with the best-equipped at The Angles.

When Hiroo Matsushima decided that he was going to develop a clan of samurai and exact tribute from the commoners of New York City, he searched his mind, and the face of the city itself, for areas of vulnerability.

The soul of crime is to succeed and to escape. Since his

need was a source of money as a motivating and enabling
factor for his disciples, he began to focus on the centers of
wealth. Naturally, the banks, the museums, the jewelers,
and the art galleries fulfilled the first imperative. On the
other hand, the presence of such concentrated wealth pro-
duces its concomitant, high security, and makes success
dubious and escape difficult.

The city provided an immediate answer to the problem
of escape. Anonymity. Among seven million citizens, and
three million transients, it is easy to get lost. The streets
are scattered with entrances to crowded subterranean tun-
nels. Thousands of enormous buildings, stores, and theaters provide instant invisibility and sanctuary. The streets
themselves, clogged with traffic, make pursuit of the
swift all but impossible. The attitude of the average citizen—
Matsushima thought it charitable to call them uninvolved—
made them willing accessories before, during, and after
the fact.

Knowing the answer to the question of escape, given a
security climate of ordinary difficulty, he focused his attention on targets of opportunity. He found his answer in
the proliferation of two new facilities—bank cash-dispensing
machines, and the wide variety of athletic outlets. It took a
while to test the waters. One had to learn which joggers
were worth robbing and which were not. Through a Japanese businessman who was keeping an expensive blonde in
an apartment on the East Side, as well as his family in
Westchester, on a salary as a sales manager for an electronics firm, he found a way to dispose of stolen jewelry
and watches. The electronics boxes came in filled with
goods for the American consumer market, and left from a
small trading company office to Hong Kong filled with
slightly used American consumer goods.

Matsushima, using the time and intelligence at his disposal, planned and blueprinted a dozen variations on the
taking of money from the bank customer who stood fool-
ishly trapped, waiting for the return of his card and receipt, with a handful of cash in front of a machine. There

were nighttime plans, and afternoon plans, plans for the East Side and the West.

Athletics offered many opportunities, Matsushima diagrammed locations and possibilities down to the timing of the last detail. While he recognized the part that luck plays in life, he was a firm believer that discipline and training, combined with stamina and the deadly weapon of the martial arts, would make the operations of the clan a success. Through his studies he had become an expert in the format and layout of most of the better-class gymnasiums and clubs in New York. It was very easy for him to have a thorough tour, and if that did not suffice, a second. He was the ideal client for the profit-making club. A highly placed foreign executive with a fat paycheck, whose dues and initiation fee would doubtless be picked up by the home office. With a little luck they might buy a corporate membership.

When he needed to see the women's facilities, he brought his wife, questioning her closely on the layout and the amenities. After six months he joined a gaudy health club in a new building on Fifty-seventh Street to legitimize his search to Mrs. Matsushima.

Among the clubs that he had cased most thoroughly was The Angles. It was less that it provided a specially tempting target financially than that it posed a fascinating intellectual challenge. After a number of visits as a potential member, and as a guest of business associates who were members, he designed a scheme which was at once elaborate and the soul of simplicity. He was pleased when it was done, but shelved it. Such a robbery was interesting as a work of art, but guaranteed no greater rewards than knocking over a smelly commercial belly-dancing studio, and entailed much greater risk.

As the weeks of inactivity piled up, Dennis Hollings found it more difficult to sleep, and descended toward the same patterns of behavior from which he had suffered prior to his entry into the Ten-do Karate-Dojo.

He had managed to finish his primary school education

in the tiny farm town of Roff, Oklahoma, having repeated both the fourth and eighth grades. His father had died in Dennis's fifth year, leaving a family of four daughters, and four sons, of which brood, Dennis was the youngest. His mother was a woman of modest character, and her health had been sapped by overwork and the close bearing of many children. Her daughters chose the same path that she had. Three were pregnant and then married before sixteen, the fourth ran away and was never heard from again. The oldest son was a brute of low morals and mentality. Like his father, he was destined to work himself to death on seventy hardscrabble acres wrenched from the dust bowl after the war. He drove his younger brothers like cattle, using the boot and the whip without a word of kindness.

As the law permitted for farm families, when Dennis finally emerged from grammar school with a certificate of completion, he was set to work from dawn to dusk of endless, ugly days, barely aware of the change in the seasons, or the passage of years.

Early on a spring morning he sat in the seat of an ancient tractor dragging a harrow through a section to be sown in alfalfa. As the sun rose and warmed the air he became drowsy and began to rock back and forth on the uncushioned metal bench. Finally, realizing that he was falling asleep, he stopped the machine and leaned forward on the wheel.

A half hour later his eldest brother came upon him as he was making rounds in his Jeep. Dennis shrieked in pain and fell with a thud to the sun-hardened earth when he jabbed him roughly in the base of the spine with a 400-volt cattle prod.

When he tried to rise, his brother lifted his hand above his head and slapped him across the face with such force that a tooth, solidly rooted in gum and bone, flew from his mouth. Something gave way in Dennis's mind. He threw a handful of dirt into his brother's eyes. When he put his hands to his face, Dennis rose from the ground like a charging bull, and drove his shoulder into his brother's midsection. His heel caught in the dirt and he fell back against the exposed curved points of the harrow blades. He yelled in shock as much as in pain, for the spikes were not embedded more than a half inch. Dennis clambered behind him and wrapped his hands around his chin. Using his weight and leverage against the rounded backs of the harrow blades, he slowly and deliberately pulled his brother backward, so that the steel spikes dug deeper and deeper into his flesh. With each attempt at resistance, gravity served to impale him more securely. Finally, one of the steel rods perforated a lung, and crimson blood spurted from his mouth. As he twisted like a moth on a pin, Dennis walked around in front of him and spat in his face, then departed to let him scream away the last half hour of his life. Dennis spent the rest of the day mending fences, then walked back to the house. One of his other brothers found the body, gray and drained of blood and of the meanness and the power that had bound them all to the soil. In a week the farm was sold for a pittance; their mother was in a roominghouse in town, and the rest of them scattered to the wind.

Dennis wandered from town to town across the Midwest, sleeping in alleyways, doing chores and washing dishes to keep body and soul together. Following the path of the harvesting season in his nineteenth summer, he worked his way from the cranberry bogs of the southern part of New Jersey to the pumpkin patches of Sussex County in the frost-filled dawns before Halloween.

When the last apples had been picked he wandered across the George Washington Bridge and arrived in New York. He took work as a stableboy in Van Cortlandt Park, sleeping in the hayloft. From time to time, he would make a foray into the city, sprouting hayseed, a target for the denizens of the dark side of life. He would occasionally sit in the theaters that featured X-rated gay films and wait for an old man to pick him up.

After he had been in the city for six months, he went for a walk by the East River, where it curves sharply into the lower part of Manhattan Island below Twenty-third Street. With no more emotion than he brought to anything else, he walked out on an old jetty and sat at its edge for a few minutes, watching the water swirl by. Then he just leaned forward, eyes wide open, to greet death.

A hand grasped the back of his collar and held him back. There was no struggle, since Dennis had not thrown himself forward. He was merely letting the course of events and gravity pull at him, as they always had, to make an end of a bad thing, his life.

"If you really want to do that, I can let go."

The voice was soft, Dennis thought; he sounds like a Mex. "It don't matter."

"You don't care whether you live or die?"

"It don't make no difference."

"Not to you."

"Especially to me. I ain't been nowhere. I ain't going nowhere."

"How about going with me? My name is Willie Lopez. Maybe you would like something to eat or drink."

"I ain't hungry. I don't eat much. I don't drink. It costs too much." He turned to look up at the face. The man, who was about his own age, turned away, so that he could see only his profile.

"Come on," the man said, tugging at his collar.

"Okay."

In a little coffee shop on Avenue D Willie asked, "What do you want to die for?"

"I don't want to die, or to live. I got no reason to do either. It's less work to be dead."

"Think about good food, sunshine, nice chicks," Willie said optimistically.

"I'm skinny. I don't like food much. I talked to you about drinks. I don't like sunshine much. I done a lot of farm work. I'm nineteen and I got squint lines in my face like an old man."

"And the chicks?"

"I never had no chick. Sometimes I go to a stag movie

and let a old man suck my thing. I don't even care about that.''

"Okay," said Willie. "I guess I'll walk you back to the pier and watch you jump in and drown."

"Would you get a kick out of that?" Dennis asked dully.

Willie shook his head. "No, not really. I'm not interested in death anymore."

Dennis raised an eyebrow. "Anymore? How come?"

"I found a reason to live. I know what I am. You want to find out why?"

Dennis Hollings shrugged. "What've I got to lose? I'm not nobody. Not nothin'."

At first, he obeyed from habit and the lack of will to resist. It was Willie who saw possibilities in him, not Matsushima. He was brought into the fold a little at a time. It was months before he was allowed to participate in the collection of tribute. Though he had been an apt pupil in the martial arts, he had more trouble than any of the others in absorbing the philosophy.

In the first weeks of the ban on activities by Matsushima, Dennis behaved in accord with the master's wishes. Then, he began to drift a bit with each meeting.

When Dennis had presented tribute to Matsushima, he had squatted before the master in his office to receive praise and to make obeisance. He had seen the drawer in which the plans for operations were kept. The night after the punishment he climbed out on the ledge of the window in the dressing room and hung there from his tiptoes and fingertips four stories above the concrete until everyone had left. As his extremities numbed, and death beckoned closer, he welcomed it more. His search for identity had come to a dead end. Without the activity provided by the collection of tribute, Dennis Hollings's source of life-giving energy receded into memories of successful adventures, Matsushima left before his grip gave out. He opened the window, stole the plans for The Angles, and shinnied down the drainpipe. He took them to a Xerox shop, had them copied, and then crawled up the system of pipes and window ledges, his fingers bleeding, and his life hanging by a thread, to return the originals.

George Pfister, the other white members of the Matsushima clan, was also its youngest adherent. He was big and young and strong. He came from Seattle. He'd left when he was fourteen, a runaway from a drunken mother and a bestial stepfather. He joined the hundreds of thousands of youngsters who swirl like flotsam in the tides of America's human sea, living and dying beneath the surface of society and largely invisible to its members. Willie had picked him out of the middle of a fight. George was almost too willing. Matsushima said that he would take the greatest patience of all, because while he was young and therefore could be formed to the clan's needs, he would be very slow to learn.

The evening he did not show up at the Ten-do Karate-Dojo George Pfister had been told by Dennis Hollings that they had secret orders from Matsushima to exact tribute from the locker rooms at The Angles.

Security at the club had been tightened since the episode at Muffy Grant's, as at every gym and health salon in New York. The number of uniformed security guards had been doubled to six. They patrolled the street level and the sidewalk around the club endlessly. One stood, stick in hand, at the side of the pretty brunette who handled the door and checked the membership cards. There was even one stationed on the tennis courts on the roof.

Following the plan, they had walked into the loft building next door at about five o'clock, just as the shift of the furniture upholstering company was leaving for the day. Once inside, they headed for a doorway that led into the narrow courtyard between the two buildings, inaccessible from either Sixtieth or Sixty-first streets because of iron fences topped by three strands of razor ribbon. At six o'clock they put their backs against one wall, and their feet against the other, and began the agonizing walk against gravity up the ten common flights of the buildings. There were no handholds. It took an hour.

When they reached the top of the wall, as previewed in the plan, Dennis, the lighter of the two, turned over and poised momentarily, his weight on George Pfister's straining body. He slid onto the roof, then reached out, took Pfister's hand, and pulled him up. They lay near the parapet for ten minutes, their muscles shaking with the strain.

The guard walked back and forth across the tennis courts twice as they lay there, then sat down on the stoop of the entrance to the building and lit a cigarette. It was the last thing he ever did. The single blow to the neck broke the atlas and axis bones at the top of the cervical column, severing the spinal cord, causing instant death.

Ignoring the staring eyes of his victim, Dennis Hollings took the key ring from his belt and opened the door to the stairwell. Both he and Pfister wore maintenance workers' uniforms under jackets that they shucked and laid next to the body of the slain guard.

They had rehearsed their next steps a hundred times. As they walked down the stairs they could hear the reverberation of the hard rubber balls bounding off the squash and racquetball courts on the next floor. They passed two spectators in gym shorts and T-shirts on the landing overlooking the players. They didn't turn their heads as Hollings and Pfister walked by.

At first, it had seemed odd to Hollings that the plan called for an assault on the women's locker room. It would have seemed more natural to enter the men's room wearing athletic equipment, and to blend in with the crowd. When he put his mind to it, he saw that there was no percentage in robbing a few lockers and getting caught by the locker boy. They would be better off with the more physically manageable women.

He checked his watch. It was precisely eight-fifteen; one half of the seven forty-five ladies' exercise class was over. The class was the club's daily highlight. The women were the loveliest, and the exercises the most rigorous. There was always a big audience.

Hollings did not hesitate. He slipped through the door of the ladies' locker room, followed by Pfister. He knew that there were two attendants, one who sat by the door, and the other who dealt with the towels. Acid rock vibrated in the air. The attendant at the door was a young black woman with close-cropped hair. She was seated reading a magazine.

According to the plan, she was to be the second and last victim of violence. Hollings struck her at the base of the neck with his fist. Slipping the magazine from her hand, he allowed her to lean forward on a pile of towels on the table. She looked as though she were alseep. They pulled on their stocking masks.

An overweight woman in her forties emerged from the shower wearing a towel around her shoulders, hiding pendulous breasts, and another held tenuously between grasping fingers, not quite encircling her waist. Her first instinct to scream was stifled by the sight of the gun in Hollings's hand, and a loud "Shhhh!"

"Listen," Hollings said, "you sit down on that bench and nobody's going to hurt you."

Pfister moved to her side and took her trembling hand. He squirted her with a drop of Krazy Glue, then held her hands against the bench. "You got the idea?" She nodded.

Pfister walked through the shower room till he saw the arch that led into the back locker area. He took a glass from the top of a sink and smashed it on the floor, stepped into an empty shower stall, and waited. In ten seconds a tiny young woman in shorts and shirt and yellow-ribboned pigtails came into the shower area and said, "Oh, fuck."

When she bent over to pick up the glass, Pfister stuck a gun in the small of her back and said, "If you say another word, it will be the last one you ever say. Walk in front of me and sit on the bench in the front room."

She did as she was told, her eyes widening even more at

the sight of the gun in Hollings's hand. Pfister glued her to
the bench beside the older woman.

Hollings had removed the locker skeleton key from the
body of the unconscious locker attendant. Leaving Pfister
to watch the door and the women, he opened the first row
of lockers with gloved hands. He pulled a plastic bag from
his back pocket and emptied the contents of purses and
pockets as fast as possible, then did the second row.

"That's all folks, we ain't greedy." He motioned to
Pfister, who tied gags around the mouths of the women on
the bench. "Don't try to go anywhere, girls. It'll just take
the skin off of your hands."

Pfister and Hollings walked through the shower into the
rear locker room. They passed the women's sauna, and
through the glass saw two elegant nude female forms. Just
past the door was the entrance to the service staircase.
They stepped inside and breathed a sigh of relief. The
second hurdle had been successfully crossed.

They returned their guns to the holsters, and stripped off
the stocking masks, climbed the stairs to the squash floor
and retracted their steps to the roof.

The door was ajar.

Dennis Hollings removed the gun from his holster and
crept close to the door. A young black gym instructor was
kneeling next to the body of the dead guard, sucking air
and trying to keep from vomiting. She was slim and wiry,
but rather a tall woman. Hollings didn't want her to make
a noise. He pushed gently against the door.

The woman looked up immediately, alerted by the light.
As Hollings's hand emerged from the door, she exploded
from her kneeling position and smashed against the swinging panel, catching his wrist. The gun fell. As she reached
for it, Hollings hurled the door open again, hitting her
outstretched arm. She kicked the gun into the darkness
even as she recoiled.

"Motherfucker," she snarled, crouched low in the position of defense, her hands held crossed before her, cal-

loused edges out. "You come near me, and I'll do you just like you did him."

Hollings leapt forward in a series of kicks. She spun to her left, and countered with a blow to the back. He evaded her. "Come on, you little shit," she said. "I'll kick your white ass."

Hollings was more audacious in his next maneuver. He leapt almost parallel to the ground and lashed out with a kick to the head. She moved her chin an inch, and the foot passed by harmlessly. As he tried to land on his hands to follow through with another kick, she struck him in the groin with clenched fingers. He crumpled at her feet. She walked forward and prodded him with her toe, then opened the door. Pfister caught her across the bridge of the nose with the barrel of his gun. As he pushed her out of the doorway and onto the dark roof, he said that she wore a black sash around the waist of a white canvas judo suit.

Hollings stank of his own vomit. "I'm bleeding inside. It hurts. I can feel it. My balls." He leaned forward and threw up again.

"Listen, we got to go. You know how the plan works. We got to go."

"I can't go."

George Pfister split Hollings's skull with the butt of his gun. To reduce the possibility of identification, he took everything from his pockets and threw it into the black plastic garbage bag. For good measure he stepped behind him, grasped his chin, and wrung his neck. There was a satisfying crack. He thought for a minute about the girl on the floor. She would know nothing. She had not seen him.

The girl was aware of only two things—pain which exuded from every nerve ending in her face, and the shadowy male shape in front of her. She bunched herself for the attack, then pushed off.

Her foot scraped slightly against the artificial powdered clay that was used to surface the court. It was enough to alert George Pfister. He spun to face her, then ducked under her fist. His shoulder caught her in the midsection.

She gasped but flung herself away from his grasp. He flung out his hand. The tips of his fingers grazed her crushed nose. She made a small scream.

He came at her again, and she stepped away in a defensive posture. He circled her, still wary. She was having trouble breathing. She knew that to survive she needed to use what strength she had left immediately. She feinted to his left and then rushed him with a series of kicks. He backed away, then stepped inside. He punched her in the breast with his fist. He could feel the crack of the underlying ribs. She slumped over his shoulder, and he flipped her over the parapet wall. Her body cartwheeled silently through the air and struck the strands of razor ribbon with the force of a ten-story fall, coming apart in pieces like a stuffed doll.

Pfister took the black bag and let himself into the service elevator with the guard's key. He walked out into the street past the garbage cans with the sack over his shoulder. The security guard looked up momentarily from his comic book, then went back to his reading.

CHAPTER

TWENTY-TWO

The first alarm was sounded by the young ladies in the steam room. "What the hell?" The first girl stood stunned. The second pulled the towels out of the mouths of the attendant and the older member whose hands had been glued to the bench.

"Let me help you," she said, pulling at the attendant's arm.

"Oww! Jesus, don't do that. They glued our hands with Krazy Glue. Quick, call Security. Use the wall phone. It's one one one."

It suddenly occurred to them that they were naked, and they fled to their lockers and pulled on some clothes haphazardly.

"Girls," the older woman said, blushing with embarrassment, "could you get my robe out of locker four one two three?" They covered her as best they could as the two security guards piled through the door.

"How the hell did somebody get in here?" Samantha Chapman yelled at the top of her lungs. "What were you doing, playing jacks?"

"Be cool, lady. We're trying to find out what happened."

"Don't give me that jive shit. You can see what happened. What gets off Krazy Glue?"

"Krazy Glue?"

"That's what's holding these ladies to the bench."

"Where's Cindy?" the blond attendant asked, almost as an afterthought.

"Who?" the security man asked.

"The towel girl," the older woman answered with exasperation. "How are you going to get me loose?" Tears started to well to her eyes for the first time, as she felt helpless and ashamed in front of the two young men.

The guard looked at the pile of towels that had fallen across the table, then pushed them aside. Cindy, the towel girl, was resting on her arms, crossed before her on the table, as though she were taking a nap. The guard reached to touch her. She was cold and clammy. He was close enough to know that her bowels and bladder had failed. "My God," he said. "She's dead."

At almost the same time, around the corner, a young man tripped as he passed an alley. He swore, looking down at the offending object. It was a human leg. He ran to a pay phone.

The call from The Angles came to the nineteenth precinct, Captain Bernard Coughlin, the commanding officer, presiding over the most affluent area of Manhattan Island, from Fifth Avenue to the East River, and from Fifty-ninth Street to Eighty-sixth Street, and most of the foreign embassies and missions.

He frowned and looked at the patrol reports. One hundred nine reported pickpocketings in one shift from eight to four. He shook his head. He should have left for home three hours earlier. The phone on his desk rang.

"Coughlin."

"This is Sergeant Cawley." The voice was apprehensive.

"Spit it out, Sergeant," Coughlin said, at once on his guard.

"Somebody hit The Angles."

"The health club? Hit how? When?"

"I don't have much. I dispatched four cars. There was an armed robbery. It looks like there are a couple of people dead."

"Dead?"

"Yes, sir, one was a security guard."

Coughlin put his hands over his eyes. He'd been to The Angles. The commissioner played ball there, sometimes. The commissioner's wife went to exercise classes there. He shuddered. Thank God he'd stayed late. At least he'd be able to put the best face on it.

"The perps?"

"That's all I have, Captain."

"Has it been on the police bands?"

"Not yet. Not the details. Just a dispatch with the street address."

"Keep it that way. Are you sure about the deaths?"

"Yes, sir."

"Okay, let's keep it down to a dull roar as long as we can." He hang up and grabbed a dog-eared address book, thumbing quickly through to the F's. "Frank, we have a mess. Somebody did an armed robbery at The Angles— that's right, the health club. There are a couple of stiffs. Who's on at HZ four tonight?"

"Four to twelves are Baxter and Hernandez."

"Who's Baxter?"

"Bright black kid. He works with Arnie Ross. John Jay College of Criminal Justice. The whole schmeer."

Coughlin chewed on a nail. "I want Ross. I don't want this to go to a kid. I don't care how smart he is. We're going to get the same shit out of this as when they knocked off the Hotel Pierre. You remember that, Frank, huh?"

Flaherty groaned. A page a day in the *Post* and the *News* for two weeks about police ineptitude. Even the *Times* front paged it. The mayor went nuts. "Ross is healing. He got shot up, you know."

"That bad?"

"Jesus, Bernie, he's just wangled his way off of sick leave to come back on the job."

"I'm asking you a favor, Frank. I need somebody that's going to get me some relief. This is going to be Excedrin headache number ninety-nine. You get me Hernandez, *and* Ross. You owe me, Frank."

Flaherty popped a Maalox into his mouth. Bernie Coughlin had been his rabbi many a time, and lent him bodies when he was short, and covered for him when he came up empty. He was the kind of cop you go to bat for. There was no way he could say no.

"I'll work something out, Bernie."

Flaherty called the private phone on the desk in his office at HZ4.

There was a pause as the phone rang five or six times, then "Lieutenant Flaherty's office. Sergeant Hernandez speaking."

"You're getting a phone call over the desk right now from Bernie Coughlin. There's been some kind of shoot-up at that fancy Angles club on Sixty-first. Some dead bodies. No details yet. It's very hot. Coughlin wants you and Arnie to handle it."

"Arnie? Frank, Arnie looks like a kid's sewing bee. He has two holes in him. He's in no shape. If he hadn't bullied Saul Rogovin, he wouldn't even be cleared for duty. Are you going to let him kill himself?"

Flaherty cleared his throat. "If Arnie is willing . . ."

"Arnie is always willing, Frank," Lou said coldly. "That's the problem. I'm not willing."

"Lou, we have to do this. We've been asked personally."

"Let me borrow Albert."

"From Finkle? Are you crazy? Not only would he say no, but then he would have something on you, on me, on Arnie, on Albert, and worse of all, on Bernie Coughlin. He'd give a year's pay to have that leverage. I'm asking you, Lou. Call Arnie." Flaherty waited while Hernandez stewed, caught on the horns of his dilemma. "Listen, Lou, it even makes good sense from a procedural point of view.

How do we know that this doesn't have something to do with the Muffy Grant case? That was a gym too.''

"Okay," Hernandez said. "Okay. I'll call him."

"What changed your mind?" Flaherty asked.

"It wasn't you, Lieutenant. If he ever found out that I let a chance go by for him to test out his theory on the martial arts murders, he'd break my chops for ten years." He hung up and dialed Arnie.

"Ross."

"You want to go out and fool around?"

"With you, *maricón*?"

"How about a robbery at The Angles with some dead bodies?"

Ross jumped up from the couch, twisting his side. "Ouch! Oh, that smarts. You shittin' me, Roach?"

"Not hardly. Listen, get dressed. I'm going to pick you up on my way."

Arnie got into the car gingerly and sat down. "Someday I got to find out how come that bullet went and hit me in the only place on my whole upper body that wasn't protected by my vest."

"Maybe it should have occurred to you not to show her your side."

"I'm sorry. My mind must have been on other things. What do you know?"

"Squat. There's silence on the band. I think they're trying to sit on it."

"Hmmf! A lot of fuckin' good that's going to do them. It might as well have happened in the center ring at Madison Square Garden."

Squad cars blocked the entrances to both Sixty-first and Sixty-second streets on First and Second avenues. Police barricades had been erected on the sidewalks.

Arnie turned to Lou and smiled. "Real low profile. See, no anti-aircraft lights, no band."

"HZ four," Lou said to the patrolman blocking his way, flashing his shield.

"No press. Get one of those investigation zone signs up. Keep 'em out."

Arnie and Lou parked in the middle of the street and walked through the canopied entrance into a scene of total bedlam. Dozens of people were yelling at the tops of their lungs, milling around in various states of undress. Every time there was a momentary hush, someone else would take up a cry: "I want to get out of here!" or "I can't stand it! I need air!" or "Why doesn't somebody do something!"

A red-faced uniformed sergeant was trying to fend off a particularly irate man in tennis shorts and T-shirt wearing a turban who kept claiming diplomatic immunity.

Ross went out to the blue and white parked in front of the door. "When did you get here?" he asked the cop behind the wheel.

"About half an hour ago."

"Were you the first."

"Yes, sir. A couple of stiffs on the roof. Also, I think somebody fell off. That's all we heard. It's a nuthouse in there. Everybody milling around."

"The perps?"

"No sign. No info."

"Give me your bull horn."

Ross walked inside with the loudspeaker, pushed his way across the crowded pillared marble entrance, and swept everything off the reception desk with a resounding crash. He climbed on top and said, "Now hear this. This is Sergeant Arnold Ross of the New York police department. Anyone who does not keep still and permit the members of my department to do their jobs will be charged with obstruction of justice and arrested. And in case you don't believe me . . ." He hesitated long enough to drag his Miranda Case card out of his wallet and read them their rights.

"I can see that some of you are still in gym clothes. I know it may be uncomfortable, but you're going to have to stay in them for a little while longer. I'm sure you're interested in making this as quick as possible. So are we.

First, let's split into two groups.'' Arnie looked at the uniformed sergeant's nameplate. ''Sergeant Block will take all of the gentlemen downstairs. As a formality, we'll be wanting the name and address of everyone who is here this evening. The ladies will stay on this floor with Sergeant Hernandez. Lou, raise your hand.''

Ross hopped off of the table and pulled Block and Hernandez aside. ''Keep them busy. Take names, addresses, and telephone numbers. Ask if they're members or guests. Very orderly. Very businesslike. Where are the stiffs, Block?''

''On the roof. There are a couple of guys from the precinct investigation unit up there now.''

''Marching around with their fuckin' flat feet,'' Arnie spat. ''Is there an elevator in this dump?''

''It's right there,'' Block pointed. ''We have a man on it.''

''Good. Keep 'em busy.''

On the roof, the guard lay eyes still open, face up, near the door. Dennis Hollings, his head at an unnatural angle, was sprawled in the midst of a tennis court. The officers had turned the court lights on, and the mercury vapor bulbs cast a cold hard light. Ross could see from where he stood that the body on the tennis court had a severely fractured skull. He leaned over the parapet and looked down. There was little light, but he could see things scattered about in the passageway. ''You call forensics?''

''Yes, Sergeant. And the M.E.''

Ross knelt by the side of the guard. He put his hand to his face to feel the skin. The head rolled away unsupported. ''Uh huh,'' he said to no one in particular. The guy on the tennis court was leaking gray matter out of a depressed fracture that covered half his head. He nudged the chin with the tip of his toe. ''Uh huh.'' There were no whole bones left in that neck.

Arnie trotted down the stairs. The scene that greeted him in the locker room was even more chaotic than the entrance hall had been.

"Get me loose!" the heavy set woman cried. "Loose!"

"Lady, we waitin' on somebody," a harassed security guard said.

She cried, "Please help me." The robe had started to slip from her shoulders, leaving her half naked and goose-pimpled. "I don't want to stay here with a dead body anymore." She began to wail in earnest.

Arnie pushed the door open and spoke in a very businesslike voice. "I'm Sergeant Ross of homicide. Where is the officer in charge?"

From the gray uniform, Arnie could see that in a moment of vaulting stupidity, somebody had sent a probationary kid not yet out of Police Academy to babysit a corpse, and half a dozen hysterical naked women in a locker room. He looked at the kid's nameplate. "Officer Ostrow, please go down to the lobby and ask Sergeant Hernandez to come up here. You stay down there and help out Sergeant Block."

Grateful and relieved, Ostrow said, "Yes, sir. Right away," and disappeared out the door.

He turned to the ladies sitting on the bench—two voluntarily, two trapped—and said, "This will be over in a few minutes." He put a comforting hand on the shoulder of the older women, pulling her robe closer around her. "What's your name, ma'am?"

She replied, "Linda Wasserman." Her voice had already dropped an octave, and the panic had began to subside. She knew a mensch when she saw one.

"Mrs. Wasserman, you're going to be free in two minutes. Young lady"—he addressed himself to the blonde who had called for help—"Do you have any nail polish remover?" Arnie moved the fleshy part of Mrs. Wasserman's hand, and the acetone crept in, dissolving the glue on contact. "Easy. A little at a time. Let the fluid do the work."

"I never thought I'd be so glad to stand up in my life," Mrs. Wasserman said. "God, I must look like a freak. May I change?"

"Certainly."

"My locker's in the back."

Ross asked, "Has anyone been back there since the robbery?"

"No," Samantha replied. "We had our clothes up here."

"Then why don't you wait a moment," he said calmly, "and let me take a look. Just procedure, you understand. I wouldn't want you to disturb any evidence."

"Of course, Sergeant Ross." Mrs. Wasserman had pushed her hair out of her face, straightened her robe, and was feeling much more like her old self.

Arnie smiled and excused himself to the others, then walked into the shower room that separated the two locker sections. The smile went with him as far as the portal. For all he knew, the perp or perps might have stashed themselves in a shower or a closet. When he was sure he couldn't be seen, he pulled the .357 Magnum from his shoulder holster and took a quick look. The place was clean. Holstering the gun, he returned to the front room, smile back in place.

"Go ahead, Mrs. Wasserman." He picked up the acetone and sat on the bench. "Next, the lady in pigtails." The kid had been quiet as hell. Once he had her free, she started to stand, took a look across the room at her dead companion, and swooned. Ross caught her before she hurt herself.

"You want to give me a hand," he said to the guard with some annoyance. "Don't just stand there like a barber pole. Lay her down."

Arnie was on his way to look at the corpse when Lou walked in. "Ladies, this is Sergeant Hernandez, also of Homicide. Miss Chapman, Miss—"

"Farrel, Sally Farrel."

"And this is—"

"Roosevelt Cole. I'm with International Security," the guard said.

"Yes, so I see. I'm sorry to find you in these circumstances, ladies."

"Lou, would you take a look at this please?" Arnie asked, standing over the seated body of the locker room attendant. Hernandez joined him and allowed Arnie to place his hand on the dead girl's neck. "The same with the other two," Arnie said.

They waited for Mrs. Wasserman, who returned in short order, makeup and hair in place. "Okay, ladies. I know it's getting late, and that you've had a hell of an evening, but you would help to protect yourselves and everybody else in this city if you'd try to remember what you saw. It may take a while. If you want to use the phone, please do it now."

It took until one in the morning to take the name of every person in the building at the time of the crimes. Arnie and Lou took the attendance sheets showing the names of the members who had been in the club at any time that day. They would be cross-referenced against the membership list. All guests of members would have to be followed up.

They walked around the corner to the blocked-off alley where a forensic team and the M.E. were standing around waiting. "Jesus," the ambulance driver said. "I thought you guys were going to leave us out here all night."

"Sorry, old buddy," Ross said, "the dead have to give way to the living. Whoever it was, it ain't in a hurry."

"This is the one that was found by the guy who went to the night club?" Lou asked.

The patrolman on duty at the barricade said, "Yes, sir. The M.E.'s covered everything with sheets to discourage gawkers."

Ross turned to him. "Well, what've we got?"

"I'm not sure. A piece here, a piece there."

Ross turned to the Forensics man. "You got a guess?"

"I don't know, Sergeant. Whoever it was fell a long way and landed in a bad place."

"Let's get rid of the drapes," the M.E. said. "Then you can see for yourself."

"My God, Arnie, it's a leg." Lou bent over hands on knees. "It looks like it's been sheared off at mid-thigh."

"The sword again?" Arnie said. "Maybe. It all fits. For those people up there, we don't need to wait for an M.E.'s report. The girl had her neck broken by a chop. The guard the same. Their heads moved around like yoyos. With the guy on the tennis court, it could have been the blunt instrument, or the broken neck. But either way, that neck was snapped by an expert."

Lou shook his head. "Same m.o. with the masks, too, and the Krazy Glue. Carefully planned. But this one wasn't done with a sword." He shined his light up and down the alleyway. "Whoever it was fell, slipped, jumped, or was pushed from that roof, and came tumbling down here"—he raised the light—"and landed on that."

The beam flickered off of the shining concertina of metal, razor-blade-thin and sharp, wound in concentric loops two feet in diameter across the top of the iron gate to discourage illegal entry.

The trunk of the body was intact, except for the left leg, which had been sheared off to land on the sidewalk, the right arm, which lay in the alley, and the head, which hung by a thread from the trunk where it was impaled upside down on the spikes at the top of the fence. The body had exsanguinated entirely, leaving a slick pool at the foot of the fence.

"It's a woman," Arnie said, "black and young. She's wearing a judo suit, Lou. Black belt." He shook his head. "Jesus . . ." He turned to the rest of the small group. "It's all yours, guys. Take it away. Hey, lots of pictures, please."

Ross didn't answer him. As they pulled away Arnie smiled with satisfaction. "Well, Roach? Is this, or is this not the same bunch that did the Grant job?"

"It only proves that intuition and dumb Jew luck are better than scientific work."

"Now, who the hell do you suppose it is?"

CHAPTER

TWENTY-THREE

Bernie Coughlin looked at the phone on his desk with the fascination of the cobra for the mongoose. He was expecting a call from the mayor. He was not disappointed.

"Captain Coughlin?"

"Yes, Your Honor."

"I'm not sure myself what to say to you. I am only grateful that this mess broke out after the eleven o'clock news was put to bed. I understand from the commissioner that the delay was caused by your precautions in using the police band radio, and the way that the scene of the crime was handled. I congratulate you."

Coughlin put his hand over the mouthpiece and closed his eyes. Even among the politicians of the city of New York there was the decency of the last meal for the condemned. He pictured himself riding a horse on a cold, lonely December morning on a bridle path in Van Cortlandt Park, or far reaches of Staten Island.

In due course the mayor let the other shoe drop. "On the other hand, as I have worked my way through the front-page story in the *Daily News*, including the full-page picture of the dismembered body, and the shots of the outside of the club, I am prompted to ask you where the patrols that are supposed to protect this part of the precinct were.''

"They were on duty, sir.''

"Where were they on duty, Captain Coughlin? Normally, I would be having this discussion with the commissioner, but it occurred to me that I would like to have this from the horse himself, regardless of which end the answer came from.'' The mayor's voice had risen a half octave, and become even more insistently nasal than usual. ''I'd like you to do something for me, Captain Coughlin. Just a small experiment in self-education and improvement.''

"Anything you say, Your Honor.''

"I'd like you to get ahold of a membership list of The Angles. Now, I've already been on the phone with Morris Goldfarb. He's the owner.''

"Yes, sir. I've spoken to him too.''

"I don't doubt it. The reason I want you to get the list—it's very strictly guarded, but Mr. Goldfarb has assured me that you can look at it—is to familiarize you with the names of the members. Now, Captain Coughlin, The Angles is not a very social club. People in the Social Register have other places to go. The club is just chock full of people with new money—Jews like me, Italians like Judge Carrano. By the way, his wife was in the exercise class last night. There are Irish, like Councilman O'Hara and Councilman Flynn, and, of course, Irishmen like Commissioner Walsh. There are models and show people. The club pays almost a million dollars a year in taxes to the city of New York alone. Mr. Goldfarb has asked me if we could translate some of those tax dollars into police protection for his club. He would feel much better if the people who perpetrated this crime were apprehended. So would I Captain Coughlin. I think, to help you along, I'd like to give you a shoulder to lean on. Why don't you keep in touch with my office directly on this.''

Bernie Coughlin put the phone down and squeezed his

eyes shut. I think I'll go and slit my wrists, he thought. Instead, he called Frank Flaherty on the phone. "I was just on with the mayor."

"And?"

"You saw the papers. Promise me you'll take care of Margaret and the children. I think I'll try to swallow my service revolver."

"Bad?"

"He was the soul of tact. Have Ross and Hernandez come in yet?"

"It's nine in the morning, Bernie. Hernandez did more than a double shift yesterday, and Ross is an invalid. When I told Saul Rogovin that I'd put Ross back on full duty, he told me he'd have my badge. They were out till three this morning."

"The mayor gets up very early," Coughlin said lugubriously.

"I'll see if I can get them in. They'll get all the help that I can spare them. Finkle's already been on my back."

"What does that son of a bitch want?"

"To make sure that I don't strip the homicide squad bare working on a case in your precinct, and leave him to rot. He brought me the God damn copies of the DD-fives on all of the open homicides in the twenty-third half an hour ago, and wasted ten minutes of my time reciting them to me. As if I didn't know that they were there, John Does and all."

"You'll find me in my office, Lieutenant Flaherty. I'll probably be drinking."

When Frank Flaherty called Arnie Ross's apartment, he got his answering machine. He left his name, and called Margarita Hernandez.

As he tried to locate them, Ross and Hernandez, showered, changed, and shaved, but red-eyed, walked the halls of the morgue on Twenty-ninth Street with Dr. Gelfand. He pulled out a rolling slab from the cooler wall and said, "Let's see if we can piece this together." He whooped at his own joke. It was the judo instructor.

Ross rolled his eyes. "It's too early, Doc. We haven't even had breakfast. What killed her?"

"The fall and the sharp stop at the bottom."

"You could say that again. That razor ribbon isn't funny."

Gelfand wrinkled his nose in distaste. "There is nothing funny about dead people. I guess that's why I am always horsing around. What killed her? Everything, Arnie. All at once. Clearly, she exsanguinated. There wasn't enough blood left in her body to dampen a sponge. All major bones were broken. She lost an arm and a leg. Spinal fractures beyond count. She was impaled on a spiked fence."

Arnie gritted his teeth and pulled back the sheet. She had been laid out in some semblance of order.

"And if that weren't enough, her head was damn near severed by that damn razor ribbon. Why don't they stick to barbed wire?"

"It's the perps, Doc," Lou replied. "They just hop right over it. They don't like to fool with this. If you make a mistake, you don't get a scratch or tear your pants, you lose a piece."

"Has anybody been to identify her yet?" Arnie asked.

"Her mother came down. Thank God, she has a brother, too, so the old lady didn't have to look at her."

Arnie shook his head. "Lucky there's a toe left to tie a tag to."

Lou peered at the youthful face, already drawn like a mummy's in the rictus of death. "Arnie, look at her nose."

Ross reached over and touched the cold face. "Doc, did that happen in the fall too?"

Gelfand shrugged. "It's possible." He adjusted his glasses and looked more closely, then shook his head. "No. I don't think so."

"So she was beat up when she went over," Arnie said.

Gelfand nodded. "I'll buy that."

It was past ten when they parked in front of the Twenty-third. There were messages for them everywhere. They went straight to Flaherty.

"Morning, Boss," Lou said. "You looking for us?"

"Please. No comedy." He pushed the three morning editions of the New York papers across the desk. "The mayor has already been chewing on Bernie Coughlin's ass. What do you know?"

"We have enough to go on to keep us chasing our tails for a week."

"You don't have a week."

"Forget it, Boss," Lou said. "This is going to be a slow one. Anything on the perp on the roof?"

"No record," Flaherty said. "No prints or pictures on file. No nothing."

"I know something."

"What's that, Arnie?"

"The guy was into martial arts."

"This is where I came in."

"This is a repeat of the Muffy Grant job. It even says so in the News. They even picked up on the use of the Krazy Glue."

Flaherty groused. "All right, I'll admit it looks the same. Especially the Krazy Glue."

"And how about the guy with no head?" Arnie pressed.

"The guy with no head? No record? No prints on file? No nothing?" Flaherty said irritated.

"Not nothing. With callouses on his hands and feet. Like the perp on the roof," Arnie said.

"All the victims were killed by expert blows of the hands. Even the perp. He was black and blue all over."

"I understand about the guard," Flaherty said. "I understand about that kid in the locker room. One smack each, and bang, lights out. But the perp?"

"Lou has a theory about that," Arnie said, turning to Hernandez.

"We just came from the ice box. That girl that was killed in a fall from the roof, she was the club's judo instructor. She was chopped up pretty bad in the fall on the fence. But besides that, it seems that before she fell, she got the stuffing kicked out of her. She was bruised all over, and her nose was smashed in.''

"You're sure it didn't happen in the fall?"

"That's what Gelfand says," Arnie interjected.

Hernandez continued. "At first, Arnie wondered whether the girl might have been the inside man. From what we can see, they were pretty security conscious. We're damned if we can figure out how they got in there. The roof of the loft next door is seven stories higher, and there are no windows adjacent."

"Human flies."

"You laugh. That's what it looks like. Anyway, the girl wasn't the only one who'd been beat on. The dead perp died of a fractured skull and severe brain damage inflicted by a blunt instrument. And his neck was snapped clean as a whistle. He was ruptured. Somebody had fetched him a collosal whack right in the balls. He was crippled. He couldn't have gone twenty feet."

"What's the guess?" Flaherty asked.

"I think that the chick came onto the roof and surprised them. We figure that she gave the first perp his hernia before the second guy decked her with that shot to the nose and pitched her off of the roof. Then, he killed his buddy to shut him up."

Flaherty nodded in appreciation. "Where do we go from here?"

"That depends on the F.B.I. If there's something on this guy, we'll follow it up. We've had him photographed. If it's okay with you, we'll have it circulated around the department. I think we ought to give it to the papers, too."

"Okay. That's good. That shows some activity. Let's do that, even if it doesn't get us a make on the asshole. It'll give City Hall something to talk about. And if you get nothing from the F.B.I.?"

Hernandez said, "I defer to my partner."

"Just how important is this, Lieutenant?"

"The mayor called personally. Is that a beginning?"

"Good. I want me and Roach, and thirteen guys off the squad."

Flaherty smiled. "You know what, Ross. You've passed the lieutenant's examination. I'll bet you could pass the captain's examination too. Nobody knows more about police procedure than Sergeant Arnold Ross. But you're going to be a sergeant forever, because you're a crazy asshole. Do you know that? Huh?" Flaherty stood up behind the desk. "I'll make you a deal. Because we have a lot of heat on our backs, I'll let you and Hernandez stick on it together. And you can have Charley and Baxter."

"And Aiello and Hannigan," Arnie said.

"All four of my sergeants on the one case? Kiss my ass, Ross."

"I do it all the time, Lieutenant. Do you want some work done on this or not?"

"Pick two others."

"Phil Chavez and Joe Siegel."

"And Albert."

"Arnie"—Flaherty's voice rose again—"are you sick? Finkle came in here this morning to remind me that I shouldn't get lost in Coughlin's work and let the good old twenty-third down."

"Frank," Lou said, "ask the new guy down in Street Crimes, please."

Flaherty threw his hands in the air. "All right. Get out of here. I'll do it now."

Once in their own office, they sat at their desks with their feet up and drank coffee from their ancient percolator, resting on the spot it had burned in the filing cabinet. "So, where do we start?"

"How are your fingers feeling?"

"A stroll through the Yellow Pages?"

"I'm going to assemble our staff, and set them on the road interviewing possible witnesses of the Angles mess. Then I'm going to take a picture of glamour boy and run it past some of my old friends from Muffy Grant's."

"What are you going to do with Albert?"

"I'm going to send him over to ruffle the feathers on those dingbat spades that were supposed to be the security at The Angles. They probably saw the bastards go in and out, and never even realized it."

Arnie was talking to Baxter and Charley Passarelli when the F.B.I. report came in. According to the government of the United States, the unknown stiff in the city morgue was unknown.

CHAPTER

TWENTY-FOUR

Hiroo Matsushima sat at his desk in downtown New York drumming his fingers on the empty polished surface. In a minute or so the telephone would ring and his secretary would inform him that his call to Junichi Hamato, his superior at the company offices in Osaka, was on the line.

On his desk there were copies of the three New York newspapers. Of particular interest was the Wall Street edition of the *Post*. On page three was a quarter-page photo of Dennis Hollings, his eyes closed in death. Beneath the photo was the bold face headline DO YOU KNOW THIS MAN?

Matsushima was not in the mood to talk to his boorish and overbearing boss. Fate had seen fit to make him trudge the colorless ladder of trade looking upward at the ungainly rump of the loud-mouthed son of a peasant. The decline in the fortunes of his samurai clan had done nothing to ameliorate his mood. Then, this! He slapped his hand at the photo in the newspaper.

"*Konichi-wa*, Hiroo-san," Hamato said. "I trust the day has not been without reward for Inyo Lines." Always

205

the silky tone, so thinly woven that the dagger beneath was always visible.

"*Konichi-wa*, Junichi-san. I hope that you have also done something to bring honor upon your house." Was there the suspicion of doubt in his tone? How could Hamato be sure?

"What are the loadings for the day?"

"They are respectable. Respect, of course, is always a matter of personal judgment."

In the office in Osaka, Hamato stared oddly at the receiver. And what, he wondered, has gotten into our little prince today? That he rankles a bit under the boot, I can understand. He is, after all, the eighteenth grandson of Tokugawa Ieyasu himself. But the boot is always applied with a very delicate touch. Hamato smiled. Or as delicate as a poor peasant boy like me is able to manage. Bah! I have no time for niceties today. Let him get on with it. There is yet London, and Puerto de la Plata to be heard from, and a dozen more.

Matsushima read the list, then said testily, "I trust that that satisfies you."

Hamato was taken aback. "It is beyond the target for the day. I am satisfied. Of course, the directors and the stockholders are never satisfied. They no doubt feel that their relationship with the New York office is more business than social."

"Then, let them look to their manners. Good day, Junichi-san." Matsushima hung the receiver in its cradle. It was a serious breach of etiquette. It is always the prerogative of the senior to hang up first, and get on last. A junior enters the car first so that the senior may be the first to be greeted at the destination. A junior never crosses his legs when seated in the presence of a senior. Of such things are the structure of Japanese social and business discipline woven. Matsushima had been purposely ill-mannered.

He pushed his chair away from his desk, angry at his own lack of self-control, and angry at the existence of the man who provoked it. He left the office without wishing anyone good night. The staff looked after him in wonder.

He loosened his body in the dark of the gymansium without turning on the lights. There was a sense of mystery, almost of boyish play. He sprang across the mats, gaining momentum with each stride, then spun into a forward sommersault. "Haiiiii-ya!" His breath exploded from his mouth as his feet struck the dummy with a force that ripped the seams. He was a soldier. He was a warrior in the forefront of his own ancestor, on the dry streambed at Sekigahara, when everything was won, and the eternity of the Tokugawa clan was defined, that day in 1603. "Haiiiii-ya!" he cried, charging the enemy with nothing but his bare hands. He sprang again, almost the height of his own head, and fell upon the practice dummy, a living buzzsaw of blows and kicks. After a time his pulse began to tell him that he was fifty-five and not fifteen. Finally, out of breath, he marched around the perimeter of the gymnasium in military fashion, pretending to accept the applause of his victorious troops.

Fifteen minutes before the time when Willie Lopez came to open the doors of the Ten-do Karate-Dojo, there was a knock at the door. Odd, he thought. He shrugged and ignored it, still walking out the heat of his exercise. It came again, more insistent.

"Who is there?" Matsushima asked.

"It's George Pfister, Matsushima-sama. May I come in?"

Matsushima undid the lock. The youngest of his disciples was wearing a clean sweatshirt over a pair of jeans. Matsushima noted that his sneakers were new. When he had closed the door, Pfister made himself very low before the master, and touched his forehead to the ground. "I wish to offer tribute to the clan, Matsushima-sama."

Ah, so. It was he who broke the rule I had made. He and the dead Dennis Hollings. It was they who extracted tribute from The Angles. How had they managed, he wondered. He glanced at the clock. In ten minutes Willie would appear, then the others, such as remained.

He sat cross-legged on the mat on the small dais. Pfister

came forward, eyes cast downward, and placed a paper bag before him. He opened the bag. It glittered, even in the tiny light of the office, like a sky turned upside down. Matsushima reached in and pulled out two rubberbanded wads of bills. There was perhaps six or seven thousand dollars. More important, there were a dozen rings with stones of meaningful size, twice as many watches, studded with stones and gleaming with gold, a couple of pins, and a bracelet that might have been painful for a slender wrist to bear, of thick gold chain, hanging with gold coins of various nationalities, the size of quarters.

"You have done well. Your tribute is accepted. It will be counted, and you shall have your share. Now you must tell me how it is that you come to me with tribute when I had expressly forbidden that it should collected."

Speaking into the floor, George Pfister said, "I know that I am not very smart, Matsushima-sama. I know that because I am the youngest, I need to be guided more than the others. I was not surprised when Dennis told me that you had given him secret orders to exact the tribute at The Angles, and that I should obey his every command."

"And how did you know how to do the things that were necessary?"

"He showed me the plans that you had given to him to make it possible. We studied them every hour of the day when we were not here. We studied for two weeks. We knew every detail of the plan by heart. We walked around the building, never together, always during rush hours when there were a lot of people. Dennis told me how proud you would be. What is a samurai who does not fight for his master? An ox. That's what it says in the old manuscript about the knights of Bushido."

"It says more. It says that he is a bull without balls. That is the same as the ox, but indicates a lesser heart. Have you a copy of the plans?"

"Oh, no, Matsushima-sama. We only looked at them twice, when Dennis said you had let him have them."

"If I show them to you, will you recognize them?"

"Of course."

Matsushima rose, and removed the plans for the raid on The Angles which he had drawn with his calligraphic brush and sealed with an ancient seal of the cormorant. He spread them out on the dais. "These?"

Pfister raised his eyes. "Yes, Matsushima-sama."

Matsushima rolled them again. "Just so. You did well. Tell me, George, were there only the two of you?"

"Yes, sir."

"How is it that you returned alone?"

"I listened to your voice in my head. It was not easy. Everything had gone according to plan. There had been the need to use force on some people. Now, when I read it in the paper, it seems that we used too much. It is hard to tell what is enough."

"It is when you are young."

"When we went to the roof with the tribute, to change and take the service elevator down, there was a woman. She was a master of the arts, Matsushima-sama. She was fast and strong. She knew more than Dennis. She crushed his balls. He couldn't even stand up. I listened for your voice, and I did what I had to do. He had no knife to commit seppuku. To use the gun would have given everything away. I stripped him of all his identification, then I split his skull with the handle of my gun. To make sure, I gave him the twist of the chin from behind. I heard the bones snap."

"You did well. What did you do with the woman?"

"I hit her in the face with my gun and threw her off of the roof. Then I left by the elevator, as the plan said."

"Just so. It is as it should be. You may go. I am pleased."

Hiroo Matsushima sat for several minutes on the dais in the empty room, the rolled operational plan for the robbery of The Angles across his knees. They would drift. Without the iron discipline that comes from the heritage and the upbringing, they would slowly revert to type. What was Dennis Hollings doing but repeating the mistakes of his

foreshortened and miserable existence? He saw that the
adventure of the samurai of Matsushima would come to an
end one way or another. He had indeed been mad to think
that a tradition could be revived among the rootless in an
atmosphere so foreign to its precepts.

He pondered on the idea of confronting them with that
sacrifice. No, he thought. They may waver. If I send them
out with the hope of return, even if the chances are nil,
they will still be purified by death. Their eternities will not
be cheated. It is not reasonable to expect that they will be
prepared to embrace death for its own sake, even Willie. I
am altogether ready. He went to his closet and took a
white silk cloth, an ink stone, and a very fine brush. He
sat at the desk and wrote in a bold fine hand of ceremonial
kanji the death poem which he had borne in his mind since
the last days of the war, when he thought the road to
eternal glory lay just before him. He folded it carefully and
laid it in the closet next to his sword.

He looked in the mirror above the desk before he went
out onto the floor. He brushed back his carefully cut hair,
graying in a distinguished manner at the temples. Out-
wardly, he looked no different than he had when he walked
into the karate-dojo. Yet, he knew, as surely as he could
see himself in the glass, that he had made his commitment
to death.

"*Kon-ban-wa*," Matsushima said to the seated members
of his clan.

They touched their foreheads to the mats. "Good evening, Matsushima-sama," they replied.

Lord Matsushima. He sat so straight that he could feel
the strain of each of the vertebrae against his thin skin. "In
a test of our will to pursue the course of the samurai, we
have abstained from exacting tribute for a period of months
so that we might study the philosophical elements of the
samurai's commitment. That time is at an end. Last night,
one of our samurai met an honorable death in the execution of my plan. Tribute was collected. When it is counted,
it will be distributed to each of you in equal shares, save

for the share of George, and the share of Dennis, both of which shall be paid to George. When it was necessary for Dennis to escape from the possibility of shame into death, George helped him. He is to be honored for his example. Let us all strive to be equal to the tasks which are before us. Tonight, we will concentrate on the building of strength. From tomorrow for a week, we will practice our arts and choose and study plans for execution. Then next week, we will act.'' He felt the ripple of excitement pass through the ten young men left to him of his clan. His eyes fell upon Willie. Other thoughts were mingled on his face with the dreams of action, of battle and tribute. Matsushima had been wise not to tell his samurai that he had set them on the path to glorious death.

CHAPTER

TWENTY-FIVE

Ethan Wyatt, the drug pusher, and ear for the twenty-third precinct, moseyed on down 110th Street not far from the Lexington Avenue local station. He was wearing shocking-pink pedal pushers and a white sweater. There were live goldfish in the water in the Lucite heels of his platform shoes. In the lobe of each ear were five pierced earrings.

"Hello, pussy," a man said, standing in a doorway. "What you got?"

"Where you going, precious, up or down?"

"I already been down, man. I want up."

"Greens do, precious?"

"Greens is fine. What's on?"

"The nigger wants six tonight."

"You shittin' me? You faggot pussy, you!"

"Nigger wants six."

"They ain't no motherfuckin' justice," the man said, counting out twenty-four dollars in rumpled bills, and taking the four capsules which looked like angry insects in

the palm of his hand. Ethan Wyatt marched on, swinging
his hips and his handbag.

"Hello, baby."

Ethan Wyatt stopped dead in his tracks. He'd know
that voice if it rumbled at him while he was passing
through the gates of hell, and he wouldn't be a bit surprised. His voice dropped a couple of octaves, he stopped
mincing, his shoulders slumped in an exasperated masculine gesture. "Shit! What you want from me man?"

"I want to have a nice little talk."

"One of these fuckin' days, you gonna get me killed."

"Ain't nobody goin' to miss a pussy like you, Ethan,
'cept your customers. And there'll be some shit-ass pusher
out there on your stroll before your body is cold."

"You a mean prick, Albert Ruggles. You know that?"

"Meet me in the alley next to the Amber Cat."

He closed his ragged overcoat up to his neck, stumbled
sloppily down 110th Street, and turned down Lex. He
came to a dark passage between two old law tenements;
the bottom floor of one was home to the Amber Cat, a
filthy, lively neighborhood bar, and the local homosexual
hangout.

Ethan Wyatt stood leaning against the back wall, almost
invisible in the shadows.

"What you want, Albert?"

"I'm lookin' for a bunch of martial arts freaks. Now,
understand me, Ethan, I ain't lookin' for a bunch of
overgrown children who think 'cause they braid their hair
in cornrows that they're tough niggers. I'm talkin' about
the real thing."

"They all brothers?"

"No. Some Spanish. A couple of honkies. Maybe even
some slopes."

"Ain't no Chinks or Japs around here, man. What's
goin' down?"

"You read the papers, Ethan."

"You mean them that jumped that health club?"

"That's what I want, Ethan."

"Shit. You an' every other dick on the force. And you gotta come up here crawlin' to me."

Albert smiled a broad gap-toothed smile. "I know what you likes in your behind, Ethan. If you don't watch yo' fuckin' manners, that passageway is gonna be the size of a thirteen shoe. Have you heard anything?"

"Albert, I can dig what you want. I ain't heard nothin'."

"Keep your eyes open. Poke around."

While Albert was setting his little intelligence network into operation in the barrio to catch wind of any martial arts freaks that might be organized enough to pull off a job like The Angles, other minds were at work on a similar problem.

Julius Strawberry was five blocks away from Albert's basketball court. He sat on a broken-down couch in the basement of a store that served as a social club for Julius and a group of his friends. They were all in their early twenties, and were holders of a number of New York's statistical records. Their specialties were truancy and juvenile delinquency, and when they graduated, welfare fraud, unemployment and unemployment fraud, and petty violent crime. They were altogether different from the refuse that Matsushima and his chief henchman, Willie Lopez, had formed into their samurai clan. They had no tutor, no philosophy, and no motivation. Of all of Willie's recruits, only the unlamented and headless Alfredo Reyes had sprung from the same roots. Like the samurai, they were slothful, disobedient, and had rap sheets, with front and profile shots and fingerprints, that filled the police blotters on which they were frequently spread. Despite a hundred arrests and thirty convictions among them, of the five, not one had done a single minute of time.

Julius was their acknowledged leader. He was a thick-lipped brute without a redeeming feature, but he could cry like the Fountain of Trevi on command in front of a judge. His size and his penchant for violence gave him precedence in their council. And he knew enough to listen to Horace Smith. Smith was to Strawberry as a pilot fish is to a shark, riding in the bow wave of the great stupid killing machine in its endless search for sustenance, exerting little energy, and eating well from the scraps.

"Julius," Horace said, "I'm not so sure it's a good idea."

"Well, you is a pussy. And you just don't know no better. You can sit here on your dead ass. But we"—his dull eyes lit on the circle of others around him—"are going to go to Eighty-sixth Street. We going to sting like a bee and dance like a butterfly." He laughed grossly, spitting. The others joined in.

"Julius," Horace said. "It's an express subway stop. There's Gimbel's on the corner. There are stores up and down the block. The place is lousy with cops."

"Sheeeeeet. Don't you never see the bright side." Julius Strawberry pulled a worn and dilapidated .32 caliber revolver from his pocket. He had had it for three days, traded for two gold watches he had acquired in a mugging. The cylinder was loose, and had he known enough to look, the rifling in the barrel was so worn that the bullet would fairly rattle as it was propelled by the powder charge, limiting its accuracy to ten or fifteen feet. "We going to go in there through the front door. We going to take out the security guard, stick up the people, and scoot out the back door, down the alley and onto Eighty-seventh Street, where old Jackie is going to be waiting in the car. We going to drive to Fifth Avenue, park the motherfucker, and just walk off into the park. Ain't nobody going to know shit."

Horace Smith started to say something, but knew when he was licked. He smiled and nodded his acquiescence, and began to make contingency plans.

Jackie dropped them on Third Avenue and Eighty-fifth Street. They strolled up the block and turned the corner toward Lex, stopping at the window of the store on the corner long enough to make sure that Jackie had made it into Eighty-seventh.

They crossed in the middle of the block, stopping traffic

as if it were their prerogative, and made a show of looking at the promotional stills of the movies that were at the Loew's. By and by they came to the curtained glass door of Mike MacMahon's Physical Culture Salon.

It was office number nineteen. Mike MacMahon was to the blue collar and the lower middle class, what Muffy Grant's was to the working girl, and The Angles to the nouveau riche. The individual attention and small classes of Muffy's and the superb physical plant of The Angles was replaced by scratched and bent cut rate rowing machines and weight pulls. Ill-assorted barbells littered a corner. The gym floor was covered with a cheap indoor-outdoor carpet stained and fetid with the perspiration of two years of flabby, out-of-shape clientele. The spa that was advertised was a tepid pool large enough to hold a third of the sixty adults who were perpetually trying to fit themselves into it. It was about five feet deep, and brown scum streaked its plastic sides.

The instructor stood in front of a floor-length mirror in a shiny pink leotard. Dark patches spread from under her arms and her crotch. Her makeup, which could have been cut with a knife, was running down her cheeks. This was her seventh forty-minute class. Another twenty-minute break, one more class, and she would be through for the day.

Julius and his friends slid into the door. Horace Smith turned the double latch to lock the door from the inside. The other three spread out against the street-side wall.

There was a male instructor who acted as the manager of the club, a bookkeeper, and the spa attendant. Julius knew that. He had spent six dollars the day after he had read about the Angles caper on the special introductory offer.

And there was the security guard. He wore a uniform and carried a night stick. His qualification for his job was that he was alive. He had been lucky enough to be the last in line to be taken when Beneficial Security was hiring one day. His ill-fitting uniform had been meant for somebody else. He was paid the minimum wage, $3.35 an hour, and was damn glad to get it.

He was dozing in the chair by the side of the bookkeeper's office, and was very surprised and frightened when he awoke with the barrel of a scratched old pistol intruding into his left nostril.

Having neutralized the threat from security, Julius motioned to his companions. Horace moved swiftly toward the office and surprised the accountant, a fat middle-aged Italian, by pulling a switchblade knife six inches long and saying, "If you talks, bitch, I'm going to cut your throat." As an afterthought, as he took the small gray metal box which contained the day's cash receipts, he pulled a stocking mask over his face.

The other two members of Julius's gang slipped into the locker room, threatened the attendant with bodily harm, and began to go through the pockets of the men's garments which hung from a plain pipe along the wall. Two pre-fab fiberglass showers dripped in the background. They tied the man up with towels, and stuffed a handkerchief in his mouth.

As they walked out of the men's locker with a bag full of wallets and watches, the manager awoke to the fact that something was wrong.

"Whot happen here?" he asked stridently.

Julius pulled the trigger, blowing off the left side of the face of the hapless security guard. Everybody screamed and fell to the floor except the manager. Julius Strawberry fired the remaining five shots from the decrepit revolver in his direction. One struck the ceiling, two the wall, and one the floor. It was the manager's bad luck that one, tumbling end over end, struck him in the mouth, knocking him from his feet and shattering his jaw.

Julius stuck his hand in his pocket and, clumsily spilling shells everywhere, managed to stuff three more into the wobbling cylinder, burning himself on the hot barrel in the process.

"Stay down, you motherfuckers," he shrilled, eyes blaz-

ing, cords standing out in his neck. "Let's go. Let's go,"
he exhorted his companions as they went through the
ladies' locker room, spraying clothes and handbags in
every direction. "That's it. Let's go." As he ran past the
prostrate female gym instructor covering her head with
her hands, he was irritated by the roundness of her buttocks, and fired a shot that severed her spinal cord.

The first shot had alerted the manager of the men's
haberdashery store that abutted the salon. He immediately
called the police. The number of the twenty-third precinct
was printed in large red crayoned letters on the wall above
the phone.

The call passed through the desk and triggered the response of the desk sergeant, who dispatched two radio
cars. When he realized that the man had said the shots had
come from a health spa, he called upstairs to Homicide
Zone Four.

Ross, Hernandez, Baxter, and Passarelli were down the
stairs, dragging their jackets and their hardware behind
them. Ross drove like a madman. Hernandez, looking at
the address on the piece of paper, used the radio to direct
patrol cars to cover the street in front, and behind it, and
both Lexington and Third avenues in case the perps should
try to make it over the roof.

Arnie pulled the car up on the sidewalk two doors
before the salon, effectively blocking any pedestrian foolish enough to wander in the way. The four detectives
fanned out on the sides of the door. As Ross approached
it, it sprang open. The policemen dropped to their knees,
their left arms thrown across their chests in a position of
protection. A fat blond woman in a sweat suit tumbled out,
having solved the problem of the lock, and screamed,
"Help, police."

Baxter dove through the door, rolled over, and came to
his feet in a crouch, sweeping the room with the barrel of
his gun. Most of the people still lay on the ground, trying
to pretend they weren't there.

"They're gone," Baxter shouted over his shoulder.

The blond woman pointed toward the door in the rear. "There!"

"The back way," Ross yelled, pushing past Baxter. Hernandez pulled his walkie-talkie from his pocket and alerted the units on the street. "Coming out on Eighty-seventh."

Julius Strawberry skidded to a halt when he turned the corner of the hall and started to head for the glass door. "Motherfucker!" he screamed as he saw his escape car burn rubber and pull away from the door as a police car came up behind him. The cop pulled away in pursuit. Julius continued toward the door, then stopped cold when a second blue and white car appeared. The officers jumped out, and drew their revolvers, shielding themselves behind the hood of the automobile, covering the door. Julius headed up the stairs, his companions hard behind him.

Horace Smith stopped at the second floor, out of breath but not wits. He listened as Julius and the other two continued their frantic dash to the roof, then slipped down the hall and waited at the end of the corridor. Several people popped their heads out of frosted glass office doors and began to wander forward to see what was going on. Horace joined them. He was stunned when Charley Passarelli, panting, his gut dangling over his belt, walked up to him and struck him across the head with the barrel of his heavy frame Colt target pistol. It had not occurred to him to take off his stocking mask.

On the roof the three remaining robbers jumped to the next building. Two of them broke their legs—a result of a four-story difference in height. Julius Strawberry was luckier. He watched them jump and heard them scream. He changed direction and headed for the building adjacent, going west rather than east.

There was only a one-story drop. His strong legs absorbed the shock with ease. He looked around and saw the ladder that ran down the back of the building.

As he headed for it he heard a warning shot and "Halt, this is the police."

Julius Strawberry had watched too much television. "Fuck you, you honky motherfucker," he yelled, spinning and firing his wretched relic. On the second shot the cylinder casing blew out, removing the fingers from his gun hand. He did not feel the pain. Ross, Hernandez, and Baxter had emptied their guns into the rest of his body.

After the mess had been cleaned up, and all of the DD-5's filled out, the questionnaire for the civilian review board had been completed, and the press had been satisfied, Flaherty, who had rushed in from his house, asked Arnie, "Well, is it all over? Is that the gang from Muffy Grant's and The Angles?"

"These assholes couldn't have stuck up the girls' bathroom at a nursery school. They were neanderthals. They have rap sheets four feet long. They read about the other capers in the papers and decided that they were good enough to pull this off. This time, I think that even Judge Wright will put the little bastards away." Ross snorted. "The Angles job. Hah! We're talking about the difference between chicken shit and chicken salad."

The M.E. took Julius Strawberry down to the morgue. His mother, a lady who did wash, looked down at him dry-eyed. "I'm glad it's over," she said. "I've been waiting for this day since he was fourteen."

The two who jumped to the roof were caged in the prison ward at Bellevue Hospital with compound fractures of the legs. Horace Smith sat with a bandage over his broken nose and his forehead in his cell on Riker's Island, kicking himself in the ass that he'd been too dumb to take off the mask. The driver joined Julius Strawberry in the morgue a couple of hours later, after trying to evade a squad car in an eighty-mile-an-hour chase up the West Side Drive. He'd missed a corner. They'd have to bury him in a shoebox.

CHAPTER

TWENTY-SIX

In the morning Arnie Ross went with Lou Hernandez to the big park overlooking Jamaica Bay. Arnie trotted along beside Lou for a half mile, loosening up his legs and raising a little sweat. There was a piece of greensward next to a playground that was flat and unlittered. Veering off, Arnie said, "See you, Roach."

"About an hour, Arnie. And take it easy." Hernandez opened his stride to the pace of a six-minute mile. Ross watched him flowing easily over the running track till he disappeared behind a clump of trees.

Arnie did a few side bends. The exercise pulled at his wounds. Lou was right. No sense in looking for trouble. He lay back on the grass, still fresh with the morning's dew, and did some sit-ups and leg lifts. He'd been afraid that he'd lose muscle tone while he was in the hospital, and sedentary afterward, but except for a tweak here and there, and a little loss of stamina, he felt okay.

After a half hour he sat up on the grass and watched two kids throwing a football back and forth. It finally landed in his lap. He flipped it back. By the time Hernandez returned, he had joined their game and was sending them out on pass routes.

"I'm going to have to steal your quarterback, guys," Lou said.

"See you guys. Thanks for the game." When they had run along a few steps, Arnie said, "I'm going to take another pass at those women who were at Muffy Grant's."

"So you told me, Arnie."

"You know what, Roach, I'll bring them all downtown and put on a show. I'll bring out the picture of the dead guy on the roof at The Angles, and as a show-stopper I'll run a line-up of those assholes that did the Mike MacMahon show."

"Arnie, you said yourself that there's no connection."

"Maybe one of them is the same. How the hell do we know?" He stopped at the car and leaned on the fender, scratching his chin. "You know what, I'm going to have the ladies that were in the locker room at The Angles too."

Lou opened the door and sat down, shaking his head. "You better check with the D.A., Arn. I don't know if that comingling of cases is going to provide a problem later in the courtroom."

"I still say that it's worth a shot."

"Do it my way. Speaking of which, I am on the third page of martial arts studios. Only three more pages to go. The Yellow Pages prints very fine."

"My God. Everybody wants to be Bruce Lee."

"From what I can tell, talking to them, half of the citizens want to learn how to rip off the other half. The other half is afraid and wants to learn how to defend itself."

"Whatever happened to sport for sport's sake, Roach?"

"It died on the I.R.T."

Arnie and Lou were in their office at the twenty-third precinct before lunch. Hernandez began his systematic telephonic interrogation of martial arts training schools, and Ross sorted the card file he had made of the witnesses to the three robberies. When they were in alphabetical order, he called the district attorney's squad for New York County. The unit commander was a detective inspector named Corrallo. He listened to Arnie till he had finished. "I don't know, Sergeant Ross. I'm a liaison officer between N.Y.P.D. and the D.A.'s office. I have a pretty good idea of what'll go and what won't. On the other hand, I'm not authorized to make this kind of decision. I don't have to tell you that one procedural misstep and these animals will all be out on the street again, laughing. I know that you're anxious to bag the perps that did the first two gyms, but if you don't handle the ones that you have under lock and key for the Eighty-sixth Street job right, you'll infringe their civil rights."

"What do you suggest, sir?"

"I'll talk to the district attorney. I think that you've got a good idea. But let's make sure that it doesn't backfire. I'll try to get back to you today. I know that there's been a lot of pressure building on this."

"Yes, sir. Direct from City Hall. Thank you."

Arnie hung up the phone, frowning.

"What's the matter?"

"Corrallo's trying to let me down easy. He's going to bat for me, but he doesn't think the D.A. will go for it. Civil rights!"

"They don't make it easy, Arnie. On the other hand, that's what we're supposed to be protecting."

"Don't start on me, Luis. No lecture today. I still think they should have hung Miranda instead of reading him his rights." Arnie thumbed through the cards. "If they're not going to let me put on a dog show," he mused, "then why don't I experiment with one witness?" The fourth card in the stack belonged to Beckman, Elizabeth Ann.

Libby Beckman was sitting at her desk in the foreign division of Citicorp, blindly pawing her way through a credit file for an agricultural project in Paraguay. Her eyes were red-rimmed, and stung from tears which she had been unable to control for the past forty-eight hours, the worst of her young life.

Nothing had been settled the night of her dinner with Willie Lopez. Far from it. The ills of the world and of their relationship had been let loose. They had had hard words, and barriers that had never existed between them in their short but intense relationship sprang like dragon's teeth from the earth. Both wounded by their sharp edges, they had retreated to the safety of Libby's apartment, and their intimacy. He had stayed with her the whole night, not leaving till she was ready to go to her office. At the door he leaned down to kiss her softly on the lips. "*Querida*," he said, just the one word.

She touched his cheek. She had no words. He walked out of the door and down the street. She wondered if she would ever see him again. When she got to the bank, she did as she had always done. She bought the *Times* and the *Wall Street Journal* at the stand in the lobby, folded them under her arm, and waited in the milling crowd for an elevator. Upstairs, she sat at her desk, checking her calendar. No meeting till half past ten. She went through the *Journal* with familiar ease, going from one section of interest to another. Finished, she laid it aside and started to pull the business section from the *Times*. In a small box, about a column inch, there was a subhead that said THE ANGELS ROBBED. THREE DEAD. A lead paragraph gave sparse details. She turned the pages shakily to the story's continuation, and read it through.

Libby felt suddenly nauseated. She got up from her desk and quick-stepped across the plush gray carpet to the ladies' room, headed for the end stall, and sat heavily with her head down. Her pulse drummed rapidly, and she began to hyperventilate.

She was afraid that for the first time in her life she was going to faint. Even the sketchy outline in the *Times* had brought terrifying memories of the Grant robbery back to vivid focus. Two words stood out like the mark of Cain. *Krazy Glue*. Jesus Christ! While she was lying there on her back with Willie's penis inside of her, panting in ecstasy, had he sent off his bunch of goons to rob another gym?

She sat up straight and leaned her head on the cool tiles of the wall. She could taste the salt on her lips from the tears that streamed down her face. The palpitations stopped, and she stood up, blotting her face with toilet paper. She went to the sink and looked in the mirror. God, Libby, you look terrible. She hadn't even brought her bag. She washed her face with soap and water, then went back to her desk.

She got through the day by staying busy. She had been supposed to stop at her parents' house after work, but called up to beg off. She couldn't imagine facing them.

Once in her apartment Libby mixed herself a drink and sat down on the couch, glancing out of the window across the street from time to time, and read and reread the story of the robbery in the *Post*. No detail was omitted. The centerfold was filled with pictures.

Libby had had no appetite, but kept refilling her glass with scotch and soda. By ten o'clock, still sitting by the window, she was no longer able to focus on the book she'd been trying to read. Pouring still another drink, she staggered across the room and tuned the TV set to the news.

"On the local scene," the anchorman said, "another in the series of wanton murders and robberies that have flared up in recent weeks at athletic clubs in New York."

Libby's eyes widened. She leaned forward at the foot of the bed, watching with rapt attention. The commentator's voice was a blur to her, but the tape showed both exterior and interior shots of Mike MacMahon's salon, and bodies being carted to waiting ambulances.

"This time the alleged perpetrators were foiled entirely. Of the five men believed to have been involved, one was shot and killed by police on the roof of the building, two were severely injured while trying to escape, and have been taken to Bellevue Hospital." The camera shifted focus to a small black man with his hands cuffed behind his back being pushed into a patrol car. "This man, tentatively identified as Horace Smith of 467 East 113th Street, Manhattan, was slightly injured and is in custody at Riker's Island prison. The fifth man, who was driving what police believe to be a getaway car, was killed during a high-speed chase that ended for him in a twisted wreck on the West Side highway."

Libby sat stunned as the commentator's face faded into a commercial. Her shoulders heaved in a sob. "Willie," she said aloud. "Willie." She pushed herself clumsily to her feet and staggered to the bathroom. She fell on her knees in front of the commode, and was violently sick, then crawled back to the bedroom and passed out.

She woke up at seven-thirty. The lights and the television had been on all night. She smelled of sickness and perspiration. She stripped off the underwear she'd had on. Her skirt would have to go to the cleaners.

She showered and dressed. She thought about breakfast, but the sight of the icebox turned her stomach. She hurried out of the house. Instead of going to the bus stop on Lexington Avenue, she walked north to Eighty-sixth Street, where there was a newsstand. She bought all the morning papers. The sidewalk across the street, where Mike MacMahon's salon was located, was cordoned off by gray wooden police barricades. A uniformed cop patrolled their perimeter.

Libby wanted to run screaming back to her house and hide under the bed. For all her education and relative maturity, Elizabeth Beckman had never been faced with a moral dilemma of such proportions. If Willie Lopez were involved, even tangentially, what responsibility did she bear for the deaths at The Angles? Or at Mike MacMahon's salon? Evil in the abstract—Hitler, Stalin, Pol Pot—is cocktail conversation. To be morally responsible, or an accessory to murder, is quite another matter.

Libby was still very shaky when she walked into the bank. She leaned against the wall of the elevator and would have missed her floor if she hadn't been nudged by a coworker. "Libby, we're here. It's time to get off."

The Foreign Loan Committee met at ten A.M. Libby sat in a chair against the wall, behind her boss, who was at the conference table, with her notes and papers close at hand if backup were needed.

It was fortunate for Libby that she was not called on during the hour and a half, for her mind was elsewhere.

She knew that Willie Lopez had not been personally involved in the robbery at The Angles. He had been with her the whole night. She was his alibi. On the other hand, only she knew for a fact that it had been he who had led the gang at Muffy Grant's that was responsible for the death of Laszlo Dushan.

Her heart skipped a beat, then the tremor of fear passed. Willie would never hurt her.

She was in a maze without an exit. What if Willie were arraigned for the Muffy Grant robbery? Would she be able to perjure herself? Would she be able to tell the truth and guarantee a life behind bars for Willie Lopez? She thought idly that a wife cannot be forced to testify against a husband.

She started violently, then looked around, conscious that she was being stared at. Embarrassed, she bent to pick up the open attaché case which her inattention had permitted to clatter to the floor, spilling its contents. It was a relief to get out of the seat, even if it meant crawling around like a fool on her hands and knees, cleaning up the mess. Marriage to Willie. Insane. Perjury. Insane. Condemning Willie to prison. Insane. Goddamnit, Libby Beckman, you can't cry in here.

When the chairman of the committee called an early recess—the meetings usually lasted until noon—she sprang from her chair and retreated to her desk quickly to avoid any conversation that would betray her lack of involvement in the proceedings. She buried her head in the pile of files that littered her In basket, making aimless notes on a yellow pad. She wasn't committing perjury if she was not under oath. On the other hand, didn't making false state-

ments to a police officer constitute a crime in and of itself?
Would that make her an accessory after the fact?

She closed her eyes, holding back another flood of
tears. She knew exactly where Willie had been during the
Angles robbery, but how about last night? Was he the one
dead in the wreck? Was he in custody in Bellevue's prison
ward? She could be sure only that he was neither the dead
man nor the man in Riker's Island. She had seen their
pictures in the paper. They were black.

She wished to hell she could talk to someone. She
wished she could talk to Willie, to know at least that he
was safe. She'd like to talk to her father. With a sigh she
opened her eyes. She'd controlled the urge to cry. Talking
to anyone was nonsense. He jaw jutted. Silly Libby. The
only salvation for you is hoping they don't catch Willie.
Then they can't ask you any questions. Anything else is
either a dream or a nightmare. Just the same, she thought
sadly, it would be nice to know that he hadn't been
involved in the other robberies after Muffy Grant. She
snorted in self-contempt. Right. Everyone uses Krazy Glue
to immobilize their victims.

She opened the file on the Paraguayan farms and tried
again to focus her attention on something more concrete,
and within the bounds of her experience. Then the phone
rang.

"Miss Beckman, Foreign Loans."

"Miss Beckman, I'm Sergeant Ross of the police department. Do you remember me?"

Libby's heart leapt.

She swallowed, a bitter, salty taste burning the back of
her throat. "Yes," she said. "Yes. I remember you."

"Miss Beckman, I'd like to ask you for some more of
your time."

"I'm sorry, Sergeant," she said, carefully modulating
her voice, "but I'm awfully busy. I've been here just
under a year. They really try to get their money's worth
out of the new kids on the block. I put in early-to-late

hours here at the office, and there isn't a night when I don't come home with a pile of work."

Ross considered the answer and the tone. Of all the people in the world you would not expect to be uncooperative, it was that nice, bright, good-natured kid. After all, hadn't she been the one who stood up to the hoods during the robbery? How odd. Arnie had been put off by experts. He brushed aside her objection. "I'm sure they're wringing the last nickel's worth of salary from you, Miss Beckman, but what I'm trying to deal with is murderers. Maybe you read something besides the financial pages from time to time. There have been two robberies at health clubs, Miss Beckman. I'm sure that the bank is worried about its money, but I have a half a dozen dead people lying in the morgue, and I'm worried that they're going to have company unless we stop whoever is doing these things." He paused to let the words sink in. "You're a nice young lady, Miss Beckman. You have a lot of courage and a good mind. You know right from wrong. I just can't picture you helping a bunch of murderers getting off scot-free by default because you don't have time to talk to me." He let that work on her mind for a moment, then added, "Listen, if it's really too much for you to come in to the precinct, I can arrange to come to visit you. Obviously," he hurried on, "I wouldn't want to disturb you at work. I could drop by any time in the evening at your house. It will take only a few minutes. I want to show you some pictures and go over your recollections of the day that Muffy Grant's was robbed."

Libby's hand trembled like a leaf. She pulled her handkerchief from her bag and pressed it against her eyes. Hurry up, Libby. He isn't going to wait all day. Jesus Christ, what if Willie shows up when he's there? She balled the handkerchief in her hand. Let's get it together, Libby. "I'm swamped at home, Sergeant, and the place is a mess. You're right, the office is out. But I don't want you to think this is not important to me. I'll come to see you at your office. Is after work all right? How about six or six-thirty?''

"That's fine. You know, I'll tell you the truth. I had a momentary worry there. The world is full of citizens who are concerned in theory, but the minute they have to budge an inch to help, their concern goes out the window. Vacations, jobs, children at school. You name it, I've heard it. I just couldn't imagine you being like that. And to tell the truth, I couldn't imagine that you'd forgotten that poor Yugoslav kid. You know, Dushan, the one they killed. Somebody ought to give him a little bit of their time. Anyway, thanks, Miss Beckman. I'll be here waiting.''

Libby went to her boss and told him she was sick as a dog.

"You don't look too well, Libby. You want to go to the nurse? You know there's a doctor here in the bank too.''

"No, thanks," she said, sounding brave as she bore up under her illness. "If it's all right with you, I think I'll just knock off for the afternoon. I'll be okay in the morning.''

"Hell, if you have to, take a couple of days off,'' he said. "Just don't forget. This is Wednesday. Next Monday you're supposed to make a presentation to the director's loan committee on our position on more credit to Paraguay. I'll want to go over it in detail well before.''

"Yes, sir. I'll keep that in mind.''

Libby stood outside of the bank's Lexington Avenue entrance in a fog of indecision. She'd had no choice with Ross. He would have smelled a rat if she'd been any more obstructive. It would have been a one-eighty from her previous attitude.

A cab let a man off right in front of her. On impulse she jumped in, and after a brief hesitation she gave the driver the address of her parents' apartment house.

CHAPTER

TWENTY-SEVEN

Willie Lopez had been stunned by Matsushima's announcement that he had instructed Hollings and Pfister to knock over The Angles all by themselves. Not only stunned, but incredulous.

It was certainly not Willie's habit to question the decisions of Matsushima-sama. In his view it was not his prerogative. Nonetheless, it appeared that he had sanctioned a rash and ill-timed way to break the prohibition on the taking of tribute. Willie shook his head in confusion.

He was lying on his bed naked. He had just finished his morning's run and shower. He was startled by a knock at his door. "Yes," he said. "Who's there?"

"It's the manager," a voice replied in a thick Hispanic accent. "You got a phone call."

"Okay. I'll be there in a minute." He slipped on a pair of trousers and pulled a sweater over his head, then stepped into his slippers. Who knew that he was here? He hadn't told Libby. No one in the clan knew.

He picked the phone from the cord where it dangled against a fly-specked wall opposite the hotel desk. "Hello."

"Willie, this is Matsushima."

"*Hai*, Matsushima-sama."

"Willie, I want you to meet me at the Karate-dojo for lunch at twelve."

"Yes, sir." The phone went dead in his hand.

During the intervening hour Willie dressed and walked toward the Ten-do Karate-Dojo. On the way he picked up the *Daily News*. There was a banner story about the shootings at Mike MacMahon's on Eighty-sixth Street. Clumsy, bungling butchers, he thought. They had been ill-trained, and had no plan. Wasteful killings, and no loot. He threw the paper in the basket in front of the gym and climbed the stairs. He was ten minutes early. It was unthinkable that Matsushima-sama should have to wait for him.

Matsushima had two white boxes tied with string. Willie made tea. Taking the chopsticks from his box, he broke them apart, and following Matsushima's lead, began to eat the sushi that was layered inside.

"You saw the papers?" Matsushima asked.

"Yes, sir."

"Bunglers," he said. "They wasted life. What were they going to do with their money? What if they had been successful? Whores? Heroin? Their deaths were like their lives, without significance."

"Of those they killed, too, Matsushima-sama?"

He waved his hand in dismissal. "What significance could there have been to their lives? Certainly, there was none to their deaths, to be slaughtered like cattle."

"They had no chance, if the paper is right."

Matsushima gave him a hard look. "The pigs who came to rob them were inspired by our work. They were sloppy. The killings are of no significance because the perpetrators were of no significance, and those who were killed were of no significance."

Willie held his tongue. How did Matsushima-sama know that the victims of the crime were of no significance? Willie had concluded that victims of the tribute-taking of the clan were in a sense ennobled by their participation in the perpetuation of an important ideal, but why were they not significant in and of themselves? Why would people killed in a senseless robbery by common hoodlums have no significance?

"Life and death are the same," Matsushima-sama repeated almost in the tone of a mantra. "Life and death are the same."

"Isn't the heart of Zen the enlightenment and the greater good," Willie asked, trying to remember the words exactly as he had heard them and seen them on the page.

Matsushima-sama rocked on his heels, as Willie knew, a sure sign of displeasure. "The greater good can be seen from very many points of view. Our heads are covered with ashes and our faces are smeared with mud. We strive for the goal when appearance is of no moment. But there are stops on the path. Death is a stop on the path. You can die a worthy death and go on. Like other worthy stops on the way to enlightenment, a worthy death must be earned."

Willie ate the rest of his meal in silence. He did not pretend to understand all that he heard or read. He was a novice, and unschooled. Nonetheless, he knew that Matsushima's answer had been no answer at all. In a period of days it seemed to Willie that Matsushima-sama's continual striving for excellence in all things had had increasingly more to do with death.

When Matsushima finished with his meal, he belched in satisfaction. Willie immediately rose to throw away the boxes and clean the tea service. When he returned, Matsushima was poring over a large sketch that he had drawn with ink and brush on piece of brown wrapping paper two feet square.

"There are but ten of you who remain to me, Willie," he said.

"I can look for more members."

"I think that is not propitious."

"We have lost. . . ."

"Yes. I know what we have lost. There is no time to train others." Matsushima saw Wilie's face cloud over, and quickly added, "Now. At another time it may be possible. Now we must act with speed and daring to sharpen the skills of those who are here. Then their skills may be used for training others."

Willie looked down at the sketch. There were six names written in a row in the corner. At the head of the list was the name of Fred Logan, the Garcia brothers were included, and George Pfister, and the tiny and agile roommates, Jorge Rodriguez and Donald Wolfe.

Matsushima answered the unspoken question. "You are not to participate. I have something more glorious in mind for you. Study the plan with me, Willie. I will take you through it step by step. You will help rehearse them. We must work very hard for a week. We will act next Sunday."

When they had gone over the plan, Willie was torn between respect for its audacity and confusion about its seemingly unresolved conclusion. He supposed that he had missed something somewhere. It would not be the first time. He was confident of Matsushima-sama's peerless eye for detail. In time Willie knew that he would understand.

He trotted back to the hotel room and sat in the worn chair at the window, reading the thoughts of Suzuki. He had decided that he must go to visit Libby this evening, if only to dissipate the cloud that had descended between them. He would tell her about his newfound faith and its source, and hope that she would understand. His faith in her would transform an act of disobedience—the breaking of the code of secrecy—into an act of valor. She was brave enough to carry the burden. He had seen that.

When he returned to his office, Matsushima found a note from the president of his host agency asking to see him at once. He frowned. What does that uncouth *geigin* want now? To beg for money? To beg to reduce service? To importune? Let him and his business be damned if he hasn't the courage to face me down. We have picked the carcass near clean as it is. It is my job to see that the year or two remaining are uninterrupted.

"Yes, Fred," he said, his voice brittle with false cordiality. "Certainly, I have time for you. Come down."

The man was beefy and overweight, with a protruding pot belly. He was in his early fifties, but looked older. His slicked-back thinning hair was streaked with gray.

Before he could open his mouth, Matsushima said, "By the way, Fred, things are slipping again in the southwest offices. There are serious questions about the service. I think we must consider adding more men." The man began to perspire at his hairline despite the air-conditioning which Matsushima always had going in his office. Matsushima noted his discomfort with quiet satisfaction.

"That's what I've come down here for, Harry."

Harry. Matsushima remained expressionless. One of the little games we play. My name is Hiroo. There have been seven Hiroos in my family. When we come to America, we find American names to suit their limited ability to deal with the phonetics of other languages. Hiroo becomes Harry. Junichi is Jack. Akira becomes Andy. A small indignity to permit them to tell us apart without butchering our given names each time they wish to address us.

"We are at the limit of our endurance. There can be no more additions to staff."

Matsushima frowned. In Japan an oaf like him would work in the kitchen, or pick up towels in the bathhouse. One simply does not say no. There are a thousand polite artifices. Perhaps it is the lack of tact and manners of the *geigin* that have permitted people like Junichi Hamato to rise above their stations. This man should be slaughtered like a bawling calf. Come on, *geigin*, unburden yourself.

"I am prepared to show you that we are losing money on your account at a rate of two to three hundred thousand dollars a month."

"So you often say, Fred," Matsushima said silkily. "We are unable to arrive at the same figures. If you would open your books to us . . ."

Fred sweated even more profusely. The great threat. Open the books. Then we will see what profit you believe you are making on each phase of your operation, permitting us to demand a reduction, even though the overall result may be a loss, which we do not doubt.

"I'm closing the Houston office in thirty days."

"That is your prerogative, Fred. The president of a company is like the general of an army. He must lead as best he can and be prepared to take the consequences. Do you know who is the president of Mitsubishi, Fred?"

"No."

"Mr. Tojo. His father was a wartime prime minister in our country, and our military leader. I believe you know that he was hanged." Matsushima broke the word into two syllables.

Fred rose to his feet, fuming with anger. "No more money, no more Houston office, and you can tell that to Jack Hamato, and to Mr. Tojo, too, if he gives a damn." He stalked out of the office.

Matsushima smiled. It was possible that he had overly provoked the fool. Well, no matter. He would turn over Fred's request to Junichi-san, who derived enormous pleasure from making him squirm. There would be a confrontation, and he would back down.

Matsushima was much more polite than he had been with Hamato in their last call. He went unrewarded.

"Hiroo-san," he said in his broken-glass voice, "it is not necessary for me to remind you that our plans for an independent operation in New York are in the future. We don't wish to have our timetable upset. You should have found a way to placate him. Well, again you have left it to me. We shall see who runs that agency, Fred or me. I will go around him to the board of directors, rattle my saber, and they will cave in as they always do, more afraid that the loss of our prestige account will scare off their other customers and ruin them than that the losses they incur in our operations will. Now, give me today's loadings."

Matsushima went over the list carefully and quickly. There were no requests for repetition.

"It will do. It must, if that's all there is. *Sayonara, Hiroo-san.*"

Good night, you oversized, awkward, big-footed peasant, Matsushima thought. *Good night, you son of a dung-carrying farm laborer.* "*Sayonara,* Junichi-san."

He looked at his watch and left his desk quickly. There was much to do at the Ten-do Karate-Dojo. Soon it would make no difference what that *eta*—that untouchable—in Osaka did or thought. Matsushima would have risen above it all.

CHAPTER

TWENTY-EIGHT

Libby let herself into her parents' apartment and went directly to the guest powder room in the hall. She locked the door and took off her jacket and blouse, filled the basin with warm water and washed her face thoroughly. She patted herself dry, and using the cosmetics that were arrayed for the use of guests in the Beckman household, she made herself up, even a little eye shadow and rouge. When she had dressed again and felt presentable, she went down the hall to the library.

Her mother looked up, startled. "Libby! For heaven's sake. You scared me half to death." She put her magazine on the couch next to her. "What brings you here in mid-afternoon in a weekday?"

"I think that flu I told you about has caught up with me. I'm feeling a little blah, so I took the afternoon off."

"I hope your boss doesn't mind."

"No, I don't think so. He even suggested I take a couple of days off if I didn't feel right." She managed a smile. "Just as long as the report on Paraguay and agriculture is ready for Monday."

"If you're really not well," her mother said casually, "you can always stay here. There would be someone to take care of you."

Libby wanted to fly across the room and throw herself in her mother's arms. Do I want to stay? Oh, God, do I want to stay. I want to have an ice cream sundae, and watch cartoons on television, and have Chinese food on a tray in my room. *My* room, with the pink ruffled bedspread and skirt, and the dressing table . . .

Marjorie Beckman stood up and crossed the room to where Libby was standing and took her by the arm. Her face was filled with concern. "You've lost some more weight, Libby."

"Terrific, isn't it?"

"I'm not so sure." She raised an eyebrow. "Look at the makeup on my businesswoman." She touched Libby's forehead with the tips of her cool manicured fingers. "I don't think you have a temperature. Just the same, I think I'll get a thermometer. Sit down." She was back in a moment, furiously shaking the mercury down the shaft of the thin glass tube. "Open," she said, sticking the thermometer under Libby's tongue. "I've always enjoyed taking your temperature. You can't talk back." She waited the prescribed two minutes, then took it out. "All is well. With your temperature, that is."

Marjorie Beckman sat on the couch and looked across at her daughter. "Now, would you like to tell me what you're doing here?"

"I told you, I wasn't feeling great. I just didn't feel like a dose of my own company."

"What happened to the lust for independence?"

Libby was starting to have second thoughts about the wisdom of her visit. She was in no shape for more pressure.

"If I don't come to visit, you complain. If I come, you suspect my motives."

"Libby, I don't suspect your motives. I just want to find out what's bothering you."

"I told you. I have the flu." If I were thirteen, Libby

thought, I could tell you that Jimmy Jones squeezed my breast in the movies, or that Billy Smith showed me his penis, or that John Doe didn't invite me to the hop. But, Mother, I have a murderer on my hands, and between my legs.

Her mother patted her cheek. "Okay. How about something to eat or drink?"

Libby ate an egg salad sandwich, drank a Coke and went to sleep on top of the pink ruffled bed in which she had spent her childhood, huddled in her down quilt. She woke at five.

When she put on her shoes and straightened her clothes, she went down the hall to the library to find her mother sitting on the couch as though she had not changed positions in the three hours since Libby had last seen her.

"I feel a lot better, now."

Her mother stood. "You sound a little better. You sure you don't want to stay?"

"Positive." Libby wrapped her arms around her mother's slender waist and gave her a crushing hug. "Thank you."

Marjorie Beckman smiled. "For the egg salad?"

"For the egg salad. Kiss Poppa for me."

Downstairs she looked at the card that Arnie Ross had left with her the night he had come to call. It was still in her wallet. She hailed a cab and gave him the address of the twenty-third precinct. Libby didn't know what she would say to Ross, but she felt better and stronger for having gone home.

Libby thought that the building should have been torn down fifty years ago as she walked through the door. "I'm looking for Sergeant Ross," she said.

"He's in homicide, lady," the desk man said. "I'll give him a call."

Ross trotted down the stairs and ushered Libby to the offices of HZ4.

"Have you ever been in a police station, Miss Beckman?"

"This is the first time. A little cheerless, isn't it?"

"You get used to it after a while. I'm getting there. It's taken twenty years. This," he said, swinging the door away from him and standing aside to admit her, "is the office of the Fourth Homicide Zone of New York." He explained its metes and bounds, and its functions. "We get all kinds." He shepherded her into his office. "I'd say excuse the mess, but for us this is pretty good. This is Sergeant Hernandez. Lou, this is Miss Beckman."

She extended her hand to the tall slender man who had risen to greet her. He was built like Willie, with the same dark olive skin and prominent cheekbones and large eyes. She found him very handsome.

"Please, sit down," Arnie said. "Let me explain what we want to do. In the past several months a number of crimes have taken place in the area of Manhattan that we cover. There are certain similarities.

"You were unfortunate enough to have been a witness to the robbery at Muffy Grant's. I'm sure that you've seen the papers. In the last few days we've had two more of the same. When the methodology starts to look the same, naturally, we begin to think that the perpetrators may be the same."

Libby sat listening intently, and watching his face. The trace of the scar and the broken nose distorted the hardened expression. She tried to probe the eyes for some warmth or sympathy. She found only flint.

"We've had a couple of gruesome murders beyond the ones that you've heard about. Oh, they appeared in the papers, but you wouldn't connect them with your case." A smile appeared on his face, and unexpectedly, Libby saw a flash of humanity in the craggy features. "As a matter of fact, there are a number of people in this department who think that there are no links at all. I have a hobby, Miss Beckman. I am a martial arts enthusiast. It provides me with both an outlet for my physical energies and a focus of concentration. Orientals are different, truly different than we are. What happens to real devotees—and I am one—is that you start to get some exercise, and you find yourself

wound up in something much more consuming. These
murders, they were one way and another, related to the
martial arts, and one way and another to . . . I suppose
you might say to Oriental philosophy. Take the business at
The Angles. You read about it, yes?''

Libby nodded.

''The perp—the robber—who was killed was very likely
killed by his own accomplice so that he wouldn't be left
behind. That's what I mean when I say different. There are
a lot of New York street scum who would kill a buddy to
save their hide, but this was . . . ritual. What I'd like to do
is to show you what pictures we have of the dead and the
living in all of the three gym robbery cases, and go over
your recollection one more time of that day at Muffy
Grant's. I know that you've been through it all before, but
sometimes, something will slip through the cracks. If we
sift it again, we catch it.''

Libby steeled herself, pressing her knees together.

Arnie took the file off of his desk. How to go about
this? One picture at a time? Just give her the file and watch
her face?

Lou bailed him out. ''What we're really trying to get at,
Miss Beckman, is a pattern. You see, a lot of criminals
are really not very bright. That's how we catch them. They
don't plan. They're clumsy. They're not careful. On the
other hand, some of them learn from the street how to be
crafty and clever. We have a lot harder time with them.
Even there, though, we have the advantage of seeing a big
picture. We aren't going to catch the little rat who breaks
into this car or that, or the guy who dresses well and
shoplifts his way through Saks and Brooks Brothers. But,
if a pickpocket works the same three bus stops on Third
Avenue every day, and his m.o.—the way he works the
crowd and runs away—is always the same, sooner or later,
we're going to nail him. You have to think about this on a
larger scale. Here is a group of possibly unrelated crimes.
Sergeant Ross, because he's been twenty years on the job,
and is good at his business, thinks he sees a connection. If

there is a pattern, we're going to be able to isolate the places and the circumstances under which the pattern can be repeated. If we can improve security, maybe we'll be able to catch the guys, maybe not. But we'll certainly be able to slow them down. You saw a group of men—three. We know they were wearing masks. But they had distinct body shapes. They were ethnic types. Some of them spoke directly to you. One was close enough to hit you. We are going to show you what we have. We want you to tell us if there are any coincidences or resemblances.''

Arnie opened the file and read Libby a brief transcript of the eyewitness account of the blond locker room attendant of the robbery at The Angles. "Does any of that sound familiar?''

Libby wished that she were a smoker. "The masks are the same. The glue is the same.''

"It was the glue that stopped us, too, Miss Beckman,'' Arnie said. "That's clever. If you don't sit still, you tear your skin. So, you sit.''

Libby's mouth was dry. "You sit,'' she repeated.

"What else?'' Arnie asked.

"Sneakers, blue jeans.''

"That's everybody. I wear 'em myself. I'm going to show you some pictures. They aren't pretty. Can you bear with me?''

Libby nodded, less sure than she indicated. The first picture was a facial shot of Dennis Hollings, dead on the roof of The Angles, his brains spilled and his eyes staring, then a full body shot.

"Does he look familiar?'' Arnie asked. "The face? The shape?''

"No.'' Libby's voice was very quiet.

"How about these?'' He showed her Julius Strawberry, and the rest of his band.

"I've never seen them before.''

"Anyone who looks like them?'' he pressed.

"No. Not ever. The people who were at Muffy Grant's were all Puerto Rican. None of them was as tall as this. . . ." She pointed at Hollings's full length shot. "These others are black. None of the people at Muffy Grant's were black." She felt better about her chances of surviving this encounter. All she had to do was tell the truth.

"Look at his neck in the close up," Arnie said, pushing the picture in front of her. "See, it's broken. His head is sort of crooked. His neck was broken by a karate hold." He slipped another picture under her nose.

She drew in a breath and fought the bile that rose in her throat. It was Laszlo Dushan, dead on a slab in the morgue. The tape had been removed from his mouth and nose, and the terrible bruises were evident.

"His face is so distorted," Libby said faintly.

"Yes. He was kicked in the face by someone trained in the sport. He died of the taping. It cut off his air. But what started him on his way to the morgue was that kick. Which one of them do you think did it?"

"I don't know," she said, barely audible. "We didn't even know he was dead till the police came to get us loose."

"I mean was it the guy who hit you? Or the leader? Or the little guy? Which one would you guess?"

"The one who hit me. It must have been him."

"That's funny," Arnie said, musing, "I would have thought it was the leader."

"Why?" Libby asked, her voice caught in her throat.

"You'd think it was the other one. Mean, surly, violent, willing to hit a helpless woman, or two or three if the chance came his way. No." Arnie shook his head. "Remember what happened. He slapped your face. He went to slap it again. The leader"—Arnie flipped through his notes—"just touched him. Those are your words. He touched him and left him holding his wrist in pain. No. The mean guy was a punk. The leader, he may be smooth and silky, but for my nickel, he's the likely candidate. He's the artist."

"How about the little one?" Libby asked hoarsely. "Why not him?"

Arnie shrugged. "When you read what all the witnesses

said, he was a gopher. If you wanted to rate them by rank,
it'd be the leader, the mean guy, and the shrimp, in that
order. And besides, it was the leader who had the gun,
wasn't it?''

Libby nodded.

"Okay. We can see that the guy on the roof was killed
by a karate blow. We can see that Laszlo Dushan was
killed by a karate blow. The next thing we find is a guy in
the East River. Another karate blow. A guy is mugged on
Madison Avenue. Somebody hits him too hard in the
throat. It's a karate blow. He dies. Then I went down to
the street crimes unit in this precinct and started to go
through some statistics. We've had an epidemic of muggings in the past six months. The bulk of the crimes have
been abetted by violence. The violence has largely taken
the form of assaults by martial arts. One disabling blow,
and gone. And then to cap it off''—Arnie pulled out
another picture, then changed his mind—"I think I'll
spare you this one. Some guy had his head cut off. It
looked ceremonial. And we could tell from the calluses on
his hands and feet that he was into martial arts. Too much
coincidence for me, even in a city this size. From the day
we found the guy with no head to The Angles job, suddenly, everything was quiet. The mugging rate in this
precinct went down to its normal level. Then, bam-
bam''—he clapped his hands together—"we get the same
kind of job pulled on successive nights.''

Libby bit at her lip, then asked, "Do you think those
two crimes were committed by the same people?''

"Very good question, Miss Beckman. That's one of the
reasons I asked you up here. You didn't see any common
features between the people who robbed you at Muffy
Grant's and the people who hit the MacMahon salon on
Eighty-sixth Street, right?''

Libby's mouth opened and shut soundlessly, her mind
racing. "I can't be sure.''

Arnie flipped through his pad again. "You seemed sure
a few minutes ago. These guys are the wrong color.''

"Yes, yes. That's right."

Arnie put down the pad and put the pictures back into the envelope. "I'm sorry. I don't mean to push you. But you can see, we don't want to have these people running around. They're violent, dangerous, and don't seem to care much who they kill. I think, Miss Beckman, that the guys who did the Grant job hid out for a while, and then came back and did The Angles. I think the goons who hit MacMahon's were amateurs trying to copy their act. Your testimony pretty much confirms that to me. What I'd like to know is where these guys are going next. The take at The Angles was pretty good: jewelry, watches, some cash. Maybe the total value to a dealer in stolen goods would be fifty, maybe seventy thousand. We have descriptions of the guys who pulled off The Angles. We have the body of one. They weren't the same as the Muffy Grant job. We're dealing with a large number of people, then. At least five. Are they on drugs? What do they do with their money? How long will they be able to subsist on the take from The Angles? All good questions with no answers. One thing's for sure, Miss Beckman—that leader is sitting someplace and dreaming up another job. I wish I could beat him to the punch before he is responsible for somebody else's death." Arnie dropped the file back into the cabinet. "Thanks, Miss Beckman, I'll see you to the door."

She was so relieved that she almost fell from her chair. Arnie gave her a hand. "You seem a little shaky."

"I took the afternoon off. I have a bug. I guess it doesn't want to go away."

At the front door Arnie said, "You know, this isn't exactly Beekman Place. Why don't you let me put you in a squad car and send you home?"

"That would be very nice, but . . ."

"No buts. Come on." He pulled her along to a car with the motor running.

"Phelan, do me a favor, take this lady wherever she wants to go."

"Right, Sergeant."

"Thank you," Libby said.

"If you think of anything that might help, Miss Beckman, I'd sure appreciate a call. From now on I'm going to consider you an honorary member of my squad."

On her way home Libby looked out of the window, dizzy with the words that had poured into her ears for the last hour, stunned by the graphic pictures. The dead parody of the smiling, open face of Laszlo Dushan. *How you doink, Libby? Vork good.* She blinked back the tears. And Sergeant Ross. He was a man to fear. That hard, uncompromising face. "I wish I could beat him to the punch," he'd said. Libby pictured that iron frame, squat and hard and brutal, facing Willie's slender body.

"Say, miss, is this the place?" the officer asked a second time.

"Oh, yes, thanks." She watched him drive away. She looked quickly across the street. Willie wasn't on the stoop. She let herself in and lay in the dark, fully clothed, on top of her bed. *I think I'll take up that offer and skip work tomorrow.* She thought about Laszlo Dushan for a while, and fell asleep on a pillow wet with her tears.

In his office at the twenty-third precinct, Arnie Ross read through the files on the gym robberies over and over again, barely seeing the words, as Lou methodically checked each of the martial arts studios in the New York phone directory.

"Arnie, you're not reading. You're just twiddling your thumbs. What's on your mind?"

"You know me too long, Roach."

"When you share underwear, you get to know someone. So?"

"The kid."

"What?"

"Nonkosher. Something is nonkosher. She is not the same person that I interviewed the day of the Muffy Grant robbery."

"Ah-ha, an impostor."

"Don't fuck around, Roach. I'm serious. The girl just isn't the same."

"How is that?"

"The kid I remember had a mouse under her eye, but was smiling and feisty. She was chubby, and very young, and very willing. A number-one good scout, Mickey Rooney's sister in an Andy Hardy movie. One of the guys brighter than that, maybe, but somebody's kid sister."

"And now? That wasn't the whore of Babylon that just walked out the door."

Ross shot a paper clip off the wall with a rubber band. "Nope. But she was uptight."

"You're a scary person, Arnold."

"More than that. She was . . . how about equivocating? She answered the questions with a teaspoon, not an open hand."

"The story still checks? It cross-references?"

"Oh, yeah. But it *sounds* different."

"Maybe she's scared that these guys will come get her. That happens. Witnesses who have a chance to think for a while about what could happen to them tend to freeze up."

Ross frowned. "Scared enough to drop twenty pounds? The walk is different. There's a different feel to her voice. The kid is gone. That's a woman." He shot another paper clip. "You know what I think, Roach? I think she's fuckin' somebody."

"If that was against the law, you would have been hung a long time ago. What, suddenly, is wrong with fucking? And what has your male nose for it have to do with her?"

Ross grinned. "The truth? I don't know." He picked up the files again and began to read in earnest.

CHAPTER

TWENTY-NINE

The sound of the door buzzer brought Libby to a sitting position on her bed, staring ahead in the darkness. She looked at the clock. It was past midnight. She had an awful taste in her mouth, and she was still dressed in the same clothes she had worn to the office in the morning. She stumbled to the door and looked through the peephole. It was Willie, his skin drawn like parchment across his prominent facial bones. She opened the door and stepped aside as he hurried in. He reached out and put his fingertips on the soft curve of her jaw. Involuntarily, she turned away.

For Willie it was as though she had struck him a blow. *"Querida?"*

"I'm sorry, Willie. I've had a long day. First, I read about the murders at that gymnasium last night, and the night before. Then I went to the office, but I couldn't stay there because I kept crying. I went to my mother's for a while. Then I went to the police."

His body went rigid. He stared at her in the half light, his pulse threatening to explode in his neck.

She raised her head and looked up at him. "They called me in. They wanted to question me about the two murders and robberies after Muffy Grant. They wanted to know if I recognized anyone." She waited in silence, watching him.

"What did you say?" His voice was flat and low and curiously calm.

As though she were in a dream, she asked, "Are you going to kill me, too, Willie? I told them nothing."

"Can you believe that I would do that? I would die first. I would kill me."

Libby took steps, closing the distance between them, and looked into his face. "You mean that, don't you?"

"In my belief, when there is shame, or there is a shame which is to come and cannot be avoided, honor demands death."

"Hara-kiri," she said. It was like a fairy tale.

"What do you know of hara-kiri, Libby? Hara-kiri is only one of the paths of seppuku."

"Asian philosophy. Sophomore year at Yale, Willie. Hara-kiri is a pretty common term. It's the way Japanese kill themselves."

"Sometimes," he said earnestly. "The stomach opening is the most difficult." He went on as though he were describing a problem in mathematics. "That is why there is always an armed witness. One must not be dishonored by crying out. The first thrust is straight to the left. The second is the turn, and the cross stroke across the abdomen. Then there is the turn upward and the stroke to the rib cage. The most gifted are able to withdraw the sword." He lifted his finger to a spot below his right ear and drew a diagonal across his throat. "And cut the throat, and the carotid artery."

"How simple you make it sound."

"Life and death are the same."

"Then, killing me shouldn't matter," Libby said.

Willie put the tips of his fingers to his temples. "Please, Libby. You are much more clever than I am. You are much more educated. It's cruel, what you are doing."

She closed her eyes and shook her head. "I don't understand you. You tell me that life has no value. You say that what you have learned tells you that there is no significance in death. I am ready to try to understand that. That's Buddhist thought. I've studied it a little. I know the basic elements. But Buddhism is a gentle religion. Nowhere that I know does it give a license to take life."

"For a samurai, the taking of life is not more important than any other part of existence. It is something to be done with purpose and dignity."

Libby sat down on the edge of the bed. "For God's sake, Willie, samurai? What samurai? I feel like Desdemona talking to Othello. Do you know who they were?"

"No."

"A general and his wife. He thought she was cheating on him. She loved him so much that she preferred to have him strangle her for something that she did not do than to watch him suffer over the possibility that she had done it. I have been asking you whether or not you are going to kill me. You say you won't. But then you give me all the rationales why it wouldn't be such a bad thing. Willie, what are you talking about?"

He took a deep breath, then sighed and sat down next to her. "I spent the first twenty years of my life surviving. I stole. I sold drugs. I mugged people. I slept in gutters and alleys. One day I met a man. In fact, I tried to mug him, with a bunch of bums just like me. He licked us all. The others ran away. I just stood there. It was like God had sent the avenging angel. I didn't care whether he killed me or not. I was very tired, Libby. I came from nowhere and had nowhere to go."

"Why didn't he just call the police? Then you would have ended up in jail."

"He knew that I was not going to jail. I was going to walk away, or die there."

"Did he have a gun?" Libby asked.

Willie shook with soft laughter. "Gun? His body is the most deadly weapon. He has taught me many things. Still, sometimes, because I am only a student, I must carry a gun. He needs only himself. When he saw that I wasn't afraid of death, he told me that I had already passed through the first portal of enlightenment. He just walked away, telling me that if I wanted to know more, I should meet him the following day.'' He turned and took Libby's hands in his. "I went to meet him and he made me free."

Libby listened to Willie for a half hour as he described the progress of his physical training, and his education in the rudiments of discipline and Zen philosophy. He spoke of gathering together the band of misfit antisocial street children who became the Matsushima clan of samurai.

Libby sat in rapt attention, shaking her head from time to time in sheer amazement. "Fagin," she said when he had finished.

"Fagin?"

"A man in another book, Willie. It isn't important. Your Zen master is Fagin, and you are the Artful Dodger. Characters in a book." She touched his cheek. "God knows, Willie, that you must be characters in a book. You can't be real."

"And you, *querida*? Where are you in this book?"

She smiled wistfully. "The only girl in that book was named Nancy. She was killed by her lover."

"Was the Artful Dodger her lover?"

Libby shook her head. "No. It was a man named Bill Sikes." God, she thought to herself, which of you plays the part of Bill Sikes? Is it you? Or is it this master of yours?

Willie smiled. "You see, even in your book I am not the one who kills."

"But you killed Laszlo Dushan, didn't you, Willie?"

"I did not. I struck him and knocked him out. The man who hit you taped his mouth and nose, and that's why he died. It said so in the paper. It was not me."

"But you're an accessory, Willie. And somewhere that man who killed Laszlo Dushan is running around free."

"Not without his head," Willie said grimly.

Libby's skin crawled with goose flesh, and her nipples contracted to the size of pencil erasers to the degree that they hurt. Her eyes widened as she looked at Willie. Is that the headless corpse of which Sergeant Ross had spoken?

"Impossible shame. Striking bound women. Stupidly killing an unconscious man. Failing to show the proper respect. Lack of self-discipline. He couldn't even be trusted to commit seppuku if ordered."

"Did you kill him yourself?" she asked in a very small voice.

"No. It was the master. But I would have."

"Willie, have you ever taken a human life?"

"Does it matter to you, *querida*? Why? I will not be a different person if I have killed or I have not. The point is that I am prepared to kill if I am ordered. I am prepared to kill if it is the honorable thing to do."

"You can be so sure? You can be so positive that you can decide whether the taking of a life is just?"

"Yes. I have been taught."

"I think I'll just lie down for a while," Libby said, crawling onto the bed. She turned and put her hands under the back of her head and stared at the ceiling.

"May I lie down next to you?" Willie asked diffidently. He had come to share his whole being with Libby. She asked questions that he could not answer. He was unsure whether she understood. When he was beside her, their bodies touching, he said, "I have tried to let you see what I am, what I have become. I wanted to share my strength and my security."

Libby closed her eyes. Oh, dear God, please look down here and take a little pity on Wilfredo Lopez and Libby Beckman. *Othello? Oliver Twist?* How about *Romeo and Juliet?* Talk about star-crossed. He's like a dog sitting before his master, wagging his tail frantically, looking for approval, his mouth smeared with blood, and a baby rabbit between his paws.

Who the hell is this master? Libby wondered. I ought to find out and turn the lunatic in. How about Willie? Shall I ask him? Shall I put him in a position where he will shame himself by answering, and then commit suicide? Shall I turn him in? I can't. She hadn't even realized that she had whimpered aloud.

He turned and put his arms around her. "You see a bad karma?"

She nodded, and all the tears that she cried in the two days before were nothing to the flood that poured from her, soaking his shirt. She couldn't speak, and for all his comforting, she could not stop. Finally, he just held her tight, and let her cry herself to sleep. When he tried to disengage himself, she clung to him, whimpering again, even whispering his name in her sleep. After an hour her grip relaxed, and he was able to get loose. Carefully, he stripped her of her wrinkled clothes, and folded them and lay them on her dresser. Before he pulled the covers over her, he looked down at her naked body and trailed his hands lightly across her sex, and her breasts, then bent to kiss her on the lips. He tucked her in and slipped out into the night, knowing in his heart that he would never see her again in this life.

CHAPTER

THIRTY

Libby Beckman played hooky for two days, and lied to her parents that she had gone to work. She sat in her old robe in the little apartment on Eighty-fourth Street and alternated between working on the report that was due for Monday and crying till there were no more tears.

It occurred to Libby Beckman that the most important thing that a parent can bequeath to a child is a sense of the difference between right and wrong. That distinction, to Libby, was a heritage in and of itself. It is the bedrock.

She ate almost nothing. From time to time she would drink some orange juice, or nibble at a piece of bread. When the report was finished, and she had reread and edited it, she felt bereft. There was nothing left but her nagging conscience.

Was Willie Lopez a clear and present danger to society? Did her failure to report him to the police make her as guilty of crimes yet uncommitted as he would be?

Laszlo Dushan was dead. She believed Willie implicitly. He was guilty of assault and of robbery, not of murder. If Willie went to jail, society would be satisfied.

But his punishment would not bring back Laszlo Dushan. If he would promise to stop his criminal activities, he would present no danger to anyone. If he promised her, she knew that he would keep his word.

"Oh, God," she shouted aloud, pounding her fists on the table in front of her. And in so doing she would force him to defy this master, whoever he was, and upset the tenuous security on which his will to live rested. He would either kill himself or shrivel and die.

Could she replace the master? Could she give Willie will and strength to pursue another course? Could she be his reason to live?

Libby walked to her closet and pushed the clothes on the hangers back and forth on the bar. It was her choice to dress in conservative plain-Jane clothes for work. There was a pretty this, and a pretty that, given by generous parents. If Libby wanted to, there was no place she could not go appropriately dressed. Where would she be left, living with a reformed Puerto Rican street hustler? It wasn't pretty dresses that she would miss.

Libby wanted the feel and the taste and smell of Willie's body. She wanted to feel him against her, inside of her, his weight posed on her in heat and passion. But it wasn't enough. Who is Fagin? Who is Othello? They are sign-posts on the streets of my life. It's where I come from and where I want to be. Those sign posts, and my sense of right and wrong, are the sum of Libby Beckman. I don't know if I can change them. I can give up the pretty clothes, and the spring dances. Not the rest.

She tried to satisfy herself that Willie had not killed. He had not been at the Angles, though by indirection he had admitted that the robbery had been performed by members of his clan. If she were simply to remain silent . . . She began to cry again. And the next time they commit a crime?

At five-thirty the following Sunday morning Libby Beckman lay in restless sleep, in a state that bordered on delirium. She had eaten almost nothing in five days, and had suffered from endless self-criticism and self-doubt. She was running a fever, and even in her waking moments she was occasionally incoherent.

About a mile from Libby's house, as the crow flies, on Eighty-ninth Street between Amsterdam and Columbus avenues, on Manhattan's Upper West Side, is the only remaining private riding stable in the borough. The building is old and cramped, and its ring is small and interrupted by eight iron posts that provide the support for the floors above, and for the stalls in which some of the horses are kept.

Frank Williams, a Jamaican who had been the chief groom at the stable for thirty years, put his feet up on an electric heater on the third floor, in the loft where the tons of hay and feed grains to maintain the sixty rental hacks and twenty-five private horses were stored.

He'd mucked all of the stalls with the help of two drunks he'd recruited from the street the night before. They all knew the deal. Five dollars and a warm place to sleep.

There were two ways to get into the stable—the electrically operated front gate securely fastened at night to the cement doorsill, and five cement steps which led to a door in the fifteen-by-twenty-foot office.

Divided by a chest-high counter, the room fronted on the ring, which was visible through the windows in a floor-to-ceiling partition. There were a few broken chairs for spectators, and standing room for those waiting for horses.

The door leading to the office from the street was bolted from the inside, as was the entrance from the ring. Behind the counter stood a massive and ancient Mosler safe.

Every weekday morning the bookkeeper emptied the old coffer, and accompanied by the regular daytime grooms walked the satchel of cash to the bank. On weekends, when eighty percent of the receipts were taken in, they were too busy during the day, and closed too late at night. On a Sunday morning the take from a fully booked

Friday and Saturday—a certainty in warm weather—could amount to fifteen or twenty thousand dollars.

Matsushima had made a thorough investigation of the facility while enjoying a favorite pastime. He had been trained to ride from the time that he could walk, in the tradition of the samurai and the nobility. He has passed hours on weekends watching his daughters schooled through the steps of dressage by the crotchety old stable manager. While watching their progress, he had made time to wander about, noting each entrance and hiding place.

He discovered the weak point in the elevator doors. All deliveries of hay and straw were made through the doors of an antique lift that occupied the western third of the building's street front. They opened both to the exterior and to the stable on all floors except the basement. The street-level door was barred and locked. The second and third floor outside doors were merely pulled shut.

Though it was summer in New York, at five-thirty in the morning, it was still dark. Fred Logan knocked out the single bulb above the stable office entrance with a broom handle. The nearest streetlamp was on the corner, a hundred feet away.

Jorge Rodriguez and Donald Wolfe appeared in the shadow of the doorway. Logan braced himself while Jorge mounted to his shoulders and stood upright. Donald, slight and agile, climbed their bodies like a monkey in a tree. When he stood atop Jorge's shoulders, he took a bent coat hanger from his belt and pulled open the second-story door the two feet he needed to insinuate his body.

The stalls on the second floor were just as Matsushima had told them. Unlike the narrow straight stalls occupied by the rental hacks in the basement, the bulk of the accommodations, at four hundred dollars a month, were taken up by the two dozen people who felt the need of a private horse in New York City. The best of the stable's horses, mostly for dressage lessons and jumping, shared their more comfortable quarters.

When Donald opened the gate and slithered through

with Jorge hard on his heels, a large bay gelding, beautifully curried and gleaming, moved restlessly in the capacious box stall across the aisle. He laid back his ears and moved away from the door.

The horse beside him, a nervous little jumper, nickered softly, and shuffled his feet, scraping at the straw, his shod hooves dragging on the worn boards.

Frank Williams heard the movement of the horses, though he was a floor above them. He cocked his head, and ground a smoldering butt under his heel. Grumbling, he picked up the baseball bat that he kept beside him for protection and walked gingerly down the ramp.

The bay in the corner stall lashed out his hind feet and kicked the wall.

"Well, well," Frank Williams said. "You just like everybody else up here. You think you're supposed to get all that hay and grain for nothing. You think them sugar cubes come free. You ain't got no balls, and you ain't got no brains. One hour a day you work, and every time it gets near seven and you think somebody's going to drop a saddle on your shiny back, you flatten them ears and get ornery." He looked across the stall. "I know you're back there getting ready to raise hell." Williams took a flashlight from his back pocket.

Jorge's first blow was to the stomach. The old man doubled over without a sound, the wind knocked out of him. The second was behind the ear. The horse in the box stall kicked in earnest and whinnied. In a moment half of the horses on the floor had taken up the cry.

Jorge and Donald hurried down the floor with the body between them, then went into the tack room behind the ramp and trussed him like a goose with the lead lines that were hanging from rings on the wall. A polishing rag served as a gag, and another as a blindfold.

Once they had descended to the ring floor, the horses quieted. They opened the door to the elevator a couple of feet on the street side and let in the Garcia brothers, Fred Logan, and George Pfister. The Garcias went to the basement and searched till they found the two bums who had mucked the stalls. They tied and gagged them without resistance. Neither awoke.

In accord with Matsushima's plan, they relaxed and waited, each in his designated place. Nothing would happen until six forty-five.

At precisely that time an old Ford station wagon pulled to the curb in front of the office. John Hoover stepped out onto the sidewalk and adjusted his snap-brim hat. He stretched and snapped his galluses, as he did every day after his drive down from the country. He looked up at the smashed light bulb. "Darn kids," he said, as close to swearing as he ever got. He shrugged it off and put the key in the lock. He'd have to get Frank to put up the ladder and replace the bulb. Darn kids.

In a lifetime of working with thousand-pound animals, John Hoover developed a certain wariness. If you don't have eyes in the back of your head, and look out for the stupid beasts, they'd be likely to take a nip out of you, or give you a hoof in the hindquarters.

He had one of those premonitions when he walked into the office and closed the door behind him. He stood perfectly still, straining his ears. I'm getting old, he thought. Suddenly, there was a terrible pain in his chest and throat.

Fred Logan had knelt in the shadow of the counter, out of the light that filtered through the cobwebbed windows. When Hoover had stepped forward, Logan had risen, using the power of his legs as well as his upper body to slam the older man with his forearm. The elbow caught his Adam's apple.

The Garcia brothers caught him and lowered him to the floor. They tied his hands and feet and took his keys from the ring on his belt. Once he was blindfolded, they dragged him behind the counter near the safe.

John Hoover thought that he was going to die for lack of air. Slowly, the bruised and contracted muscles had relaxed, and he had begun to breathe normally. His heart pounded like a trip-hammer, but the pain had begun to ebb enough so that he could think.

"Listen, mister," a voice said. Hoover tried to listen very carefully, so that he would remember it. It was muffled by a stocking mask, "I want you to give me the combination to the safe. I'm going to take out the gag, and you're going to tell me."

Hoover drew in a breath. The moment the gag moved, he started to yell. His voice was stifled by a blow to the mouth that split his lips and broke his dentures. He turned his head to the side, spitting and sputtering, trying not to choke.

"That was dumb," the voice said. Hoover heard a snap of fingers. Hands pulled at his trousers, undoing his fly, then pulled at his private parts.

"These are the pliers that they use to pull horseshoe nails," the voice said. Hoover cringed as he felt the cold touch of the metal against his skin. He could picture the nail nippers, open jaws that touched only where the two blades, four inches across, met. "I'm putting them on your balls, mister. If you don't tell me the combination, I'm going to squeeze. Like this, only harder."

Hoover's eyes widened behind the blindfold. Even a gentle pressure caused excruciating pain. My God, he thought, am I nuts? Let them have the money.

"Eight left three times." He waited till he could hear the clicking. "Twenty-six right three times. Nine left twice. Sixty-one right once, then back to the left. Now turn the handle." The safe opened and the nail nippers were removed. Hoover licked his bloody lips. "Don't kill me. I haven't seen you." The gag was stuffed back into his mouth, and he was pushed against the floor next to the counter, face down.

"Not a sound. Not a twitch. Then, you'll stay alive." Logan looked at his watch. Seven sharp. "It's late. Let's go."

George Pfister scuttled out of the office and waved his arm. Jorge Rodriguez, standing at the bottom of the ramp, raced up to get Donald Wolfe. Hector Garcia headed to the basement to get his brother.

As Logan picked up the bag of cash and valuables, the door of the office flew open with a bang.

"Hey, what the fuck is going on here?" The man in the door was six feet tall and weighed two hundred and thirty ill-distributed pounds. His stomach stuck out like a melon through the made-to-measure fawn doeskin riding breeches and tweed hacking coat. An enormous cigar protruded at an aggressive angle from the corner of his mouth.

Marvin Goldstein had made a late and large fortune by buying bits and pieces of inherited jewelry from poor people all over the United States. He paid ninety percent of the day's quotation for the weight of the gold. The stones were thrown in for free.

When Fred Logan sprang at him, the man turned just enough to avoid the full brunt of a blow to the face. An elbow caught him on the ear painfully. He pushed Logan away with a strong hand.

As Logan turned back to strike him again, Goldstein fired his .25 caliber pistol at point-blank range into his head. George Pfister was at the door of the office and rushing toward Goldstein when he stumbled into Logan's falling body. Goldstein spit out his cigar and emptied the gun into Pfister's head. It was the last thing he ever did. He dropped the gun and reached for the door as the Garcia brothers crossed the floor. He struggled against them with his advantage in weight and size. Hector blinded him with his thumbs. His gurgling scream was cut off when his windpipe was smashed.

Phil Teitelbaum was Marvin Goldstein's youngest nephew. He was also his chauffeur and bodyguard. When he heard the first shot, he sprang out of the stretch Lincoln limousine. Unlike his uncle, the gun he carried was no pocket toy. It was a Colt .45 caliber pistol.

His first shot blew off Hector Garcia's right kneecap, the second, the back of his head.

The three remaining members of the Matsushima clan ran pell-mell up the ramp to the second floor, bullets ricocheting off the walls behind them. They hid behind the first stall, waiting.

Teitelbaum, after checking his uncle's body, grabbed the phone and dialed 911.

"We got to get out," Oscar Garcia said.

"Let the horses loose," Donald Wolfe suggested. They ran down the aisles dropping the ropes at the back of the straight stalls and swinging open the gates of the boxes. Whooping and hollering and waving their hands, they drove the panicked horses down the ramp into the ring.

Teitelbaum fired his last two shots futilely across the ring from the office. When he saw that he had missed, he dove out of the door and ran back to his car. The howl of the sirens presaged by seconds the arrival of three squad cars.

Donald Wolfe pushed the button and the gate rolled up to the ceiling. Startled, the horses milled about for a moment, then thirty-five strong poured out into the street, galloping first this way and then that, in a maddened frightened mob. Oscar Garcia ran toward the river, trying to hide in the midst of the crowd. Shielded from the police, he made it nearly to the corner. His foot landed on a piece of fresh manure, and he fell heavily on his back. Despite their efforts, the horses were unable to avoid him. By the time that they had passed, he was a lifeless pulp.

With the confusion and the horses, and the blockage of the street, Donald Wolfe and Jorge Rodriguez were given an opportunity to use their greatest asset, speed afoot. Without a backward glance, they sped out of the door on the heels of the horses, their arms pumping like pistons and turned in the opposite direction from the herd, eastward toward Central Park. They dodged across Columbus Avenue, not even checking for traffic. The green of the shrubbery beckoned to them, offering refuge.

A rookie policeman named Galen Royce had spent four

years running track on city champion high school teams, and he'd grown up in the ghetto. When he saw Donald and Jorge running toward the park, he knew he wasn't looking at athletes. They were escapees.

Despite the impediment of his service shoes, Royce took off after them. He still did ten miles a day.

As they strained for every ounce of speed, leaving the pandemonium of the stable behind them, Donald and Jorge gained the last block separating them from the park. As they came to its end, they could hear the sound of running feet reverberating off of the walls of the silent buildings. Sneakers don't make noise.

Jorge Rodriguez looked quickly over his shoulder. He was running as fast as he could without leaving Donald behind, and he could see that the policeman was gaining. "Come on, Donald," he panted.

They crossed Central Park West and came to the granite wall that bordered the park. Jorge cupped his hands. "Step in here. Hurry up." He glanced down the block. The cop was less than fifty yards away. Donald stepped into his hand, and he boosted him to the top of the wall. He climbed up himself just as the cop began to cross the avenue.

"Go, Donald," Jorge exhorted him. "Go. You can do it." They climbed an outcropping of rocks and galloped downhill, almost stumbling into an open field.

Donald began to lag. "Leave me," he panted. "You go. I can't keep up."

Jorge grabbed Donald's tee shirt and dragged him along. "I ain't going to leave you nowhere. You're all I got."

"Please, Jorge. I just can't."

"Come *on*!"

They made it halfway across the field before the cop broke from the cover behind them. For all of their conditioning, they'd been sprinting at top speed for a half mile, and were wheezing painfully. Their legs were starting to cramp from lack of oxygen.

Galen Royce had the advantage of them. Where they

were short and agile, with quick small strides, he was tall and spare, with a long gait. He closed within twenty yards, and yelled, "Halt, Police."

Jorge, dragging Donald with him, swerved suddenly across the field, and into the bushes that border the Eighty-sixth Street transverse. At the edge of the wall, they looked down a dozen feet to the pavement.

"Jump, Donald," Jorge exhorted, his voice shaking with emotion and exertion.

Donald hesitated a fracton of a second, more from fear that Jorge wouldn't follow him than from the height. He was the only person he had ever loved in his whole eighteen years of life.

"Hold it right there," Royce said, his voice ragged with effort. His gun was drawn.

"Go," Jorge said to Donald a last time, then turned to face Royce.

Galen Royce had never taken his gun from his holster in the line of duty. There were two of them, and he was alone. When Jorge whirled on him, the gun fired almost by itself.

Jorge was shot in the chest and was dead before he hit the ground. Royce stood dumbstuck, staring at the smoking barrel of his revolver, and then at the boy on the ground. Bone dry throughout the chase, he was suddenly soaked in perspiration as he realized that he had taken a human life.

The blond boy at the edge of the wall looked to be fourteen or fifteen. Silent tears poured down his cheeks. He sat on the ground next to the corpse and took it in his arms, and began rocking it like a doll. After a moment, he shook with sobs.

The sounds of his anguish brought Officer Royce back to reality. "Okay, get up and put your hands on top of your head." The boy ignored him. "Are you deaf?" Royce said, his voice unsteady. Jesus, I don't want to use this gun again. "Let him go. Stand up, and put up your hands."

Donald Wolfe looked up at Galen Royce, then bent, and kissed Jorge Rodriguez's dead lips. Then he pulled a knife from a shealth on his belt and cut his own throat.

CHAPTER

THIRTY-ONE

Ross and Hernandez had finally knocked off at three on Saturday night. They flopped fully dressed onto the bed and the couch in Arnie's apartment on Eighty-sixth Street. The theory of regular rotation of manpower, and regular hours in detective work is tenuous under the best of circumstances. When there is a case that hits the papers, or there is heat from Police Plaza, or the Mayor's Office, or Borough Command, the theory vaporizes in the crucible of reality. The heat had kept them working sixteen or eighteen hours a day since The Angles was hit the previous Tuesday. They were uncertain of the situation that awaited them as a result of the unexpected phone call this Sunday morning, but had little reason for optimism.

The scene at Eighty-ninth Street had the elements of a Brueghel painting. The street was scattered with police barricades erected in seemingly random array. As Arnie parked the car on Columbus, a riderless brown gelding flecked with foam, his eyes rolling in terror, barreled across the avenue and jumped the hood, clattering and slipping on the sidewalk, and hurtled west toward the stable, home, and safety.

Ross and Hernandez looked at each other speechlessly, then followed the horse. There was a cacophony of sirens and horns as vehicles of every description, ambulances, squad cars, and a truck from the A.S.P.C.A. assembled in the area. Horses of various descriptions ran or walked alone or in groups as the spirit moved them, on the open plains of Manhattan's Upper West Side.

"Look out," Hernandez said, pulling Ross with him as another animal plunged by, his steel shoes striking sparks on the cement. As they got to the stable door there was a screech of brakes and a juddering thud. At the corner a horse had been struck by an oncoming produce truck. The driver, in an effort to avoid the animal, had spun his wheel. It had been too late for both. The horse, screaming whinnies of pain, tried to drag itself along on its forelegs, both hind ones broken and bleeding. The vehicle had turned on its side, and smoked furiously from its engine.

The people in the street, police included, stood frozen in horror.

"Come on," Ross said, already running. He stopped long enough to put a bullet into the horse's forehead. Lou and Arnie climbed on the top of the truck cab and tugged at the door.

"*Hijo de puta*," Lou spat. "The frame's bent, Arn."

"Break the glass, Roach. This fucker's going to burn. Where are the firemen?"

Lou pointed his chin up Amsterdam in the direction of the firehouse that shared the space of the twenty-fourth precinct on West 100th Street. He tugged again, straining against the side of the cab to pull the door up toward him, The driver had tumbled to the passenger side, and lay still against the door, limp as a doll, and bleeding. "They're coming, Arnie," he grunted.

"Fuck it, Roach. It's burning, man." Ross jumped off the truck and pulled his gun. "Get off. Roach."

Hernandez dropped to the pavement. "Do it. I'll grab him."

Ross fired three times through the windshield, making sure that the bullets would lodge in the cushioned seats. The glass splintered, and crazed, but held together. He kicked his foot through and pulled the crumbling edges apart. "Now, Luis!"

They put their hands onto the inert body and pulled it through the opening in the windshield, dragging the injured man across the street. As the fire truck pulled to a halt, there was a popping sound, and flames belched from the engine block.

"Shit," Arnie said as they reached the corner. "Down!"

As Ross and Hernandez hit the sidewalk, the cab of the truck burst into flame, and seconds later the drumlike fifty-gallon gas tank exploded, sending a gust of fire ten stories into the air.

The firemen pulled their masks over their faces and charged, like a squad of infantry rushing a bunker, across the pavement with chemical extinguishers. Windows had shattered, and the few tenants of the neighborhood who had not already leaned out to watch the show appeared.

The two detectives got up slowly, their charge still unstirring on the sidewalk at their feet. "Christ, Lou, I hope we didn't kill the poor bastard."

"If we did, it's got to beat the shit out of being in there." The truck was a smoking ruin. Debris was scattered over the street, and some pieces of body work had been lifted and had fallen over the sprawled carcass of the horse.

It wasn't until ten that Ross and Hernandez had managed to take all of the names, separate the dead from the living, and the perpetrators from the victims. The street was choked with vehicles from all of New York's uniformed services including sanitation. Mounted patrolmen were still looking for three horses that had escaped into the park and were roaming at large.

Ross had finally gotten his way. Both Sergeants Aiello

and Hannigan had been assigned to help him on the case—the full complement of HZ4. Baxter and Passarelli were in Central Park working on the two dead boys there. Flaherty, cursing like a boatload of sailors, appeared in knickers and a tam o'shanter.

"I think I'm going mad," Flaherty said. "I think it may really be time to toss in the old badge. Does anybody have an explanation?"

Ross turned to Hernandez. "All right," Lou said. "I'll take a stab. A number of perps—our initial estimate is six—broke into the stable. They decked and tied up the night watchman, then waylaid the manager and forced him to open the safe. An early morning rider showed up too early. His name was Goldstein. He was a jeweler with a licensed pistol. He surprised the perps, and shot two of them dead. The others jumped him, poked out his eyes, crushed his windpipe, and broke his neck. Goldstein's combination nephew-chauffeur-bodyguard had an unlicensed pistol, and blew away another perp. He's the one who called nine one one.

"The remaining three perps let the horses loose to give themselves cover. One got trampled, the other two made it to the park. A cop ran them down. He shot and killed one. When he tried to arrest the other one, he committed suicide. That's what happened."

"Is that all?" Flaherty said. "We should have sold tickets." He watched as the A.S.P.C.A. dragged the dead horse down the middle of Amsterdam Avenue. The produce truck was still sending up wisps of smoke. Bubble gum lights on top of squad cars revolved eccentrically at every corner and intersection in sight.

"Not suicide, Lou," Arnie interjected.

"What do you mean?" Flaherty asked.

"Not suicide—seppuku." He repeated the description of Donald Wolfe's death as told by Officer Royce. "He had him under the gun. He just sat there rocking the other kid's body back and forth. Royce kept the gun on him. He kept telling him to stick up his hands. When the kid pulled the knife, Royce says, he was too surprised to fire. He's never drawn his gun before on duty. He said the kid just pulled the knife and slit his throat.'' Arnie drew his finger across his own neck. ''Got the carotid artery. He was dead in seconds. Seppuku, the fourth stroke. Japanese suicide.''

''Six dead,'' Flaherty said with finality. ''You wonder why they didn't just clear out. They had all of the money. Why didn't they just run? It has the look of professional work.''

''I think they were on a tight schedule,'' Arnie said thoughtfully. ''They just didn't have room for the contingency. Hey, Baxter,'' he bellowed.

The tall black detective had been on a day off too. He was wearing tennis clothes under a pair of sweat pants. ''Yes, Sergeant.''

''Go find George Ruditz. Tell him to get his fat ass in gear. I want usable pictures of the perps, looking pretty, in two hours. Eight-by-tens.''

''It's Sunday.''

''Are you speaking for him or for you?''

''I'm already here,'' Baxter said indignantly. ''There isn't anything else you can do to me.''

Ross flipped him his address book, ''It's in there. He lives in Cedarhurst. Call him. He'll be asleep. Give him my love. And Marvin, don't bet I can't think of something to do to you.''

CHAPTER

THIRTY-TWO

Joe Beckman's Sunday routine was sacrosanct. He arose at nine-thirty, two hours later than his regular schedule permitted, descended to the newsstand on Eighty-sixth and Lex, where his trade had been entertained for thirty years, and bought the *Sunday Times* and the *Sunday News*.

Marjorie had stayed in the country with friends overnight, so at ten o'clock he sat at the dining room table in solitary splendor before a plate of waffles cooked to crisp perfection, and eight pieces of bacon.

Next to the dish was a brace of needle-sharp number-two pencils and a white plastic German-made eraser which was used for no other purpose. And there was the crossword puzzle of the *New York Times*.

The puzzle irritated him. It was the kind with a key. It took the best part of an hour to find his way through. Once solved, the rest was a breeze. Chortling, he headed for the telephone.

"Well," he asked his son, "how far are you from the end?"

Barry Beckman said a single word. "Hylacine." He paused, then said, "Have a nice day, Poppa."

"Hmph," Joe Beckman said, resting the phone in its cradle, mortally offended. Hylacine: Australian marsupial wolf. If you got that—it was 56 Down—the rest was a snap. Barry had at least tied him in the race to finish the puzzle.

"Ah, well," he said aloud. "He's entitled to a lucky Sunday." He picked up the phone again, wondering if Libby had done in her poor old father too.

The phone rang a half-dozen times. Odd, he thought, then let it go on another half-dozen. He looked at his watch. A quarter till noon. Was he his daughter's keeper? All the same, he hadn't spoken to her since Wednesday, and she hadn't told either him or Marjorie that she was going anyplace. Maybe he'd dialed the wrong number. He tried again.

For the first time in her life Libby Beckman had done all of the wrong things.

She hadn't eaten properly in a week. After a weight loss of nearly twenty pounds on a controlled diet, she had cut her calorie intake to nothing. Exacerbating the problem, Libby, who normally took a couple of weak drinks during the course of an entire week, had managed to empty her bar of its contents—two bottles of scotch, a bottle of vodka, and a bottle of gin—in five days. Wandering around cockeyed, or sleeping off her drinks in the nude, alternately sweating and chilled to the bone from the evaporation, the flu she had begun with entrenched itself in her body and fluid began to collect in her lungs. By the time that Joe Beckman called his daughter on the phone that Sunday morning, she lay naked and semi-coherent on her bed with a temperature of 104 degrees and a serious case of pneumonia.

Joe Beckman let the phone ring another dozen times. As he was about to throw in the towel, Libby turned, and fumbling, knocked the phone from the hook.

"Libby?" Joe Beckman said. All he could hear was

congested breathing, sounding like interference on the phone.
"Libby, it's Poppa."

She heard his voice dully, as though it were being
strained through a cloth. She wanted to respond, but her
throat hurt and she felt groggy. "Pop," she said, the
syllable barely a breath.

Joe Beckman frowned. "Libby, are you all right? This
is Poppa, Libby."

"Poppa." She tried harder, but the words stuck in her
throat. Her chest hurt, and she had a terrible headache.

"Libby." His voice was serious but calm. "Libby,
listen to me. Are you all right? Is there something wrong?"

"I don't feel so good, Poppa," Libby said. The phone
slipped out of her hand and hit the floor as she dropped
back into a fevered coma.

The words had been unintelligible to Joe Beckman.
Libby's voice was garbled and her breathing labored.

He called her name several times. When there was no
response, he hung up. He debated his course of action
briefly, then dialed a number.

"May I speak to Dr. Lerner, please."

"I'm sorry," a cultured Caribbean voice replied. "Dr.
Lerner is not available for the moment."

"Vincent, this is Joe Beckman. You tell Dr. Lerner to
stop playing bridge. I want to talk to him right away. I
mean *right* now."

There was a brief pause, and then, "Goddamn it, Joe,
it's lunchtime Sunday. You know what I do lunchtime
Sunday."

"Yes, you try to lose all of the money you steal from
your patients during the week to Herb Roberts, Jack
Wasserman, and Herman Chaikin. Well, today you're going
to do without. There's something wrong with Libby. I
want you to meet me at her apartment in ten minutes." He
gave him the address. "You'll be there, Sylvan?"

"Of course." Sylvan Lerner rushed to the hall closet,
shouted his regrets to his partners, and took his bag. For
more than fifty years, man and boy, Joe Beckman had

been his friend. Never once in all those years had he called upon him in an emergency. Dr. Lerner waited impatiently for the elevator, and, like Joe Beckman, was sore afraid.

They arrived within seconds of each other at the door of Libby's apartment in the small building. Joe Beckman rang the bell, gently at first, then insistently. "Libby," he called out, "Libby, can you hear me." He pounded with his fist. Finally, transgressing rules of personal privacy which he had taught his children were sacred, he pulled the extra key to Libby's apartment, always at hand but never used, from his pocket, and opened the door. The door stopped at the end of the chain. He looked through the narrow aperture and saw that the apartment was in a shambles. He called out again, to no avail. Filled with dread, he let the door swing free to give some play to the chain, then leaned back and put his shoulder to it. It took a half a dozen hard jars to rip the fixture from the door buck. He stumbled, falling forward as the door gave suddenly.

He and Dr. Lerner entered the dark apartment, closing the door behind them. Beckman felt about for the wall switch and flipped it up.

"God! Libby."

The phone was still on the floor, off the hook, and just out of her reach. She was nude and stretched across the bed, her head hanging nearly to the floor. Her body glistened with a fine film of perspiration.

All business, Sylvan Lerner put down the bag and said, "Come on and help me pull her up on the bed."

Beckman did as he was told, and was stunned to find how light she was. Her complexion was pasty, and her breathing labored. Lerner pushed him aside firmly and put a stethoscope to her chest and a hand to her forehead.

"She's a sick girl, Joe. Is she allergic to penicillin? Does Marjorie know?"

"I don't know. She's at the Gages in the country. I called. She went out for a ride. I don't know when she'll get the message, or when she'll be back to town. She's not supposed to be back before dinner.''

Lerner shrugged. ''I'm not going to wait to find out.'' He pulled two syringes from his bag, and two ampules. ''Where's the john?'' He followed Beckman's directions, and rapidly washed his hands. He stripped the covers from the needles of the disposable syringes and filled one with the entirety of a bottle of milk-white antibiotic, and the other with a dose of Adrenalin. He stuck her first in one arm and then the other.

''Pull the covers over her, Joe, and try to keep her warm. I'm going to call Doctor's. It's the nearest.'' He sat down on the floor next to the bed and rang a number. ''Yes, this is Sylvan Lerner.'' There was respect on the other end. He was a senior attending physician. He gave the address and said, ''Let there be no dawdling.''

The emergency entrance was six blocks away. It took a total of less than five minutes from the end of the call to get Libby Beckman on a stretcher, into the ambulance, and on her way, with both her anxious father and Dr. Lerner riding beside her.

Across the street, hovering in the lee of a brownstone stoop, Wilfredo Lopez watched with trepidation as the two men broke into the apartment. At first, he had been tempted to interfere. He could see clearly enough that Libby's features had come to her from the thinner of the two men. He peered nervously, trying to see through the slats of the blinds, but without success.

He had been sitting on the stoop since eight o'clock. He had gone for an early morning run, restless and bored. As he had padded up the concrete path that borders the river, he had turned his radio earphones away from the Latin music station and to the news. By the time he had reached Gracie Square Park, it was apparent that the attempt of the Matsushima clan on the stable had been a calamity. All six, nameless to the news as yet, but brothers to him, were dead, one by his own hand. Another bystander had died, and others had been injured.

"Is there a degree to loyalty?" Matsushima-sama had asked. "Can a task be well done if half done? Is half a response the answer to a question?" All these things he had wanted to know. The inference was clear. "If I smear my head with ashes, and yet powder my face like a geisha, I have served only to call greater attention to myself, and to stand away from a oneness with the universe. Better to deny and to disobey, and to honorably take one's life, than to seek dishonor in half truths and half-done deeds."

When a plan was ordered for execution, Matsushima intended that it should be played out as it had been designed. Willie could see that. By not making latitude for change, he was committing his samurai to a course of action which would end in death. Is that what we are seeking, death?

CHAPTER

THIRTY-THREE

Albert Ruggles had prowled the streets of the barrio from one in the morning until the sun had begun to cast a glow in the east. He was tired and thirsty and discouraged.

It had been the usual Saturday-night lineup. A couple of fights, a couple of robberies. With the flow of beer and booze, a dozen noisy family disturbances had broken out.

He had not seen Ethan Wyatt the whole evening, though he had sought him out in his favorite haunts. It was unlike him to deviate from his pattern. Albert shrugged. He could have found himself a new boyfriend, or he could have been ripped off by a supplier or a seller, or as Albert had prophesied to him more than once, he could have ended up dead in a gutter someplace. Life in the street isn't full of rewards.

Albert reached inside his ratty coat and moved the butt of the heavy service revolver where it had been digging into his paunch. He wanted a glass of cold beer. He wanted to go home. A flash of color caught his eye coming down Madison Avenue. The streets were all but empty, and except for the occasional squawk of a ghetto blaster, the music had died down. Albert pushed his cap up on his forehead and squinted into the gloom. Streetlights in Harlem have short lives. This block was no exception. Albert smiled as he saw the figure duck into a store-front church.

Albert ambled over to the door and pulled it aside. A large dude with cornrows on his head and a droopy moustache held up a hand of interdiction and growled, "Is there something I can do for you?"

Albert smiled. "I can see that you is bad, real bad. I don't mean no harm. I just want to see that skinny little faggot that just walked in here. Name of Ethan Wyatt."

"I don't think he'd have anything to say to you, brother. This is a private club, a religious establishment. Now, why don't you just mosey along?"

"Would you ask him, please?" Albert said politely.

Ethan was sitting perched on a barstool, putting on a fresh layer of hot pink lipstick. When the bouncer approached him, he looked up and said, "Oh, he's all right. Let him in. He's an old friend of the family."

Albert, looking very retarded, sat down on an accompanying stool and said, "Could I have something to drink?"

"Certainly, my man. What would please you?" Ethan asked.

"A cold beer."

"Give my man here a cold beer, George," Ethan said to the bartender in his squeaky feminine voice.

"You come down, Ethan, consortin' with that," the bartender said, sliding a glass and a bottle of Miller's down the counter to a dead halt in front of Albert.

Albert doffed his hat and ducked his head subserviently. "Thank you," he said. He downed the bottle in a single continuous swig, not bothering with the glass. When he was done, he slammed the bottle on the counter and emitted a cavernous belch. "Better."

"Good boy," Ethan said aloud, then muttered, "outside around the corner, ten minutes." As Albert shambled off he said, "You-all be a good boy now, you hear." When he was gone, Ethan said to the bartender. "Sad case. He don't mean no harm."

"Anyway," the bartender said, "my grandma always said being nice to dummies was a service to the Lord, and brought good luck."

Ethan showed up at the appropriate time. Albert was seated on a half of a chair somebody had thrown out, leaned up against the wall. "I'm grateful to you, Ethan. I was very thirsty. One of the reasons that I was very thirsty was that I been walking these poor dogs of mine off the whole night looking for your skinny faggot ass. Where you been, son?"

"It just so happens. That I been out doing you some good."

Albert leaned forward and pushed up his cap. "What you got?"

"Little Puerto Rican girl scared shitless out of her fuckin' mind. She was doing it for a very bad person. All for love, you understand."

"Her pimp?"

"No. She was only doing it for him. He was a bad dude, and into weirdness of all kinds."

Albert snorted. "You should talk."

Ethan shook his head. "This was the real thing. He was a pain person. Very special. A bully. All kinds of bad shit is what the Spanish chick says."

"So what? Sounds like your average citizen to me." Albert waved his arm, indicating the squalor surrounding them.

Ethan gave him a piece of paper. "Does that address mean anything to you?"

"Housing development over by the river, isn't it?"

"It is. That's all it means?"

"I hate games," Albert said grumpily. Then his eyes widened. "Isn't that where they found the stiff with no head."

"You got it. The chick is by the name of Alvarez. She

lives in the place with her stepfather.'' He leered. ''The dude would call on her sometimes.''

''How did you run this down?''

''I did what you asked. I sniffed around.''

''Don't jive me, Ethan,'' Albert said, annoyed. ''I shook that neighborhood like a lollipop tree. Ross and Hernandez went over it with a comb, and besides, I know for a fact that Charles Passarelli and Marvin Baxter interviewed every swingin' dick in that building. A big fat zero.''

Ethan preened like a bird. ''Well, you ain't supplying them like I am, honey. The stepfather buys a little herb from time to time. He sends the girl to do his errands.''

''You got the names?''

''On the other side of the paper.''

As Ethan Wyatt sashayed down the street Ruggles called out after him, ''Don't catch anything I wouldn't catch.''

''I stay away from the dirty old holes, honey. That's the secret to my long life and success.''

When Ross and Hernandez returned to the twenty-third precinct four hours later from the debacle at the stable, they found Albert Ruggles snoring loudly, fast asleep, sprawled out on their desks.

''Albert,'' Ross said, shaking his arm, ''wake up. It's the police.''

Albert opened a single baleful eye. ''I'm tired. Come back in a week.''

Hernandez rattled the percolator. There was something left sloshing around. He poured a cup and put it on the desk. ''It's the best I can do for you.''

''Milk and sugar.''

''Okay. You got anything.''

Albert yawned enormously and stretched his ham hands in the air. ''Not much. Just a make on the guy with no head.'' He picked up the cup and made a face as he sucked at the stale brew. ''At least it's hot.''

''Albert, please don't break my balls,'' Ross pleaded. ''I haven't been sleeping a lot either.''

Albert fished in his pocket and handed him the piece of

paper. "On one side is the address, which you ought to be familiar with. On the other side is the name and apartment number of a chick who can make the corpse with no head."

"Albert, would you be embarrassed if I kissed you?"

"Only if you promise not to tell, Arnie." He heaved himself to his feet. "Let's stop fuckin' around and go get her."

As they entered the building in the development by the river, kids ran by on the ill-kempt grass, laughing and jumping and throwing balls. When the door closed, it seemed to shut their life and gaiety out with the sunshine. The hall of the building, though it was less than ten years old, had the look of a city subject to house-to-house combat in a war. Fixtures were broken, and no portion of the walls within arm's reach was not defaced by graffiti of some sort. The linoleum tiles were clean, but smelled of institutional disinfectant, which had always reminded Arnie of vomit.

"Tell me why she didn't say anything before?" Arnie asked as they waited for the elevator.

"I got this from an ear. He says she's just plain scared. I suppose it's no skin off her ass anyway. Why would she want to come mix with the fuzz?"

Eventually, the sole working car out of the bank of three lurched to a halt in front of them and spilled a full load of pungent humanity into the hall. Dodging them, the three detectives just managed to get in before the door shut again. The car stopped at every floor up to the twelfth, where they got off.

"Alvarez is her name," Arnie said, holding the piece of paper.

"No," Albert said. "That's the stepfather. Her name is Toreno. Carmelita Toreno."

They strolled up the hall checking names and numbers on the doors. The paint was scratched with key marks, sometimes names or dirty words, other times just ragged scrapes. From some apartments there was a sound of

laughter or music, or a television set. A few were quiet.
Near the end of the hall they came to a door through which
they heard the familiar sound of a hand striking flesh, and
a scream, followed by a torrent of Spanish in both male
and female voices.

"This is it," Ross said sourly, looking at the number
stenciled on the doorframe. He winced as there was another slap and another scream.

Ross knocked on the door.

"*Chupame maricón!*" the male voice from the apartment said vulgarly.

Hernandez pushed his way forward between the other
detectives, rapped sharply, and said in Spanish, "This is
the police. If you don't open the door, you won't have
anything for anybody to suck on."

There was a hurried and hushed conference behind the
door. Hernandez rapped again. "Let's go."

The door opened on a small room dominated by a
modernistic large screen console television set. The rest of
the furniture would not have been accepted by Goodwill
Industries as a donation.

The man who opened the door was in his early forties.
His thinning hair was tousled. He wore an undershirt and a
pair of filthy khaki work pants; his feet flopped in rubber
zorris. "What you want?"

Ross muscled his way past the man and looked around.
"We want to talk to your stepdaughter. Where is she?"

"She ain't here," the man said.

"Uh-huh," Albert said, pushing him out of the way. He
walked across the room and turned a door handle.

"Hey! This is my house," the man said. "You can't
pull that shit. Show me your warrant. . . ." He moved
toward Albert. Hernandez tripped him flat on his face.

"Please excuse me, sir," Lou said solicitously in Spanish, picking the man up like a rag doll and brushing him
off with bone-shaking pats on the back. "I hope you were
not hurt."

Ruggles wrinkled his nose. The bedroom was worse

than the living room. It smelled of stale sweat. There were two beds—one single, one double. The sheets were gray and rumpled. Oddments of clothing lay everywhere.

The girl sat on the edge of the bed, a defiant look on her face. One cheek was red and puffed, half again the size of the other. She was wearing a dirty pink slip. The little strip of lace was half torn from the top, exposing small breasts to the dark brown nipples. Her hair was thick and untended.

Albert looked out into the room and motioned to Hernandez. Arnie walked forward, but Albert waved him off.

When Hernandez closed the door behind him, the girl winced involuntarily, then a stony look of resignation came over her face.

"I am not going to hurt you."

"Sure. Like he doesn't hurt me." She sneered at the door. "I'll bet you're a cop. This is some kind of game, right? He beats my ass cause I won't go down on him. Then, he gets three johns to come work me over. Listen, I got to fuck the other two guys, too?"

Hernandez pulled out his badge and his I.D. card. "I'm tired. Can I sit down?" She gave back the identification, and moved over. Hernandez sat next to her on the bed. "How old are you?" he asked.

"Twenty," she lied.

"Fourteen?"

"Fifteen."

"How are you related to that man?"

"He was married to my old lady."

"Where is she?"

"She split about six months ago. He used to beat on her, too. She worked in a grocery store. He works—when he works—in a bar, cleaning up. You know, dishes and shit like that. I guess she just got tired of him. So one day, when he was at work, she put her stuff in two shopping bags, and beat it."

"Where were you?"

"School. I go to Julia Richman."

"How come she didn't take you?"

"I guess she didn't want me where she was. She started trickin' for a spade pimp. Some john offed her about three months ago." Hernandez searched for a tear. I guess there just aren't any left, he thought to himself. "Listen, you want to get away from him?" Hernandez asked.

"You mean some juvenile home?" The girl smiled a hard smile. "At least I know his cock. I go to one of them places, if the hacks don't chew my pussy off, I end up with some queen in the bed next door." When Hernandez started to protest she continued. "Never mind the fairy stories about getting a nice foster home, or adopted by somebody on Park Avenue. I grew out of that when I was seven. No, you leave me here. At least I got a hole to call my own." She looked into his face. "Hey, listen, you ain't with no juvenile authority. What you really want with me?"

"You used to have a boyfriend."

"I got lotsa boyfriends," she said, showing her tits.

"Have all of them lost their heads?"

The arrogant smile slipped from her face, and was replaced by a mask of fear. She shook her head silently, then said, "I don't know what you're talking about."

"You know the guy who was found downstairs a couple of months ago with no head. He used to come to see you." Hernandez got up. "Look, if you don't want to talk about it, I can always ask him."

She grabbed his hand and pulled it against her. "Don't do that. He'll beat my ass."

"I don't need much. Do you know his name? Where he lived? Anything about who he hung out with? Was he your first boyfriend? Is that what it was?"

The smile crept back, but without confidence, sad and wise. She pointed at the door with her thumb. "You funny, man. He popped my cherry when I was eleven. He came in while I was taking a bath, soaped my box and just popped me like that." She snapped her fingers. She sighed and looked up at him. "You ain't going to let me go, are you?"

"Not until you tell me what I want to know about that boy."

"His name was Alfredo Reyes." Hernandez took his pad out of his pocket and began to take notes.

"Where did he live?"

"I don't know. He lived with a bunch of guys he called his clan brothers. I never met any of them."

"What was he like? How old?"

"He was big, over six feet. He was built. He was hung like a horse, man. He was mean. He liked to hurt. He was a real jock. Shit, I mean he was strong. That's one reason why that asshole out there hated him. He made a move on Alfredo one time. He kick his fuckin' ass like a drum, man. Just a touch of the hands." She shuddered. "He could make you scream just by he touch you with two fingers. He was into karate and jiujitsu and shit like that. He was twenty-something. I don't know for sure. He always had bread. He said he was learning to be a philosopher." She smiled the sad smile again. "I don't even know what a philosopher does. I guess he ripped off the bread."

"What did he look like?"

She got off the bed and pulled out a drawer from the cigarette-burned dresser. There was a picture taped to the bottom. "That's him on the left. Him and me at Coney Island last July Fourth."

"Can I have this for a while?" Hernandez said, trying to keep his tone casual. "I'll give it back."

"You keep it," the girl said. "It ain't going to do neither of us any good. Say, I'm not going to get into any trouble, am I?"

Hernandez shook his head. "You been telling me the truth? That's all you know? You don't know any names or addresses or places that we could connect with Alfredo Reyes?"

"No," she said. "I don't know nothin' else. I never met no one with him."

"Where did you meet?"

"He picked me up in the park at a concert. I just walked down to Seventy-ninth Street myself to get away from the old man. I guess in his way he wasn't so bad. He used to give me a few bucks and buy me dinner out. He even bought me a dress once. You want to see it?" Her voice brightened.

"Sure," Lou said. It was pink with ruffles and much too old for her. "It's beautiful. I'll bet you look terrific in it."

When she put the dress back into the closet, her spirit seemed to stay in the dark with it. "Anything else?"

"No," he said, getting up and heading to the door. He slipped the pad and the picture into his jacket pocket. His elder daughter was her age.

"Well, you get what you want?" the stepfather said with a sneer.

"Yes. We can go now." Lou motioned Arnie and Albert to the door, then turned back for a minute. He put his hand on the front of the man's undershirt and turned it till it constricted around his throat. "I'm going to be around. I'm going to be in touch. If you ever hurt her, and I find out about it, I'm going to see that you never walk again." Because he spoke so quietly and clearly, his words were more menacing. *"Entiende?"* He twisted the shirt another ten degrees, till the man's face turned a little blue, and his tongue began to protrude. Hernandez abruptly let go, turned on his heel, and slammed the door behind him.

Lou waited till they were in the car again before he read them his notes and showed the picture. "Where to now, Arnie?"

Ross held the picture up in the light. "We show it to some witnesses. Let's start with Elizabeth Beckman. Take me back to the precinct. Hey, Albert, this is hot shit, man."

"What would you honkies do without me?" Albert asked disdainfully. "I think I'll go home."

Ross called Libby Beckman's apartment ten times over the course of the next hour and a half. By two o'clock Lou Hernandez couldn't stand his company anymore.

"Listen, Arnold, the lady has the right to go somewhere on a beautiful Sunday afternoon in the summer. You're making me crazy like you. Now, why don't you shut up and sit down and write DD-5's to pass your time. You're further behind in your laundry than Phyllis Diller."

"Go ahead, tell me I'm wrong and that it all doesn't tie together. This picture could be the missing link." He pulled the phone off the hook and rang the desk. "Did those pictures come in for me from Forensics yet?" He jumped to his feet, slammed the phone onto the cradle, and ran out the door.

"I guess they must be there," Lou said, looking after Arnie. He tapped the eraser of his pencil against his forehead. "That man has got to get his circus under a tent."

Ross burst back through the door, panting, in less than a minute, ripping open a brown envelope. "Ah-ha, there they are. Good stuff. All recognizable. You think that she's going to make them, Roach?"

Hernandez bounced the pencil off Ross's head. "How am I supposed to know, you crazy person? How am I supposed to guess? I am only a humble Puerto Rican police detective. I am not Arnold Ross, who sees the extra sets of eyes, and who is a magician—a fucking magician."

Ross looked at him in mock horror. "You swore. Luis Emile Fernando Hernandez, you swore. What would your mother say?"

"It's your fault. Something else to confess. You made me do it. You are a profound pain in the ass."

"I want to talk to her!" Ross shouted at no one in particular.

Lou gestured in the direction of the Almighty. "I give up. Let's go and sit in front of her house in the car. We'll ring the doorbell. Maybe her phone is broken. Anything to get out of here. I can't stand being in a cage with you anymore, Ross. Not another minute.''

"Now you're talking, Roach." He grabbed Lou and dragged him down the stairs after him, the envelope full of pictures tucked securely under his other arm.

They parked in front of Libby Beckman's house and knocked on the door. Arnie was so insistent that a woman who lived in the apartment above finally came to the window to look down at the street. Arnie smiled up at her. With a withering glance she turned away and slammed the window.

To escape from Arnie's fulminating nerves, Hernandez left him baby-sitting Libby Beckman's door and walked around till he found a newsstand and bought a paper.

When he came back and slid into the seat, Ross was staring at Libby's door, positively willing something to happen. Lou turned wordlessly to the paper and began to read. After about ten minutes, as he became absorbed in the day's events and began to forget about his partner's neuroses, Ross gave him a painful whack in the ribs with his elbow.

"Shhhh! Look, Roach."

A dignified man in a sport jacket and slacks was letting himself into Libby Beckman's apartment. He remained inside for ten minutes. Ross's foot tapped like a woodpecker's beak against the floorboards of the car.

"Who do you think that is?"

"I am not God, Arnie. I can't see through stone walls. I don't have the faintest idea who that is."

"Why does he have a key?"

"Maybe he's the maid."

"Don't be funny, Roach."

"He's maybe sixty, right. He's got the key to her apartment. It's probably her father. She's not the type to be kept by a sixty-year-old man."

Arnie opened the door and said, "Enough of this shit," and strode across the street. He knocked at the door. It opened instantly. Joe Beckman stood in front of Ross, obviously just on his way out, with a small suitcase in his hand.

"Yes?" Beckman said.

"I'm Sergeant Ross of the police department. I'm looking for Elizabeth Beckman.

"She's very ill," Beckman replied shortly. "I'm taking these things to her at the hospital."

"I'm very sorry to hear that. You are . . ."

"I am Joseph Beckman, her father. Now," he said, closing the door behind him, "if you will please excuse me, I must go."

"Mr. Beckman, this is a very important matter. It has to do with a number of homicides."

"I am sure, Sergeant Ross," Beckman said politely, but in a tone that brooked no nonsense, "that when Elizabeth is better, she will be only too glad to cooperate with you."

"Mr. Beckman, we may not have the luxury of that time."

"Officer, my daughter is deathly ill. I am an attorney. I would like very much to cooperate, but it is not possible."

"I just want to show her a picture."

"She's in a coma, Officer. She wouldn't be able to see it, much less identify it." He started toward the curb, clearly looking for a cab.

"I'll drop you off. My car's across the street."

Reluctantly, Beckman followed Ross across to the Porsche. He stopped cold when he saw the rumpled blue-jowled Puerto Rican sitting in the car.

Lou Hernandez had been looking at Anglos looking at him that way all of his life. Smoothly, he drew out his identification and held it out to Beckman, so he could see it clearly. "We've been up for almost two days, sir. Please forgive our untidy appearance," Hernandez said. He opened the door, slipped around into the tiny backseat, and let Beckman in.

"What's the matter with your daughter, Mr. Beckman," Ross asked as he started up the block. "She's a very nice young lady, and very bright."

"She has pneumonia. She's lost a lot of weight lately. It seems to have weakened her system. I called her this morning. When she didn't answer, I called again. She sounded so . . . so . . . sick on the phone. I called my doctor. We found her. She's very sick." It was a relief for this terribly private and reserved man to be able to vent his concerns to a stranger, and he babbled as he would never have been able to in the presence of an acquaintance or even his wife. Ross listened quietly. It was a familiar phenomenon. In a sense, it was almost as though, for Mr. Beckman, he and Lou were not real people, just receptors for his emotional outburst.

"It's so strange. She's a very healthy girl. Robust, you might say. Other than childhood illnesses, she's never been sick a day." Beckman looked aside at Ross. "How do you come to know my daughter?" He wrinkled his brow as though he had not heard properly what had been said before. "What do you mean, homicides?"

"The Muffy Grant salon, Mr. Beckman."

"Oh, yes. Yes, of course. How foolish of me." He wiped his brow with the back of his hand. "I'm not all there today. Did I say it was Doctor's Hospital?"

"No, sir. You didn't." Ross continued on his way till he reached East End Avenue, then turned north.

Ross pulled up in front of the hospital, diagonal to the curb in one of the slots reserved for doctors. He dropped his visor so that his police parking permit showed, and followed Mr. Beckman inside.

Beckman shook his head. "Really, Sergeant, I don't want to be an obstructionist, but you may be endangering my daughter's life."

"Mr. Beckman, if I don't talk to your daughter, and show her the new material I have, we may be endangering the lives of a lot of people. The perpetrators at the Muffy Grant salon may be responsible in one way or another for at least a dozen deaths we know about—and maybe more that we don't."

Beckman pushed insistently at the elevator call button.

"Mr. Beckman, did you listen to the radio or watch television today?"

"Not really." He pushed the button again, wishing the policeman would go away and leave him alone.

"There was a robbery at the stable on the West Side, Mr. Beckman. Seven people died, half a dozen injured. It's these same people, Mr. Beckman. The same ones."

A laconic operator sat bored and indifferent on a stool in the large elevator. He ignored Ross, Beckman, and Hernandez when they walked in.

"You can talk to the doctor, Sergeant Ross," Mr. Beckman said. "But if there is the slightest question of my daughter's well-being, you are simply going to have to wait, or get a court order." His voice was as firm as his intentions. "Operator, could we get going?"

"I have my schedule," the man replied in an arrogant Jamaican twang.

Ross stuck his badge under his nose and said, "Six, and make it snappy."

The car stopped at the sixth floor, and Ross, Beckman, and Hernandez emerged in a hall opposite a waiting room with wooden floors and a carpet, and couches, chairs, and tables more reminiscent of a private salon than an institution.

As the two detectives followed Mr. Beckman down the hall, they had no occasion to notice a slender dark-haired young man in a jogging suit sitting in a corner, reading a magazine. He held it at eye level to hide his face, and its peculiar distinguishing triangular scar.

Sylvan Lerner, M.D., was leaning against the counter of the floor nurses' station, writing on a chart affixed to a clipboard. When he heard the footsteps, he looked up. "Hello, Joe," he said somberly.

Beckman's face was full of concern at the sound of his voice. "She's all right, isn't she, Sylvan?"

"I think so. She certainly hasn't been treating herself very well, Joe." He looked queryingly back and forth between the policemen and Beckman.

Beckman sighed. "I'm sorry. Dr. Sylvan Lerner, this is

Sergeant Ross and this is Sergeant Hernandez. They are police detectives. They want to question Libby."

"For the moment it's not a possibility," Dr. Lerner said with a tinge of hostility.

"Why?" Ross asked.

"Because she's a damn sick girl. That's why, Sergeant."

"This isn't about a parking ticket, Doctor," Ross said. "It's about murder. Just how sick is she?"

Lerner, confused, looked to Beckman for guidance. He sighed. "Go ahead, Sylvan, you were in the midst of telling me anyway."

"Okay. Libby has not been taking care of herself. To begin with, there's a lot of alcohol in her bloodstream."

"Alcohol?"

"Alcohol. One of the reasons she's comatose is that she's absolutely pickled. Blood level is about point five. That's five times legally drunk. She has nothing in her stomach, so she's thrown up or excreted everything she's consumed. The rest of her digestive tract is just as empty. It's been days since she's had any solid food. In addition, she hasn't even been drinking water or other fluids. Her electrolytes are completely out of balance, and she's suffering from extreme dehydration. That's further complicated by high temperature, which has excreted what little fluid there was in her body through her pores in an attempt by the body to cool itself through evaporation. With her resistance down, she got an upper respiratory bug. Lying around naked in a draft, and cockeyed, it got to her lungs, and they started to fill. She's got a pretty nasty pneumonia. She's all dried out, and besides—and I never thought I'd live long enough to say this about Libby—she's just undernourished. She's weak as a kitten."

"But she'll be all right?"

"Absolutely. But she's damn sick, Joe. It must be the pressure of the new job."

"How long is she going to be in here, Sylvan?" Beckman asked.

"It's hard to say. I have to see how she responds. A

week wouldn't be a bad guess, ten days at the outside. But
then, depending on what we see, it'll be a couple of weeks
of R and R, Joe. Jesus, I've never seen her take a drink.''

Beckman shook his head in wonderment. "I don't know.
You think you know everything, then . . . Well, I've
never seen her take a drink seriously either. Just a little
pale scotch and soda to be sociable.''

Ross cleared his throat. "Would it be all right if we
looked in on her?''

"Sergeant," Dr. Lerner said, "you are being a pain in
the ass. You just heard me describe the patient's condition.
She's in an oxygen tent. She has an intravenous infusion in
her arm, and a urinary catheter. She's running a 104-degree
fever, and she's out like a light. You want me to draw you
a picture?''

Ross's face hardened. "It's tough everywhere out there,
Doctor. People are dying out there, Mr. Beckman, I talked
to Libby. She knows all about social responsibility. She
says you taught her. I think that she'd be the first to want
to help in this case. She doesn't want these goons running
around New York killing people. That Laszlo Dushan who
was murdered at her gym was her friend.''

Dr. Lerner's mouth set in a hard, angry line. "Come
with me, Sergeant Ross." He walked away down the hall
without a backward look. The other men followed after
him.

A nurse looked up from a chair in the corner where she
was sitting. Libby lay in the oxygen tent, her head back on
the pillow, her eyes closed. The metal skeleton of the
parenteral set cast a shadow across the white sheets, supporting the bottle from which the saline/glucose solution
dripped into her arm. Libby coughed hoarsely, and tossed
her head.

"Go ahead, Sergeant, ask her all the questions you
want," Dr. Lerner said. "I would be interested to hear her
answers.''

"How long is she going to be like that?" Ross asked.

"I am only a physician. With the restoration of her

fluids, and the reduction in temperature, and the restoration of her chemical balances . . . hell, I still don't know. Certainly, by morning she ought to be coherent. Maybe a few hours. I'm not in a position to tell you."

"I'll wait in the hall," Ross said. Dr. Lerner started to say something, then looked at Ross's face and gave up.

Lerner shrugged. "Suit yourself. But you don't come in to see my patient until I give you clearance. You aren't going to jeopardize her health."

"I'll wait. You tell me. I'll listen."

"As you wish. I'm going home. I'll be back around six. If she wakes before then, Nurse, you can reach me at home. The switchboard has my number. No one is to go in until I have given the okay. Right?"

"Yes, Doctor."

Lerner walked out of the door with his train of visitors behind him. They stopped in front of the waiting room to talk. "Joe," Dr. Lerner said, "I hope that you get a little rest yourself. You're gray."

"Thank you, Sylvan. I think I'll go home."

"I'll be here," Ross said. "Lou, why don't you give Mr. Beckman a ride?"

Hernandez nodded in agreement. "Then I'm going to go home. I'll go up to the precinct and have one of the guys in the patrol cars drop off the Porsche downstairs. He'll leave the keys at the desk. If you need me, you know where to find me."

As they waited, exchanging a last few words at the elevator, Wilfredo Lopez slipped out of the waiting room and down the hall, eyes shifting anxiously till they lit upon a red exit sign. Checking to see that he was unobserved, he let himself into the staircase and breathed a sigh of relief.

For three hours Arnie Ross read and then reread the pile of stale magazines that lay on the coffee table in the waiting room. From time to time he would get up to see if the nurse had emerged from Libby Beckman's room to notify the doctor that his patient was awake. After his fifth request, the hard-bitten Irish head nurse, blue eyes spitting fire and indignation under a cap perched on glistening white curls, said, "We'll let you know when something happens, Sergeant. You're standing in the way of our work here," Ross stomped back to the waiting area and flopped down in the chair again. He was starting to lose the battle against exhaustion, and found himself blinking, and dozing off, his head rolling and nodding on his shoulders.

The staircase in which Willie was hiding was between the nurses' station and the waiting room. On several occasions, as he heard footsteps, he had been forced to run either up or down a couple of flights of steps to avoid detection. Only twice had he stuck his head out of the door. The second time he had seen Arnie Ross's broad back retreating down the hall.

What was wrong with Libby? His concern excluded all other thoughts from his mind? Why was Libby sick? She would need him. She would need his love. From the stoop across the street from Libby's apartment he had seen the ambulance and the attendants. He had started running. It was a half-dozen blocks from her apartment to Doctor's. He was panting like an animal, crouched near the big emergency dock when the ambulance roared in, siren wailing. He had seen the pale form bundled in blankets on the rolling stretcher—his Libby.

At five-fifteen Willie's endurance and self-discipline gave way at the same time. He got up from the steps, opened the door, and strode resolutely into the hall as though he had something to do, and a place to go. He walked past the nurses' station without a glance. He was ignored.

Libby's room was at the end of the corridor, which turned off again to the left. He saw her name on the door, and the large sign in red forbidding visitors. He paused only a second, then heard a scraping noise inside and scuttled down the hall in the other direction. He looked over his shoulder to find the nurse leaving Libby's room. He hesitated only a moment, then turned back.

He peered around the corner, down the hall at the nurses' station. Libby's nurse had picked up the telephone. Boldly, he walked across the polished tile floor and entered the room.

"Mother of God, Libby!" he said in a hushed voice, full of pain and fear. "Libby."

Her eyes were half open, and she saw in a mist. She felt hot, and her arm hurt. She tried to move it, but was unable, strapped as it was to a board. Things seemed hazy to her. She tried to blink away the fog, then realized that it was the plastic around her. It slowly registered in her mind that she was in an oxygen tent. She coughed dryly. Her chest hurt and she was thirsty. She wanted to tell someone to get her some water. She raised her head a little from the pillow. She managed a little smile. "Willie, I'm thirsty, honey." She had no idea where she was or why, but she was happy he was there.

"*Carida*," the word was a caress. He poured water from the Thermos at the bedside into a cup. Clumsily he lifted the hem of the oxygen tent and held the cup out.

"I can't," she whispered, too tired to lift her free arm.

He slipped his hand under her neck and lifted her a little from the pillow, and fed her a little at a time. She choked a little, at first, but then was grateful for the cool trickle. When she had finished, he asked, "Would you like some more?"

"Please." Her voice was a little stronger. She finished another half cup, then lay back and closed her eyes. "I'm so tired." Then she looked up and said, "Don't go, Willie!"

He sat at the edge of the bed, holding the hot dry hand. "I have to. You'll be all right now. I know. I had to know that."

A tear rolled down her cheek. "You won't come back."

"There will be other times," he lied. "There will be other places." But not on this earth Libby, who I love. I must go now. I must run. I think I will run to eternity. He looked out of the window at the flowing river. I think I will submerge myself in eternity. After this morning's end of the clan of Matsushima, and the knowledge that their love could not be more than a dream, Willie believed that he finally understood the master. They had tried. They had failed. In the face of failure, and dishonor, it is reasonable to seek another level of the universe in dignified death. Willie pulled the plastic curtain up and leaned across Libby's body. Cupping her breast in his hand, he kissed her lightly on the lips. Then covered her again, and backed away from the bed.

"What the hell . . ." the nurse said, as she opened the door, seeing Willie fondling the prostrate form, "guard," she bellowed, "guards!!!"

Ross was awake in an instant and hurtling down the hall. The nurse screamed again. Arnie shoved the door of the room open, striking her in the back and pitching her into the arms of Wilfredo Lopez. Instinctively, Willie grabbed her, turning her body to use it as a shield. He looked over her shoulder into the granite face he had seen across the street at Libby's apartment.

"Let her go, chico. I'm a cop. You just put the lady down, and everything is going to be just fine."

Willie took a last look at Libby. She was trying to raise herself from the pillow on her free arm, her eyes wide and shining, her mouth moving without sound. He divorced himself from that dream, and plunged into the reality of the situation.

"Back off, Officer," Willie said menacingly. "Back off. I'm leaving. Do you want it to be over her dead body?"

Ross crouched a little, reached behind him, and slowly drew the revolver from the back of his trousers. Willie put his hand into his jacket pocket and took out his own.

"It's a tie, Mr. Policeman. But I have a shield."

"I can shoot your eye out right over her shoulder, sonny," Ross snarled. "The only thing that will happen to her is that she'll need to have your shit-for-blood washed out of her uniform." He extended the gun.

"Stop," the nurse croaked, pointing her finger at the green sign that said NO SMOKING—OXYGEN.

Ross was pushed forward as a uniformed guard bulled his way into the room. "Out," Ross said, "out."

Willie loosened his hold on the nurse's throat. "If there's a spark," she said, "the tent will explode. The whole room will burn. The patient."

Ross stood upright and returned the gun to its holster. "Okay, chico, you shoot."

He knew, Willie thought to himself with a bleak smile. Somehow he knew.

Ross watched the kid carefully, looking into those large brown eyes. So this was the leader of the gang that robbed Muffy Grant's salon. So this was Libby Beckman's lover. So this was why she had been torn in two by love on the one hand and conscience on the other. Is he going to shoot his way out of this room? If he does, then Libby Beckman would pay the final price for her own judgment. She would be burned to death because he wanted his freedom more.

Willie threw the nurse at Ross's feet like a sack of wheat, and slipped the gun back into his pocket. He moved gracefully into the center of the small open space in the room and took up the first posture of defense.

Arnie helped the nurse up and pushed her out of the door, closing it behind her. "You're sure you want this, chico?"

"My name is Wilfredo. "You can call me Willie."

Ross made a small bow. His first stroke was the classic one-step kick to the head. The boy took a half-step back, avoiding it, then turning, caught Ross on the point of the hip with his heel.

Ross bowed in appreciation. Trying to use his greater bulk, he forced Willie toward the corner with two feinted kicks. Willie sprang from the floor and thrust a foot at his chin. Ross lashed out with a balled fist and struck the calf muscle as it passed his face.

Willie landed upright, crouching. He tried to put weight on the leg, but it was a knot of pain.

Ross sensed the opening and moved forward with another series of kicks. Willie dropped to his knees and struck a blow to the thigh. Ross inhaled sharply at the pain, but followed through, striking Willie across the back with the edge of his hand.

Willie wanted to be sick. He could feel that he had wet his pants. He could barely breathe. His kidney was ruined. He gathered himself and flew at Ross in a series of blows with the edge of the hand and the feet. Each blow was met with a block and a counterblow. Willie slumped heavily against the wall in the corner. Hope ebbed from his eyes. Even this decent death was going to be denied him. The policeman was of the same caliber as the master, but bigger, younger, and stronger. Ross would beat him senseless, then Willie would spend the rest of his life in prison without hope.

"You don't want her to see me whip you, Willie. You don't want her to remember you that way."

"Back away," Willie said, taking out his revolver. "Back away."

Ross was stunned. "You won't."

"You ready to bet on it?" Willie gasped. The hemorrhage in his back was an agony. He backed into the corner. "I need air," he said, pulling up the window, the wavering gun pointed at Ross's midsection. He looked across at Libby, and tears rolled slowly down his cheeks. "In another world I will love you forever." He turned to Ross. "And I will be your match."

Ross reached out to him with his hand. Wilfredo Lopez threw his pistol out of the window to the street six stories below, then threw his life after it.

CHAPTER

THIRTY-FOUR

Hiroo Matsushima pondered on the idea that news, both good and bad, can be delivered in so many ways that one is often stunned by their multiplicity. A wife whom one has neglected is thought of satisfying her urges either in the sublimation of the rearing of children, or the more direct means of self-gratification. A single glance is passed over the dinner table, a relaxed smile overcomes her as she slips off to sleep, and it is announced that the void has been filled. No words are spoken. No offense is intended, given, or taken.

The Japanese imperial government, rigidly affixed atop the rubble of the country, is unable to announce or to accept the concept of defeat, a circumstance that has never been visited upon Japan in its two-thousand-year existence. The announcement is brought home by the incineration of one hundred fifty thousand citizens, in two flashes of light too brief to measure.

The newspaper announces Tokyo 6, Sendai 5 in eleven innings.

At nine o'clock on that Sunday evening Hiroo Matsushima

sat cross-legged on the dais of the gymnasium floor at the Ten-do Karate-Dojo. He had been sitting there for two hours, since the meeting was supposed to have come to order.

In listening to the radio during the day, it had become apparent that the raid on the stable had been both a success and a failure. Tribute was taken, there was a battle of some moment, the samurai had acquitted themselves nicely, and had perished in an honorable manner. He was particularly touched by the seppuku of Donald Wolfe.

The emptiness of the room before him was a news announncement of a different kind. The four remaining samurai, including even the redoubtable Wilfredo Lopez, had failed to respond to the scheduled meeting. The other three, well, they were the newest of the recruits. If they failed him—really, failed themselves—they would have to bear that shame. Willie would have to bear the shame of recruiting them, and his own disobedience.

As the story of the stable had unfolded over the morning, Matsushima had experienced moments of increased lucidity, flickering in and out like a windblown candle in the confusion that had overtaken his mind. Of all the questions with which he tormented himself, the one he could answer least was the reason for his misplacement in the skein of time. He began to feel a sense of guilt, for he could only suppose that this life was the punishment for an earlier and unremembered life in which he had acted with dishonor.

At eleven o'clock he turned on the small transistor radio at his side and listened to a news broadcast that announced the death of Willie Lopez.

"Lopez, who was believed to be about twenty-two, was the suspected mastermind of the series of robberies of athletic facilities in the New York metropolitan area over the past several months which culminated this morning in the robbery of the Central Park stable and deaths of six gang members. The suspect was discovered in the hospital room of Elizabeth Beckman, an employee of the foreign loan department of Citicorp. Miss Beckman, who is recovering from pneumonia, was among the victims of the robbery some months ago at the Muffy Grant Slimtronics Salon on Madison Avenue. The suspect was discovered in Miss Beckman's room at Doctor's Hospital by Detective Sergeant Arnold Ross of Homicide Zone Four. According to eyewitnesses, Lopez was armed. The room's atmosphere was charged with oxygen because Miss Beckman was in an oxygen tent. Because of the danger of explosion, neither the officer nor the suspect fired. A brutal battle took place between Sergeant Ross, who is a karate expert, and the suspect, who was, according to Ross and a hospital guard who was a witness, also trained in martial arts. According to the private nurse, Miss Beatrice Waltham, who was present through the entire episode, when it was clear that Sergeant Ross had injured Lopez, and that he was going to be subdued and captured, he opened the window and jumped six floors to his death."

"Just so," Matsushima said aloud. "A death with courage and dignity. Then it was not in vain."

"Sergeant Ross explained to reporters at the hospital, including our own Juliet Klausner, that Lopez was the suspected mastermind behind the string of daring assaults on fashionable gyms like The Angles and Muffy Grant's. He was unable to say whether any of the other members of the Lopez gang were still at large."

Late in the night Hiroo Matsushima finished the numerous tasks that he had set for himself at the desk in the Ten-do Karate-Dojo. His eyes were very tired. He had used the ink stone and the pen and the brush, and nearly all of his remaining parchment rice paper. He had composed a will and a narrative of the activities of the clan. He had written a letter of formal resignation to the president of his company, asking his forgiveness for failure to complete his task. He had written to his father, and to his wife, and to his daughters. He had laid out all of his plans for the robberies performed and unperformed, so that they could

be appreciated. Last, he had written a letter to Sergeant
Arnold Ross of Homicide Zone Four.

"If you are only a policeman, you can come and find
me at the Ten-do Karate-Dojo. It will be waiting for you,
and you may claim my body. If you are a samurai who
fought bravely and defeated Wilfredo Lopez, whom I trained
myself, then you may join me for dinner tomorrow. We
will test our skills, to see who is the greater warrior. Then
you may claim my body. It was not Willie, but I who
planned the robberies." He left the note unsigned, save
for the ancient seal of his family. The invitation was for
seven P.M. On his way home Matsushima stopped on Third
Avenue and 102nd Street and walked down the block. He
left the envelope addressed to Sergeant Ross lodged in the
old precinct door.

In the morning, though he had enjoyed only a few hours
sleep, he expressed upon his wife the lust which he had
shared lately only with Han, the Korean whore. She bowed
to him in gratitude, and stood at the door in her kimono
waving to him as he drove away to the city.

Arnie Ross slept from eleven o'clock on Sunday night
until noon on Monday. All of him ached. He felt old and
used. He looked at the practice dummy in the corner of his
bedroom, and was not tempted to test himself against it.
Yesterday had been altogether enough. That smile of resignation, and the young body hurling silently through the air
to bounce like a stuffed toy on the cement below.

He shaved and pulled on slacks a shirt and a sweater.
When he was dressed he called Lou at home. "I need a
schwitz. Did you run, yet?"

"I ran this morning. What happened?"

"I'm not sure. Meet me at the Y?"

"Forty-five minutes. In the steam room."

Arnie sat on a long slotted bench perspiration welling
from every pore. Lou walked in with his towel over his
shoulder. No wonder Margarita looked at him with those
eyes. God knows well which one of us had aged the most.
It's that runner's shape, that no-bulk lankiness. It comes

out in your personality. My body is bulky and stolid, so is my mind. His intellect is as fluid as his movements.

Arnie told him about the hospital.

"What are you going to do about the girl?"

Arnie shook his head. "I don't know. Nothing. What should I do?"

"She is guilty of harboring a fugitive, and withholding evidence."

"Is she? She is guilty of fucking a fugitive. He wasn't living there. She had no evidence that we know of. We can't force her to incriminate herself. At best, she knew what he had done, and didn't say anything about it."

"If she had talked, Arnie, maybe some of those people wouldn't be dead."

"Maybe." Arnie was quiet, his face without expression.

"It's its own punishment, isn't it, Arnie?"

"To love someone who is bad is its own punishment. Who will be served?"

"No one will be served. Not even justice. We taking the day off?"

"I want to drop in and see if there's anything else. Okay?"

"Sure."

The letter was sitting on Ross's desk, addressed in exquisite *romanji* calligraphy. Ross felt the paper with appreciation. Lou looked on curiously.

"What is it?"

Ross opened and read it, and without hesitation, put it in his pocket. "Just an invitation to a judo school. Say, did you run across the Ten-do Karate-Dojo in your travels through the Yellow Pages?"

"Not to my memory. Let me look at the list." Lou pulled out the directory and leafed through the worn pages, referring to his notes at the same time. "I called a couple of times, and got no answer. It's downtown on Sixth Avenue."

Ross glanced over his shoulder and made a mental note.

"You want to grab a sandwich, Arnie? I'm starved."

"I'll sit and watch, if you like. I don't really feel like eating, Roach."

"Suit yourself, my man."

They had a chance to talk to Flaherty for an hour after they came back from the deli. It was just routine. There was a feeling on the part of the people at the top that there had been a job well done. Even Finkle was happy, because his precinct would get the bust on Willie Lopez. Since he was the ringleader he figured it as more than a number. He had expressed interest in wanting to be at the award ceremony when Ross got his commendation.

"What do you think, Arnie?" Flaherty asked. "You've been awfully quiet, for you. Is it finally all over?"

"I think we can put it to bed tonight, Frank."

Hernandez invited Arnie to come home with him for dinner. "I don't think so, Roach. Listen, we're off tomorrow, it's nice out. How about we do a clambake in the backyard?"

"Terrific. I'll set it up. Plenty of beer. We'll take Wednesday, too, unless you really want all of that overtime."

Arnie smiled. "Let 'em keep their friggin' money. Sounds great. Love to everybody. Good night, Lou."

Arnie arrived on the third floor of the building on Sixth Avenue at precisely seven o'clock. He removed his shoes and put them at the side of the door on the rack that was provided. He took off his coat and strode barefooted across the mats in his best judo suit, the black belt of the seventh dan tied securely about its middle. He came to the figure squatting on the dais and bowed.

"I am Arnold Ross."

"I am Hiroo Matsushima." He stood and bowed. Ross saw that about his waist was the red and white belt of the master. When he sat again, Ross sat opposite him.

"We are men of a time that no longer exists, Sergeant Ross."

"How is that?"

"Direct action is no longer appreciated. Life is a continuum of subterfuge. All is sham and illusion."

"And we . . ."

"Our heads are covered with ashes. . . ."

"Our faces are smeared with mud," Ross finished. "Is that really so?"

"Just so. I don't know the answer. I have been searching in myself the whole day as I cleaned out my desk and tidied my affairs. Naturally, one does not want to leave things in unmanageable condition for one's successors."

"Naturally. Are you so sure that you are . . . finished?"

"I think so. You have no proof, of course. You would be unable to trace my activities back to me."

"Was it your ego that made you write to me? Did you feel that Willie didn't deserve the credit?"

"Credit?" Matsushima smiled sadly. "The activities of a madman. To that conclusion I have already come. I am quite mad. No. I did not want all of the opprobrium to fall on that poor and already overburdened spirit. And of course, there is the girl."

"Did you know about the girl?"

"Only in my heart. He never mentioned her existence to me. But, I could see. He was the most perfect of all samurai. What he was too young to know was that even the most perfect of samurai are still men. In the end, he was destroyed by his loyalty to me and his love for the girl. He could not endure the loss of either and, therefore, was doomed to lose both. She should know this."

"I cannot tell her. If I do, I will admit that I know she is a criminal."

"By your standards?"

"By the standards of the law which I represent."

"Well then, Ross-san, you are not so different than I, after all. But, you have made a better compromise." He stood. "Come and test your skills."

Ross stood and bowed and took the first position of defense. Matsushima, slight and elegant across the floor, extended a slender fist pointed between Ross's eyes, his legs in the half squatting stance.

"Will I die, Matsushima-sama?" Ross asked.

"In time, Ross-san." It seemed to Arnie that he floated from the floor, though his movement was as quick as a hummingbird's. The upraised hand swung in an arc just beyond the reach of Arnie's blocking forearm. The touch to his neck was as light as a kiss.

"Size, Ross-san, is not an excuse for lack of speed. Clumsiness is not pardoned by death, simply acknowledged."

Ross marched across at him with five high kicks of each foot. At the end of the fifth kick, Matsushima was no longer in front of him. He felt a tap at the base of his spine. He swung his body, and was tantalized by the brushing of his fingertips against cloth.

"Given that you would have survived the blow to your kidneys, you were very near to my heart with the stiff-fingered blow," Matsushima said in a dry analytical tone.

It occurred to Arnie that he was being played with like a toy. At any moment those unlanded blows, the feinted kicks could become real. And he would most certainly die. He barreled across the floor to catch Matsushima by surprise with a football tackle. He stepped aside like a matador and stung Ross sharply across the ear. He fell heavily to the mats, but rolled and came to his feet.

Matsushima clucked his tongue. "A clumsy *geigin* thrust deserves punishment. Let your stinging ear remind you that all has been imagined, all has been received. Nothing has been left without a solution, or a countermove, especially nothing so crude."

Matsushima spun into a whirlwind of activity as he had the day he pretended that he was in the forefront of the army of his ancestor. Instead of a canvas dummy, he practiced his art on Arnold Ross, black belt of the seventh dan, who was helpless before him. Each crushing kick or blow, each disabling and crippling movement of the attack, ended in a tap or a pat. In a finale Matsushima seemed to fly upward into the air, parallel to the ground.

Ross stumbled backward off balance, the balled fist hurtled, with all of the body's weight behind it, toward the point between Ross's eyes, to crush the bone, sending the splinters into the frontal lobe of the brain. The blow ended in a caress.

Matsushima bowed to Ross, who was seated exhausted and beaten on his rump on the mat. "It has been my pleasure, Ross-san. Shall we dine?"

Ross sat in front of the table as Matsushima laid the tray out before him. "I have been shot a number of times. As you can see, I have been stabbed. I have never been so close to death as I was tonight."

"You are a worthy opponent. You would be a superlative student. Look further into the martial arts, Ross-san. You may find the salvation of your soul there. Sadly, I have not."

Matsushima pulled a paper cover from the top of the tray. It was an elegant refinement of the art of Japanese food preparation. Fish of all kinds were appliquéd over the china in the shape of the chrysanthemum, and of the crane, the symbol of long life. At the center of the plate there was a small round dish in which tiny slices of a fleshy tan substance were carved to transparency.

The men broke apart their chopsticks. Ross reached forward, taking a chunk of the light green ball of wasabi. "May I be permitted?"

Matsushima bowed. "Of course." He watched as Ross broke the spicy substance in his dipping bowl and mixed it with soy sauce. "Thank you," he said when the mixture was still a lethal greenish-brown. Ross mixed an equally potent blend for himself.

Matsushima removed a tokura of saki from a pot of hot water at his side, and filled the two shallow cups. "*Kampei!*" he said.

"*Kampei*," Arnie replied. Empty glass. They threw the warm pungent rice wine down. "How did it begin, Matsushima-sama?"

"I am the eighteenth grandson of Tokugawa Ieyasu. I

am without money, without castles, without rice fields, without samurai. I am what a French intellectual would call the daimyo *manqué*. My spirit is of another century. But I was born after Mutsuhito—the Meiji emperor, and after MacArthur, the white shogun. My father lives on our empty island in a sea of memory. I am a clerk.''

''A clerk?''

''Indeed. I am the general manager of a large steamship line. I live in the suburbs. My daughters are valley girls. My wife shops at Bloomingdale's and I play golf.'' He looked up at Ross under hooded brows. ''And my dignity, where shall I seek that? At the Pizza Hut? Or a McDonalds? We have them on the Ginza now, you know.''

''Is it our civilization?''

''No. It is the evolution of ours. It is that conclusion that led me to ask you to dinner this evening. I have erred. My mind—I have a good mind, Sergeant Ross—has slipped. I have moments of burning insight, and moments of complete despair, and visions of what cannot be. I have seen, that more and more, I have been overtaken by my insanity.''

''If you know this, how can you be insane?''

''I gathered to me a fine young man. He tried to rob me. He was a mugger. But buried under the shards that misery had made of his life was the spirit of a samurai, of a good man. He was loyal. In his way he was honest to a fault. He bore good will and affection to those for whom he cared. If he was indifferent to the pain and suffering of others, you may attribute that to the indifference that the world showed him.'' Matsushima motioned. ''Please eat. Don't let my rambling prevent your enjoyment of the meal.'' Matsushima brought a small plate from under the table. ''Willie needed only the proper banner to follow. I gave him mine. My banner has not flown in too many centuries to be of use now.''

''They flew it at Pearl Harbor.''

''They flew it at Hiroshima.''

Arnie smiles. ''It sells cars.''

''For the Pearl Harbor of Toyota, there will be a Hiroshima too. I was not born for this world." Matsushima raised an eyebrow, "Neither, then, were you."

"I am the son of the lowest dog. My father was a common criminal. I have spent my life disproving the bad genes."

"You have no family?"

"For fear that the genes lie hidden."

"My fear was that the genes that made the history of my family and my country had been altogether dissipated. I set out to prove that this was not so." Matsushima proffered the small dish. "Take only a single piece. Only a touch of spice is necessary."

Arnie dropped the tiny piece of firm flesh onto his plate, then dipped it into the sauce gingerly and popped it into his mouth. After a split-second his fingers and toes tingled, his lips were numbed. It was like an electric shock. He saw that Matsushima was watching him, and feigned indifference.

"So, Ross-san, I taught Wilfredo Lopez the martial arts. I began, with some success, to teach him the way of Bushido, and the philosophy of Zen. He brought others to me: the homeless, the unloved, those with no allegiance, and I gave them a home for their wanadering spirits. But instead of making samurai of them, I made brigands. And when I saw what I had done, that their acts and mine must be judged in the context of the world we live in, not the world as I wished it to be, I sent them off to their deaths. All of them except Willie. He perceived himself, and made his own ceremonial death. You will find all of the plans, all of the names, all that I had wanted them to do, on the desk in the office in the corner. You may do with them as you see fit. I have written a will, and a confession. They are both on the desk. I have written farewell messages to my wife and children. I have simply said that the world in which we live overwhelmed me, and that I have passed on to the next." He smiled again. "You must not look at me so. I am in the end only a master criminal. I have not been a leader of men, I have been a killer of men.

I, who sought a glorious destiny, have succeeded only in drowning in my own pride and shame. Please, let us finish our meal.''

Ross ate of the beautiful designs till there was little else to eat. He had not eaten since he had received the invitation in midday, and had been sorely tested by the strenuous bout with Matsushima.

"I find this particularly interesting, Matsushima-sama," Ross said, pointing to the slices of tan fish.

"You must have another, then. But only one. It is always the most attractive fish on the plate." He watched Ross eat the sliver of fish and react with combined pleasure and curiosity. "You must take my *tachi* with you. It is a gift from one samurai to another. It has been in my family for two hundred years. You are worthy." Matsushima took the remaining slices of tan fish, dipped them into the wasabi, and wolfed them down. "Ah," he said. "I see the open door." Two small round objects remained on the plate. He ate them as well.

"What is that strange fish?"

"Ah, so. The tiger fugu. Blowfish. Very common in all of the waters of the world. Here in America they gut them and clean them, and only the pure white flesh by the backbone is eaten. It is no more interesting than the halibut. What you have done, Sergeant Ross, is to participate in the Japanese national pastime of flirting with death. The internal organs of the blow fish, particularly the ovaries and the liver, contain a virulent poison which affects the nervous system. Those two small bits you ate were shavings of the liver. Your lips were numb, were they not?" Ross nodded in agreement. "And of course the tingling in the extremities, and the tip of the penis. Yes, it is exciting to flirt with death at the dinner table." Matsushima rose and stepped back, bowing slightly, then sat again against the wall. "I have not flirted, I have embraced the lady. The liver and both ovaries. I bid you sayonara, Sergeant Ross." His smile became fixed. Ross watched him for a moment in fascination, then realized he was dead.

For a few minutes, Ross went through the papers that Matsushima had laid out on the desk. He went into the closet to look for the ceremonial sword. It gleamed like a mirror as he slid it from its scabbard.

He thrust it home again, and slipped it through the folds of the belt on his waist. He looked at himself in the mirror, a barefooted warrior, prepared for battle. He looked at the plans. Who would know if he just threw them away? Who would care if he left the reputation unsullied? Would it make any difference? It could all be an accident. He had only to burn all of the letters and the plans.

Ross took the sword from the belt and laid it on the table, then walked out and looked at the smiling figure, upright and unblinking in death. I would know, and Libby Beckman would know, and the shade of Willie Lopez would know. Ross walked across the room and kicked Matsushima's corpse over, and left it sprawled on the floor, bereft of its illegitimate dignity, and went to call the cops.

BESTSELLING BOOKS FROM TOR

MORE BESTSELLERS FROM TOR

☐ 58827-4 *Cry Havoc* by Barry Sadler $3.50
    58828-2   Canada $3.95

☐ 51025-9 *Designated Hitter* by Walter Wager $3.50
    51026-7   Canada $3.95

☐ 51600-1 *The Inheritor* by Marion Zimmer Bradley $3.50
    51601-X   Canada $3.95

☐ 50282-5 *The Kremlin Connection* by Jonathan Evans $3.95
    50283-3   Canada $4.50

☐ 58250-0 *The Lost American* by Brian Freemantle $3.50
    58251-9   Canada $3.95

☐ 58825-8 *Phu Nham* by Barry Sadler $3.50
    58826-6   Canada $3.95

☐ 58552-6 *Wake·in Darkness* by Donald E. McQuinn $3.95
    58553-4   Canada $4.50

☐ 50279-5 *The Solitary Man* by Jonathan Evans $3.95
    50280-9   Canada $4.50

☐ 51858-6 *Shadoweyes* by Kathryn Ptacek $3.50
    51859-4   Canada $3.95

☐ 52543-4 *Cast a Cold Eye* by Alan Ryan $3.95
    52544-2   Canada $4.50

☐ 52193-5 *The Pariah* by Graham Masterton $3.50
    52194-3   Canada $3.95

Buy them at your local bookstore or use this handy coupon:
Clip and mail this page with your order

TOR BOOKS—Reader Service Dept.
49 W. 24 Street, 9th Floor, New York, NY 10010

Please send me the book(s) I have checked above. I am enclosing
$_____ (please add $1.00 to cover postage and handling).
Send check or money order only—no cash or C.O.D.'s.

Mr./Mrs./Miss _____

Address _____

City _____ State/Zip _____

Please allow six weeks for delivery. Prices subject to change without
notice.